The Morley Mythology

By the same author

Camden's Eyes (1969)

First Persons (1973)

The Morley

Mythology

Austin Wright

Harper & Row, Publishers
NEW YORK
HAGERSTOWN
SAN FRANCISCO
LONDON

Grateful acknowledgment is made for permission to reprint the following:

Excerpts from *The Flagstad Manuscript* by Louis Biancolli. Reprinted by permission of the author. Excerpts from *Geological Evolution of North America,* second edition, by Thomas H. Clark and Colin W. Stearn. Copyright © 1968 by The Ronald Press Company. Excerpts from *Physical Geology* by Chester R. Longwell, Richard Foster Flint, and John E. Sanders. Reprinted by permission of John Wiley & Sons, Inc. Excerpt from *Flagstad: A Personal Memoir* by Edwin McArthur. Copyright © 1965 by Edwin McArthur. Reprinted by permission of Alfred A. Knopf, Inc. Excerpt from *The Singing Voice* by Robert Rushmore. Reprinted by permission of Dodd, Mead & Company. Excerpts from the *New York Times.* Copyright 1935 by The New York Times Company. Reprinted by permission. Excerpt from *Michelin Guide,* Paris edition, 1967. Used by permission. Excerpt from vocal score of Wagner's *Tristan and Isolde.* Copyright 1906 by G. Schirmer, Inc. Copyright renewed 1934 by G. Schirmer, Inc. Used by permission.

Photo credits: UPI Photo, Inc.: page 77; William King Covell: page 146; Joanna Louise Wright, page 151; New York World-Telegram: pages 108, 163, and 172.

 For information address Harper & Row, Publishers, Inc., 10 East 53rd Street, New York, N.Y. 10022. Published simultaneously in Canada by Fitzhenry & Whiteside Limited, Toronto.

FIRST EDITION

Designed by Sidney Feinberg

Library of Congress Catalog Card Number: 76–5553
ISBN: 0–06–014751–2

---

77 78 79 80 10 9 8 7 6 5 4 3 2 1

Author's Note

Those who knew me long ago will recognize the Favorites in Michael Morley's Mythology. They are people and things taken from the real world, where they played a part in my own childhood similar to the part they play in Morley's. I salute them, living and dead.

Except for them, this novel is as fictional as any other. Whether the poet would call this an imaginary garden with real toads or a real garden with imaginary toads, the characters—Macurdy, Horace, Claudia, the two Ruths, Morley himself (except for the graft on his childhood), and the rest—are as fictional as characters in a novel can be. They have no counterparts in real life that I know of.

The Morley Mythology

PART ONE

1

Lately I have been talking to myself. Not out loud, unless I am alone, but I hear myself, and I hear me listening to myself. Perhaps I have always done this, but now that I am fifty I notice. I can distinguish between the speaker and the listener and between one speaker and another. The most important speaker is this *narrator* who tells me who I am, where I have been, where I am going. Pulls his stories out from the words and pictures in my head, links them up with gadgets of cause and effect, making narratives for us all to look at. The narrator is one speaker. There is also a *father,* as well as a *mother,* a *brother,* a *sister,* and a *wife.* The *manager* runs things. He is distinct from the *boss,* for whom he works. There are others too, and they all talk inside me from time to time.

They all claim to speak *for* me, and they appropriate my first person for their use. They say, "I thought so-and-so," when they really should say, "The father said so-and-so," or "The brother said so-and-so." It was the narrator who first noticed them, and now he tries to keep their identities clear, speaking of himself as "the narrator" and the manager and the boss and the father as themselves, and reserving the "I" for us all together.

If there is a narrator, there must also be a *reader,* and the narrator recognizes his voice too. The reader asks if this talking to myself in different voices doesn't represent disintegration of the personality. The narrator says no, the control of brain over surroundings has never been so good. Regards this as his own job—he himself ties things together, making them connect. Yet there are times—as the reader knows—when the narrator runs wild. Defies the manager. Drags out old pictures from the past and interrupts the business of the boss. The boss complains to the manager: Why do you let him loose like that? Can't help it, says the manager. When he does that I lose all control. Seems to think he's the boss himself. The boss warns: Just don't lose sight of me, he says.

2

Tell about my fiftieth birthday. Now it was November again, with overcast sky and chilly air as he came out of the office in the late afternoon (said this narrator) and the chilliness of the air warned of hard times to come. But the narrator insulated him like an overcoat, directing him to his car, which was parked in front of Old Main University Hall accumulating cold through a day of dropping temperature with warning smell of snow, while the sharpened edge of the November wind scraped against his nose, cheeks, eyebrows, under his glasses, down the back of his neck inside his overcoat where the collar hung open. All this physical terror (said the boy) kept out by the narrator, who found the car and directed him home in the late-afternoon traffic. Home again, said the narrator, to where Claudia waits, practicing the piano. This is the afternoon she comes home early, and tonight you take her out to dinner.

While he (said the narrator, speaking of me) waited for the light to change, the forthcoming winter tragedy blew up and down the street past the early lights in the shop fronts, whistled and cried against the slits of the car windows waiting in line or looking for parking among the meters, shivered around the car radios raising a shield of music against tragedy. No one noticed the tragedy yet, while the narrator spoke of his wife waiting and the plan to go out. And his success: Well, you made it to fifty, said the narrator.

The narrator regarded this as a triumph, but there was a disagreement. As I turned (finally) at the traffic light and made my way in bunching traffic down the shopping street, jamming the brake to save pedestrians flying between cars, I heard the brother growl: What's so great about being fifty?

We were stopped by the traffic in front of the movie theater, then the butcher shop, then the savings and loan office, then the drugstore. A neon sign in the window of the drugstore, bloody red. Winter hemorrhage, said the brother. How sad for you, he said, you're walking down a long hill—down, down, down. Fifty, the beginning of the end. When all that might have been ahead is not even behind. Sums of winter addition and subtraction, said the brother: fifty minus twenty is thirty, which was not so long ago when you remember early marriage days with Claudia, with Nancy and Bobby both infants, and you walked with them in a stroller to the playground and taught two sections of Introductory Geology. Fifty *plus* twenty is seventy, which was your father at seventy white and almost blind sitting on the porch and listening to birds. Yourself at fifty, said the brother, describing what was left of Michael Morley's gray hair, his potbelly, his deep eye pouches, his once good eyes that now need not merely reading glasses but bifocals. Can't run, jog, trot, without caving in the chest. Tiredness sets in early. Body has weights attached. The brother looks at his face, at the backs of his hands, and speaks of the rust and decay. How disgusting to be old, says the brother.

The narrator waited his chance to reply. Meanwhile I turned into the street where we lived. The narrator pointed to the Dean's house. That should shut the brother up. Michael Morley, Dean of the College. Make the brother look at it, this newly acquired house consequent upon this newly acquired deanship at age forty-nine.

Not usually available to younger men. Its large spread of lawn now brown—but see it in the spring, its lustrous green, with a hired man to mow it. Show the brother, and also the father and even the boy, this house, old and vast with a circular tower with curved windows (like the pilothouse windows of an old steamboat) and a porch with curved corners around three sides of the house (like the promenade deck of such a steamboat), mixing styles with walls of brown shingles and great stones. As the Dean turned his car up the driveway, the house said, Well done, Dean.

Almost every afternoon when he came home, the house said this. Well done, Dean. With a footnote about the joint success and combined salaries of a Dean of the College and a wife who was head of the Piano Department in the School of Music. Up the driveway through the old porte-cochere, back to the garage: the long garden hose coiled on the wall, the wheelbarrow, the mower, rakes and shovels. Six beagles come running when we come into the house, and Claudia stops practicing.

The boss felt better. As we dressed, the narrator encouraged him. This is the true prime of life, he said, when the well-developed man has his full powers, intellect is most keen, wisdom most functional, experience counts most—now before you begin to lose strength. Rather be this age than any other. Yes, the boss agreed. He was always passing contemptuous judgments on the years of Michael Morley's past: how naïve he was then (he would say), how stupid, ignorant. The narrator explained why: namely that this whole complex edifice of Michael Morley, Professor of Geology and Dean of the College, husband of Claudia the musician, father of Nancy and Bobby, college students—this whole construction that bore Michael Morley's name had only recently been finished. Work of a lifetime. Michael Morley is a better person than ever before, said the narrator. The reason is that the boss has more control over the parts than he ever had before. Never had those parts been less rebellious, less contentious, less disorderly. Never had Michael Morley's administration been so smooth.

The six dogs tried to block our way when we were ready to go. Tonight there were seven, actually: Claudia had brought in another one from the kennels. This dog's name was Ethelred. We could hear them howling when we left the house. As we drove to the restaurant, conscious of being well dressed, of the still-deepening winter chill and the warmth of clothes returning the warmth of blood, the narrator anticipated the celebratory evening. Described in advance the quiet of the table in the corner, and the martinis and the soup, the good wine and the good dinner, the pleasant waitress, and told how Michael and Claudia would find many things in their life today to talk about, things from the day, the University, the School of Music, the dogs, the questions students had for both of them—and everything will be as it should be, assured the narrator, and the boss was pleased.

3

Only one bad moment. While they were talking, someone called the narrator's attention to a piece of restaurant décor—the stylized image of a Greek helmet with a plume upon a circular shield, posted on the wall over the opposite tables. And flashed suddenly in the narrator's eyes, like a card:

DIOMEDES. Son of Tydeus. Greek hero of the Trojan War, prominent in the *Iliad.* Sometimes called Diomed. King of Argos, second to Agamemnon in numbers of ships under his command. Companion to Odysseus on several adventures. Dared to attack the god Ares and the goddess Aphrodite in battle. Sometimes called "The bravest of the Greeks."

(From *The Morley Mythology*)

"Look at that," I said suddenly. Interrupting Claudia, who was talking about . . . what was she talking about? She stopped and looked at me.

Come to attention, said the boss. Annoyed by this distraction, alarmed, afraid the narrator was running wild again. The narrator was urging the manager: Tell her, tell her about Diomedes, son of Tydeus. The boss and the manager struggled to hold him. You're out of my mind, said the boss.

"Look at what?" said Claudia.

"That Greek shield and helmet." She turned, surprised and puzzled. "Reminds me of—" The manager cut him off, censoring the explicit mention of Diomedes, son of Tydeus. "It reminds me of the pictures in a child's book of the *Iliad* I once had."

She looked at the helmet and shield, trying to understand. Turned to us with a funny look. "Oh?" she said.

"That's nice," said she.

"I interrupted what you were talking about."

"I've forgotten," she said.

Meanwhile the narrator, having been subdued, was apologizing. Said it wasn't really himself—not the narrator—who was running wild with irrelevancies and trivial distractions, it was not his own madness. It looks like the old *boy king,* he said, taking possession for a moment. The boss was alarmed. The boy king? he asked. Waking up after all these years?

The reader remembered the boy king, but had not heard of him in more than thirty years. That was a time long before the present boss came to power, a time when we were children and the world was legend. In those days, said the reader, the ruler was a boy and the boy was king. He ruled by choosing Favorites from the world around him, heroes who became his delegates, his ambassadors, personifications of his kingship. Like this Diomedes, son of Tydeus, said the reader, who was the boy king's Favorite hero in the Trojan War. No one could remember why Diomedes was the Favorite rather than Achilles or Hector or Odysseus—the choosing was lost in prehistory. But the whole world was stretched out like a map by the pins of the boy king's Favorites. When the boy king had to abdicate, the memory of the Favorites was stored in what the reader (archivist) called his Mythology—*The Michael Morley Mythology*—with a few remains preserved in old papers in the Dean's file. Not to be confused with the Greek Mythology, for sure, despite Diomedes. It was full of public figures, ballplayers, heroes, machines, and mountains. They all slept safe in the boy king's sleep, deep below the years of geological superstructure. No one had expected the boy king to rise again. No wonder the boss was alarmed—this kidnapping of the narrator, these wakenings by the king's old Favorites.

Now the reader remembered Diomedes as if he had never died. He remembered a colored picture in the child's *Iliad* captioned "DIOMED CASTING HIS SPEAR AGAINST ARES." It showed him standing on a chariot with his arm drawn back to cast a spear, wearing a helmet with a gold fringe. Red hair is visible over his forehead, over the top of the circular white shield which conceals his face and body above his short tunic, while the goddess Athene stands behind him dressed in green, urging him on. The picture was fresh and new. For almost an hour it remained vivid in the narrator's eyes before it began to fade and fall back into the king's sleep.

Fortunately Claudia did not know what had happened. Afterward the narrator could tell how they came home, warm with food and drink and talk and feelings, and the boss smiled and said, Don't mind me, and they turned out the lights in the room with the curved windows in the corner of the house under the old tower.

Later in the night the narrator woke up and went to work because the boss was worried about prowlers and termites. Perhaps he was also worried about usurpation. The narrator brought in sightseers instead, to lead through the interior of the Dean. We have a deanship here, he said, a ship of Dean, with displays and exhibits. The name in the front of the catalogue where the administrative offices are listed, and also alphabetical in the faculty list with title following. Reappears in lists of university and college committees, *ex officio* as Dean of the College.

The narrator took the sightseers to the office in Old Main University Hall, past the outer office with the secretaries and the office on the side for the Assistant Dean (Fred Whorsky) to the office in the back with the white letters on the black sign: "OFFICE OF THE

DEAN." Pointed out the rug on the floor, the large desk, the curtains, the old family paintings, and finally the Dean himself, sitting mostly bald but with some gray around the sides, behind his desk, plump and smiling. Benevolent. Michael Morley—ex-boy, ex-geologist. Gaining weight, glasses with dark frames, competent (said the narrator) and kindly. Once again the narrator told the familiar story of how he became Dean, chosen by a committee from a field of candidates: how surprised everybody was, for Michael Morley was not your run-of-the-mill political type but a true professor of geology, and how glad that it wasn't either of the others who got the appointment.

When the reader asked what vantage point would most vividly display the Sights of the Dean, the narrator said it would have to be in the past, before Michael Morley became an ex-boy or at any rate an ex-geologist. Now they gathered all those sightseers out of the past into the auditorium to applaud. They were all there: the boy and the student, the graduate student and the young geologist. The young father and the lieutenant. The summer vacationist and the young professor and the son and the older brother. The disorganized lover and also the clown. The paranoid was there and the coward. They all looked at the Dean and expressed their admiration for what a grand and capacious ship it was. When the narrator told them that the Dean had now been occupied by Michael Morley, they were impressed, saying what a tribute to him. Vindicating their faith against those who scoffed or ignored. Against those who could not see where Michael Morley (quiet, slow and steady, falsely called a bore) would go when he reached the prime of life, those great deanbuildings.

The applause rang out. It was a standing ovation. It rang into the night, into the sleep, into the next day, all the next day. It was still ringing, the narrator remembered, all over the shining obliterated page of the geology textbook he was reading the next evening and ringing at the moment when the telephone ringing distinguished itself from it.

4

The Dean was reading the geology textbook to keep up in his field, for he was afraid of falling behind since becoming an administrator. That was the evening (said the narrator) of the first anonymous telephone call, interrupting his reading. It was not the first interruption that night. The first came as the Dean settled down to read—another slide flashed upon the screen:

RICHARD II (1367–1400). King of England, son of Edward the Black Prince. Came to throne in 1377 at age of ten. Quieted the Peasants' Revolt, but later errors in judgment led to his deposition and abdication in 1399. Replaced by Henry of Bolingbroke, crowned Henry IV. Died in prison, 1400. Patron of Chaucer. Inventor of the handkerchief.

(From *The Morley Mythology*)

The boy king again, announcing his intention to revolt with an image of himself? Ignore him, said the manager, sink into your reading and swim. The Dean read:

The hypothesis that the sea floor is spreading laterally from active ridges grew out of the discovery that. The latest version of the hypotheosis combines conviction conversion convolution, continental drift, and the origin of. It states that new oceanic crust keeps appearing keeps appearing keeps appearing above, corruption within the mantle at the crest of an active old age.

Somewhere a distant argument, voices dragging downward, but the woman ignored him, ignored the argument. In the sea, she forgot the argument altogether. Spoke of the sea mostly green-gray shading into blue in the distance. Flecks of sea water, sun shining on the sea water. Bright and blinding, eyes squint. She remembered the dazzling sea water, and spoke now of the earth, of geology, of the mind of the earth, of the earth's unconscious, roiling around beneath the crust. He's in there, cried the boy, hiding in there, peeking out. And the earth itself under the sea, she said, the bright sea in the sunlight. Work hard, she said. Read well.

Then it spreads laterally across the sea floor, and disappears slowly fading away dying singing (Liebestod) where a cool, descending conviction current beneath a sea-floor trench drags it downward

The pages shone in artificial light, obliterating words. The sea surface glistened, and the sky spread clear and blue and enormous to all horizons, with only a few puffs of dark-gray clouds near the edge, down low, in one direction. He's under the surface, said the boy, the water rat, the dwarf, Alberich. The sky was blank. The sky had nothing to say, she said. Only in the middle of the view, steaming down toward us, heavy smoke pouring up into the sky, the big white steamer in the middle of a flat sea, paddles churning, bearing down upon us. She gripped the rail. Read, insisted the manager.

The ocean crust is disposable, in a continual state of flux (full of sex), and can be renewed completely every career can be renewed completely life can be every 200 to 300 million years. While all this activity takes place on the sea floor all this partying all this celebration all this ringing of bells (praising the Dean) the continental mosses the incontinent messes the catholic masses drift passively along (we all drift) souls houses deans drift passively along not on the surface but at a depth of 100km or so

She did not know the time, but reached to turn it off, while the boss said praises ringing for the Dean and the narrator said the tele and the manager said read it right while the narrator said the telephone and the boss was saying who is calling with praises for the Dean? until the narrator repeated, Telephone!

The narrator took over. On that evening (said the narrator) after his fiftieth birthday, Dean Michael Morley sat in the living room reading a geology textbook. He sat in the large brown armchair to the left of the fireplace, while his wife, Claudia, sat in the armchair (dark blue and red) on the other side. It was a quiet evening, although the Dean was aware that it was cold out, with snow falling, the sound of the distant traffic hushed in the falling of the snow. All these evenings were quiet (said the narrator) now that the children had gone away to college, and Claudia chose not to practice at night. It was into just such silence that the telephone jabbed, cruel yet eager, offering a promise or a threat—guess which? The Dean resisted the impulse to leap and run (toward or away). He moved with dignity appropriate to his rank and years. He set his book down deliberately, glanced at Claudia, and walked quietly to the phone, which stood on the little table between the living room and the dining room. Picked up the receiver and spoke courteously:

"Hello?"

The telephone did not reply. There was a silence, said the narrator (silence filling up rapidly, water pouring over the edge of the continental shelf into the oceanic basin, filling up the ocean in a flood with steam and geysers, and then all flattening into the sudden hush of the telephone again, and he heard the telephone holding its breath, the shocked silence of the telephone, unable to speak because of the noise in the deanship at that moment), only the silence of the unspeaking receiver in his ear, and the slight, at first most mild, most delicate, barely noticeable shock (said the narrator) that comes from not getting any of the responses you naturally expect. Now, who could that be? Well, it doesn't seem to be anybody, said the manager, unless someone is too shocked to speak. Or the connection is not working.

"Hello," I repeated.

Again the telephone failed to respond, and the silence pushed through the sea with a heavy bow wave, and he heard the malice of the telephone in refusing to perform its function.

I tried once more, though he knew it was futile, and I said for the third time, "Hello." With a quaver in the voice, said the manager, disgusted—so disgusted that when the silence again replied, he did not wait, but put the phone down hard. Slam, said the manager. Catching the slithering silence with an ax just as it was trying to get away—cutting off its head. Because he was just beginning to get a glimpse of him, said the watchman, the little ratty punk at the other end of the line, the dirty eyes, the long pointed nose, the cigarette stub dangling from his lip.

"What was that?" said Claudia.

"Nobody," I said.

The first time something like that happens, the manager tries to give everybody the benefit of the doubt, devise the explanation that disturbs least the calm movement of time leading into it. Censoring the watchman's warning of enemy and danger, ruling against anything that would throw the crowd into a panic. The manager denied all enemies, ruled out even a malfunction of the telephone, and called it only an accident, a human error by some caller who got the wrong number and was too paralyzed by confusion to apologize, explain, or even hang up when he heard your unfamiliar voice. With such calm words the manager quieted the crowd, and we resumed our reading:

While all this activity takes place on the sea floor the continental masses drift passively along, not on the surface as was formerly supposed but on the top of the low-velocity zone in the upper mantle at a depth of 100km or so. The relationships of Greenland and Rockall Bank to the Reykjanes Ridge southwest of Iceland illustrate banking hours dean hours telephone hours time taken from work traveling Greenland to Rockall Bank by boat to hear the singers singing the saga illustrate the simplest example of spreading drift and corruption (Fig. 22-18, A)

Focus:

If we assume that Greenland and Rockall Bank were joined together about 60 million years ago when the basalts of the Thulean Province were extruded and that they began to drift apart soon afterward

King of the Thulean Province basso Queen of the Thulean soprano married Claudia soprano and Horace basso Ruth mezzo and Michael tenor about 60 million years ago and began to drift apart Horace and Ruth on collision course sinking ships

Come back:

then their average rate of drift has been 2cm/year. A continuous rate of spreading of 1cm/year yields a close fit between anomaly curves and polarity episodes (Fig. 22–18, B) anomaly fits between close curves and naked polarity episodes between naked anomaly curves and close fits

How does this history of the Ringing Ridge compare with the first ringing of the Ringing Telephone newly again the naked caller ringing Does evidence elsewhere agree that interruptions of ringing again distract and interrupt the spreading and drift that twice thrice is ringing again?

Right, said the manager, it's the telephone. The narrator said, This is the second call in five minutes. The boss said, We must answer it nevertheless as if there had been no other. As I walked (deliberately slow) to the telephone, the manager was saying, Easy boy, we don't know anything yet, and the father was asking, Why is he fluttering? With his big sturdy old house overlooking a broad descending lawn, comfortably deaned in his living room on a quiet evening with only a telephone to irritate the nerves.

"Hello?"

So it was not a mistake, a wrong number. Not a malfunctioning, either, said the narrator. Someone is deliberately—said the narrator. Still the manager gave them every chance.

"Who are you calling?" he asked.

No answer.

"Hello," he said again.

No sound. And yet the line is not dead, said the watchman. He listened for breathing and heard nothing, yet knew there was a living presence at the other end. How do you know that? asked the reader. Somehow, said the watchman. One of those things a watchman knows. A living presence. Meanwhile I hung up and said to Claudia, "Again."

"Oh, dear," she said. "Are we going to have this to put up with again?"

(For it has happened before, said the narrator. Prank calls, crank calls, sick calls, the calls everyone receives from time to time, said the narrator, making the least of them.)

Resumed reading, but the crowd was clamoring now, the reporters asking questions, while the manager tried to calm them with a speech.

How does the history of the Reykjanes Ridge compare with the rest of the Mid-Atlantic Ridge? Does evidence elsewhere agree that 1,200km of new sea floor have been created since the end of Cretaceous time? The only answer we can give in Cretaceous time is that someone wanted to annoy us (but did not speak obscenely did not threaten did not extort did not abuse did not blackmail) we have no idea who and until we have evidence the only fair assumption is that this voice was a Cretaceous voice out of the ancient abysmal plain

With the phone ringing once again that evening, to make three times altogether. The manager gave the mob more leeway, and the mob said, "God damn!" She looked up from her reading and said, "Would you like me to answer it?"

"All right." Watched her go to the phone, and then her low soft beautiful voice. "Hello?" Watched as she waited and without speaking again quietly lowered the phone onto the hook. "What shall we do?" she said.

I mumbled, "If it continues—"

She sat down and said, "If we don't offer any encouragement—"

"Right," I said.

Once again the Dean read his geology.

The latest version of the hypotheosis states that nothing can be done. The oceanic crust is in a continual state of flux, and you can cuss them out and expel them and prosecute them and call the police and set up a trap, and if nothing else works you can get an unlisted number (which you give only to your friends and you can keep a list of those to whom you have given the number and thus you can tell if he calls again) a number which can be renewed completely every 200 to 300 million years.

Meanwhile the narrator drew a sketch. Described a young man, a kid, with stringy reddish hair, a thin throat, and a prominent Adam's apple. Placed him by a telephone on a wooden chair in a small room like a closet, hunched him over the telephone, wire twisted around his arms, legs crossed and double-crossed, body all knots, smirking and keeping silent his chortle. Waiting and listening to the ringing of the number he had dialed, and the quiet voice that said, "Hello." Now his little eyes narrowed, his mouth opened, he gripped his thigh and waited through the second and third tense and frightened "Hello," until the click of the phone and the dial tone released him, and he let it out in a harsh noise: "Haw! Haw! Haw!"

Hoar, hoar, hoar, yourself! roared the sheriff. Then the narrator described how the sheriff went in the night, late when the streets were dark, down to the back-street area where the call originated, down among the barrels and the warehouses, went up the stairs silently, listened through the door to the dialing of the phone and the ringing, and then burst in. He stood over him where he huddled over the telephone in knots and said in a loud voice: "Hello!"

The punk fell backward in his chair and banged his head against the woodwork. Don't kill me, he begged, please! The sheriff laughed.

5

The next night there were two more calls of the same kind, and the narrator knew that something had begun. After that the calls kept coming, and they were all the same. They came in the prime of the evening, between ten and eleven when it was quiet and peaceful, the dinner and the dishes done, my wife and I reading in our spacious living room in the time left before retiring. They came on the third, fourth, fifth, sixth, seventh days, one two or three calls a night, all of them the same, each a silence alive yet not breathing, into which my "Hello" (always friendly yet getting edgy) or Claudia's sank and died.

They went into the next week, and weeks became more weeks with more of the same. We learned to recognize the silence the moment we heard it, the moment it came silent in the receiver to our ears. We learned to recognize it in the ring of the telephone, although never quickly enough to avoiding answering. I said to Claudia, "We mustn't give him the satisfaction. If he doesn't answer, hang up."

"Right," she said. "And if he should say something—don't answer."

He had tricks and we had responses: he called twice in quick succession. We let him ring. We took him off the hook, and left him off the hook all night. When we did this, the dial tone began to complain, peep peep peep peep! Pain in the machine, a cat yowling. Still the calls came. One night I said to the silence, "I'm going to get an unlisted number." The silence did not reply. "It won't do any good to tell him that," said Claudia.

Later the narrator would look back upon those days and recall the uneasy arguments over what the silence was trying to say. The manager said it was only an irritation, a nuisance, no need to be afraid. But the narrator kept asking: Why would someone call you on the telephone and give you only silence? Because he has it in for you, said the brother. Out to get you. Why should anyone be out to get you? asked the mother, who could never understand such things. But there were the calls to prove it, and the only possible inference is that the caller expects you to be frightened and is determined to make you so. If it is a stranger, how frightening for the craziness of it, but if it is someone you know, how much the worse. And if you don't believe he has scared you, said the brother, notice how the heart chonks and sloshes about whenever the telephone rings during the accustomed evening hours. And afterward how you go back to your armchair with your insides going chonk chonk chonk.

Sometimes the reader asked the narrator to justify these queasy fears. So the narrator described how the caller would grow impatient with simply annoying you over the phone. You would become aware of eyes watching you through crowds of students in university corridors. Then a threat. Go to such-and-such a phone booth to find out what's good for you. Someone shoves you in a crowd downtown. You dodge out of an elevator. At night the dogs whine, shivering, something outside the window, in the bushes. You wake at night, the shape of a man standing over the bed, huge, leaning over you, whispering: Why didn't you speak to me when I called you on the phone?

The word came down from above: an order against anxiety. The boss was against fear. He was sick of it and thought our deanship should protect us against it. The narrator's sketch of the boss's rise to power looked like a path through swamps of fear, most of which had been needless. Fear of failures—but look at us now. Fear of accident, illness, loss of children, trouble with Claudia. Fear of war, disease, doomsday. All groundless. The boss said his power was based mainly upon the conquest of fear. Let no silent caller take this away from us.

Nevertheless—the narrator pointed out to the boss how afraid he was of fear itself. There's always something to be afraid of—said the narrator to the boss—as long as you live in time, swimming in a present with a future ahead of you and a past trailing off behind you. This was one of the narrator's functions, he said, to sketch the fears of what might happen and to erase the unrewarded fears from the record of the past.

Maybe it's the god of narrative retribution, said the narrator, calling you because he heard you boasting of your success in the prime of life. Complacency leads to comeuppance, by all narrative laws. You could always have an accident: fall, break something. Car crash. Drop dead of a heart attack. Consider paralysis. Or blindness. Suppose you go blind? Or it could happen to Claudia. Or Nancy or Bobby. Maybe the caller wants to warn you of the coming of old-age disease and pain. The loss of your mind, the downward slide toward senility, or, if you prefer, some faster crash into a bright madness peculiar and appropriate to *you.* The boss resisted these suggestions. The boss wished to believe that no fear was worth admitting except useful fears, fears capable of ordering protective action.

Meanwhile the narrator, caught in his own gloom, said the whole world is turning gray. Spoke of the old horror that would come out of the sky, pointed and ready in somebody's silo. If that is too obvious, consider things breaking up from the inside out instead of outside in. States of guerrilla war down the street. Bombs in buses and in city squares. Collapse of the economy. Telephones all go dead. Money is suddenly worthless. No gasoline for the car, no way to get out of the house. Doomsday rumors in the Morley mind—always present somewhere in the house, and sometimes the narrator would intercept them and show them to the boss, who would always say, Take them away.

The manager called this distraction and directed the narrator to find his gloom rather in immediate specific personal things. The question of whether Mr. Runzel the neighbor will soon complain about the collapsing retaining wall between our properties. The question of whether the Department of Romance Languages will make trouble because you cut their budget more than that of the German Department. The question whether Helen Mehring in the outer office has aroused so much antagonism among the younger faculty by her manner that you will have to speak to her. These and other things, said the manager, weary and turning away.

The narrator objected: It's not a question of loose general anxiety; it's a question of a specific silent stranger who is harassing you over the phone. Right, said the brother. A specific blackmail plot that has to be coped with. The reader jumped. Blackmail? he demanded. Who said anything about blackmail? The narrator groaned with a new fright, and then suddenly there was a roar and in came the sheriff on his motorcycle, asking what the hell was the matter with us to let some foreigner get the better of us like this. The sheriff's mood was lynch. His bull neck was red, inflamed, incandescent with outrage at the punky stranger without a voice who thought he could frighten us by a mere presence. The sheriff's outrage grew whenever the telephone rang, whenever the word *Hello* went unanswered and he heard the telltale fearing chonk

chonk chonk. His big hands were shaped for strangling. Just let me get hold of him, he said.

The sheriff wrote a speech that he wanted the manager to read into the telephone, words that would burn the punk up from a distance. Saying: This is a Dean you are trying to scare. Do you think a Dean cares for your silence, your heavy breathing, that is to say your not breathing at all? Do you think the things that frighten you would frighten *him*? Have you ever felt the scorn of a Dean?

Neither fear nor rage was authorized by the boss. The boss's policy was always to be calm and restrained, above all panic emotions. The father agreed with him. You are a Dean, he said, you symbolize something to him. Who knows what? Perhaps he is a student or a graduate, or one who failed to graduate, or perhaps just a citizen of the town. You symbolize authority, or his own father. You represent the institution, or he sees in you the personal embodiment of the cause of his failures. You stand for the fine house you live in and his idea of money, his idea of age or of middle-class values. To him, you may be the devil himself, and you don't even know him. There are no limits to what he might think you are, said the father.

The only problem to worry about, repeated the manager, is the question what to do. What, if *anything*. You could scare him, suggested the boy—bluff, fake him out. Next time the phone rings, say quickly as if you had a hookup with the police: "Here it is, officer, this one. Got it?" The mother said you should be gentle: a madman like that must be suffering, she said. Can you even *begin* to imagine how much? Surprise him with sympathy, she said. Next time he calls, tell him, "I understand how lonely you must feel." Recommend a psychiatrist. The sister said madmen don't yield to persuasion or sympathy. The only way is to be practical, take the measures that will force them to stop. Call the police, she said, and arrange a trap. Or get an unlisted number. The sheriff said that this would be a surrender to the outlaw. The father agreed. Why should you let a mad stranger cut you off from the unknown, from forgotten friends, geologists from other universities, cousins passing through town? The father said the best way would be just to give no satisfaction, let time go its natural way, let him get tired of it himself. Follow the advice in the telephone book:

What to do about obscene or harassing phone calls.

1. *Don't talk.*
   What this kind of caller really wants is an audience. Don't be that audience.

2. *Hang up.*
   Hang up if the caller doesn't say anything.
   Hang up at the first obscene word or improper question.
   Hang up if the caller doesn't identify himself to your satisfaction.

3. *Call police.*
   Call the police if any kind of threat is made.

4. *Call us.*
   If obscene or harassing calls persist, please call the Telephone Company Business Office. We're quite concerned about these calls. We want to do everything we can to help stop them and to assist police in the apprehension of persistent offenders.

6

The boss kept the narrator busy in those days trying to shape the silence into a person, with face, body, eyes, hair, and character of some kind. For the first two or three weeks, he attached the long-nosed, red-haired punk firmly to the other end of the line. He composed the kid's raspy breathing in the nonbreathing silence, and the stillness, the hush, moved in the shadow of the punk gnawing his fingernails and picking his nose. Soon the narrator reminded the boss where the punk had come from. Telling how he had come into his office on the day of the first call, this student (long nose, red hair with a straight lock hanging across his forehead but cut otherwise short for these times), summoned because he was charged by his English professor with plagiarism. The narrator surveyed the painful discussion that ensued, the inarticulate kid who would neither admit nor deny that he knew what plagiarism was. "Do you know what I'm talking about?" said the Dean. Finally the kid said, "I'm no writer. I want to be an accountant. I ain't much for all this words and style and shit." And all the while the narrator made him look shrewd and foxlike out of his little eyes, squirming in his blue jeans. Inarticulate, said the narrator, as he slouched out of the office at the end of the interview, looking for an inarticulate way to express what he felt. The boss objected to the identification. He said even a punk is innocent until proven guilty. The narrator clung to the kid, though, because it was in character.

The brother urged him to consider other candidates. Find a person and attach him to the call, see if he fits. The doctor said you couldn't tell by appearance: such calls were the product of concealed madness, and the thing that made concealed madness hard to recognize was that it was concealed. So the caller might be anybody. The brother suggested possibilities you (narrator) would least expect. Try Nina Herring, his secretary—how would she look ringing up his number and holding her breath while he answered and looked for a reply? Or Reuben Gorman, the exceptionally friendly Ph.D. student in geology, who kept stopping him in the halls to talk? Or the mail carrier who brought the campus mail to the office every morning with a strange staring look and sullen manner? Or the teller at the bank who always looked down, avoiding his eyes?

During the day now the narrator watched them—these and others: the cashier in the faculty lunchroom, the student member of the long-range planning committee who had a way of looking at him curiously. One afternoon at a meeting his suspicion lit upon President Walnutt himself, who might have a secret madness like any of the rest of us (why should we assume he does not?). Might he not get kicks out of haunting his subordinates in unguessed ways at odd hours of the night?

Then suddenly one night in January there came out of the silence a voice. First, the now familiar ringing of the phone. The goddammit weary rising from the chair while Claudia looks up from her book, and the usual quickening of the heart. He picked up the phone and heard music. It was the soaring voice of a dramatic soprano, riding a full orchestra, operatic, grand, Germanic, and familiar. He knew the music; they had the record. It was not Claudia's music but his own, or rather that of the dormant boy king—but in front of the music he recognized the same familiar enemy silence. "Hello? Hello?" No answer, only the music. He lingered before hanging up, to catch a few more phrases, though the sister reminded him that if he wanted to hear the music he could play it on his own set and not give the madman the satisfaction.

And then suddenly a sound in the foreground, a giggle, a stifled laugh. Girlish. It caught the narrator, the sound of it, and he listened, trying for more. In an instant the connection was severed between the plagiarizing punk and the silent telephone. The narrator stared at the image that was filling up the blankness that was left. Staring, his eyes took in names on the bookshelf over the telephone table: green guides to Austria, Switzerland, Germany, Paris, while the silence reshaped itself into a woman's face, a woman's mind, black hair, eyelashes, bangs low over the forehead, a woman's richly decorated face slowly smiling at him to remind him of things—things she did not want to let the narrator forget. My God, could it be *she?* asked the manager, in a frozen voice.

Blackmail! whispered the brother. So it's blackmail, not madness, or it's blackmail and madness together. Now the boss was truly frightened. He asked the manager, If it is *she,* what will you do to protect me? The father objected. She wouldn't do that, he said. Like hell she wouldn't! said the brother. She'll do anything. The sister said, This is ridiculous. Even a crazy woman wouldn't blackmail you by silent long-distance calls to no purpose, two or three calls per night—it would cost a fortune. All this, while the manager to steady his panic spoke again (low, whispering, with a glance at Claudia) to that sound of giggle he had heard—asked her to come forth, said, "Is that you, Ruth?"

There was a gasp, then a kind of a squeal, and she said, "Who did you say?"

Wrong, said the narrator. That's not Ruth. He said, "Who is this?"

"Who do you think it is?" she said.

"I'm asking you." The sheriff coming in.

After a pause she said, "Don't you recognize me?" Not offended, but as if it were funny. The narrator recognized nothing in her voice, which was light, soft, balancing close to the edge of laughter, no doubt young. He groped through the files looking for the voice that would not fit. Ran through Nancy, Penny, Nina Herring, his secretary, even Mother, though Mother is dead, looking for a match, though knowing in advance that none would fit. Meanwhile she said, "You called me Roof."

"That was a mistake." Cover your tracks, said the watchman. "I was expecting a call."

"Aw, come on," she teased. "How did you know my name?"

"I don't know your name."

"You called me Roof. Roofie."

"Is that your name?"

Now she laughed, high-pitched, a light furry laugh that reached like arms around his neck. Prostitute! said the mother. Someone is trying to embarrass you sexually, said the brother. Only the father held out, concerned by our failure to recognize someone who claimed to know us. Who will be hurt by our forgetting.

Which you will simply have to risk, said the manager.

Suddenly the sheriff asked: "Who are you calling?"

"Why, you, baby, no one but you."

Brother whispered, It could be a student trying to screw the Dean into something stupid. "You have the wrong number," said the manager.

"No I don't. It's you I'm calling. You know me."

"Not unless you identify yourself. I don't recognize you."

"Roof. Roofie, I told you. You knew my name."

"I don't know any Ruth."

"Aw—ho ho ho. I don't believe *that,* no, sir."

"Well, I don't know you."

"Too bad," she said.

"I'm going to hang up unless you tell me what you want."

"I just wanted to hear you talk."

Drunk? Dope? Try this, suggested the lawyer: "Do you want to speak to Claudia?"

"Who? Who's Claudia?" She started to laugh, then caught herself: "Oh!" And laughed again, this time high and hilarious. "No, honey, just you."

Sheriff again: "Then we have nothing to talk about, do we?"

There was a moment of pain that made the girl cry as he snipped the strange voice off, but the manager said it had to be done.

"Who was that?" said Claudia.

The Dean came out of conference to reply. "Some sassy kid calling herself Ruth."

She gave me a look full of memory, but all she said was, "Is that the one who has been calling?" The narrator guessed she was, some crazy student at the University, probably. He wondered at the coincidence that gave her the name of Ruth.

7

The manager asked the narrator, What made you call her Ruth? You shouldn't pull surprises on me like that. The boss was displeased too: he did not like to have the reader's clear and cleanly ended story undermined by the narrator's endless uncertainties. What is it you are so nervous about? asked the boss.

So once again the narrator sent the reader back to check it out. Back to the bright still room upstairs in his sister Penny's summer cottage, with the sun on the curtains lifted ever so gently by the light breeze, and a light buzzing sound from the yellow fields outside. With Ruth, Horace's young third wife, lying on the bed, propped on one elbow, smoking a cigarette, wearing no clothes. Her skin was bright in the sunny afternoon room, her dark hair fell in low bangs just above her eyes, her eyes themselves were decorated and violet as she looked at him thoughtfully, wonderingly, doubtfully.

And then, said the reader, this last thing stands out: how when Claudia found out about it this October, she went out to the car and drove away. It was a Saturday, and not until evening did he learn that she had gone to the beagle farm. Calling him up in the late afternoon: "Go to a restaurant and get your dinner," she said. "I can't talk to you yet." She came back at midnight. It was the next day before she could talk. She denied that her flight had anything to do with what he had told her. "I had work to do," she said. But then it came out: "Is it that you want a divorce?" *Morley:* No no no, it was nothing, nothing, only a summer afternoon (or two) while you were away. *Claudia:* Nothing? Nothing? How could it be nothing?

They talked all afternoon, and the reader hid most of what they said in the confidential file, where only fragments could leak out. *Claudia:* I don't understand, I don't understand. . . . *Claudia:* You never put anything like this between us before. Were you thinking of me at all? . . . *Claudia:* I don't want to be a goddamn jealous possessive wife. But god *damn!*

The reader told her that it was over, cleanly over, and the manager said it would not happen again. She said, "You say so, it damn well better." The talk stopped. The narrator said it was dangerous ground and criticized the reader for calling it a clean end. Look again at the narrative, said the narrator; it was a messy end.

The reader reread the messiness of the end. He saw it gathering during both the summers in which they met, Ruth saying, repeating, "Will you help me?" "What kind of help do you want?" "You must help me stand up to Horace when the time comes." She detected the brother's reservations. "So I'm just a summer afternoon, right?" she said. With bitterness she said, "Nothing must disturb our happy marriage to Claudia." It made the boss angry. Right, he said, nothing must. Asked the lawyer what claim she had. The lawyer denied she had any claims at all and blamed it on the youth, who must have given her secret promises. The youth said he never promised her anything but his happy self on a sunny afternoon. Meanwhile the manager tried to soothe her melancholy. "I'd like to help you if I could," he said. She smiled ironically. "If you could," she said.

The reader reviewed one day last summer when Ruth said, "I'll probably leave Horace when we get back to New York. If I do, will you leave Claudia?" My God, how they clamored to answer her. Sheriff in the lead, telling her, Certainly not, we have no intention of leaving her, never did. The sheriff called it an arrogant suggestion. The narrator explained that the boss loved Claudia and so did the father and sister and the narrator himself, and she was a strong member of the organization. "Yes," said Ruth grimly, "I knew you would say something like that." The unspoken words that passed between the husband of Claudia and the wife of Horace—unspoken across the table, past, around, and under the live presences of Penny and George, of Horace, of all the children—were angry.

In the reader's most polished account, it was Ruth herself who was to blame, but when the father or the narrator pressed the reader to dig out a more candid report, the reader usually put the blame on the youth. This youth had not been seen for many years. He had been the ruler once, long ago, at some time after the boy king and before the boss took over—a brief adventurous rule. Who reappeared now, unexpectedly, on a sunny summer day, year before last, the day that the reader was afterward to designate as the Beginning. That was the day that Ruth and the future Dean were left alone (convenient details enumerated by the youth: Claudia gone for two weeks—as she annually was—to the Valley Summer Music Festival, Penny and George on an all-day trip to Bangor to visit an old friend, Horace deep-sea fishing with all the children). And why didn't the Dean go deep-sea fishing? asked the lawyer. Because he was expecting a long-distance call from the University, said the Dean, and it was a good opportunity to do some of the office work he had brought along. And Ruth? Because she gets seasick, said the reader.

The reader's record for that morning shows the Dean doing his opportune work on a table on the porch. It shows Ruth coming onto the porch several times and the Dean responsive to her apologies, full of assurances that she was not disturbing him, not at all. She wore jeans and a red kerchief over her black hair, and she leaned against his table with an amused look on her face. The talk grew lively, with a momentum that destroyed the Dean's opportunity to work. It was personal, and the Dean was not accustomed to learning so many private things about a person so quickly. She talked frankly about Horace. What he expected of her. How she became involved with him. Certain disappointments. Certain fears. The sickening slow discovery that you have made a mistake. And she spoke of other men in her life, affairs she had had. She spoke also of him, of Michael Morley the brother, how she knew him vicariously through Horace. And the happiness of the Morley childhood, such a contrast to her own.

Sitting on the edge of his table, she was so close, so free, it was easy for the narrator and the manager, who thrived with talk, though the boss held back, always doubtful. The boss said, she doesn't know us as well as she thinks, and he was a little offended. She mentioned a half-brother she had who lived in the Dean's own home town—a real estate agent. "Let me give you his number," she said. "You two would like each other." The manager took the name politely, but the boss was annoyed. How could she imagine that he and her half-brother the real estate agent would like each other? The boss maintained his aloofness, but the youth was looking at her breasts in her navy-blue sweater, at her jeans, at her violet eyes and her low black bangs. The youth returned the frank direct look in her eyes with the hint of a challenge in them. Suddenly the youth announced in a loud voice: *It's all right.* What's all right? said the manager. I tell you it's all right, said the youth. Through lunch, while they ate sandwiches in the kitchen, the youth repeated it: It's all right. I promise you it's all right—as if the youth had secret knowledge. And after lunch when they returned to the porch, still talking (as if talk itself were an organism with a life of its own), again the youth said it: Goddammit, it's all right! It was her eyes, staring at him, asking him, Do you dare?

The reader told how the manager's fear was overcome by the youth's confidence. Just as she turned to go, the manager reached out to her. She stopped, looked at him, came closer. He moved his hand up from her waist. She was quivering, her eyes searching. The youth said, I told you it was all right. She said, "You don't want to involve me in another mess, do you?" Her eyes said something else, though. She said, "Should you be worrying about Claudia?" When the youth slipped his hand under her sweater she said, "Let's go upstairs." She was pulling off the sweater on the way up, while the brother following gave warnings about her complexity, her unhappiness, the expectations she would have, the complications that would ensue. The brother was not reassured by her trembling smile. Don't think you are going upstairs for a casual afternoon adventure, he said. But he was overruled by the youth, who cried, It's all right, with even more conviction when he saw her lying naked on the bed and with triumph—*It's all right! Ah hah!*—as he came close and leaned over her. The word *adultery* sounded faintly, sadly, in the distance, and someone mourning for Claudia, but it was drowned out by the thumping calisthenics of the youth.

There was a lot of grief that afternoon, mourning by the father and mother, the wife, the husband, and the boss himself, as if Claudia had died. Soon there was also this anxiety of brother and lawyer about Ruth's mood and her expectations. But it was all muffled by the strident gloating of the youth. The narrator himself joined in the youth's celebration, leaving the manager, his normal impulses pushed around in several directions, confused. During the remainder of those two weeks these contenders struggled with each other. After the summer was over, the narrator gave the whole episode to the reader to stow away in the files—something for the past. The following summer brought an attenuated replay, but it was no longer the youth's show. It was taken over by the manager for the sake of peace with Ruth, who said she had been expecting it, assuming it. There was little support from the rest of us, except a vague loosely identified man of the woods, who chewed his cud and said she was a fine sexual woman even if she was discontented and angry about it.

The sheriff was angered by the audacity of her anger, all through the short two weeks of their second summer. The mutual anger was difficult for the manager to conceal when the visit came to an end and they had to say goodbye, all of them standing in front of Penny's cottage with everybody—Penny, George, Horace, the children—shaking hands and kissing. The narrator remembered the straight, unsmiling, unforgiving stare with which Ruth's violet eyes attacked his own at the moment when, to please the others, he shook her hand.

The reader said it was cleanly ended, but the narrator could not erase the smudge of Claudia's pain, her cry, her humiliation, when she heard about it. How could you have dared? said the narrator to the youth. To risk so much for so little? The manager promised solemnly, Never again. (The youth said Claudia had no grounds for complaint, but they shut him up—this youth who had seen nothing, knew nothing of twenty-five years of history that had accumulated since his time.) Claudia—and that last dark velvet dominating and destroying stare by Ruth. The narrator heard that stare in moments of deepest silence. He heard it in the silence of the telephone.

8

Though the narrator knew that the strange caller was not Ruth, he could not get rid of the idea that there was some connection. The youth would not listen to this. He had been wakened by the provocative girlish voice of the caller and wished she would call again. The narrator was shocked and warned the manager not to listen to the youth. Even if there is no connection to Ruth, that girl's voice can only be dangerous, he said. The father stayed calm: Most probably just a teasing kid, dangerous only if the youth or someone else makes her so.

This lasted a couple of days. Then again the telephone. I said: "Hello?"

A pause, long enough to recognize the silence again, filled now with the imagined face of an unknown girl, and I held a moment longer than usual on the chance she might break the silence again. And the silence did break. It broke upon a voice that quietly replied, "Hello"—only it was a man's voice. I did not recognize it.

"Who are you calling?"

"You," said the man.

The narrator said this was the silent caller at last—before the manager reminded him that we had already discovered the silent caller, who was a lecherous young girl. Who had answered the same question in the same way. Are there two of them? asked the father.

"What do you want?" I said.

A long pause. The manager was afraid the caller would not speak again, until he said, "I thought it was time to introduce myself."

"Yes? Who are you?"

Another silence, while the narrator reiterated his belief that we now had the true silent caller, that the girl the other time was someone else, an impostor. The man's voice said, "I thought it was time for you to hear the sound of my voice." Words spoken quietly, slowly, without color, the voice nasal. Over that stillness, the narrator boasted of his proof, while I, pushing the inquiry, asked as naïvely as I could: "Why should I want to hear the sound of your voice?"

"Haven't you been trying to?"

The manager came to. Gave a clear order: Hang up—now. The

order didn't get through, however, because of the shouting of the narrator, while the crowd mobbed the barrier, anxious to see (and the youth's question—the girl? what about her—was drowned out). I said: "Are you the one, then?"

Voice gave a brief dry laugh. "Which *one* do you mean?"

Tell him, said the sheriff, rub it in. "The one who has been calling this number without speaking, making a goddamn nuisance of himself."

"I knew you'd rather hear me speak," said the voice.

Now you got him, give him warning, said the sheriff. "What is it you want to say to me? Because I have one thing to say to you."

"You first," said the voice.

The sheriff stood behind the Dean and said: "If you continue to harass us on the telephone, I mean to have the law after you." Is that an empty threat? asked the brother, nervously, because if it is, it may only provoke him to more harassment.

"Is that all you got to say to me?" said the voice. "Well, I got a question for you. Would you like to hear it?"

The manager read the words from the telephone book: *Hang up at the first obscene word or improper question.*

"Are you ready for my question? I really want to know, and maybe you can help me."

"What question?"

"Listen carefully now. The question is: Who was Judge Piggers?"

The boy king, startled awake, caught another name, one of his own, which interfered with the manager's hearing. The narrator had never heard of Judge Piggers, so he said: "I beg your pardon?"

"Who was Jaw Edge Pitgers?" Again the boy king deflected the name with one of his own, which the narrator denied, and for a moment we all paused and watched the name, Jaw Edge Pitgers, rise up out of the grasp of the voices, spin and sail and circulate in the air, ricocheting against the edges of the sky before it came down and landed within hearing, its shape confirmed not as Jaw Edge Pitgers, but what the king had heard all along:

GEORGE PIPGRAS (1899–). Pitcher for the New York Yankees and the Boston Red Sox. Pitched for the Yankees from 1927 to 1933; sold to the Red Sox in 1933. Elbow injury ended career in 1933, though not given release until 1935. Won three games in the World Series of 1927, 1928, and 1932.

(From *The Morley Mythology*)

"You know, don't you?" said the voice.

The boss ordered extreme caution. The manager kept guard. "I've heard of him," he said.

"Yes, well, who was he?"

The boy king wanted to tell him everything that was on the slide, but the manager, stingy, said: "He used to pitch for the New York Yankees."

"Ah, good, I knew you could tell me."

The manager's slow question: "How did you know?"

"Just a hunch." The man laughed. "Pretty good pitcher, was he? Not as good as Waite Hoyt, though."

"Perhaps not," said the boy king, held back by the manager.

"Ever see him pitch?"

"Twice," said the boy king before the manager could catch him.

"Did you really? And you must have been pretty young, weren't you? Tell me—"

"Who are you?" I said.

"Let's not worry about trivial—"

"I insist that you tell me who you are." Sheriff.

"Not until I try another question on you."

"I think you should tell me—"

"Wait now, listen to my question."

"Who are you?"

"Listen carefully. The name is Dorothee Manski. Who was Dorothee Manski?" This time the boy king, prepared, caught the name full in the face, and converted it immediately into one of his own, complete with the distinctive spelling of the first name, so concretely that the manager and narrator lost the real name and could only grope for alternatives that might have been: Dora Tay

Magazine? Dotty Muskie? Doctor Day Monster? The boy king insisted there was no mistake and flashed the card on the screen:

DOROTHEE MANSKI (1891 or 1895–1967). German operatic soprano, Metropolitan Opera Company 1927–1940. Sang minor roles and occasionally substituted in major roles in the Wagner and Strauss repertoire. Known for versatility. Celebrated as the Witch in *Hänsel und Gretel.*

(From *The Morley Mythology*)

The name belonged to the boy king, one of the oldest in his collection, regarded as a very private name. It embarrassed the manager and he could not bring himself to pronounce it in public. He said, "What did you say?"

This time, with everyone listening carefully to catch any variation, the stranger repeated it, and it was perfectly clear, spelling and all: "I said, Who was Dorothee Manski?"

Pointless to resist. The manager said humbly, "She was a minor singer at the Metropolitan Opera in the thirties."

"No kidding," said the stranger, with a long pause. "And was she also very good?"

It was the boy king's privacy that made the manager reluctant to respond—along with the sheriff's insistence that he extort some civility out of this man. And the narrator's dazzled terror.

"I don't know how good she was," said the Dean.

"You *don't?*" Was that real or feigned incredulity? "You never heard her sing?"

"I was too young to distinguish how good the singers were."

"What a shame," said the stranger. "I was hoping you could give me a good analytical description of her work."

"What for? What do you want that for?" Wrong question, said the manager. You shouldn't be fooling around like this. You should be remembering the situation and insisting—

"Curiosity. You know I have a great curiosity about all things. Don't you?"

"I insist you tell me where you got those names."

"Don't insist so much. Okay?"

The father read from the telephone book: *Hang up if the caller doesn't identify himself to your satisfaction.*

"You seem to know me. I want to know how."

"Who knows?" Then he said, "It's been a pleasure to make your acquaintance. I feel as if I'd known you for a long time."

Afterward Claudia said, "What was that all about?"

I told her. I said, "How strange. Where did he get those names?"

"What names?"

"He asked me about my childhood favorites."

"Childhood?"

"He asked me who was George Pipgras."

"Who?"

"George Pipgras. He pitched for the New York Yankees from 1927 to 1933."

"He asked you that?"

"Then he asked me—" The manager was embarrassed. He asked the narrator to remember if he had ever in all their closeness revealed this much of the boy king's secrets to Claudia, ever in their twenty-five intimate years? Respectful of the boy king's privacy, he hesitated now, before telling: "Then he asked, Who was Dorothee Manski?"

"Who was who?"

"She was an opera singer who sang minor roles at the Metropolitan in the thirties."

"Was she one of your favorites too?"

"Yes indeed."

"A baseball pitcher and an opera singer?" She smiled. "How old were you?"

"Ten or twelve. Who can he be, to know things like that?"

"Well, who have you told about them?"

The narrator reflected. "When I was a kid, everybody. But that was forty years ago. Nowadays, nobody."

"You never mentioned them to me," she said. "I thought Kirsten Flagstad was your favorite singer."

"That was later, when I knew something about singing."

She thought a moment. "But if this man is asking all these questions," she said, "what then was that other call?"

"The girl by the name of Ruth? That must be unrelated. Some prank. I hope it was unrelated."

9

When the telephone rang the next evening, the narrator actually hoped that it was the stranger calling again. The manager and the brother were afraid, working with the hired detective, but the narrator was simply curious and wanted to know more.

"I got some more questions for you," said the stranger. "Interested?"

"That depends. . . ."

"Ha! Okay, listen. How about Priscilla? Tell me about Priscilla." Spoken in an insinuating tone, allusive, complicit. The boy king recognized a name—

PRISCILLA (1894–1938?). Paddle-wheel steamship of the Fall River Line. 440′6″ long overall, 95′ breadth over guards. Gross tonnage 5292. Two black smokestacks, four passenger decks over guards. Sailed nightly between New York, Newport, and Fall River.

(From *The Morley Mythology*)

—but the manager ignored him and searched for the young woman that the stranger meant. Called the narrator, who looked over the girls of long ago, before Claudia, and found none. He said, "I don't know any Priscilla."

"Come on, now," said the voice.

"I truly can't remember anyone named Priscilla."

"Up and down Long Island Sound every night?"

"Oh, hell!" said the manager.

"Now you know? Okay, tell me."

"I don't need to," said Morley.

"Don't want to talk about it?" said the stranger.

"I'd like to know who you are and how you got these names."

"Just happen to be interested, that's all. Okay, you don't want to talk about Priscilla, let's talk about Denise."

Who?

"Denise."

This time the boy king had no response. The name suggested nothing. The boy king was disappointed and so, actually, was the narrator, and they poked around in the shed for something, but the manager rejoiced to be able to say (truthfully now): "Denise? The name means nothing to me."

"That's what you always say."

"This time I mean it. I make no connections to Denise."

"What? You deny Denise? From Poland?"

Poland? Now, while the narrator continued to deny, the boy king did catch something. He found a vivid design in brown and white like a map on a soft and furry hide, and the screen flashed another name on a black slate nailed to a board—

DANUSIA (?–?) . . . on a Polish farm . . .

(From *The Morley Mythology*)

—blocked, censored by the manager, who said Denise, not Danusia, was the name given.

"I know no Denise, from Poland or anywhere else."

"That so?" The stranger was not disturbed. "Well, okay." Then (while the narrator whispered to the manager that he probably *did* mean Danusia, an error which only magnified the mystery), he said, "Here's one you'll know. Who was Christian flustered?"

I beg your pardon? But even while the manager begged, the name sailed up and around through its alternatives, changing color in the sky, moment to moment, from Christian flustered to Clear stream flocks dead to Keer steen flack stead, to the name which the boy king had already heard so clearly that he thought he had been expecting it always, from the moment the stranger had made his first raid upon the files of the Mythology:

KIRSTEN FLAGSTAD (1895–1962). Norwegian soprano, sang at the Metropolitan Opera 1935–1941 and 1951–1952. . . . One of the great Wagnerian sopranos. . . . Center of political controversy after World War II . . .

"Yes, I remember her," said Michael Morley.

"Pretty good, wasn't she?"

"Yes."

"Which was better, Kirsten Flagstad or Dorothee Manski?"

"Flagstad."

"Okay," said the stranger. "You've got these big German operas and all this Siegfried stuff. Tell me, was she a Nazi?"

"Who?"

"Flagstad. You remember the talk."

The boy king was outraged, familiarly. "Certainly not," he said. "That's a notorious slander."

"Slander," said the man, quite smooth. "Good. I'm glad to hear you put it so forcefully."

The boy king wanted to nail it down, to recapitulate for this stranger all the evidence and arguments he had used years ago to show the singer's innocence and liberate her from the old controversy, but the manager said, Peace! Adding in a whisper, Don't forget who he is. Who is he? said the reader. That's what we mustn't forget, said the manager.

"But what about Wagner himself?" said the voice. "Wasn't he one?"

It stirred up more uncomfortable rumors, and the boy king answered with indignation. "How could he be? He died forty years before the Nazis. He composed *music.*"

"I heard he was a Nazi."

The boy king gave his explanation, while the manager still urged, Peace! "The Nazis used him. They misused him. It wasn't the music's fault, what they did to him. Just because the music was effective, powerful . . ." Peace!

"I insist you tell me who you are," said the manager. The narrator noticed that the insistence lacked the sheriff's old urgency—it sounded routine.

Again the man laughed—mildly. "Well, I don't know as that's so important. Seems to me we have interesting conversations, just as we are. What more do we need?"

This frustrated the sheriff, and he slammed down the phone. He was angry with everybody.

10

While others argued about what attitude to take (should it be alarm or indifference, curiosity or terror?), the detective tried to cope with the facts. Hired by the manager and making use of the narrator's resources, he investigated: Who in all the world, he asked, could know enough about the long-ago childhood of Michael Morley to bring up such names from a twelve-year-old's book of heroes as George Pipgras (Yankee pitcher) and Dorothee Manski (second-string opera singer)? Names that might not have appeared in a newspaper in twenty years, one dead and the other might be. Who knew enough to combine these with the names of the old steamboat *Priscilla,* the celebrated singer Flagstad, and the unknown, humble Polish Danusia, which the stranger himself had garbled? Some of the names, noted the detective, unknown even to your wife.

Of course you will have mentioned George Pipgras somewhere in casual, nostalgic baseball talk, said the detective. But would you have mentioned Pipgras to the same person you mentioned Manski to, and would you also have named *Priscilla,* or combined all five, including Danusia, in nostalgia with anybody at all? No doubt some friend from long ago might remember your support of Flagstad, whose achievement was a public matter, but who ever heard of your commitment to Danusia, with her dark and resonant, familiar but unknown voice?

The parents knew those names. But they would not have told, and now they are gone. Penny knew once, and so did Horace. If they remembered, perhaps her husband or his wives had also heard them. The narrator confessed (to the detective) boasting of old memories, with more than one of Horace's wives, in the euphoria of summer nostalgia and families coming together. But had he spoken of the Mythology? Had he given names out of its pages? Could he have mentioned so many, and if he had, would anyone have remembered? And even then, demanded the detective, what line would have connected sister, brother, or forgotten friend to a harassing stranger on the telephone so many years later?

Yet the fact is clear, said the detective. Some living person, some person of today, has facts from your inner life in its most distant past. With enough hate to want to frighten you with his knowledge from a concealed position.

Like a devil, said the mother. The father objected to devils, but the detective said that devil was exactly what he wanted you to believe, with his deliberate mystery and suggestions of power. To scare hell out of you. Meanwhile the mother worried about the *hate* the detective had mentioned. It shocked her. Someone hates my Michael? Perhaps he doesn't hate us all, suggested the father. Perhaps he only hates the Dean, or the manager, or maybe the sheriff, or at worst the boss. The mother would not distinguish, however. She stared at the stranger's hate, like a bloody bone with a rag around it: the coming revolution of the mob of hate, its assault on all the good, the gentle, the reasonable, and the polite.

So it was—those days while the calls kept coming—between the detective, who kept looking for an explanation; the mother, who gazed at the hate; the father, who saw the understandable human smallness to be pitied rather than feared; the brother, who kept talking traps to outwit the enemy; and the boss, who made speeches about our work, our career, our substance as man in the world and the home. We are being pestered by a fly, said the boss. Swat him with our tail.

Now the stranger always talked. There were no more silent calls. Nor calls from the girl named Roof. Once when the phone appeared to be silent, the Dean hung up. The phone rang again, and he heard the stranger saying, "Don't hang up like that. I want to talk to you." The sheriff demanded, "Well, who the hell do you think you are?" It made the stranger cheerful. He said, "Well, who the hell do *you* think I am?"

He would say, "Are you puzzled how I could know so much? I am sure I would be, if I were in your place. Perhaps if we talk long enough you'll find out what you want to know. We'll become friends. Maybe we can meet someday. I look forward to that, don't you? Aren't you eager to see if I look like what you imagine?"

Even the father called the stranger's questions impertinent, and he and the mother and the sheriff all for different reasons asked the manager to cut him off. The manager could not obey. The brother kept saying that something big was coming, a suspended ax, he called it, hanging out of sight. The narrator kept looking for it. Sometimes he thought he caught a glimpse in the bland tone of the stranger's questions—a glimpse of steel, high up in the trees, though nothing fell and it might have been only early sunrise. The stranger would say, "This is fun, isn't it? Talking to a stranger you don't know anything about? We can talk about the most intimate things you couldn't say to a friend. You can tell me, because I'm a stranger, things no friend would dare say. I hope you'll take advantage of this opportunity. It isn't often two strangers have a chance for a relationship like this."

Once he asked, "How did it happen that someone like you, with such a diversity of childhood interests, so varied and colorful—so in a certain way precocious and yet so also childlike—how did you happen to settle for geology as your career?"

"What's wrong with geology?" said the geologist.

"Oh, nothing at all; I meant no disparagement. Your career is notable for its success; I have only admiration. I find it curious, though, the connections, you know, between the child and the adult, the growth of the little childish mind into the adult professional mind."

The manager wondered if he was being mocked and did not try to answer. The reader could not sit still, though. He felt challenged in his specialty. Later that night he went to look again at that large family house in the Westchester suburb, which backed over the edge of the woody ravine. To visit again the third-floor room of Michael the boy, looking out into the woods. He brought the telephone stranger along to watch while he displayed the boy's equipment: the recording mind already filled with bird books and astronomy books and books about trains and steamships. Eyes focused on the material world about him, substance, the phenomena of concreteness. The reader revealed the boy in his room as he drew up in tables his record of bird sightings this spring as compared to last spring—keeping both records in a black-and-white mottled notebook. In the second spring there were more details noted as well as species sighted, along with an improvement in the handwriting. Studies in statistics. Michael Morley was statistical, numerical, orderly. The reader recalled how his mother had classified them: If Penny is our politician, she would say, Michael is our scientist. Maybe Horace will be our artist.

The boy scientist kept records of baseball players, whose skill was reducible to decimals. The reader preserved his work as scorekeeper for the high school baseball team and took him from there to college, where he decided to become a geologist. Sometimes the young scientist heard the Name admonishing him. You must find your genius, said the Name, and make Michael Morley famous, so that the world will know that he lived in it once and gave it a home inside his eyes. For a time, then, the Name sought quick ways to bring this about, with plans for spectacular artistic or political careers, before deciding that was not where his genius lay. Would the stranger ask him about that? Why did a young man like you, with so much ambition and so many eccentric interests, decide to become a geologist? To bore his life into the earth, to dwell amid rocks, to live in the strata of petrified time. The world turned rock, the rockman striking his head against it like a hammer against outcrops on a field trip: quick heavy blows to prove the solidity of existence, of the stricken rock and the hammer too.

The narrator remembered a letter home from college, the geologist son to his ornithologist father:

> A modest science, not difficult, with a respectable tradition. Geologists can teach in colleges or work for the government or for mining or oil companies. There are oil geologists and mineralogists who study the nature of minerals, and seismologists who study earthquakes, and paleontologists who study ancient life forms in the earth, and structural geologists who study the arrangements of the strata. If I become a geologist I'll have a lot of time for outdoor work in summer.

The reader made it all converge, to show the stranger how the notations of birds seen and bird songs heard, the cumulated baseball averages, the classified listings of railroad locomotive numbers, the systematic filings of drawers full of travel folders, all gathered into an academic curriculum of courses dealing with rocks. From that convergence it was a straight line. From college to graduate school, from graduate school (with a specialization in paleontology—that is, fossils) to an instructorship, thence up the ranks to our present eminence. Straight, anyway, until this recent shift from geology into positions of administration and power.

"And you married a geologist's daughter too," said the stranger, one night in his probing of the Dean's career. "That was a help, wasn't it?"

The lawyer saw a hint in this, and warned the manager that it might not be wholly innocent. So, while the Dean ignored the comment, the reader went back again to look up Morrison Field, the great geologist of the old school who was Claudia's father. He wanted to set the stranger straight, if the manager would only permit, on why he was hired by the Department of Geology. The reason (repeating) that Michael Morley was hired by the Department of Geology all those years ago, said the reader, was for his reported excellence in teaching, two geological articles, the book he was working on (whatever became of that? asked the brother), and because there was a particular vacancy to be filled. Tell how the old man took him into the kitchen to explain (privately, while the others listened to Claudia at the piano) how he had deliberately and conspicuously absented himself from the departmental discussions. What a surprise (and what a delight) to the old man when they came out after the meeting and told him they had decided to offer young Morley the appointment. And if you are not too proud, said Morrison Field, you can stay and grow in this department, just as I did many years ago, and make as big a geological name for yourself as if you were in an Eastern university. And you can come every Sunday to dinner.

And the old man's senility. It fixed on his obsession in his last five years with writing his autobiography. He believed that his autobiography was necessary to his fame and would be of great value to all young would-be scientists. It was to be called *The Education of Morrison Field.* The old man was by now blind, and he wrote the autobiography by dictating it. He had a secretary take dictation, but sometimes he made his wife do it, and often he asked his Sunday dinner guests to take dictation for an hour or two. He never checked his last dictation to connect with what he dictated next, and if anyone tried to do it for him, he got angry, saying it was all in his head and the natural order was best. The secretary told us that he had repeated certain incidents often, but she didn't dare irritate him by reminding him.

One Sunday afternoon I took his dictation myself.

My Aunt Louise was my mother's stepsister. She was the daughter of my grandfather's first wife, so that her maiden name was Gross like my mother's and her mother was a Brookridge. She invited me to come and look at the pebbles in her walk, and she used to express great interest in my collection, but her interest was aesthetic, I am sorry to say, rather than scientific. Like all the people on my mother's side, she had very little scientific blood. Most of my mother's people had religious blood. My grandfather was a minister in the Presbyterian church and his brother was a missionary to the Far East. His sister was a musician, and this musical blood—it is interesting to note—has reappeared in my daughter. But my geological blood appears to have come mostly from my father's side, although even there we find very few if any true geologists. The most direct source of my geological blood is no doubt that of the naturalist, my uncle Joseph. He was a botanist, concerned with the classification of species of trees. The Brookridges had craftsmen's blood—old Mr. Brookridge was an engraver and his brother was an undertaker—but of course this could have had no effect on me since he was not related to me by blood.

When he died—suddenly one Sunday morning in his living room chair after breakfast—his autobiography, 2,237 pages long (fairly represented in the sample above, said the narrator), was given to Claudia for safekeeping. It occupies a drawer in the attic, because no one wants to throw it out.

11

The brother warned: He's snooping into Claudia too. The stranger asked: "Is it true that your wife gave up a promising musical career in order to marry you?" The question angered the wife and brought the sheriff: "She *has* a musical career," he said. "She has an active career right now."

"Oh, forgive me. I only meant the more prominent career she *might* have had—the chance to be *nationally known*—if it hadn't been for marrying you and raising a family. I mean, she did make sacrifices, didn't she?"

The manager said, on advice of the lawyer: "This is a private matter between my wife and myself."

"Of course it is. I only thought you might want to give your side of the case, in view of the question that has been raised."

"I repeat"—lawyer in control again—"it's a matter between my wife and myself."

"And I respect that privacy," said the stranger. "I'm sure your marriage has been a very romantic one."

The reader kept that legend too, telling how it was the narrator himself who found Michael Morley a wife at the Rocky Mountain Summer Geology Field Camp, where he was summer teaching at the beginning of his career. Six weeks of field trips in a caravan of seven station wagons, giving instruction in how to chip rocks, collect outcrops, draw maps. She was an undergraduate from a New York college near his own, and she was not even a geology major, she was a music student and a pianist. She was also the daughter of Morrison Field, the eminent, and took this summer course in the Rocky Mountains to see what her father's work was like. Everyone in the camp knew that she was Morrison Field's daughter, and it embarrassed her and made her shy. Every evening she worked on the piano in the lodge, as if to prove that she was not a geologist. She had a boyfriend during the six-week session, and her instructor, Mr. Morley, kept his distance.

The real beginning of the legend was the return trip east in Jackson's car. She had lost her ride and wanted to ride with them. Three in an old blue Chevrolet—the twenty-year-old undergraduate and the two twenty-five-year-old geology instructors. The reader recapitulated her in the legend: thin and tall, with large intelligent dark eyes and a smooth sweep of light-brown hair, who wore dungarees on field trips and light skirts and sweaters on the trip home. The trip took three days. There was talk, singing, jokes, narrative, description, rhetoric—over Nebraska milk shakes, in the back seat while Jackson drove, in the front seat while Jackson, stony and geological, disapproved in the back. They talked of past and future, and on the second night, at a place called the Euphoria Motel, the new-born legend reached its first climax. "Don't make trouble for yourself, boy," warned Jackson, but the youth (a cowboy then, who had only recently liberated his horse from the old corral and was raring to go) said, *I think* it's all right, and he went and knocked on her door. She opened it partway, wearing a furry white bathrobe.

"I was just about to take a shower," she said.

"I'm sorry! I was going to suggest we take a walk."

She looked at him a moment. "Well, come in anyway," she said.

There was a time later when the narrator's memory of the

legend of the Euphoria Motel roused him to jealousy: asking whose foolish advice it was to ignore the recent boyfriend whose lessons had prepared her so well for that night at the motel, so that now, waiting for her to come home, he had to wonder what she was doing in the practice rooms of the music school in the evening. Later still, the narrator instructed the reader to put that memory of jealousy out of mind: You have decided that nothing ever happened in those rooms but practice and there is no need to reopen that discussion.

Through the years, the reader brought out new editions of the legend. At first it was a glamorous sequence that he liked to reread, not knowing what was coming, delighting in its outcome. Later it looked stale: less gratifying to the reader than alternatives that might have happened, in which he had moved more intelligently, or (perhaps) had allowed the cowboy more adventures before marriage. There was an edition in which the legend was a mere dull tale, not worth rereading, and others, when times were hard, in which the legendary outcome was ironic or tragic, a cautionary tale of the blind step and the enormous consequences. This too passed: in another edition the regret itself was regrettable. Later editions treated the sequence that began in the Euphoria Motel as inevitable, a journey traveled by young people unconscious of how time takes care of you and converts future choice into past necessity. Now there was neither pride nor regret—the legend was the past itself, when we were children and not as we are now. It was the beginning of the long narrative that we shared with Claudia—which our reader could verify at any point by consulting *her* reader—confirmable through the three-room apartment in the beginning, the six-room one they moved into five years later, the small house that followed, and now their great big one. Through infancies of children, through diapering and bottling babies in the night, and picnics with small children, and family visits to the elementary school on parents' night. Through movies, dinners out, subscriptions to theater and concert, vacation trips, trips to Europe. Through advancements of career, his promotions, her step-by-step return to music. Through cameras: the old box camera, the movie camera, the new slide camera. Through cats and tropical fish and hamsters. Through beagles, dog shows, obedience trials, veterinarians. Through insult and anger, suspicion and jealousy, reconciliations and jokes and crying and comfort. Through deaths. And doesn't this past make her (herself) a part of you, make you love her and be glad you married her? said the narrator. Yes, said the reader. Then tell the stranger, said the narrator.

And if he asks again about the sacrifice of her musical career, said the reader, tell about the letter she got from the Musical Institute of Connecticut. How much had grown out of those early days in the apartment when she practiced the piano in the late afternoon, with the snow gathering outside, and the child inside her. Or the neighbors' children taking lessons in the living room in the late afternoon when Michael Morley, then assistant professor of geology, came home. Out of those late afternoons, those pupils' recitals with engraved programs in January and June, those young years before she joined the School of Music, on her way to becoming Chairman of Piano. With an annual downtown recital of her own in the fall.

The letter from Connecticut asked if she was interested in applying for the directorship. Well, yes, she wrote back, she might. Tell that stranger who is worried about her sacrifice how important a position that directorship is. The famous and powerful Institute; whoever got that position would be in charge of everything —policy, hiring, instruction, supervising the publications, the programs of teaching and concerts. . . . A name known all over the country. Even more important than your deanship, then? said the stranger. Hush, said the manager. We don't discuss questions like that.

The reader himself had to ask: What if they actually offer her that job? The wife and some unknown child began to cry, muffled somewhere. *Narrator:* What an honor that would be. *Reader:* Would she accept it? *Narrator:* No need to decide yet. *Reader:* What if she does take it? *Narrator:* It would be a great distinction for her, a vindication, a reward, a pinnacle. *Stranger* (intervening):

You would not, however, allow her to have it. *Reader:* Why not? Would she have to move to Connecticut? *Narrator:* That's a detail. Details can be settled later. *Reader:* Would she give up her kennels, all her beagles? *Narrator:* An honor like that, a way can be found. *Reader:* Would she have to leave you? *Stranger* (to the reader): Press it home. Force him to answer. *Narrator:* A solution will turn up. *Stranger:* Of course you'll make her turn it down. *Reader:* Could you do that? *Narrator:* There's no need to worry. *Stranger:* Because she probably won't get the offer anyway? *Narrator:* Because an honor like that, yet far in the future, a solution can always be found.

12

Still from night to night the stranger's questions probed, with unaccountable knowledge of the narrator's secrets. He seemed to have raided the Morley archives—stealing from the child's hall of private fame names and shapes that once, long ago, landmarked the inner Morley geography. He asked: "Do you know what pitcher led the American League in games won in 1928—tied, I mean, with Lefty Grove?" The boy king knew, because it was important in the Mythology, even though 1928 was before the boy king knew baseball.

The stranger said: "Here's a bit of historical diddley-doo that you can help me with. In 1933 there was a performance of this *Die Walküre,* you know. And in the third act there was an accident. . . ."

(Already, though the manager could not know, nor the narrator, the boy king knew what was coming.)

"There was this soprano singing the lead—singing Brünnhilde, right?—alone on the stage with Wotan at the time, and he's punishing her for disobedience, okay? And the singer wasn't Christian flustered and it wasn't Dorothee Manski, because Dorothee Manski was only a minor spear maiden and had just left the stage, but it was another singer, some German whose name was Free Delivery—"

"Frida Leider."

"Good! I knew you'd know. It seems this Frida Leider got a frog in her throat and couldn't sing. At that moment everything is quiet and suddenly the singer is supposed to sing alone without orchestra. She begins to plead. *'War es so schmälich?'* she sings, which can be translated, 'Was it so shameful, what I have done?' starting a series of turns upward as the orchestra comes in. Right? Only suddenly this Frida Leider had a frog in her throat and couldn't sing. Now, my question is, what happened then? Do you happen to know?"

"I guess I do," said the boy king, over reluctance.

"Good. I wondered if you could tell me. More than forty years ago, such an obscure incident. Am I correct in understanding that another singer took over from the wings? Spotting Brünnhilde's difficulty, in an instant she came in, singing the lines from offstage with amazing cool, the voice filling the silence until Frida could recover and carry on. Is that right?"

"Yes," I admitted.

"I call that quick thinking, don't you? Remarkable! Were you there at the time?"

"No."

"How did you hear about it."

"How did *you* hear about it?" asked the manager.

The stranger laughed. "Okay," he said. "Then tell me this. Do you know the name of the singer whose quick thinking and guts saved that performance?"

Long pause before the manager had to admit: "Yes."

"Will you tell me?"

"I don't need to tell you," said the sheriff.

The stranger laughed. "Okay, okay! But we know, don't we?"

One night the stranger said, "I want to apologize for those Nazi questions the other night. I happen to like that old music myself. I like the old Kraut."

"You mean Wagner?"

"Yeah, him. All that grandeur, all that passion, all that movement. Listen, your wife is a musician. Does she like him?"

"Not so much."

"That's a shame." A pause, then a hushed question: "Your marriage to Claudia is a happy marriage, right?"

"Right," said the manager, after a pause.

"Years and years without trouble, you and Claudia, loving each other, always true."

Enter sheriff. "This is none of your business."

"You mean it's not all that happy."

"No, I mean it's our business, not yours."

"Privacy, yes. I do respect privacy. Nothing in life is as important to a person as his privacy. The most important virtue, don't you think?"

"I wouldn't call it a virtue."

"Surely it's not a vice?"

It's a—what is it? said the manager. A right, said the father. Privilege? said the sister. Meanwhile the stranger: "Anyway, it's not like your brother Horace's life, is it?"

"What are you talking about?"

"His three marriages and three divorces, right? A mess of women and affairs. Whereas you and Claudia—twenty-five years without a breath of anything. I mean like scandal, that's what I mean: without a breath of scandal."

The manager said nothing. Why should he?

"The question is whether Claudia believes that."

"Believes what?"

"Believes that you have always been faithful to her."

Here it comes, said the brother, here comes that ax you saw hanging in the forest, down, down, down! Yet there was no sound, and on the advice of counsel, the manager repeated, "That's none of your business."

"You mean she doesn't know?"

"Doesn't—know—what?"

"Doesn't know—whatever there is to know."

The lawyer controlled the sheriff. "My relations with my wife are no one's concern but my own."

"And hers. You're perfectly right. My only concern is—" Pause again. Wait, said the lawyer, for him to say what his concern is. But then the stranger decided to wait too.

"Yes?" said the mother.

"Yep," said the stranger, as if that settled it. "Well, then—so she doesn't know?"

"What?"

"Okay, she *does* know, then. You've talked it over with her and reached an understanding."

"Know what?"

"About any possible—how do you say it? Straying? Adventuring? I don't like the word *cheating* —it's so *negative.*"

The detective said, He is trying to find out by trapping you. The lawyer asked, Find out what? The detective said, He wants you to think he knows and therefore trick you into revealing it. Reveal what? said the lawyer. The detective said, He is trying to slip you into a confession. Confess nothing, said the lawyer.

"Tell me, does your brother know?"

Ruth! cried the brother. He knows everything! While the sheriff grabbed the phone and slammed it down.

You shouldn't have done that, said the lawyer. Why not? said the sheriff, fierce, regretting only that he hadn't hung up earlier. Quivering, the lawyer said that slamming at that point amounted to a confession of guilt. Call him back, said the manager. Interpret the slamming, say simply that we were getting fed up with this invasion of privacy. Can't call him back, said the narrator. Don't know his number, not even his name. Now you'll just have to wait, said the brother.

The phone rang. Now tell him, said the lawyer.

"You must not hang up on me," said the stranger.

While the brother was observing, Yes, that is the voice of power, of blackmail about to begin, the manager tried to defy: "I was getting tired of—"

And the stranger, drawing back: "Sorry I touched a sensitive spot." The sharp power edge was clothed again in the stranger's familiar nasal ease. "I assure you—" He didn't say what he was assuring you of. He said, "I don't wish to pry into your secrets, I didn't mean to pry into that one."

"What one?"

"That one. The one that made you hang up on me."

"Secret? I was merely getting—"

"Don't apologize," he said. "Only I beg of you don't hang up on me. I think we know each other quite well by now, and you ought to trust me. You know I don't want to offend you, and I do enjoy our conversations about so many things, private things you couldn't possibly say to someone you actually know. You know?"

The stranger sounded abject. He asked to be forgiven. The manager refused to give him that satisfaction, although he allowed the conversation to follow the usual course, which amounted to the same thing. Later, the lawyer said, It proves you are vulnerable to blackmail. Better give that some good hard thought. It's only because the stranger is maybe not quite ready that he didn't go on and put the screws on you this time. How could that be? said the manager, since Claudia and I discussed it and the incident is closed?

Doesn't matter, said the lawyer. If you tremble when a stranger brings it up or merely hints, you're vulnerable to blackmail.

13

Then the calls stopped. There have been no calls for a week, said the narrator. Then it was two weeks. So we handled it right, said the manager, and he got tired of us. The boss was relieved. The mother was disappointed, for she was attached to all familiar things, and the detective was also disappointed, because of the unresolved mystery, but the manager said we should be glad to let little mysteries go unsolved, greater evils to avoid.

The narrator picked up a piece of time with a forward thrust, turning into an event, after the secretary came into the dean's office and said, "There's a Mr. Macurdy who wants to see you." The event itself was a man in a business suit, round-faced, conservative, short-haired. Later the narrator described him to the reader, a man in his thirties or forties, wearing horn-rimmed glasses, and fat. The narrator thought he might be a book salesman or an insurance salesman, although the brother said that he looked like a dealer in pornographic goods. He sat down in the soft leather chair by which the Dean consoled students called in to see him. The lower lids of his eyes drooped, leaving white space below the irises. The man's mouth was tense, and his eyes stared.

"My name is Edward Macurdy," he said. The voice was soft. It could have been louder, said the narrator, but it wasn't.

"What can I do for you?"

The man stared awhile and said, "Do you know me?"

"I'm afraid I don't remember you. . . ."

"You don't know me? Don't recognize me? My name? My voice?"

The Dean gazed back at this staring man—embarrassed, said the mother, because you have forgotten somebody who expects you to remember him. The narrator repeated his quick hunt through the files and came up with nothing.

"I'm very sorry," said the Dean. "I can't place you. . . ."

"Don't worry about it," said the man quickly. "There's no reason for you to recognize me." Yet adding as if he did not believe himself, "You're sure you don't?"

For a few moments, there was only this stare. Then two narrators diverged to tell it differently. According to one, there was a quality in the voice, or maybe only in the situation, this being stared at, the strange words, the silence presented by a tangible human presence, which was familiar. He made the connection and whispered to the manager: He's here! The man himself. Sitting here in his own fat flesh. The father reacted: Impossible! You're obsessed with him. The second narrator denied the other by saying that it never occurred to him to connect this man with the enemy on the telephone. It simply did not enter my head.

Meanwhile the man—Edward Macurdy—said: "I owe you an apology."

While one narrator said, He's going to apologize for those telephone calls, the other closed his eyes and kept an open mind.

"Apology? What for?"

"Yes," said Macurdy. He looked at the floor and clasped his hands across his stomach. "Things I've done. Things I'm sorry for." Gloomy?

The Dean consulted with his advisers, being careful not to react too quickly to one assumption or another. "What things have you done?"

"That, I can't tell you," said Macurdy.

"Then how can I accept your apology?"

"Accept it on faith."

"Faith?" exclaimed the Dean. "Faith in what?"

"Faith that I owe you an apology." The narrator saw a brief amusement in the man's white-rimmed eyes, quickly fading.

"I can't accept your apology without knowing what you're apologizing for."

"You can't?" said Macurdy. Disappointed in his eyes, as if baffled, looking to the Dean to solve his problem. "I can't tell you what for, because if you don't accept my apology, then . . ."

"Then what?"

"Then we're in trouble," said Macurdy.

"You mean *you're* in trouble?"

"*You* might think so." After a moment: "I can't afford to take that chance. I mean, I can afford to but I'd rather not." Another pause. "I'd like you to know I'm sorry for any distress I may have caused you. As far as you are concerned, I've forgiven you for everything."

"*You've* forgiven *me?*" said the Dean.

"I just want to let bygones be and be friends," said the man with the gloomy eyes.

The Dean studied him, while the narrators tried to compare his voice with the taped memory of the telephone voice, now apparently mislaid. Finally he said: "I don't understand a word you're talking about."

"It's all right," said Macurdy, waving it away. "I've forgiven you, and I'd like you to forgive me."

The sheriff intervened: "I've never done anything to you that needs to be forgiven," and the father added: "As far as I know."

"I promise never to mention it again," said the man.

"I don't know you from Adam," said the Dean.

"You know me. I just think it's time for you and me to see what we look like and be friends."

Oh! said the narrator, spreading the news wildly. It's *him,* it's him, all right, it's got to be him, it couldn't be anybody but him.

Shall we catch him? said the manager. Is it safe? Careful, said the lawyer. Take the advantage, said the sheriff, move fast, make a quick arrest. Wait, said the lawyer, checking it out. But he found nothing, and so the manager said—slowly, carefully: "What you want to be forgiven for is those calls on the telephone, isn't it?" (Which *has* been known from the beginning, said the narrator, revisionist, or even from before the beginning, from the moment the secretary first announced his name, a name you'd never heard before, and our minds all made the immediate inevitable leap.) And now watched the man to see the effect.

The narrator saw the masked change of expression, the passage of knowledge moving within features that remained frozen. The narrator guessed it was relief, and then something was taken away from the man's face and everything closed down and hid again, as he said, "What calls?"

Now for a long time they stared at each other while the manager heard the conflicting arguments of those who said the man was merely a liar and those who were humiliated by the mistake, and the watchman looked for some sign in the man's face. Finally the manager retreated: "Someone has been harassing us on the telephone, and I thought you were talking about that," he said.

"You're not still upset about that, are you?"

"So it *was* you. . . ."

"I thought our conversations got pretty interesting after a while, didn't you?"

"Interesting?" Now at last the sheriff was released, free to ride in joyful rage with all the right on his side. "Interesting, you say? I'd like to know by what right—who the hell you think you are—what impertinence—what arrogance—" Suddenly the sheriff realized that he had been sent on this ride by the lawyer, that his rage was more dutiful and tactical than natural. The narrator noticed the man looking at him as calm and sag-eyed as a vulture, and felt the deflation of energy from the Dean's voice as his angry speech collapsed. Ended up in the manager's question: "What is it you want of me?"

"All I want is your friendship and good will," said the man.

Manager's exasperation yielded to the narrator, who said: "I need to know who you are, how you found out so much about me." As he watched, it seemed now to the narrator as if the cold face had relaxed, the frozen stare melted, the rigid body softened. The face was looking at him now almost smiling, and he looked like a boy—a fat boy, self-indulgent, a bully, untrustworthy, but nevertheless a boy, whose dawning grin might actually be playful.

"I don't mind telling you—sometime," he said. "Right now I have to know if I can trust you."

"You trust *me?"*

"I'm in your power, you see," said Macurdy. "At least, you think I am."

"There are heavy penalties—"

"So you say. You could file charges against me. But let me remind you that I came here voluntarily, as I said. Nobody compelled me to come. And I have offered you my apology for any offense I may have given and hope you will not hold anything against me. I hope you'll appreciate the *risk* I took in coming here."

The Dean said, "I could have you arrested. Call the police—"

"I am politely asking you not to."

"Why should you think I won't?"

"You're not that kind of a guy. I know you, and everyone calls you a *truly* decent guy. If my friendship has been an annoyance to you, I am *genuinely* sorry. I want to be your friend, and I'm taking the chance that you won't injure me, that's all." Fat smile, shrug of shoulders, spreading hands.

The sheriff said, If he was scared at first, he's over it now. His confidence is perfect. Shake him up a little, see what makes him so sure of himself. The Dean said, "You've been a great nuisance, and I regard your assaults on my privacy with the greatest seriousness. I see no excuse and no reason why I should not call the police."

Reached for the phone, despite the lawyer's alarm. Wait! We're not ready, we don't know enough. Calmly Macurdy watched the Dean's hand at the phone, and it was as if his calmness itself made the Dean stop, wait, fail to lift it from the hook.

Macurdy said: "You don't want to do that."

While the lawyer held back the Dean's hand, waiting to hear the man's reason, the sheriff urged the simple insult of his words: "What makes you think I don't? I have every intention of turning you in." Too late, the lawyer objected to the absolute statement.

"I hoped you wouldn't take it like that," said Macurdy.

"Whatever gave you reason to hope that?"

"Because we know each other so well." The reply came quickly, as if prepared in advance. "Like good friends," he added.

"I don't know you," said the Dean, aware that he had said this before, "and I don't consider you my friend."

"But I know you *very* well," said Macurdy. Suddenly the lawyer put the narrator on the watch for this man's blackmail potential, which he thought he had heard at last in the tone of his words.

"You think you know me well?" said Michael.

"You should know how much I admire you," said Macurdy. "Everything I've heard about you confirms how good you are. I also admire your wife." He was looking at the floor as he said these words, as if eyes were unable to bear them. "My girlfriend admires you both too, and we'd like to invite you to dinner at a good restaurant sometime soon."

Crazy enough to make the Dean smile. "You're out of your mind."

"Do you know The Great Wall of China?" asked Macurdy. "A great Chinese restaurant. Terrific food. Atmosphere. We want you to eat there with us sometime."

They actually forced a laugh out of the Dean at this point. He said, "If you think we'd go out to dinner with you, you really must be crazy."

"Why are you so hostile?"

"What?"

"I said, why do you talk to me as if I were an enemy? As if it were an outrage for me to speak to you? As if I were scum. Why do you do that?"

The mother woke up, startled by the sudden new tone. Anxiously she asked, Is this sincere? Are we really being unreasonable and excessively suspicious? Is there something in his case we ought to understand and do not? Not at all, said the brother. Anyone who would do what this man has done is dangerous by definition, and his words could only be ironic—or mad.

So the Dean explained why he was hostile. "Because you won't answer any of the necessary questions I've asked." Is that enough? asked the sheriff, who kept thinking of more complaints. That's enough, said the lawyer.

"What questions do you have in mind?"

"Why have you been haunting me?"

"Because you're interesting to me. Your life is interesting."

"That's not enough. My life is dull and ordinary. Why should you take such an interest?"

"Maybe I can tell you later, when we know each other better."

"What is your purpose?"

"I told you, I have no purpose except to be friends."

"And I told you, that's not enough. How did you learn so much about me?"

Macurdy, smiling: "Much? Surely you don't think I know very *much* about you. What, you mean things like George Pipgras?"
"Yes."
"Or Dorothee Manski?"
"Yes!"
"Or the S.S. *Priscilla?*"
"Yes!"
"Well, come to The Great Wall of China for dinner and maybe I'll tell you."
"No, sir!" Abrupt pause, while the narrator tried to determine the direction of things. In this pause the brother came forward, all gross and swollen, asking about his fear. Can he blackmail us? Is he going to try? So loud that the manager decided to go to the question directly. He asked: "Are you trying to blackmail me?"
The look on Macurdy's face was surprise, but no one knew if it was real or feigned.
"Blackmail? Why should I blackmail you?"
"I don't know."
"What do you have that would be worth blackmailing you for?"
"Damn little!"
"What have you done that you could be blackmailed for? Naughty secrets, eh?"
What a relief! said the mother, though the lawyer said that our question had betrayed anxiety and weakness, and the brother warned us not to believe him anyway.
"I will not be blackmailed," said the sheriff.
"Good man," said Macurdy.
After a moment, Macurdy said, "Actually, I probably could blackmail you if I wanted to. But why should I? I'm a nice guy; I don't approve of things like that. All I want is to be friends. You see? It proves the sincerity of my motives toward you."
"*What* proves it?"
"The fact I wouldn't think of blackmailing you. Even though."
"Even though what?"
"Even though I probably could."
". . . How?"

"Oh . . . let that suffice."

"No, sir! If you mean to intimidate me, you'd better come up with something more specific."

"I'm *not* trying to intimidate you."

Now as they stared at each other, as he saw the man's pale eyes looking at him, measuring and playing games—this man whose face had been totally strange only a few minutes ago but was already as familiar as a lifetime—as the narrator calculated the exchanges of power in a combat carried on entirely in words (thus far), he recognized the word that he had already applied to this man, the word *enemy:* this man, this Macurdy, is not merely the stranger, he is the enemy, said the narrator. And though we sit in chairs in an office merely speaking words, what is happening is a battle, a fight, like two swordsmen facing each other. And all we have ever used were words and silence. The narrator recognized the man's eyes, looking at him across the gap, as *human* eyes, like his own, same species, alive in the same room and same time, with voices interacting in the same language both had learned from childhood in the same way, yet true mortal enemies like savages, who were also human and faced each other across a space. The physical distance between them, across a mere desk, seemed to the narrator like a whole world crushed into inches by a great smash. Compare the warm and friendly struggles of familiar people inside the capacious room of our self, said the narrator—but this stranger, this enemy, is outside, visible and explicit, and he means to do us harm. You are looking, said the narrator, at a man who means harm.

"Not in the least," said Macurdy. "I want to *assure* you. Every way I can." Then a more casual tone. "I realize it's a shock to you. But after a while . . . And The Great Wall of China—it's a good restaurant—and my girlfriend—you'll like her too. We both admire you and would like to know you better. Later, when you've had a decent chance to think it over . . ."

While Macurdy was talking he was fishing in his coat pocket for something, which after a moment he brought out. It was a small piece of twine tied into a loop with a knot at one end. He put the loop on his finger, and then he took out of his breast pocket a pencil which he inserted in the loop and, removing his finger, began to spin—vibrating the pencil so as to make the loop rotate rapidly around it. After a moment he noticed Michael looking at it, and he stopped speaking. Spun the loop faster, holding the pencil up in front of his face.

"This how you do it?" he asked.

Another trick designed to shock, said the narrator. The deepest and most secret of all. The manager watched while Macurdy quietly put the loop of twine and the pencil back in his pocket and pulled on his coat.

"You know someone who knew me as a child," said Michael Morley.

Macurdy shrugged. "Someday," he said, "if you decide not to reject my friendship—if you *should* decide to come to The Great Wall of China—I might let you in on a thing or two."

"I don't mean to be deliberately unfriendly," said Michael.

"I understand."

"You must see how it seems, when you say so little to make it clear . . ."

"I see perfectly," said Macurdy. "A natural caution. Okay." He was getting up. Yes, he was getting ready to go. "I'll be in touch with you. Maybe later you'll change your mind."

"About what?"

"About having dinner with us at The Great Wall. You and Claudia. That's what I meant. Did you have anything else in mind?"

"No, nothing."

Macurdy got up and then suddenly sat down again. "Oh, can you tell me one more thing? Your brother Horace."

"What?"

"His three wives."

"What about them?"

"What was the name of the third one?"

Watch out! said the brother. Alert, everybody. Still, the Dean kept his control. "Don't you know?" he asked.

"Was it Ruth?" asked Macurdy.

"Of course it was Ruth!"

"I thought so. Well, tell me, is she still married to him?"

"You don't know that?"

"I thought you might know."

"Why should I know?" exclaimed the Dean.

"Well, he is your brother," said Macurdy solemnly. He shrugged his shoulders, got up again, said goodbye politely, and then he was gone.

So that's what he intends, said the brother, that's what he means. But he can't blackmail you over Ruth, said the father. Why not? said the lawyer. He can't, said the manager. What could he know? He knows everything, said the narrator. That's impossible, said the manager.

You'd better get ready, said the manager to the narrator. It's going to be busy times ahead, you're going to need all your wits to keep us together now. The narrator looked behind and ahead, in all directions, slow, careful, as ready as he could be.

PART TWO

14

To understand this encounter with Macurdy, the reader asked the narrator to dig holes in the past. Some parts were easy, because the narrator was constantly reviewing them: the blackmail question, for instance, for the narrator kept repeating it—that brief connection with Horace's young third wife, how it was forgiven, and the case with Claudia was closed. What it was for Horace or for Ruth herself the narrator didn't know. The reader could understand this fear, vague though the actual threat might be.

It was harder with the other matters. Pipgras, Manski, *Priscilla,* the boy king and his Mythology. Though the narrator had given explanations, the reader felt how doubtful they were. And now this little trick that the man had played with his pencil and looped knot of twine. If the reader had ever known, the narrator had taken away that knowledge long ago. And now had to bring it back —what was, said the narrator, simply the boy Michael Morley's most private secret, buried so well that even the narrator himself had forgotten, so that it came back to him now with a shock. The secret (said the narrator) was the boy's knowledge (known only to himself) that he was really insane, with private madness spinning around a pencil on a looped knot of twine. It was what separated him, as only the boy then knew, from everybody else. Actually—the narrator now realized—the boy's madness was the narrator's as well: it was narrative insanity. And it was related (wasn't it?) to the upwellings of madness that had been threatening the narrator only recently: these sudden impulses in the narrator to run wild, which he blamed on rebellion by the boy king.

The narrator enjoyed explaining it to the reader. It wasn't his fault that the boss had censored it for so many years. Now explaining it to the reader seemed to give license to the wildness and madness itself.

The narrator showed the reader a scene: a twelve-year-old boy (or eight, or seventeen) sitting at his desk, holding the pencil tightly in his right hand, vibrating it so as to make the loop of string, weighted with a knot, rotate around it. There he sits, rotating the knotted loop, making it go fast, his eyes blank, more inward than outward. It goes on and on and on. Sometimes the loop gets away, flies off the pencil, up against the books. The boy retrieves it and resumes. The narrator points out the callus on his index finger where he grips the pencil. As they watch, he tells the reader how the boy has been doing this since the beginning of memory. Doing it daily in arranged-for time, an hour, sometimes two or three hours at a time. Can't do it at school, or with his friends or family, so he has to find time alone each day, for he feels desperate if prevented. Like a drug, says the narrator. He does it at his desk, as you see him now. He takes it to bed with him at night and does it under the sheets before going to sleep.

Masturbation? asked the reader. No, said the narrator, distinguishing. The boy knew about that too, but this was a different thing. The spinning loop was a matter between his fingers and his brain. His penis expressed no interest. Displaced masturbation? suggested the reader—but the suggestion bored the narrator, who said there were more interesting things than that to know.

The spinning loop burrs against the facets of the pencil like a motor. The reader notes the boy's staring eyes and asks, What's going on inside? The narrator is embarrassed and deprecates:

Some boyish fantasy, quite banal. In this case he is a railroad engineer driving a locomotive. Yet see how he conducts this banal fantasy, says the narrator. Look how the boy with his burring loop hedges it in. A controlled fantasy; not a free-flowing reverie, but a tight act of will putting into order images that in some sense his will commands. He drives the locomotive step by step from Boston to Woods Hole—by the stations and through the countryside. Which makes him a narrator like yourself, observed the reader.

The narrator told how the boy narrator—after taking his loop and pencil from the desk and checking to make sure no one was around—first of all laid down the conditions for his adventure. This will be in the future, he said, and I am an engineer on the Woods Hole branch of the New Haven Railroad. Ignore how I became an engineer and whether I do other work as well. Ignore the question of change—whether the countryside or the railroad itself will be different in time to come. Let it be as it is now, except that I am in the engine.

The locomotive is No. 1001, class I-1, a 4-6-2 ("Pacific") type, assigned to the morning train from South Station, Boston, down to the Cape. He sits in the cab of the locomotive, backing it up to the train, which waits at the platform. Engine now hooked up. Leans out the window, looking back at the coaches, waiting for the signal to start. A five-car train—two baggage cars, followed by three dark-green steel-riveted passenger cars. Let time pass. Engineer looks at his watch, looks at the signal down the track ahead, takes the wave from the conductor, and opens the throttle. Hissing steam, a slow movement of the piston and the drivers, then *chuff!* Wheels turn a little more, then *chuff!* again. And *chuff* and *chuff*. (Meanwhile the loop spins at high speed on the pencil, burring against the facets like a motor.) Chuff. Chuff. Chuff chuff. Chuff chuff chuff chuff. Chuffchuffchufchufchufchuf. Chuchuchu. Chichichichi. Shishishishishi. Shshshshsh. Slowly, then gathering speed, the tracks glide in toward the locomotive. Clickety switches bear us through the left side of the yards and then we are in the clear, on a double track going fast through the suburbs south of Boston. Whistling for grade crossings. Passing at seventy miles per hour through suburban stations: Braintree, South Braintree, Holbrook, Avon, Montello . . .

Not knowing those suburbs south of Boston, the boy has to make them up, using the names that appear in the timetable and fragments of old memories. Since this gets tiresome, let more time pass. Arrive at the Buzzards Bay station, observe No. 1024, waiting on a siding. Cross the Canal Bridge, slowly, and let time pass again. Single-track now, the line passes between fields and clumps of woods and shingled summer cottages. Off to the right are glimpses of the beach and the silver bay. Close to the track the fence goes through clumps of berry bushes and the telegraph wires rise and sink rhythmically between the low tilting poles beyond the trackside gully. A bend to the right, straightaway on a slight grade—the engineer sees the rural station he knows best at the top of the rise, cuts the throttle, applies the brake, whistles, and stops short of the station, just before the siding switch. The brakeman walks ahead to turn the switch, and the engineer moves the train onto the right-hand track, stopping with the engine blocking the road just beyond the station. Panting and clanking while passengers get off, stepping across the left-hand track to the station platform. Engineer steps across to the fireman's side (left) to watch: bags of mail unloaded onto a hand-drawn truck, station wagons, people in bathing suits watching from the parking lot. Long grass in the fields behind the houses across the street. When the conductor signals, he pulls forward to wait on the siding beyond the station for the other train. Hears the other train whistling for crossings. Soon it arrives and passes cautiously on the left—No. 1015. When it is past, the brakeman goes ahead to throw the switch, and the journey resumes—*chuff*—through fields with high grass and summer cottages—*chuff chuff.*

The boy always tried (said the narrator) to construct the experience as realistically as he could. To place himself in time and space, composing images of things in space and making time move second by second. The spinning loop was the machine that erected the experience and propelled it through time—it drove the train from Boston to the Cape. It wasn't easy. There were always dull spots and ignorant spots to be skipped over. The actual train trip from Boston to the Cape took two hours, but the boy seldom gave it that much time. He skipped to the interesting parts —the arrival in Buzzards Bay, the stop at his village, the final approach into Woods Hole. Often it was hard to get the train moving at all. Leaving a station, the boy sometimes found it so hard to control the time that he would have to start over again. And then it was hard to keep the acceleration of the chuffs even, neither unrealistically fast nor slow. It was still more difficult to observe the even acceleration in the rate at which the countryside glided by or to control the difference between the speed of near and distant things—the fences nearby, the houses and trees in the middle distance, the sand dunes far away—and to keep all this in phase with the steaming of the locomotive and the spinning of its driving wheels. The images kept going wrong, something moved too fast—or too slow—or it just didn't look right, or he forgot something that should have been included. Or his mind went off the track—distracted by another thought—and when he came back he would land in a different place or time, often one that he had already been through. Yet the spinning loop helped him control it and stamped it with the quality of reality, unlike his ordinary reveries. He had more freedom than in real experience. As he drove the train, he could also watch it from across the fields or coming into the station, or project himself into a passenger to look out the window at the same countryside that he also watched from the engine cab. Such shifts of viewpoint required no changes in his preliminary rules: they happened automatically, involuntarily. His narrative was most vivid when it had this kind of freedom. But whenever he imagined himself looking directly at something, he had the same difficulty that he had with the speed of the passing countryside. How big was the engine (No. 1001) when you got to Woods Hole and stood back and looked at it? He would look and suddenly his powers of visualization failed. It did not look big enough, perhaps it looked like a toy or a picture from a book—so he would make it bigger. And still bigger. Suddenly it was too big, impossibly big, as big as the station itself, its chimney reaching the level of a three-story building, its length extending for a city block. Won't do. He tried to shrink it, but the more he tried to focus, the more unreal it became. The only way to restore realism was to back off a little, blur the focus, shift the point of view, squint at it from an angle. He kept trying to give his constructed images the crystalline reality of actual memories where the whole picture is seen in one glimpse, as a whole.

And all the while, the spinning loop burrs around the jiggling pencil to keep the experience alive, just as the turning reel of the projector keeps the movie alive and the turntable of the record player keeps the music alive. Then—says the narrator—suddenly an interruption, footsteps, his father coming up the stairs. The boy shoves the spinning loop with the pencil into the open desk drawer. His father appears in the hall, going to the bathroom. Guilty and afraid, the boy searches the miscellaneous surface of his desk for something plausible to explain what he has been doing. Yet his father knows—the boy can tell from the dark look on his face. He does not speak of it, though. The boy waits for him to come out and go downstairs again, before continuing his journey to Woods Hole.

15

His mother called it a *habit*: something you keep doing, that you can't help doing, an activity that generates its own repetition. Like a drug, but without a chemical—just the two necessary tools: the vibrating axis and the eccentric wheel. The boy tried to develop good habits (brushing teeth, virtue) and to break bad habits (chewing fingernails, laziness). This spinning loop was a bad habit, which his mother and father wanted him to break.

The name of this habit was "needle and ring." The name came from the original tools: a long white knitting needle and a metal egg-poaching ring. It preserved the ancient myth that explained the origin of the habit. In the myth they were sitting in the kitchen near the beginning of time, and the boy's father picked up a knitting needle and put it through the poaching ring and jiggled it to make the ring spin. A demonstration, perhaps an elementary physics lesson for the child (three, four, five years old, whatever he was), to show the nature of forces and how they are converted from one form into another. See how the back-and-forth (reciprocating) motion of the needle is translated into the circling (centrifugal-centripetal) motion of the ring. Just as in a steam engine the reciprocating motion of a piston generates the circular motion of the driving wheel. The child discovered he could do it too. Once the fingers had felt what it was like to translate reciprocating motion into centrifugal-centripetal motion, the child was hooked.

At first there was no secret about it. He would practice his habit in the kitchen while his mother cooked dinner. Then the reciprocating motion of the needle began to generate the narrative force of his imagination, and the child, vaguely ashamed, began to conceal it. Someone decided the habit was bad and ought to be broken. His parents tried to forbid it. His mother said: "You mean you can't *think* without it?" Her alarm frightened the child and made him more secret than before. He had given birth to a narrator, but the narrator, hooked up to a steam engine, was ashamed. Later his parents changed their tactics and tried to be tolerant. But it was too late for the boy not to hide guiltily, nor could his father conceal his irritation when he observed the boy's startled guilt. Rituals of evasion were developed: the boy became skillful at concealing the habit, his parents at concealing their knowledge of it.

He went through a variety of tools after the original knitting needle and poaching ring, though he continued to call it "needle and ring." For the axis, a pencil would do. He preferred one with faceted edges, for the sake of the vibration, the motor effect, that concentrated the narrative process. For the rotating object, he used almost anything that could be spun, weighted on one side: a large paper clip, a small padlock, a knotted loop in a reasonably heavy piece of twine. The callus on the index finger of his right hand stayed with him through childhood. Mark of his shame, his madness, the fact, discovered by his mother, that he could not think without it. This made him different from everybody else, incapacitated from leading a normal life. He kept his madness a secret, concealed from others and from many parts of himself.

He did not use the word *insane.* That was for the people in the *insane asylum,* what his friends called the old gray Victorian building back in the woods. Crazy people who according to legend (he never saw them) had intense staring eyes, talked to themselves, supposed that they were Napoleon or Caesar or Jesus Christ. People in magazine photographs who sat in corners huddled against the wall or—like Robert Schumann (said Mrs. Graham)—*lost their minds.* Insanity was losing your mind—it flies away in the wind, leaving an empty house. The madness of needle and ring was different. It was worse, because it was so secret, so private.

Well, every child spins fantasies, said the reader. Not like this, said the narrator, insisting on peculiarity. His madness showed in his inability to understand how normal people could do *without* needle and ring. How empty their lives must be, how pale, how fluid. Fluid? said the reader, challenging the narrator to describe the unanchored quality, the waste of experience, the passing away of time, the fate of life that escaped without being swallowed and digested by the act of needle and ring.

You mean you couldn't *live* without it? echoed the reader. The narrator remembered about dreams, how you dream in order to flush your mind of the day's waste. It was similar with needle and ring, except that it wasn't to get rid of things, it was to save and use them. Every day the boy saw things, learned things, sometimes had adventures. Then he would revise them, extend them, review them from other viewpoints, always using needle and ring. Everything that went into his mind this way came out in a new shape through the motorized imaginings of needle and ring. He ran them through needle and ring to make them his. It required him to observe the world keenly: he had to remember as much detail as possible, to stock the needle and ring narratives that would follow.

So you watched the passage of trains by the local station, or the boats by the bridge—said the reader—or went to an opera or a ball game or read a book about birds. Was the real experience too intense, too uncontrolled, too dominated by uncertain future and outside people, so that you had to drive through a second time under your own control on the centrifugal momentum of the ring upon the vibrating needle? Yet the boy never simply duplicated his actual experiences. Most of his needled narratives were postulated as things to come. They placed him in the center, sometimes with skill and knowledge and years, as when he drove the train or commanded the ship, and sometimes as he actually was, observing things as they happened. Some were located in an imaginary country whose relationship to the real world he had worked out carefully. Sometimes he would adopt the identity of someone else so as to partake of an experience unlikely for himself. Sometimes the fantasy was almost impersonal—he did not place himself in it at all.

Most of the needled fantasies tried to evoke the feel of actual experience. Sometimes they tried to discover what an experience would be like. He traveled to outer space and on sailing ships in storms. Once he became by secret formula—temporarily, with protection against cats—a bird to live for a day the life of a wild creature (wood thrush) in the trees and bushes of the backyard. With the vibrating needle he flew from branch to branch, returned to the nest, stopped to sing, while a boy with a notebook watched, followed, and lost him. Often he was the conductor of a performance of an opera. He was also in the audience watching himself conduct, and sometimes he was singing too. Sometimes he disappeared altogether into the music, sounding through his head, with himself only as listener—for the needle's interest more and more moved from the ego of the imaginer to the experience itself, to the time and what moved in it.

Still the reader complained about the plainness, the lack of romanticism in these fantasies of everyday life. What is the use of fantasies—he asked—if they don't transport you into a different world, beautiful and strange, to make up what we lack down here? Well, the narrator remembered that the boy did put in time as one of King Arthur's knights, he fought at Troy and lived on Mount Olympus—but that was no answer. Despite the romantic worlds of books he remembered, the boy seldom composed such worlds for needle and ring—it was not what his madness needed. It was not to escape from his life (suggested the adult narrator looking back), but to become more conscious of living in it. The world was around him, but the boy never knew what it would do next. He took his needle and ring and by converting reciprocal motion into centrifugal produced his own image of that world.

Still, it was a bad habit, said the narrator, which a child ought to get rid of. Because it will make you nervous, his parents said. The boy never knew what they meant. Later he found another reason: Because it takes too much time, said the narrator, time other children would use for books or friends, exercise, practice, or work. The narrator contrasted him to some opposite child—competent, practical, and ambitious, looking ahead always to a career in a realistic future—the child he might have been were it not for needle and ring.

Encouraged by his mother, he got rid of other habits. There were techniques for breaking habits. But needle and ring was too deep for techniques. So how did you get over it? asked the reader. The narrator could not remember. He could not remember a last time, nor a decision, nor even the year in which it ended. It must have stopped by itself, he said, when the need stopped. Maybe when he began to smoke . . . And the demands upon his time, the greater urgency of adult work. A more social life, suggested the narrator. New friends. Women. Roles to be filled, positions occupied—he was an army officer, he became a graduate student and teacher. The boss was taking over from the boy king's successors, trying to establish a regime with authority and dignity, responsibility and respect. At this time, also, the *writer* was most active: he kept a journal filled with sketches, memoirs, stories, poems. No doubt the writer interfered with the graduate geologist, but he did more than any other to render the needle and ring superfluous. The narrator gave him credit—somewhat wistfully, for eventually the boss subdued the writer, or at any rate bought him off. This too was a censored story. The writer was still alive, taking his notebook with him on the summer field trips to the Rocky Mountain Summer Geology Field Camp, even when Claudia Field entered his life, but the boss considered him subversive and through the years imposed more and more restrictions on him. This left only the narrator free—busy, respected, and useful, but with no official status. Finally, adds the narrator, the boss got tired even of the geologist and became a pure boss, which is to say administrator and Dean, and then the writer died.

And so you got over the needle and ring with no hangovers, no secret desires to tie a piece of string into a knot and give it a twirl for old time's sake? said the reader. None whatever, said the narrator. The impulse is dead and the machinery has rusted away. Nor do you have (asked the reader) any vestigial need to ride a narrative fancy as the boy used to do, to solidify the experiences of your day?

The narrator assured the reader that everything was in good order, functioning well for a good deanship and fatherhood of a successfully grown-up family, with the boss securely in command. Yet something was wrong—the narrator felt it inside himself, even as the reader accepted his assurance. The fit was coming on—the narrative obsession again, threatening to break loose. Was it an infection picked up from Macurdy? Or some self-generated or congenital disease in the narrator himself, emerging now after all these years, to which Macurdy was a mere coincidence or ironic accident? His narrative membranes tingled with old excitement. The names were luminous on their slides. George Pipgras. Dorothee Manski. Danusia. The king was awake. He was taking over the narrator, who once again felt the feverish intensity of old interests. The Mythology was coming to life.

In his fit, the narrator seized upon the reader. Let me show you in detail—if you pay enough attention to detail you can get interested in anything. Here are the deep and permanent landmarks of the Morley mind, images of the source of life, of Michael Morley himself, and if you wish to know this world, this mind (said the narrator to the reader), you must look at them closely, in their detail and with his eyes.

The narrator had gone mad again, but he could not help it. He opened up the pages of the king's Mythology and began reading to the reader.

16

Favorite Baseball Player

The narrator looks back over a wreckage of needle and ring narratives, finds himself with the king somewhere in middle time. He is seated in the open stadium with a friend, looking out over the bright unnatural green to the opposite stands in the great shadow beneath the upper deck. All that openness between our seat and those opposite, stretching away from first base toward right field, and all through that shadowed space the smoke of thousands of cigars, filmy upward. From the double decks of the stadium, under the ornamented stone pediments hanging from the roof, thousands of voices roar together—the roar bursting and subsiding with the motions of the figures on the green, dressed in white or gray. Numbers on their backs, to be checked against the programs in our hands. Out to the left, sunshine glitters on the center field bleachers and the apartment buildings beyond, with a crowd of speckles watching from the roof, and the elevated station, with every now and then a train. The white and gray figures grow bigger as you look at them. One team is white with black pin stripes and black socks, caps, and numerals, the other gray with black lettering and numbers and socks striped variously in red, white, and black. As they play, the boy watches the man in a black suit who stands behind first base. Whenever the ball beats the runner to first base, he crouches and raises his fist before his face, and when the runner gets there first, he spreads his hands out, palms down. The Yankee first baseman is a tall man wearing the number 4. The umpire is not as tall, yet the boy watches him closely, every move. Especially when a stray ball between innings drifts down the first base line and the umpire picks it up. He watches the umpire's motion as he throws it back, a deliberate overhand movement like the aged voice of a retired opera singer sounded experimentally, without forming a tone—for the name of the umpire is George Pipgras, and he is all that is left of the hero of many a game of needle and ring. In that slow tossing motion the boy looks for vestiges of the old art, some indication of what his arm looked like in old days when arm was a fast ball and knuckle ball sustained through nine innings with enough mastery and skill to bewilder a team of batters—when arm was the perfection of art.

During most of his residence in the Mythology (as narrator explains to reader), this George Pipgras was already finished as a player, and the problem was what to do with a disappearing career. The beginning was the best. This was one of the root events in the Mythology, archetype and source, listed by the king as the First Baseball Game. His father's purpose was to show him Babe Ruth, Star of Stars. But on the scorecard, Babe Ruth's name was on a level with the others, all of whom were mythological, who would in later years be remembered in the newspapers and by the narrators of unforeseen friends, though the boy king had no knowledge of their status at the time. The line-up as announced by the scorecard was as follows:

1	Combs,	cf
	Lary,	ss
3	Ruth,	rf
4	Gehrig,	lb
22	Lazzeri,	2b
6	Chapman,	lf
	Sewell,	3b
8	Dickey,	c

In the ninth slot, five pitchers were listed:

10 Pipgras,
11 Gomez,
Ruffing,
Pennock,
Allen,

(The narrator omits numbers where these are not remembered, for the sake of accuracy and loyalty to the boy king.)

The boy understood that the pitchers rotated from day to day, and the pitcher on this particular day was number 10, Pipgras. The gray team were the Chicago White Sox, in seventh place in the American League. The Yankees, who were in first place, won easily. The score was 6–0, the pitcher Pipgras pitching what the writers called a shutout. The next day the paper had a picture of him and said it was his second shutout of the season.

So the boy, looking over the line-up for a Favorite, picked Pipgras. He followed the games in the paper and observed the rotation of Pipgras with the other pitchers. He saw that pitchers got credit for winning and losing games, and Pipgras won more than he lost. He was the second or third most reliable among the major pitchers on the team. Later in the season the boy went to another game, this a doubleheader with the Detroit Tigers. Pipgras appeared as starting pitcher in the second game. He did not look quite as the boy remembered him, although only a few weeks had passed: his memory of the first Pipgras was tall and thin, whereas this Pipgras was huskier and more solid. He did not do so well, either. One of his pitches struck a Detroit batter on the head, and the victim had to be helped from the field. Later he faltered and had to be replaced by a relief pitcher. The Yankees won, but the relief pitcher was given the victory.

His father invented a game of imaginary baseball for him. He composed imaginary teams and snapped a spinner on a board to see what the players did. The line-up of one of the teams his father invented for him was as follows:

Gapspir, rf
Pasgrip, cf
Ispgrap, 3b
Prigsap, 2b
Grippas, 1b
Rippgas, lf
Aspprig, ss
Sargpip, c
Pipgras, p

The real Pipgras had a good season that year, and the imaginary Pipgras, said the king, was sensational. The imaginary Pipgras won almost every game (not quite all, the boy king was careful to note), and pitched several shutouts and a couple of no-hit games. The real Pipgras worked hard every fourth or so day, standing on the pitcher's mound practicing his art, and won sixteen games and lost nine. His team won the pennant, and Pipgras won the third game in the World Series, although he had to be relieved by Pennock in the ninth inning.

The next year, the Yankees sold him to the Boston Red Sox, and the king followed, switching his allegiance to the new team, even though they were in last place at the time. In the middle of the season he was struck on the elbow by a batted ball, and his elbow was shattered. The papers said he would be out for the rest of the season. Thereafter, week after week, the king watched the line of print that was his record in the column of pitching averages—frozen while the records of the other pitchers kept adding and growing and changing and living around him:

	G	IP	H	BB	SO	ERA	W	L	PCT
Pipgras, NY-Bos	26	161	172	57	70	3.90	11	10	.524

Now the question was whether the Favorite could make a comeback. It was a long, hard time. The following year the king watched the papers regularly, looking at Red Sox box scores, searching out the name Pipgras, which seldom appeared. The king worried on his behalf. In the season after his injury Pipgras pitched only three innings. Still they kept him another year, but it did not work, and finally a small item in the paper announced his unconditional release. End of career for George Pipgras. Not quite, actually, because he did come back as an umpire. The boy watched him that day to see what was left of his artistic arm tossing loose balls back to home plate, and he watched the box scores for the names of the umpires down at the bottom. Then Pipgras stopped umpiring. The last the boy knew, he was a scout for the Red Sox, but he has heard nothing of him for a long time and does not know what has become of him.

So it was for only a short time that Pipgras the pitcher actually practiced his art under the king's observation. After that he lived mainly in games of needle and ring, where the king tried to construct a comeback for him. When this was no longer realistically conceivable, he entered the Mythology as a figure from the past. While the king watched the name of Pipgras the umpire around the country at the bottom of box scores, he studied the historical Pipgras the pitcher through records fixed for all time in encyclopedias and baseball almanacs. The best years for Pipgras had been before the king's own time—although the king's first season had been a good year too. The historical Pipgras came into his own with the 1927 Yankees, which some sports writers of a later day, nostalgic, called the greatest team of all time. This was mainly because of Babe Ruth and Lou Gehrig. Well, said the king to the reader, George Pipgras was a member of that team too. He pitched the second game of the World Series that year and won easily. For years (perhaps forever after) the king watched for references to that team, and he was skillful in scanning familiar names quickly (Ruth, Gehrig, Meusel, Lazzeri, Combs, Pennock, Hoyt) in search of the Pipgras which usually did appear if enough names were listed.

Michael Morley's own baseball career began after George Pipgras's was finished, said the narrator. The boy practiced pitching in his own name with his friend Guy. They went out to the aqueduct path behind the houses and measured off the distance and practiced fast balls and curves and knuckle balls, counting balls and strikes. Michael Morley had a good windup and a stylish preparatory motion. By flinging his body into it, he worked up a pretty good fast ball, though he could seldom get Guy to call it a strike. The main problem was to keep it enough under control so that Guy would not have to run back to the fence for it. That was about as far as he got. He never got to pitch for a team. In games with friends he usually played right field.

Then he would go home and in the privacy of needle and ring bring a different class of pitchers to life. After Pipgras became ineligible for fantasies of the future, he was often replaced thus:

11 Morley, p

But he had trouble with the needle and ring making the ball move properly from the pitcher to the plate. He tried to visualize it concretely, the sequence of gestures in which is concentrated the pitcher's essential art. Right foot clamps against the pitching block, arms swing up and down, body rocks back as the arms go up, then as the pitching arm sweeps back prior to the throw, the left leg kicks forward and up. Sometimes in the needling, the motion would go wrong: the pitcher's legs would tangle or his arms get reversed or one ankle would trip the other, and the boy king would have to do it over. The biggest problem was after the release of the ball. It would slow down in midair, begin to dance. It would sink teasingly as the batter pushed out his bat to meet it. The king would try again. He wanted to create a proper impression of speed, to make the pitcher's prowess convincing. Actually, it was easy for the king to zip the ball to the catcher at any speed he liked. Trouble was, no matter how fast he made it go, it never seemed fast. The faster it got, the less of a ball there was. There was no heat at any speed, no sense of weight or difficulty or reality in the pitcher's challenge. As with the locomotive, the only way was to back off a little and squint at the pitch from an angle.

Meanwhile, with nothing to show for his own baseball career, the king watched the works of art crafted by professional ballplayers in the newspapers. This was the true object of a baseball game, said the narrator to the reader: a collaboration of eighteen artists to make a box score that will last. Just as reciprocal motion is transformed into centrifugal and this in turn into images concretely displayed to the mind, so the motions of players on a bright green field in the sunlight are converted into a fix of statistical print, a master score with a variety of subclassified contributories. And just as every game was fulfilled in a box score, so every player became a line of differentiated figures which grew steadily through the weeks (while shifting position from time to time in relation to the lines of other players) until frozen finally at the end of the season. And as the seasons passed, so every player's life became an accumulation of these lines, and when the player's career came to an end, this accumulation was his monument, the meaning of his name—the player himself.

So what kind of a monument did George Pipgras build in that first season when you watched him? asked the reader. The king listed figures, with comparisons to make their significance clear:

That year Pipgras was the starting pitcher in 27 games, of which he completed 14 without having to be relieved. He won 16 games and lost 9. His earned run average was 4.19. (This, explained the boy narrator, indicates the average number of runs allowed in a game. The lower the better.) He pitched a total of 219 innings, in which he struck out 111 men, gave up 87 bases on balls, and allowed 235 hits. He pitched two shutouts (of which the king witnessed one). Compare these figures with those of the other leading pitchers on the team:

	PIPGRAS	Gomez	Ruffing	Pennock	Allen
Games started–completed	27–14	31–21	29–22	21–9	21–13
Won–lost	16–9	24–7	18–7	9–5	17–4
Earned run	4.19	4.21	3.09	4.60	3.70
Innings	219	265	259	147	192
Strikeouts–walks	111–87	176–105	190–115	54–38	109–76
Hits	235	266	219	191	162
Shutouts	2	1	3	1	3

But you should see him in 1928, said the king. That year Pipgras pitched more innings (301) than any other Yankee pitcher, and he tied with Lefty Grove of Philadelphia to lead the league in games won (24). The king said 20 victories in a season is the sign of an ace pitcher at his best. He was proud of Pipgras's 24-game season, which proved his distinction. That season also he won the second game of the World Series, giving up three runs and four hits.

The king took credit for these achievements. This was what being a Favorite meant. It meant that Pipgras was the king's representative in the public world of baseball. He was a public incarnation of the king himself, an other self at work in the baseball world, so that when the king scanned the papers and found his name, he had found his own name. Just as he took credit for the achievements of Pipgras, so also he took responsibility for the humiliations and frustrations. And shared with him the unanswerable question of whether, if he had not shattered his elbow in 1933, he might not have had a career long and distinguished enough, like Herb Pennock or Red Ruffing, to put him in the Hall of Fame.

The king never met George Pipgras, never saw him except those three times, far away in the sun-shadowed cigar smoke. He never knew enough to give him a personality, for though he watched the papers closely, Pipgras anecdotes were scarce. He hardly even knows what Pipgras looked like, for he was distant on the playing field, and it was long ago, and pictures were scarce. The picture on the bubble-gum card could have been almost anybody: a tall man with a square and probably good-natured face. The boy king said that he must be intelligent and reliable, as indicated by his becoming an umpire after his career was done, but the narrator said in fact you know nothing, and the only Pipgras that counts is his art as fixed in the record book:

CAREER TOTALS	G	GS	CG	IP	H	BB	SO	ShO
	276	189	93	1488	1529	598	714	15
	W	L	PCT	ERA				
	102	73	.583	4.09				

17

Portfolio of Favorites from The Michael Morley Mythology

First Series. Here are the major Favorites (said the narrator)—objects of interest, goals of study, chief protagonists for the needle and ring narratives of the king. Permanent occupants of the Morley house. Arranged chronologically, in the order of their original nomination as Favorites by the boy king.

PRISCILLA (1894–1938?). Paddle-wheel steamship of the Fall River Line. 440′6″ long overall, 95′ breadth over guards. Gross tonnage 5292. Two black smokestacks, four passenger decks over guards. Sailed nightly between New York, Newport, and Fall River. *Favorite steamship.*

GEORGE PIPGRAS (1899–). Pitcher for the New York Yankees and the Boston Red Sox. Pitched for the Yankees from 1927 to 1933; sold to the Red Sox in 1933. Elbow injury ended career in 1933, though not given release until 1935. Won three games in the World Series of 1927, 1928, and 1932. *Favorite baseball player.*

1001 (1907–?). Steam passenger locomotive of the New Haven Railroad. Class, 4–6–2 ("Pacific") wheel arrangement. Driving wheels 73″. Tractive effort 31,550 lbs. Tender capacity 14 tons, 6,000 gals. Believed to have served in late career in local and light express service out of Boston. *Favorite railroad engine.*

DOROTHEE MANSKI (1891 or 1895–1967). German operatic soprano, Metropolitan Opera Company 1927–1940. Sang minor roles and occasionally substituted in major roles in the Wagner and Strauss repertoire. Known for versatility. Celebrated as the Witch in *Hänsel und Gretel. Favorite opera singer (First Series).*

SATURNIA (1927–1965). Italian passenger motor vessel. Gross tonnage 24,346. Length 630.1′, breadth 79.8′. Served ordinarily during long career between Trieste and other Italian ports and New York. Acquired by U.S. during war and served as a hospital ship before being returned to Italy for passenger service. Traveled on by the boy king during height of his reign. *Favorite ocean liner.*

Second Series. Here are some minor Favorites, selected objects of occasional intense but less continuous attention than those of the First Series. Some of these were stronger Favorites than others. They still attract the narrator's attention when he meets them in reference books—he likes to look them up and talk about them, and he sees the stamp of the boy king's selection upon them. Arranged alphabetically.

ATHENE. Greek goddess of wisdom and war. Helped the Greeks during the Trojan War, especially helpful to Diomedes, and Odysseus. Sprang full-grown from the brow of Zeus. *Favorite goddess.*

BALDCAP PEAK. Elevation 3090 ft. Tree-covered mountain at Shelburne, New Hampshire, overlooking the Androscoggin valley. Connected to Baldcap Dome. *Favorite White Mountain of New Hampshire.*

DANUSIA (1926?–?). Guernsey cow, Mosty Wielkie, Poland. Brown and white design, veteran member of 32-cow herd, occupied middle stall in group of five similarly decorated brown and white cows. *Favorite cow.*

DIOMEDES. Son of Tydeus. Greek hero of the Trojan War, prominent in the *Iliad.* King of Argos, second to Agamemnon in numbers of ships under his command. Sometimes called Diomed. Companion of Odysseus on several adventures. Dared to attack the god Ares and the goddess Aphrodite in battle. Sometimes called "The bravest of the Greeks." *Favorite Greek.*

EIGER. Elevation 13,036 ft. Peak in the Bernese Oberland in the Swiss Alps. Third in the chain of peaks with the Jungfrau and the Mönch. The north face is a notorious hazard seldom conquered by mountain climbers. The Jungfraujoch Railway tunnels through the Eiger on its way up to the Jungfraujoch. *Favorite Alp.*

ELIZABETH I (1533–1603). Queen of England. Succeeded her older sister, known as Bloody Mary, by whom she had been imprisoned. Reign marked by a flowering of English pride, commerce, and power. Age of William Shakespeare, as well as Sir Walter Raleigh, Sir Francis Drake, and others. *Favorite queen.*

EQUIPOISE (dates unknown). Race horse owned by C. V. Whitney. Active in 1933. Won a variety of big-money races, including a special match race with Questionnaire. *Favorite race horse.*

FOMALHAUT. Star in the constellation Piscis Austrinus. Magnitude 1.19. Distance from earth 22.6 light-years. Visible in the evening sky near the southern horizon in the autumn months. *Favorite star.*

SIR LAUNCELOT DU LAKE. Knight of the Round Table of King Arthur's court. Celebrated for valor, greatest of the Round Table knights, though marred by flaws. In love with Guinevere. Had accidental affair with Elaine, the Lily Maid of Astolat. Ended career doing penance for sins in a monastery. Reputed father of Sir Galahad, who was purer. *Favorite knight.*

LOUIS XI (1423–1483). King of France. Known for being wily, crafty, rather nasty. Possibly hunchback. Prominent in *Quentin Durward. Favorite French king.*

CLIFF MONTGOMERY (dates unknown). Quarterback, Columbia University football team in 1932 and 1933. Played in the Rose Bowl game. Later became professional. *Favorite football player.*

PAUNPECK (dates unknown). Ferryboat, with paddle wheel and walking beam, Yonkers Ferry, crossing the Hudson River between Yonkers, N.Y., and Alpine, New Jersey (a ten-minute trip), in the early 1930's. Dark reddish-brown in color, with name painted in gold letters, sister of the *Musconetcong. Favorite ferryboat.*

RICHARD II (1367–1400). King of England, son of Edward the Black Prince. Came to throne in 1377 at the age of ten. Quieted the Peasants' Revolt, but later errors in judgment led to his deposition and abdication in 1399. Replaced by Henry of Bolingbroke, crowned Henry IV. Died in prison, 1400. Patron of Chaucer. Inventor of the handkerchief. *Favorite boy king.*

TERIBUS (dates unknown). Steam locomotive on the London and North Eastern Railway (number 9906), formerly of the North British Railway. Member of the class of Reid North British "Atlantics" (wheel arrangement 4–4–2), celebrated for working passenger trains in northern England and Scotland. Seen by boy king in Perth, Scotland, in 1934, painted green. A whole book was written about the North British Atlantics in later years. *Favorite British railway engine.*

TIGER. Scientific name, *Panthera tigris.* Animal of the cat family, gold with black stripes, celebrated for ferocity, majesty, and power. Two primary varieties, the Bengal tiger and the Siberian tiger. Subject of a poem by William Blake. Popular in zoos and circuses, but the wild tiger is a threatened species. *Favorite wild animal.*

WOOD THRUSH. Scientific name, *Hylocichla mustelina.* Songbird, approximately 8 1/2″ long (somewhat smaller than a robin). Brown upper parts, white underparts, with black spots on the breast and sides. Breeds in northern United States, prefers woodlands, but also flourishes well in residential areas. Member of the most musical branch of the thrush family. Its song, an elaborate series of musical phrases, varies from one individual to another, and is surpassed in musical interest (according to most authorities) only by its close cousin the hermit thrush. *Favorite bird.*

10001. Electric interurban trolley car running between villages on the Belgian coast (Ostend and vicinity) in the 1930s. Most of these trains consisted of one car with an overhead electrical pickup, towing a second smaller car. Designated a favorite probably because of resemblance of number (differing by one zero) to the Favorite on the New Haven Railroad back home (q.v., above). *Favorite Belgian trolley car.*

Third Series. These are a few strong Favorites, who came later, after the king's needle and ring rule had largely ended. They differ from the foregoing in that the king recognized some real superiority—some merit, beauty, or authentic championship—before he made them Favorites. They were chosen because of their supremacy. In most cases, this happened after the king's rule had been destroyed. Even from his prison sleep the boy king sent out to give them the same obsessive attention that he had given earlier to the First and Second Series. Arranged roughly in descending order of lasting strength as Favorites.

KIRSTEN FLAGSTAD (1895–1962). Norwegian soprano, sang at the Metropolitan Opera 1935–1941 and 1951–1952. Made a celebrated debut in 1935 at the Metropolitan after a long career of obscurity in Scandinavia, and quickly became recognized as one of the great Wagnerian sopranos of all time. Center of political controversy after World War II, but reestablished herself. Sometimes advertised as "The World's Greatest Singer." *Favorite singer.*

TRISTAN UND ISOLDE. Composed 1859. Music-drama by Richard Wagner in three acts, with roles for soprano, mezzo-soprano, one heldentenor, one baritone, one bass, three minor tenors, and a minor bass. Noted for difficulty of performance in early days. Celebrated for innovative harmonic development and for dealing at greater length and intensity than previous operas with concentrated human emotions. *Favorite opera.*

THE POINT. Shingled house on peninsula at village on Cape Cod, that formerly belonged to the Morley grandfather. Porch on two sides. Main stairs and back stairs. Three bedrooms facing the harbor on the second floor. Lawn with a sprinkler going on clear summer days. Lawn slopes down to bushes, through which a path goes to the garden and through the garden to the dock at the harbor. Sold thirty-five years ago. *Favorite house.*

LOUIS ARMSTRONG (1900–1971). Trumpeter and jazz singer. During his long career he was regarded as the champion jazz trumpeter and singer, and performed at various times with a great variety of different kinds of musical groups. In the early days he was celebrated for elaborate virtuoso trumpet improvisations, in later years for his gravel-voiced jazz singing and for the impact of his personality upon jazz. Strong influence upon jazz musicians. *Favorite jazz musician.*

TED WILLIAMS (1918–). Baseball player who played entire career (1939–1960) with Boston Red Sox. Last batter ever to achieve a season batting average over .400. Led the league in batting in '41, '42, '47, '48, '57, '58, in runs batted in in '39, '42, '47, '49, in home runs in '41, '42, '47, '49. Most valuable player in '46, '49. Famous for his studied scientific attitude toward the art of hitting, criticized sometimes (perhaps unjustly) for concentrating on this to the exclusion of everything else. Wished to be remembered as the greatest hitter that ever lived. *Favorite hitter.*

JOE LOUIS (1914–). Prize fighter, heavyweight champion of the world, 1937–1949. Successfully defended the title against more challengers than any other champion, and was famous for knocking out many of his opponents in one round. A powerful slugger, admired also for his grace and dignity, especially in the hard times that befell him after his career as a fighter was ended. *Favorite fighter.*

The narrator explained the marks of a Favorite: how it leaps to mind ahead of other associations, whenever the chance presents. If the manager should enter a discussion of singing, the king will intrude with knowledge of the Favorite Singer, because she is singing to the king. If it is a discussion of the sea, the king will appear with his Favorite Steamship or his Favorite Ocean Liner or any of his Favorite lesser vessels not mentioned in this portfolio —because the ships float and manifest the king's conquest of the sea. The king has stock in all his Favorites, and is careful to guard this interest. He wishes to make all his subjects, all his readers, look at his Favorites with the same concentrated attention that he does. He does this instead of making them give their attention to him. It is as if he has dispersed himself among his Favorites and lives there, rather than in the Michael Morley self that you are looking at.

18

Looking over the Mythology, the narrator said that the real biography of the boy was the biography of the careers of the Favorites as they spun their way through needle and ring. Who in the earlier days were journeymen, workmen, and in the later days champions. Narrator and boy king building history in a world whose geography even now surrounded and enclosed the geography of the office of the Dean. He looked up from his chair at the desk to the door into the outer office, where the secretaries were. With white posts and a white net railing and the late-afternoon sunlight on the waters of the city harbor. You walk forward up to where the deck curves around and lets you see over the bow of the ship as she moves slowly out from the pier into the harbor and turns south. The reader asks, Where are we now? Inside his mind, says the narrator. Mind of the Dean? says the reader. I hope not, says the Dean. The mind of the Dean is occupied with administrative matters, letters to be written, problems to be solved—such as this of the man named Macurdy.

Then whose mind is this big white steamboat? asks the reader. The narrator looks about, surprised how familiar everything seems. As if it were my own, he says.

One evening the narrator found us in The Great Wall of China having dinner with this man Macurdy and the girl he called his research assistant. After all. On a rainy evening before spring began but with the winter bitterness washed out of the air by the rain, and mud around the edges of the sidewalks and in the lawns. This was while my wife, Claudia, was in Connecticut, where she had been called for an interview about the directorship of the Musical Institute.

The narrator discovered us, Michael Morley the Dean, sitting in a booth in the restaurant, colored by rosy light, facing Macurdy and the girl named Ruthie. (*Ruthie?* said the detective when Macurdy introduced her. This Ruthie wore blue jeans and wire-rimmed glasses and looked like a student, smiling brightly as if they were old friends. Ask her, said the detective.) The narrator was embarrassed and said, We're going to have to work out an explanation for this. The boss said, You damn well better. It was dark and ornate in The Great Wall of China, with ironwork posts and corners and a low shadowy ceiling, with filigree along the partitions between the booths and sections of the restaurant, and rose-colored paper lanterns and iron dragons, and the waiter was Chinese and wore a white coat. Sitting opposite, Macurdy (round face with heavy eyes in heavy glasses and threads of hair streaking back across his baldness) looked at the menu and said, "I recommend the sweet and sour pork, the egg foo yung, the beef chow mein." He talked about Chinese cooking. He said the distinction of Chinese cooking, apart from rice, was how they did the vegetables, waiting until the last minute and cooking them just enough to take the rawness out, to give them that crisp, fresh, new-cooked taste. Especially fond of bean sprouts, said Macurdy. Crazy wild about bean sprouts, he said.

Meanwhile the narrator was hunting back through the last half hour or so. Discovered them, a few minutes before, as they walked along the sidewalk, three abreast, on the way to the restaurant. With the Dean on the inside and Macurdy in the middle and the girl his assistant on the outside, next to the parked cars shining in the drizzly late-afternoon light which came partly from the sky, partly from streetlights and shopwindows and moving automobiles and signs. The narrator was watching how Macurdy walked, this not very tall fat man, with his coat rounded over his shoulders, noticing how heavily he came down on each foot and how the feet themselves pointed outward as they splashed and his walk made his middle swing slightly from side to side. The narrator noticed this awkward physicality and tried to connect to what had originally been merely a silence on the telephone and after that an unidentified voice and was still mostly a mystery in his mind, living there for speculation, indefinite threat, unknown purpose—even while he clumped along stiffly, toes pointed out, wearing a dark-blue raincoat that looked as if it had been stuffed with a pillow, with his collar turned up to protect his tie.

And walked so carelessly that he kept crowding the girl into the gutter. She was wearing an army coat, and she looked very thin and light, and she walked with rapid little steps and her head bent downward, as if it was difficult to walk beside him, and she kept her feet narrowly close together as if she wanted to make just one single line of tracks, skipping to change her pace the way a soldier does to get back into cadence. Every now and then she went down with one foot into the gutter and bounced back like a bird without seeming to notice.

Now he sat opposite them in the booth and looked at them both while the narrator tried to figure out how he got there. They gave their orders to the waiter, who first brought them cocktails. "So here we are in China," said Macurdy. Looked across the table at the Dean, slightly grinning, his glasses magnifying the whites of his eyes. Slightly grinning, though most of what he thought and felt was hidden in the plumpness of his face. He said, "Let's enjoy the strangeness of being here." The girl's face, which had been blank and bored, showed surprise, and she puckered as if to laugh but held it back. With her gold-rimmed glasses, she had a clean young face without make-up. The narrator wanted to ask what it meant to be the research assistant to Macurdy, and he wondered how old she was—eighteen, nineteen, or twenty-five? She wore a green T-shirt with the word "*DARTMOUTH*" in white letters across her breasts, and he wondered what her Dartmouth connection was, so far from here.

Macurdy continuing on the strangeness of being here: "Not really China, but it might as well be. I eat foreign food to bring foreign places to me." He patted his stomach. "Home," he said. "Here. Good as traveling. Feeds me too, just like home food. Do you realize that when you eat something like this egg roll, this beef in oyster sauce, these bean sprouts, you are eating food that is just as real to your stomach, with proteins, fats, and seasonings, as any equivalent American dish? Did you ever think of that?"

"No," said the Dean. "I never did." The girl gave him a quick companionable grin.

"Never?" said Macurdy. "You *never* thought of that?"

The narrator said, You will have to explain to Claudia how you allowed yourself to come in spite of all good sense. The narrator rehearsed the sequence. He came out of his office when they were closing up, and the manager said to the boss, You'll have to go out to dinner by yourself tonight because Claudia is in Connecticut. You take care of it, said the boss. The secretary said, "Good night, sir." Meanwhile Macurdy carried on: "That is why I like to eat in foreign restaurants, especially Chinese. Because they are opposite to us. Even though they are real people, just like you, just like me, just like Ruthie here."

The Dean saw the waiter, a young man in a white coat, across the room, writing an order on a small pad. The girl Ruthie Thomas followed his glance and looked also at the waiter, while Macurdy continued: "They eat food just like us, with their human stomachs. Not like the horse or the dog. You and I, we are not *equipped* to eat grass like a horse; if we tried we could not do it." Suddenly her face was all wrinkled by amusement again, which she shared with him, and he again wondered what it meant to be research assistant to Macurdy. She licked her fingers, wiped them on the napkin. Macurdy said, "Horse food, no, but Chinese food—now, that tastes good to us. Even though it's as opposite as you can get. Much more opposite than Italian food or French food. That's Western culture, to which we all belong—you, I, even Ruthie. But Chinese food, Eastern food, now, that's another world—a complete other world. Yet it's good. Taste it, these saucy meats, these crisp and lightly cooked vegetables. Now you know what the Chinese stomach feels, the Chinese palate tastes. In all those cities and restaurants and homes on the other side of the globe so far away."

Narrator admitted, the food did taste good.

"Of course China is not the perfect opposite," said Macurdy. "If you dug a hole, you would not come out in China."

"Where would you come out?" asked Ruthie, mouth full, sprouting bean sprouts.

"Indian Ocean," said Macurdy. "Out beyond the southwest tip of Australia. If you went through a hole in the earth you'd drown. So our true opposites are not the Chinese but the whales."

She looked at the Dean with her face relaxing again into a companionable amused state, and said, "He likes to be profound."

Macurdy nodded and continued: "The Chinese are opposites to us in day and night, but they share the same hemisphere. Opposites aren't interesting unless they have something in common. Whales aren't very interesting as opposites because they have so little in common with us, there's not much to imagine about them. Even so, they *are* mammals, and they have some brain, and they travel about, which is something. Fish are more opposite than whales. Clams and mussels are even more opposite—but they are correspondingly less interesting. The most extreme opposite—well, Ruthie, what do you think the most extreme opposite would be?"

She seemed as if sleeping. "Opposite to what?"

"Opposite to us."

"Us? You and me? Or him too?"—pointing to the Dean.

"Human beings. You weren't paying attention. It doesn't matter. It's merely an interesting idea to explore. The most extreme opposite to us would be—"

"A log," she broke in, grinning, and her mouth stuffed with rice.

"Ah," said Macurdy. "That's pretty good, but if you really want to follow through, the ultimate opposite would have to be a stone, a rock, which has no life at all. Now, the Chinese, they are human beings still, yet opposite—that's my whole point—*human* opposites. And they *share* the northern hemisphere, which helps even more: they share the seasons. That's what makes their oppositeness truly interesting."

Looking boldly at the Dean, she asked, "Does this interest *you?*"

"Of course it does," said Macurdy. "Dean Morley is an intellectual. Like me. You are not an intellectual—not yet. Maybe someday you will grow into it. An intellectual is interested in the life of the mind, as the Dean and I are. The Dean studies rocks, I study people. In that way we are different kinds of intellectuals—opposites—but we have a lot in common. Don't you agree, Dean?"

The sister looked to see if Ruthie was annoyed by Macurdy's remarks, but she showed no sign. The brother asked whether there was something impertinent in the way the man called him "Dean." Suddenly Macurdy turned to Ruthie and said in a tone of casual explanation, "The Dean is being careful because he is not sure we know each other well enough."

Boss to manager: What's the trouble here—can't you loosen me up a little? Manager: We have to keep the guards posted. (Meanwhile the narrator had gone back to the sequence he was trying to construct for Claudia, to the gap that remained after the Dean came into the outer office and remarked to the secretary that we would be eating alone tonight. He saw Macurdy sitting there, waiting for him. "Hello," said Macurdy. "Remember me?" *Yes, I remember you,* said the Dean, wishing that he didn't. Macurdy stood up. "I was hoping I wasn't too late." *What do you want?* "I just wondered if you might like to have dinner with us at The Great Wall of China. This"—as now the Dean noticed the slight girl in the glasses, the jeans, the Dartmouth shirt—"this is my research assistant, Ruthie Thomas." Who looked shy, too shy to smile or do more than tilt her head or slightly nod. Later, said the narrator, she would not seem so shy.)

"I hope you don't think I've been pursuing you," said Macurdy.

The Dean spoke to that: "Well, yes, I do. In fact, I do."

Now Macurdy smiled. (His face does not naturally shape into a smile, said the mother. It looks like a deformity.) "I'd like to be of service to you."

The Dean said, "There *is* no service I need from you." The sheriff's tone was full of policy, uncompromising, though the father was ashamed, considering that we were dining together—a social occasion. (He said, "I know your wife is away and you have to eat somewhere." They were outside the Dean's office then, and the Dean had locked the door and turned off the lights. "I recommend The Great Wall of China. I assure you—I only mean to be friendly." The brother was full of warning—remember what he did—while the man walked beside him with the girl skipping along, adjusting her pace, up from the campus toward the block of shops, and the man kept assuring him of his good will. So that when they came suddenly to the door of a restaurant and Macurdy swung around to face us—)

Macurdy said, "I know you think I owe you an explanation. I'd like to give you one." He said, "I'd like to bring everything out all clear and open and honest, so that you can see for yourself. Okay?" The carefully constructed smile in the plump face did not soothe the watchman, while the brother's suspicion actually increased. (While Macurdy swung around and said, "Here we are, right here! The Great Wall of China! Come in and eat with us." He demanded, "Is there any good reason not to have dinner with us?" As they went in, seeing the red paper lanterns and the ironwork dragons, the wife said, Claudia will think you are crazy. How will you explain it?)

Meanwhile, Macurdy kept his smile and said, "You see, I've always had an exaggerated interest in people."

There was a mechanical sound in these words, something rehearsed, prepared in advance, as if the truth was missing, though it was not necessarily a lie. When Macurdy continued—"An exaggerated interest in people. You can call it an obsession if you want to"—the narrator recognized it: he was being addressed by another narrator, putting things into a sequence. Not an actual lie, perhaps, but a manipulation, in a tone that was slick and embarrassingly familiar. The narrator was being addressed by Macurdy's own narrator, a cousin, telling a smooth and easy tale in the rosy light of The Great Wall of China, with the ironwork dragons and pictures of pagodas on the walls, and Ruthie, who leaned on her elbow and looked away, bored by it all.

From this "exaggerated interest in people" which he called an "obsession," Macurdy's narrator shot back to "beginnings in childhood" looking for a source—while our own narrator tried to judge, from his own experience as a narrator, how much skepticism was needed. There was an image presented of the boy Macurdy (already plump, already with heavy-rimmed glasses) prowling around neighborhood houses in the evenings, peering into windows. Full of the simplest curiosity, said Macurdy's narrator, provoked originally by the comings and goings of a girl who lived nearby, a few houses down the suburban block in which Macurdy grew up. She was three years older than Macurdy, popular with older men as well as boys her own age, the object of much masculine competition. This excited the plump Macurdy boy's curiosity, and stirred him to action. Seeing her go out one night with one boy, and the next night with another, the young spy discovered that it was possible to follow her movements without her being aware. This became most interesting one evening when from the bushes across the street he saw one boy deliver her home, after which another man in a car came and took her out again. He began to keep a record of her dates. Her name was Lena, and he called it his Lena Diary, his notebook with a daily and nightly account of her movements out of the house. At first he kept merely a general record of whether she was in or out, checked by the light in her room. Soon, without spending so much time on the watch, he developed an instinct for the right time to watch her leave and come home again. His Lena Diary became more coherent and complex, with records for every day, and distinctions between the different men who took her out. Some returned frequently, while others were strangers, and then some of the strangers grew familiar too. At first he gave them made-up names, but then his narrative curiosity led him to research their real names. It was purely a spectator sport, said Macurdy's narrator. Although he was fascinated with Lena's popularity and the life she led, the plump boy felt no desire to be a part of it, no wish to enter into the competition himself. His desires were served by entering their names in his notebook.

Yet his curiosity grew more ambitious as he discovered what he could do. He began following—always discreetly—in the secondhand car his parents had given him. He tracked them to movies, to dances, to bars across the river, to the roller-skating rink, sometimes to the drive-in hamburger stand. Different escorts took her to different places. There was a middle-aged man with spectacles who took her once a week to an old apartment over a store with an outside staircase, where they stayed in a lighted room behind a drawn shade for three hours before he took her home.

Going deeper, he worked with license plates and street addresses and the city directory. He conducted discreet inquiries and soon got the names of almost all the men he saw. It was easier when he got his friend Jerry Millis to help. With two working together, it was possible to keep a much more thorough watch and acquire much more interesting information. One night they decided to find out what went on with the man in spectacles in the little apartment over the store. (He was, they now knew, a real estate agent, a friend of Lena's father, a man with a wife and four children, whose name was Clayburn Rennig.) That night, knowing that Rennig would be taking Lena there, Macurdy broke into the apartment ahead of time by slipping the latch with his knife, while Jerry Millis stood guard. He cut a small hole in the shade in the window. Later, when the couple entered the apartment and drew the shades, he climbed the back-stairs and watched everything, while Jerry Millis waited below. According to Macurdy's narrator, that was his initiation; all later things followed from that. Afterward he wanted to know if Lena treated her other boyfriends the same way. He investigated and found that the real estate agent was in fact more privileged than the rest. He wondered why, which was a more difficult kind of question, since it required looking beyond the movements of people into their actual relationships. He never got far into it because one night a gang of youths caught him spying, trapped his car in a dead-end alley, pulled him out, and beat him up.

Macurdy's narrator did not say whether the beating actually stopped him from watching Lena or merely made him more careful. The important thing was how interested he got in the process of finding things out. An obsession, really, just like yours. The things you could discover if you make an effort. He went to movies about private detectives and read books about private eyes. Through high school and college, he gave his spare time to investigation, spying and detection. The inferences you could draw from clues. The checks by which you test your conclusions and eliminate alternatives. This was much more interesting to Macurdy's narrator than the things themselves, much more interesting to keep track of Lena's dates than to date her himself (in which case he would merely be one of those kept track of). Only years later, said Macurdy's narrator, did he begin to think of doing the things he had observed. A girl who came to live in his mother's house—teachable, who wanted to learn from him what he had learned from watching Lena . . . but that is another story, said Macurdy's narrator, and it was nothing to this deep satisfaction, this power that comes from setting up great curiosities and satisfying them, all in secret, unknown to those concerned.

In college he was good at writing research papers, said Macurdy's narrator, and he thought of becoming a scholar, except that scholarly subjects lacked for him the personal feelings, the dramatic sense of power that come from finding out about living people. The objects of his curiosity chose themselves—gave signals, he did not know how. His mind was attracted, would narrow and lock upon someone, compelling him to investigate. It might be a professor, sometimes a fellow student. For a while it was a girl who was clerking in the library. Some casual question might occur to him—why, for instance, did his biology professor seem to linger after the class as if waitng for someone, and was that girl also lingering in the back of the room? Such questions had a way of growing in the Macurdy mind like the beanstalk. Though he might often begin with a potential scandal, his curiosity usually outgrew that. He became interested in the professor's life for its own sake, as if to put himself into it. He wanted to know how the professor lived, when he got up in the morning, what he did in the afternoon and evening, what kinds of friends he had, his family life. He wanted to know about the subject's childhood, and when his interest was most keen, he wanted to write the professor's biography. This was a game with rules: the object was to base the biography on inferences from a distance—from spying and surreptitious investigation—and then compare with the real-life story (if he could ever get hold of it).

He became a real estate agent himself, he said, to make money and give him a feeling of solidarity with the man he used to spy upon. It gave him also a good look at the insides of a number of houses, a glimpse of family lives. And on the side—well, he had this little private detective business on a part-time basis. The narrator wondered why he didn't make it full time, since it was such an obsession. Well, said Macurdy's narrator, it was better to have a cover. Besides, his work as a private detective was really a hobby, an avocation, done, as he said, not for clients but to satisfy himself, to answer whatever stirred his curiosity. "There's no question you can't answer, if you have the guts," said Macurdy's narrator.

"So you see," said Macurdy's narrator, as if that made it all clear.

"So you've written my biography and now you want to check it out?" said Michael Morley.

Macurdy shook his head. "Nah," he said. "I got over that."

"Well, why did you investigate me?" said Michael Morley.

"Don't you think you're important enough?" said Macurdy. He dipped his egg roll in the hot mustard. "You're a public figure now," he said.

19

Was that all he would say? The Dean watched him manipulate his chopsticks. The Dean used a fork. So did Ruthie. Finally Macurdy said, "I predicted your appointment as Dean. Didn't I, Ruthie?"

She said, "You wrote it on a piece of paper and sealed it in an envelope." Looked at me. "He seals lots of things in envelopes. His desk drawer is full of sealed envelopes."

Are you saying (asked the narrator in disbelief) that was what made Michael Morley interesting to investigate? Because you were interested in who would be Dean? Macurdy grinned. Who knows? Or maybe it was what we found when we looked into your case. Why not?

"In my preliminary investigation," said Macurdy, "I detected something a little different in you. I detected a kinship, and I wanted to look into it." A kinship with Macurdy? The brother recoiled; even the narrator was shocked. "You had some pretty good obsessions yourself," said Macurdy's narrator. Was that what he meant? A kinship between his obsession with private detection, snooping into people's lives, and Michael Morley's childhood obsession with Favorites whose careers he used to ride on a game of needle and ring? But even if there were such a kinship (which our narrator wished to deny)—what could it explain? How could the private detective have discovered Michael Morley's Mythology without already having investigated deeply into his life? How could he have known it was there, without looking for it first? Who knows? said Macurdy's narrator, as if it were a mystery to him too.

That night at The Great Wall of China (and at later meetings also, which the narrator cannot always distinguish among), Macurdy or his narrator suggested ways in which he might have been investigating Michael Morley. To show his good faith, he said, though there was something equivocal in these good-faith revelations. Every revelation was in the form of *might have been* rather than *was.* As if to protect the secrecy of his working methods. It all sounded slightly fictionalized, like everything Macurdy's narrator said. How *such an investigation* might start with the ordinary biographical data collected from a university vita sheet or publicity release. How the investigator's interest might have been aroused by mention of the Westchester town where the subject grew up, which was near the investigator's own original places. There must have been traveling ("Lots of traveling—I travel compulsively," said Macurdy), with visits to those original places. Collecting addresses and going to the old streets to see what they looked like. Gathering names for interviews. ("Yes, we interview many people, always—in depth. We have our ways.") Letters of inquiry, phone calls, under a variety of false pretenses. Posing as a credit investigator ("Your name was given as a reference") or an FBI man (or woman, since Ruthie was in on this too) conducting a security check for undisclosable reasons. Such ruses would have elicited mostly simple facts, nothing especially secret or private, though from these a detective might put together a pretty long list of important dates and names in the subject's life. And sometimes, no doubt, he could dig deeper. Now Macurdy's narrator began to talk in questions. Was there in fact an interview, long and friendly, between your sister Penny and an ostensible reporter who was preparing an in-depth personal profile of the new Dean for some special publication? If so, how had this reporter managed to persuade Penny not to mention the interview to Michael himself? Could he have led her to believe (or if not Penny, Horace, or perhaps Horace's wife Ruth?) that Michael was being considered for a special award, for which interesting personal information of a private kind, not derogatory, would be desired? Could he have elicited in this way such buried matters of childhood as needle and ring and the Mythology of Favorites from a Penny or Horace or Ruth? (*Or their equivalents,* said Macurdy with a smile, to emphasize the hypothetical in all this—as if there were equivalents to one's brother, one's sister, or one's sister-in-law.) The narrator staggered between hypotheses provoked by Macurdy's narrator, none of which seemed very good. Would it have been Ruth, perhaps, discovered by the investigator to be the least guarded, teased into revealing the funny little human things she had learned (maybe) from Horace? Would she have said, "I understand he had this habit which worried his parents when he was a kid"? Could this have come without some prod from Macurdy, tipped off by another source to look for it? But what would the other source have been? Did he say, perhaps, "Are there any unstable things you know of, any childhood problems that might have been an issue, peculiarities that might have set him off as a child, predictive of his success?" Could this have drawn her into saying, "Well, his brother (my husband) tells of this habit which they called needle and ring, but I doubt that he'd like it to be made public." Of course the interviewer would be considerate ("I wouldn't dream of mentioning it"), dropping the issue (hot potato) as far as Ruth (if it was Ruth) was concerned, but pursuing it with another relative, say Penny or even Horace: "Can you tell me about this needle and ring thing? Does it indicate some intrinsic instability that the committee should know about?" Might this have caused Horace (if it was Horace) to describe needle and ring and even mention the portfolio of Favorites ("Well, yes, there was a baseball player named George Pipgras and an opera singer named Dorothee Manski and a steamboat named *Priscilla* and a Polish cow named Danusia") while trying to prove that there was no disabling instability? If this was possible, said the narrator, then it would be easy to follow Macurdy's narrator the rest of the way as he looks up those names in newspapers and reference works and old programs, going wrong only with the name of the cow. Yet Macurdy's own suggestions seemed almost deliberately to emphasize their unlikelihood. There was only the unarguable fact that Macurdy had indeed discovered all these things. There was the additional problem of why none of these sources (neither Penny nor Ruth nor Horace nor their *equivalents*) had ever told him that they had been interviewed by the FBI or the dean's search committee or a reporter writing a profile. Now, though, you could track it down, said the manager. You could write to Penny or Horace to ask if they had given any interviews. But though there were to be several more meetings with Macurdy, the manager kept postponing this inquiry—as if he preferred to accept Macurdy's good-faith revelations on faith. Or didn't want any more mysteries.

"And now I'd like to do some service for you," said Macurdy. When the manager backed away, he said, "I'm harmless, believe me." Insisted that it was merely the purest form of curiosity. "I like to put myself in other people's places. I fix on someone and I have to know. It ends up having dinner with you like this, telling you the whole truth. And if there's any investigating you'd like me to do—me and Ruthie—I'd like to put my facilities at your disposal."

Then he added, heavily: "We have nothing but the highest admiration—"

So the narrator asked: "How do you explain those silent phone calls?"

Macurdy looked surprised. "Why, that's over. That was another phase."

The narrator pushed. "That doesn't sound like pure admiring curiosity. That was harassment. That was hostile."

Macurdy considered. "I suppose those calls did not strike you as very friendly."

"You're damn right they struck me as not very friendly," said the sheriff.

Still Macurdy considered. He ran his hand once over his baldness—a gesture he had not displayed before. "Yes," he said. "Well, I suppose at that time we had not yet decided what approach to make. It was trial and error. Hit or miss. You see what I mean?"

"Hit or miss?" said the Dean. "No. I don't see what you mean."

"Ruthie can explain," said Macurdy.

"Who, me?" she said. They looked at each other. "Hit or miss? Yes. You know," she said. "You know." You know. "In the beginning he wanted to hear the sound of your voice—"

"*We* wanted," said Macurdy.

"We wanted. After digging up all that dirt about you, he wanted—we wanted—you know." You know. "To see what you sounded like. You know." You know.

Then Macurdy angrily, as if the question were unworthy of his time: "We called you up first to hear the sound of your voice. We wanted to see how you would react under some minor stress. Then also Ruthie—" (You know?) "You must make allowance for an element of capriciousness in such things. Every serious venture should have its lighter side." (You know.)

"And now as a result—" You know. And hurrying forward, anger buried again in plumpness: "And I'd like you to know how much we appreciate—how much we both appreciate your—" He hesitated. You know.

While Ruthie picked up her Chinese teacup in her fingers and drained it. Amusement always in her eyes. You know. (The sister was curious about her—who she was, how he found her, how he got her involved in his insanity. The sister said Ruthie looked intelligent and lively in her eyes and seemed to share the ironic frankness of the natural generation. She asked what a girl like Ruthie could see in a man like Macurdy—what kind of hold he had.)

"Your courtesy and restraint," said Macurdy suddenly. It made Ruthie giggle. You're going to have to explain to Claudia, said the manager to the narrator.

20

Favorite Opera Singer

Again the narrator leads the reader back to the boy king in a primal event. This is the First Opera, and the king is ten years old, sitting in the top balcony with his father and sister, looking down through the dark to the bright stage where the two children who are really women dance and send their sweet clear voices through the full sound of the orchestra. The king is attentive. Fixed on the colored light on the scenery and the shaded lights in the orchestra pit and the waves of the music as it thrusts forward, carrying the singers with it. He listens to the sound of their singing, not the words, which are German, incomprehensible and exotic. The children are chased from the house to gather berries by their angry, work-weary mother. The scene is changed and now they are in a wood with soft green light on flats of painted bushes and hanging trees. The light changes to blue as night comes on, and the children settle down to sleep while silvery angels descend a staircase to surround them. An intermission and then it is morning in the wood, and a decorated gingerbread house is revealed. An old witch with a pointed hat sticks her head through the upper half of a door to observe the children as they dance about the house, closes the top, and then opens the door to come forward down the stage to surprise and capture them. She is an old crone, dressed in dark gray—hunched over, she stoops and shrieks and cackles in intricate nasal phrases. Halts them with her wand when they try to escape. Dances about the stage when she has them in a cage and flies through the sky to music with thunder and lightning. Goes too far and ends up in the oven herself instead of Gretel. The oven explodes, and all the cooked children come out revived, to sing in chorus a happy ending in German. And is the witch dead? No, for when they come before the curtains to take their bows, she reappears, bowing with the others, holding the children her colleagues by the hand.

The boy king studied the cast as listed in the program:

HAENSEL	EDITHA FLEISCHER
GRETEL	QUEENA MARIO
THE WITCH	DOROTHEE MANSKI
GERTRUDE	HENRIETTA WAKEFIELD
THE SANDMAN	ROSE BAMPTON
THE DEWMAN	PEARL BESUNER
PETER	GUSTAV SCHUETZENDORF
CONDUCTOR	KARL RIEDEL

On another page of the program he noticed the listings of the week's operas. A different opera each night, and different singers for each opera. Some of the same names reappeared. He saw the name Fleischer in the listings again, also Schuetzendorf, also Manski. He was surprised that a thing so complex and grand as this opera could be followed the next night by another opera, and that the same singers could appear in different roles.

During the next few days he discovered that the newspaper always carried listings of the scheduled operas and singers for the week ahead. He watched and became curious as to what operas would come next and what singers would reappear. The operas were reviewed in the paper. The critic passed judgments on the performances of the singers—so-and-so was the best, so-and-so was not so good, so-and-so was in poor voice. Like the scores of the baseball games, the singer's performance could be measured, could be scored. To cope with such a world, the king needed a Favorite—a representative in opera, like Pipgras in baseball. He picked Manski and followed her from the world of Germanic fairy tale to the world of Germanic myth, guilty gods, and Wagnerian passions.

Mrs. Graham helped. She explained leitmotifs and gave him books. She said, "Did you listen to *Lohengrin* Saturday? Rethberg was flat." The king learned quickly. He learned about the guilty god, who tried to break his contract with the giants. He learned about the unfortunate brother-sister lovers and the battle maiden who disobeyed the god by trying to save the brother and was punished by being put to sleep on a mountaintop surrounded by magic fire after a sad farewell. Then the hefty young offspring, who killed the dragon and the dwarf and broke through the fire to win the maiden, only to be tricked into breaking his own vows by a malignant plot, which ended in the downfall of the gods themselves. He learned the motifs upon which the music of these stories was built—the Fate motif and the Ring and the Rhine and the Renunciation of Love, and he knew the Love Music and the Magic Fire Music, and the murmurs of the forest and the Forest Bird and the journey through the Rhine. He listened on the old radio (two pieces, the circular speaker bulging in the middle with a leafy design over the fabric), and he read the papers and learned what kinds of singers sang the different roles: what the heavy *dramatic* sopranos sang (Isolde and Brünnhilde), the lighter sopranos, the mezzos, the heldentenors, the baritones, the bassos. He grew familiar with names such as Göta Ljungberg and Lotte Lehmann and Frida Leider, Gertrude Kappel and Elisabeth Rethberg and Maria Müller, Maria Olszewska, Karin Branzell, and Doris Doe. Also Lauritz Melchior and Paul Althouse, Marek Windheim and Hans Clemens, Friedrich Schorr, Gustav Schützendorf, Ludwig Hofmann and Emanuel List, Siegfried Tappolet and George Cehanovsky, with conductors such as Artur Bodanzky and Karl Riedel.

All this—the stories, the music, the singers, the ads, the casts, the reviews, the joining of careers into a common enterprise—was rich material for the churning digestion of needle and ring. There it was revised and brought under the king's control. The narrator remembers the boy king's year more vividly than he remembers Michael Morley's year—the debuts of Frida Leider and Maria Olszewska in *Tristan,* the farewell of Antonio Scotti, the matinee *Ring* cycle, the substitution of one singer for another—a chronicle of events followed daily in the paper just as he had followed the Yankee season and Pipgras the summer before. The narrator has to look beyond the king to rediscover the outside world, picking up from the ten-year-old boy some recollection of walking to school on the aqueduct, of sloppy wet muddy days of early spring, of boys who were friends running down a path behind the houses to the athletic field, with the frozen ground, plotting and dodging other boys who were not friends. Finding also afternoons of sitting in a stiff chair in a large room while Mrs. Graham organized the pupils into a rhythm band—tense, uneasy, with the four or five other children, boys and girls, who seemed to know more about something, though what they knew more about he did not know. Rediscovered pain and fear mingled in the drizzly days, the cloudy skies, dumbly felt through the shouts of children, some of whom were friends, some not—while he kept mostly to himself the king's singers and reviews and mythological music. Shared with Mrs. Graham (who explained things)—but not the other kids, who did not know his kingdom and would probably consider it sissy.

The reader wonders why the king picked Manski for the Favorite. Not for her voice, said the narrator. The king in fact never knew just what her voice sounded like: when she sang the Witch it was distorted, and when she sang in broadcasts of other operas

Dorothee Manski, One-Woman Wagner,
Knows Every Note of All His Opera

World-Telegram Staff Ph

Dorothee Manski, the one-woman Wagner.

the only way he could identify her was by following the German words in the libretto. To him her voice was not distinguishable from the voices of other secondary singers.

Was it her witchdom itself? asked the reader. Was it to show that he wasn't frightened of the Witch because he knew there was a singer in that costume who had mastered the music? Or was the music itself a magic he had mastered? Did her musical witchery signify for the child the operatic process—as if the opera itself were an attack upon you like the Witch who eats children, yet was made to behave and be funny and above all musical by virtue of her conversion into a singer named Dorothee Manski? Or was it merely that the evil old woman who had been thrown into the oven was able to come out and take her bows holding hands with the others? That the distorted, nasal, shrieking voice could be listed in the paper as "soprano" and would appear later as the goddess of youth and beauty and as the beautiful Gibichung daughter who lures the hero away from his true bride and toward his death?

There were also the interesting things she did in those first few weeks. It was in the paper, what Macurdy discovered forty years later, how Brünnhilde lost her voice and was saved from the wings by one of the Valkyries. Dorothee Manski. The following week the same star was *indisposed* (new word for a boy's vocabulary) and it was the same Dorothee Manski who took her place in the next opera of the series as the sleeping Brünnhilde, wakened in the sunlight by the hero after he has killed the dragon. Though she was the same wicked witch who had eaten so many children a few weeks before, the critic praised her for "an intelligent and communicative performance," and the king knew she would be fine material for a Favorite.

In the papers, the advertisements, the announcements, the reviews, the news items, he looked always for references to Manski. She was the center, the point of view. He learned about the operas, how to run an operatic season, how to shape an operatic career, by following Manski. This was the purpose of a Favorite—as it had been with Pipgras. He followed her career as if it were his own, entering the operatic world through her. The narrator said it was better for the Favorite not to be a star, not to have that aura of personality that would surround a star. Manski's obscurity would make it easier to see how it all worked. A clearer lens. Being secondary, she had to struggle for attention. This made her more interesting than the stars who already had attention. As he followed the Favorite's career in the papers, the boy king wished for her to rise, to become a star. Then he could rise with her—but how could he rise if she already was a star?

She never did become one. Still, she was a good Favorite and gave him a fine obscure career that lasted through most of the boy king's childhood. Piece by piece she put herself together for him. At first he did not know what she looked like, for the Witch's costume concealed her, as the Witch's voice disguised her voice. He saw no picture for two years. Ultimately there were several, and he thought he might recognize her if he saw her: a large woman, fortyish, with black hair, large oval face, and easy amiable smile. Certain small parts belonged to her. Besides the Witch and the goddess Freia and the maiden Gutrune, she was the Walküre Helmwige (top soprano in the ensemble of eight) and the Third Norn, in whose hands the rope of Fate breaks at the beginning of the downfall of the gods. She was the duenna in *Rosenkavalier* (praised by a critic for being comical), the Overseer of the Slaves in *Elektra,* and sometimes Herodias in *Salome.* Occasionally she did bigger things. Once she sang Elsa, the baffled and dreamy heroine of *Lohengrin,* and a few years later she sang Ortrud, the wicked mezzo in the same opera. Sometimes she was Venus, goddess of love, in *Tannhäuser.* There was always a chance she would get a big part as a substitute. One Sunday afternoon the boy king listened as she took over the soprano roles in a broadcast Wagner concert conducted by Bruno Walter.

The reviewers seldom gave her more than a word: "competent," "adequate." When she sang Elsa she was described as "sympathetic . . . ample in voice and acting well within the traditions . . . not always able to avoid overstressing her tones."

The longest review the king ever saw was written by the critic of the *New York Times* when she sang the final scene from *Salome* at the Cincinnati May Festival. It was the high point of the king's Manski career:

> Miss Manski seemed able, on her part, to ride the orchestral wave at will, to provide, on occasion, tones that wove through inner parts of the harmony or that now and then merged into a kind of song-speech. . . . Because of her performance, and in spite of the wealth of instrumental commentary, the passage remained what it should be—one of lyrical melody and song.

A few years later the *New York Times* was less appreciative. Venus was criticized for "wavering sounds." Another reviewer disposed of her: "Miss Manski's Gutrune? No!" One by one she dropped even the standard small parts she had always taken. She remained only as the battle maiden Helmwige, singing "Hojotoho" for a few minutes at the beginning of the third act of *Die Walküre.*

She retired in 1940, eight years after the boy king had made her Favorite. After her retirement she went to teach in the opera workshop at the University of Indiana. Once in the mid-fifties he saw a picture of her in *Life,* her name misspelled, mouth wide open, teaching a young woman whose mouth was also open. She had a daughter who sang for a year or two at the Metropolitan.

According to the reference books, she came from Germany (though one book said she was born in New York). The boy king does not know if she ever went back. She had been dead a long time before he knew that she had died. He found it in the index of a book about singing, where her name was listed with the parentheses filled in: "Manski, Dorothee (1891 or 1895–1967)." So there was a mystery about her birth date too.

Once long ago, she was featured in an interview in a New York paper, along with a large picture. The headline read:

> Dorothee Manski, One-Woman Wagner,
> Knows Every Note of All His Operas

The interview described her clowning to liven up rehearsals, bringing a smile even to the face of that stand-no-nonsense conductor Mr. Bodanzky. It spoke of her versatility, her readiness to sing any part at short notice. "I could even," she said, "sing the Swan in *Lohengrin.*" She had a dog who could play the piano.

The king took credit for her as he took credit for Pipgras's record. Years later he wondered if she had followed her notices in the paper as closely as he had. He guessed she probably had.

21

A day or so later Macurdy came again with Ruthie to the office of the Dean. The secretary announced him through the intercom. When they came in Ruthie went directly to the window to look at the bird feeder that the Dean kept, tended by the secretaries. She turned her back to them and sat down to watch the birds. Macurdy had a large Manila envelope. "I thought you'd like to see these things we found—Ruthie and I—which ought to be of interest to you," said Macurdy. The narrator wondered: Is this the beginning of the blackmail?

First there was an envelope of pictures from the town in which Michael, Penny, and Horace Morley had grown up. Snapshots—"Ruthie and I took these last fall"—showing the aqueduct (the level path by the backyards of houses, crossing ravines and gullies on an embankment, on which the Morley children had walked years ago on their way to school) and the athletic field as it now was, and the residential streets that curled their way around the sides of the three hills on which the town was built. Pictures also of the elementary school and the high school as they now looked, and the downtown business street (called "the village"), which Macurdy compared with another picture he had found of the same street when Michael Morley had lived there. "Recognize this?" he said, showing pictures of the Morleys' own house, which backed over the ravine. The house was still there, said Macurdy, though the woods of the ravine were invaded, in the pictures, by new houses, modern and costly, whose large windows overlooked gardens. When Michael Morley asked how much of the woods remained, Macurdy took the three snapshots and examined them.

"Well, obviously," he said, "we must go back and take another look. We must plan to do that, Ruthie."

"Pittipittipitti!" said Ruthie. "Look how that little bird chases the big one off!"

Then Macurdy produced other things. He had a picture of George Pipgras standing on his left foot, having just thrown the ball at high speed. He had a Xerox copy of the interview that Michael the boy king himself had clipped years ago from the *New York World-Telegram*, dated Wednesday, January 9, 1935, with the heading: "Dorothee Manski, One-Woman Wagner, Knows Every Note of All His Operas." He had a deck plan of the steamer *Priscilla* of the Fall River Line. "Look at these," he said. "Tell me about them. What was it like?"

Subverted by this former stranger, it was hard for the manager to control his crazy narrator. Though the manager tried to hold him back, the narrator had to talk—hesitantly, in staggers. Looking for anecdotes that would sanitize the flow of memory that the stranger had stirred, pacify the manager, and still communicate to Macurdy what it *had* been like. Faltered trying to describe it, lying in the upper berth watching the lights move in the mirror over the stateroom sink, how these lights reversed their direction and he knew the steamer was turning, and confused this memory with waiting in the top balcony of the opera house, in the hot muffled smell of powder and perfume, as he sat in red plush and listened to the tuning up of the orchestra and looked down at the curtains, closed with the footlights upon them. He tried to pin down memory under stakes of communicable fact. He said: "I wonder what became of George Pipgras—whether he is still alive."

Macurdy was quick. "We'll look into that." Added: "We'll dig up anything you want."

He said, "For example. Dorothee Manski is reported to have died in 1967. Yet we couldn't find an obituary in the *New York Times.* We'll look further into that."

Possible research projects began to appear, and no one was clear where they originated, with Macurdy or the narrator or the interaction. Let's find out what became of the I–1 locomotives on the New Haven Railroad—when each one was withdrawn from service. Try to get a complete list of Flagstad's recordings. See if you can discover some pirate recording of an old broadcast preserving the Manski voice (never recorded commercially, said Morley, as far as he knew).

"What we must do," said Macurdy, after a while, "is write a book about all this."

"What?"

"The Morley Mythology," said Macurdy. "A book of *detail.* All the facts we can discover along with memories and impressions of these Favorites that made your childhood so singular. Put together the detail that made it live."

The boss was shocked. The brother searched Macurdy's face for proof of the mockery that must be there. The proof failed to come, however, and the king jumped up, exclaiming: Just what I've been saying all along. A book, a book, you must put it in a book! The father wondered: How did Macurdy know what the boy king wanted, buried so deep? The detective answered: You must have given it away unconsciously. Or revealed it through the same source, who ever that was, from whom he learned it all in the first place.

Meanwhile up on top the manager was saying, "Ridiculous."

"Not so ridiculous," said Macurdy. "A book of facts. You could write it and we could research it for you. Or you could talk to me and I could write it. Or you could write your view of these things and I could write another view, for a three-dimensional effect. You could have illustrations, photographs. A section on the steamboat and a section on a singer, and a record of the ballplayer. You have a *human* mind. If you're interested enough, you can arouse anybody's interest."

"That's a fallacy," murmured the critic.

"What use is anybody going to have for an obscure steamboat?" said the Dean. "Michael Morley's childhood. Who the hell cares?"

Macurdy looked as if shocked by the Dean's doubts. "The thing about you is that you are a fan," he said. "I am a fan too. The world is full of fans. You are a baseball fan and a steamboat fan and an opera fan and a railroad fan. There are many other fans of each of these kinds. There are hundreds of *other* kinds of fans too. There are movie fans and football fans. Sailing fans and soccer fans and television fans. Clothes fans and airplane fans and architecture fans and Gothic cathedral fans. Astronomy fans and astrology fans and antique fans and string quartet fans. And stereo fans and home movie fans and pornography fans and Greek vase fans. Tropical fish fans and modern poetry fans and Oriental rug fans and dog show fans and brass pot fans. Bird watchers and automobile fans—"

"I want a bird feeder," said Ruthie (back turned).

"—and horse fans and insect fans. And fans of Mao Tse-tung and Democrats and specialists in the seventeenth century. Listen: A fan is a fan who finds a little world to stand for the big one. Finds his identity, defines himself there. Usually he finds a favorite in it —favorite team, favorite star—to represent himself, and that way shares his life with other people."

The mother noticed that Ruthie (back turned) had put her hands over her ears. The father was surprised to hear this man, thought to be so dangerous, talking like this. Certainly you should give him a hearing, said the father, hear what he thinks.

"Typically the fan cares only for his own thing, the game of baseball or whatever he is a fan of. He doesn't care for what a hockey fan cares about. That's because only the one thing stands for himself. Somebody else's thing, that stands for somebody else." Macurdy paused. "I suppose that makes a difficulty for your book."

Seeing the perplexity on Macurdy's face, the boy king was disappointed. But in a moment it cleared.

"Let's make *The Morley Mythology* a book for all fans. We'll admit that every fan has his own particular interests, but let's invite him to consider *these* details—*your* mythology—as typical of *all* mythologies. If he pays enough attention . . . And if he doesn't," added Macurdy suddenly, "so what? Who cares about the reader anyhow?"

He looked at the Dean. "How about it?"

The idea was that the Dean should give Macurdy a number of interviews, when times were free, talking into a tape recorder about items in the Mythology. Meanwhile Macurdy would continue researching detail, and eventually—well—we shall see.

The Dean did not agree to this proposal. Partly because the brother was still suspicious. Wait and see what he asks in return, warned the brother. The Dean was also worried about decorum, about attaching his name publicly to so personal a project. "That's no problem," said Macurdy. "Wait and see what comes out." Still the Dean held back.

On the other hand, he did not reject it, either.

22

Favorite Cow

This was on the original Trip to Europe, a couple of weeks after the performance of *Rigoletto* in Paris, a few weeks before the performance of *Das Rheingold* in Vienna. There were the boy with his notebook, his sister, and his baby brother, traveling with their father and mother. It was near the city of Lwow in a part of Poland that was later to be absorbed into Russia, into the Ukraine. They were met at the station by a groom with a horse and buggy, for the station was a long distance from the farm. The groom smiled politely but spoke no English, nor did they speak Polish, so there was no conversation. They rode in the buggy behind the horse down long straight dirt roads flat between fields, past kilometer posts which the boy counted off. They turned off the road and crossed a broad field to another dirt road beyond a clump of trees and traveled another distance before they came to the farmhouse—sprawling and spacious, with a semicircular drive and a lawn in front and a view across fields and a meandering stream lined by trees beyond. The trip from the station took an hour. It established the basic mythology for the Russian novels that were to come later in the Morley history.

In the first twilight they went out of the house, down the muddy path past the first barn, containing horses, to the second, which housed the cows. There in the sweet milky shitty muddy smell of the barn in the half light, the boy looked at the backs of the cows in their stalls, lined up on both sides of the barn. Watched the stocky peasant women in bare feet, sitting on stools, spraying milk into singing cans, while a man with a ledger book recorded the amount delivered by each cow. In his suburban life at home the boy with his notebook had only the most fragmentary memories of farms. The smell and the light and the gritty grainy floor of the barn, and the long distance from the station covered by horse, rested him as much as the dim beams of colored light in the dark chapels in the backs of visited cathedrals, and the boy felt friendly toward the cows.

Still, cows were only cows until the host pointed out the writing in chalk on the slates above each stall. Each cow had a name. Furthermore, as the host managed to explain, each cow's name began with a letter signifying the year of her birth, so that all cows whose names began with *A* were born one year, those whose names began with *B*, the next, and so on. This woke up the boy king. We have a group of cows here, he said, distinguished from each other by meaningful names. We also have a man who records in a book the daily performance of each cow. Since we'll be staying here two weeks, the situation calls for a Favorite.

The next day he went out into the pasture to study the cows and select a Favorite. There were several kinds. Some were decorated

in patterns of brown and white. Others were black and white. There were other, more muddled types—light gray, or milky white, or pale tan, or white with black speckles. The boy chose for Favorite a cleanly designed brown and white cow. She looked like his idea of a Guernsey. Whether there could be a Guernsey cow on a farm in Poland near the Ukraine he did not know. He learned to recognize her design on both sides. On her left flank she had a red-brown patch shaped like the Spanish peninsula and the coast of France. When they went back to the barn that evening she took the middle stall in a group of five brown cows opposite the door. The slate over her stall bore the name *Danusia.* That meant she would be approximately eight years old.

The boy king did not catch up on his journal until later. Then he recorded the names of all the cows with the colors of those he could remember, going counterclockwise around the barn from the left door as you entered:

Jagna	black and white	Fatma	brown and white
Iskra		Fala	brown and white
Ikra		Danusia	brown and white
Flona		Janka	brown and white
Flora	brown	Halka	brown and white
Frania		Ela	
Guishka	gray	Berta	
Gotka	white with black	Herta	
Dorota			
Ida			
Alfa	dark brown		

Through Danusia, the king studied the life of cows on a farm in Poland, her going out to pasture and her coming back to the stall, and her circulation among the other cows in the society. He wanted to take a look at the records of the man with the clipboard, so as to judge her performance in comparison with the others, but he dared not ask. Once he managed to ask one of the peasant women which cow was the best milker. When she caught on, she grinned and slapped heavily the rear of the cow named Halka, who had, certainly, an enormous milk bag.

Inspired by the boy king's revival, one day the narrator dug out the king's old journal and found the following:

> Jagna was a friendly black and white cow. As she was next to the door of the barn, in which the cows were in, I could pat her. Guishka was a big gray cow. Her hoof grew too long so they had to cut part of it off, one day. They kept her indoors after that, and finally put a bandage on her foot. Poor cow! Gotka was Mother's favorite. She was white with some black. She did not behave properly. Fala was brown and white. She milked the best milk. The last day we were there she had a big cut in the side which I think will be a permanent scar. It was evidently from a butting cow of some sort. Danusia was a very long, fat cow. When we were in the fields I took many photographs of her. She never milked much and she never was one of the first in the barn but I liked her best anyway. Once when I was patting her she looked up at me and snorted. Janka was Penny's favorite. She was short but fat, and had a scar in the side. She was a good milker.

Considering that neither the aristocratic host, tall and stiff and grandfatherly, nor the peasants spoke any English, and neither the boy nor the boy king spoke anything else, the narrator cannot recall how it was communicated to him that the cows' names indicated their years of birth, or that Halka was the best milker, or that Fala gave the best milk.

23

One night in the same season came a new narrator, feeding the Morley narrator a chunk of new material. This was Ruth's narrator —Horace's Ruth, the famous Ruth, not to be confused with little Ruthie, Macurdy's sidekick.

(Ringing she came, sounding across the table—

Plumber: Heffner	772–5834
Peacock	465–9926
Psychiatric Inst	455–7000

—and out of the row of thin green guides to Austria, Switzerland, Germany, Paris, turning them into the voice that he had been afraid to hear in all the silences of the winter past.)

First she said, "Michael? This is Ruth." Immediate identification, straightforward, giving the lie to the nervous narrators of the silence. The name came back from everybody: It's Ruth said the mother, Ruth said the wife, Ruth said the brother, the detective, the sister, Ruth said Ruth. What can she want? Reckoning, said the brother. She will explain Macurdy. Partners, said the detective, just as we predicted. Now comes the blackmail message: "I'm calling because Horace is in the hospital and I thought you should know."

Slowly, almost reluctantly, the detective put away his file on the blackmailer, the lawyer put his briefcase back in the corner, the brother climbed down from the shelf and crept back to bed. Slowly Ruth's narrator came into view, wearing a nurse's uniform. The mother and father arose and told the narrator to pay attention to her. Horace is in the hospital. The narrator asked.

There was Ruth herself, a telephone voice, and speaking through her Ruth's narrator (and filtered somewhere in the distance also Horace's narrator), and receiving them was our own narrator, taking her sense and making it into his sense. Adapting it for history.

The narrator reconstructed what Horace's narrator must have said about the darkness that overwhelmed him—how he gave up after giving up. First there was his decision not to fight any longer, the humiliating fight. If they wanted to get rid of him, let them—even if it was unfair and illegal. It was not for him anymore, and Horace's narrator would have known it. Would have known what he meant by his own change in his teaching habits, recognized the provocations he had been raising—knew that he wanted them to get rid of him, that it was not their whim alone that produced this attack against him but that he had invited it, wanted it. And now, since it had not worked, Horace's narrator would know that he had wanted to be rid of them, the job, the students whom he did not like, whose empty faces sneered and insulted him—and said to himself, If I am to be a failure, I might as well be a failure in something I like, and not in this degradation.

So instead of fighting he quit—suddenly—a month ago (said Ruth—and nobody had bothered to write Michael Morley, who did not even know until now that there had been a fight). Make them drop their proceedings by letting them win, lose face but be free, private at last. End the downward slide with surrender, no way to go now but up (said Horace's narrator through Ruth).

He thought then that if he quit teaching (Limewood Country Day School), gave up defending his tenure, got a casual job with even less ego in it, perhaps he could stop asking whether his life constituted success or failure, and henceforth life would be better, kinder, easier to feel. Got a job too—bottom-level editorial in a textbook-publishing firm—found for him by someone who liked him well enough. All that in the last four weeks, said the narrators.

According to the reader, this was the fourth great change in Horace's career, each following closely upon a change in wife. Highly educated with a closely crafted specialty and a Ph.D., he began on the ladder toward a college professorship in mathematics. Abandoned that along with his first wife after a few years (great noise in the family) to become a Unitarian minister (family reconciled by the idealism this was thought to represent). Gave this up to try his hand in a business venture (book and art store—with a mistress to replace the second wife). Returned to education to teach mathematics to children in the Limewood Country Day School (while mistress became third wife—we have now arrived at Ruth). Now that too was over and Ruth cut loose, and he said to himself, Henceforth I am going to live life without goals. A new habit of thought the members of his family could never understand, said Horace's narrator. Contrary to his own habits also, despite the veerings and changes of his careers. Warned himself how difficult it would be to manage his life without goals, without the old currency of success and failure. But since it was now desperate, he resolved to keep his attention on this new renunciation of self, lest he forget and begin to feel depressed again. Compared himself to the animals, who knew how to enjoy life as given by nature—knew it long before reading and writing and men with self came along, animals living without worrying whether they were failures or not. That's how he'll live, said Horace to Horace's narrator, quietly and plainly, with his stereo and books, and after a while a woman, earning the little he needs as quietly as he can, not caring who never heard of him.

(In the hospital, she said. She explained how she got the message late at night after she came home to the apartment. For she was no longer living with him—you knew that, I believe? You may remember from last summer—which otherwise we won't go into now, will we?—how she had been planning to leave him for some time, waiting only to find the least disruptive way. Not wanting to abandon him in the midst of the Limewood ugliness. Only—I have to tell you this—there was this other man who came along, a lawyer, a sweet guy unhappily married and divorced, advanced in years, almost your age in fact, a lover of music, frail in health. They fell in love, she said, using those words, and that was when she decided to let Horace fight Limewood by himself. A fight he had brought on himself, after all. Only it didn't work out with the lawyer lover. He couldn't abandon his ailing wife and went back to her—as so many married men do, said Ruth, when the chips are down—which raised the question of whether she should go back to hers too. Decided not to. Having once made the break which she had so struggled to make, she could not reverse herself merely because the particular man on whom she counted had failed her. Decided to keep her new apartment, for it was impossible to think of going through all that again. All this was only recently, and she was living now in her apartment, alone and rather depressed. She had gone out that night with a young man she knew from before, a former lover if you want to know, which you don't, of course. Dinner, theater, ultimately back to her apartment with him—yes, that too, which doesn't mean, by the way, that he was what you would call "serious" in her life, but only companionable, useful for comfort on a lonely night. What else would you have her do? she demanded, as if someone had criticized her for it. Meanwhile the hospital had been trying to reach her for the last hour when she arrived, but of course she couldn't know that when they came in at twelve-thirty and put on a record and had a drink and embraced and undressed. [So the narrator rebuilt the events from Ruth's words that stopped short of what her own narrator knew, as she moved directly to the telephone call that startled her out of bed a few minutes later—rebuilt by the narrator's quick discovery that what she meant but had not actually said was that it startled them both out of bed.] The telephone call from the hospital saying that her husband had been brought in in critical condition.)

Now Horace's narrator spoke to all the other narrators through the deed itself. It must have been a great disappointment to him, she said, translating. All the energy of his decision exhausting itself in about two weeks. His new freedom, petering out in two weeks like a dying campfire. He discovered that he could not remember what was supposed to reconcile him to the unimportance of failure —and having forgotten this was forced to confront yet again all his failures, reconfirmed. Now his job became menial. He remembered the people who had turned their backs on him: three wives gone, his brother lost in importance (Dean), his sister gone in politics, his mother (who alone retained the notion that everyone considered him a genius) dead, and then came yesterday, which happened to be a dark day—and suddenly he realized what a dark day it was. She reproduced the weather: gray and gloomy, yet not bad enough to produce energy—an enervating afternoon, with a low overcast and chilly air, damp without rain or even drizzle, uncomfortable yet not enough to justify complaint. Through her narrative you saw how that dull afternoon faded into night so imperceptibly that no one noticed, and his workday at the office ended and he took the train and went home without the lift or change of mood that he wanted to feel when he went home. So he stops in a neighborhood lunchroom to have soup and hamburger and coffee for supper and when he gets to his house he goes into the kitchen and mixes himself a martini—thinking how little it matters whether he has his martini before or after dinner. He turns on the stereo, thinking to soothe himself, but immediately turns it off again to avoid the irritating effect of first sounds in his living room, threatening his mood, as if trying to make him forget what he has already forgotten. He sits for a half hour on the couch with only one light in the corner, allowing the record (which he has not bothered to select, but has drawn without looking from its jacket) to spin to its end in silence with the speakers off, sits wondering what has made him so suddenly irritable and allergic to music, which is like being allergic to himself. Then as if he has found an answer, he goes upstairs to the attic without turning on the lights.

(The man in her bed, who is naked and almost ready, groans and says, "What the hell, he's not your husband anymore, he has no claim on you." Arousal turned to indignation, he sits up in bed and wraps himself in a robe, arguing: "It's all a plot to get you back." She dresses while he sits on the edge of the bed in his robe. "It's easy to get you back," he says. "It's easy to manipulate you, make you do anything. Okay, maybe I'll try it myself. Put myself in the hospital too. Then you can come and visit me. . . . Why the hell can't you let him commit suicide if he wants to?" She pays no attention, dressing, while the voice from the hospital returns in her mind: "Are you Mrs. Horace G. Morley? We have your husband in emergency, critical. We don't know what happened.")

In the attic he turns on the one bare light in the middle and begins to look. Sees the old empty trunks. Opens one, lets the top hang open like an open jaw. Looks at the jaw, judges its weight, gets down on his knees, lowers his head and rests his neck against the edge of the trunk like a French aristocrat. Reaches with his hand to test the upper half of the trunk, finds it very light, laughs, gets up. Sees the empty socket on the wall. Goes to it, studies the copper casing with threads inside, open to receive light bulb, plug, or finger. Goes to the other light bulb and switches it off, so as to partake of the darkness. Then to the window, opens it, and leans out. The porch roof slopes, two stories below. Beyond it, the lawn.

Says to himself, No. He shuts the window and goes downstairs to the bathroom. Looks at the bathtub, feels the hard porcelain surface, cold. Medicine cabinet: a pack of razor blades. Removes one from the pack, holds it in his fingers. Sits down on the closed toilet seat looking at the razor blade and thinking. Lifts it to the edge of his eye, shudders, and jerks it away. He stands before the mirror and watches himself as he touches the blade to his Adam's apple. Declines to press. He holds the blade in his right hand and looks at his wrists, at the two bulging veins which make a lopsided inverted Y on his left wrist. Sits down on the toilet seat again to think about that. He winces from imagined pain or squeamishness. Then aware that he has winced, and as if to challenge that feeling, he opens his pants and takes it out and moves the blade up close —but not close enough to touch. Then as if afraid he might hurt himself by accident, he puts it back, zips up his pants, and puts the blade back on the shelf. He puts the bottle of pills in his pocket. Leaves the bathroom, turns off the light, goes down to the first floor, where all is dark. Sees the faint glow in the living room window, the glare of the city, notices the merged sound of the trucks and cars, trains and ambulances and fire engines. Then the kitchen, where he turns on the light over the sink.

(When she is dressed and ready to go, the lover—whom she never actually mentioned except twice—jumps up naked and says, "By God, I'm not letting you go anywhere without me. If you go to the hospital I'm going with you." So she has to wait while he dresses and sprays his armpits and groin with perfumed deodorant and brushes his teeth. They drive to the hospital in his car. At the emergency entrance, he says, "I mustn't go in. I mustn't be seen with you." "What will you do then?" she asks. "Will you wait in the waiting room?" "No," he says. "I mustn't be seen." She says, "I'll probably be quite a while. Will you wait in the parking lot?" "Parking lot!" he cries. "You expect me to wait hours alone in the parking lot in the middle of the night?" "Well, I'm sorry," she says. "I didn't know that you couldn't be seen with me. I didn't ask you to bring me." He says, "I'll go on home. Christ, what the hell do you want me to do, waiting around in the parking lot for you? I'll go home and when you're ready to leave you can call and I'll come and get you." "I didn't ask you to bring me to the hospital," she says. "I would much rather have come in my own car." He says, "I'm perfectly willing to come and get you. It's already past one A.M., and you probably won't be finished until three or four, so I've got to go to bed. Jesus, I have to get some sleep. I've got a busy working day ahead of me tomorrow with the alarm going off as usual, but *I said* I'm perfectly willing to be waked up in the middle of the night at three A.M. to come and get you. You can't expect me to let you drive over here to the hospital in the middle of the night all by yourself, can you?" "I would much have preferred to drive my own car," she says. "Well, Christ, what do you want me to do, take you home again so you can come over here in your own car?" "Let me out," she says. "Fine," he says. "You call when you're ready. Just let it ring a little. Don't mind my lost sleep. I'll come. Christ, what the hell do you think I am?")

In the kitchen he observes the gas stove. Opens the oven door and looks in. Looks behind the refrigerator at the coils. In the drawer at the carving knives, the bread knife, the paring knives, the ice pick. Stares for a long time. Then turns off the light. Goes to the cellar stairs and turns on the cellar light. Looks down. Notes the garden tools on the landing: a pair of shears, clippers, a spade, a rake against the wall, a sickle hanging on a peg. Teeters at the edge as if about to fall. Teeters again deliberately and, simulating the need to grab something for balance, reaches toward the rake, which stands next to the sickle. Studies the positions of rake, sickle, and himself, as a billiard player would. Then as if forgetting it all, he goes down into the cellar. Looks first at the gas furnace. Then the water pipe overhead. Spends a long time on that. He finds a coil of rope in the corner and tosses it up to the pipe, but he cannot make it pass over the pipe. He gets a ladder and climbs up to pass the rope over the pipe. Pulls on the rope a few times, testing, though some caution in him will not allow him to pull hard. Anxiously he studies the joints in the pipe as he pulls, and also the attachments that hold the pipe to the ceiling. Ties a loop in the rope. With the loop around his neck he climbs to the fourth step of the ladder. Pauses a moment, closes his eyes, and jumps. Lands on his feet while the rope spinning free coils up on the floor around him. Again he climbs the ladder to pass the rope over the pipe and looks for something to tie the other end to. Sees the water meter, considers how to tie the rope to the heavy pipe that goes into the meter from the wall. But as he studies it, his mind seems to change. Eyes go blank. Shrugs his shoulders, winces again, takes the rope off his neck. Flings it into the corner, and goes upstairs again, cursing quietly. The house is totally dark now, only the red glow of the city through the living room windows. He finds his coat in the closet in the dark, puts it on, puts the bottle of pills which he is still carrying into the pocket. He goes out, walks down the sidewalk to the corner, to the avenue. Watches the cars coming fast down the avenue in the night. Walks two blocks to the Jack and Jill Tavern. Goes in and orders a drink at the bar.

(The nurse at the desk asked her questions and began filling out forms. "Can you tell me what is the matter with my husband?" she asked. "That's what the doctor will find out when he gets here," said the nurse. "You don't know what's wrong? Then why is he here?" she asks. Not hearing the question, the nurse asks whether her husband's parents are still living and what they died of. She tells the nurse about that. The nurse asks if he has ever been hospitalized before and has he any drug problems? Is there insurance and who will pay? She tells the nurse that she is separated from her husband. "A legal separation?" asks the nurse. Not yet, she replies, but a separation nevertheless. The nurse shrugs her shoulders with a slight look of disgust. "Well, why are you here?" she asks. "Because they called me," says Ruth. The nurse says, "Do you mean you won't take responsibility for your husband?" She asks, Responsibility? The nurse says, "Somebody has to answer these questions so I can fill out these forms." She says, "Well, I can answer the questions for you." The nurse says, "Someone has to be notified in case of death or accident." She says, "Well, it's all right to notify me." The nurse says, "Someone has to give permission if anything has to be operated on." Ruth says, "I'm not sure I can do that, but I guess I can." The nurse says, "Someone has to take financial responsibility, promise to pay." She says, "I don't see how I can do that—or why I should." The nurse says, "If someone can't take financial responsibility we can't admit him." She says, "How can you not admit him? You've already got him." The nurse says, "We're only admitting him now. That's what you and I are doing." Ruth says, "Well, I don't have any money. I don't see how I can take financial responsibility." "Has he got any money?" asks the nurse. "He has Blue Cross," says Ruth, "I mean, he has it if he still has it." "What do you mean by that?" says the nurse. Ruth hesitates, anticipating trouble if she tells the nurse that he has just changed jobs. Does this mean he lost his Blue Cross too? So she says, "Nothing." The nurse says, "Has he got anything besides Blue Cross?" "He has a savings account," says Ruth. "Okay," says the nurse. "We'll take that." "Take it?" says Ruth. "I mean, we'll put it down in this space in the form. Right here." She points to a blank line and Ruth nods. "Another question," says the nurse. "Who's going to take responsibility for the body if he should—" "My God," says Ruth, "is he that bad?" "I haven't the slightest idea," says the nurse. "A hospital has to be prepared. We have to know what to do in case he *should.* It doesn't mean he necessarily *will.* Will you?" asks the nurse. "Please, ask someone else—his brother, or his sister," says Ruth. "I'm only here because I'm naturally concerned." The nurse is sympathetic. "I understand," she says. "What could be more natural than to be naturally concerned?" Another nurse comes in. "That your husband?" she asks Ruth. "Who? Who are you talking about?" "That's the one," says the first nurse. "The one who came in the ambulance. She's separated from him," she explains to the second nurse, "but she came to fill out the forms and take responsibility. She's here because she's naturally concerned." "I wouldn't want to take credit for him, myself," says the nurse. "Why?" asks Ruth. "How is he?" "Not good," says the second nurse. "Will you tell me what's wrong with him?" says Ruth. "Nobody's told me anything. Was it a heart attack?" The second nurse wrinkles her nose. "Looks to me like he had too much to drink," she says. "To drink?" exclaims Ruth. "You brought him to the hospital and put him in emergency because he had too much to drink?" The nurse shrugs. "Drink isn't always harmless, you know," she says, lecturing. "People do die of it. Alcohol poisoning. But we'll have to wait and see what the doctor says.")

He sat at the bar and ordered a drink. He did not speak to anybody, they said, but sat brooding, staring at things they could not see. When he had finished the first drink he ordered a second. From time to time his brooding is marked by face changes, lip movements, talking to someone who is not there, arguing his case, explaining himself. He orders a third drink. Maybe there was also a fourth—no one was keeping track. He went to the men's room. As he makes his way among the tables his steps are unsteady, and he braces himself with his hand against the backs of chairs. He stays in the men's room a long time, but no one notices. There are other customers in the bar, also brooding or talking quietly, and though they recognize his face because he has been there before, no one has a clear impression of him. When he comes back, though, his steps are even more unsteady than before. He lurches into his seat and orders another drink. His hand drops on the counter. As his fingers relax, the empty pill bottle rolls out, his head sinks on his arm, and his body slumps to the floor. "God damn," says the bartender. Two men pick him up under the shoulders and take him to a table. "Should we throw him out?" says one. "Naw," says the bartender. "Let him be." Then they notice the empty pill bottle. The bartender thinks about that. "What are these?" he asks. One of the men looking at them tells him. "What was he doing with them?" asks the bartender. "Maybe he was trying to kill himself," says one of the men. The others laugh, except the bartender, who looks at him asleep on the table where they have placed him. He goes over with the bottle in his hand and shakes him by the shoulder, trying to wake him up. He stirs a little and the bartender shouts at him: "What are you doing with this?" The bartender has to ask three times before the words reach him —reach deep enough to stir some thought that is still alive down there, that has never agreed with the rest of him or the decision he supposes he has made. Stirring to life enough to make him suddenly force his eyes open to look at the bartender and the bottle. "Yes," he says, "those." "What are you doing with them?" asks the bartender. "All," he says. "Jesus!" says the bartender. "You better get me to the hospital," he says. "What did you do that for?" asks the bartender. "Ask them," he says. "Who?" says the bartender. "Them. Ask them. I don't know. *They* know." The bartender called the ambulance. Meanwhile he passed out again and was out when the ambulance arrived. At the hospital they got Ruth's number from the identification card in his wallet.

So it was a close call, she said, but they got him in time, and his condition was bad but his life was saved, and you could be thankful for the bartender who had the sense not to dismiss him as simply another drunk. Be thankful also that he was careless enough to display the empty pill bottle in the bar—which was a careless way to save his life too, since it depended on the sensible bartender. She told how they let her look at him asleep in one of the emergency rooms, and how she talked to the doctor, who said he would be all right, and how she visited him next day in the hospital room —sitting up, depressed. The doctor told her they would keep him for a few days and put the psychiatrist on him, since he had (after all) tried to commit suicide. But then, said the doctor, they would let him go, and then what would become of him?

"So what does become of him?" asked Ruth. "They're going to let him out in three days!" That's too soon, says the brother. The sister disputed that, pointing out the evidence that he didn't really mean to kill himself. The brother said he almost did kill himself whether he meant to or not. And when he comes out of the hospital in three days, asks the brother, how can any psychiatrist change the world they are sending him back to? Going back to it, just as fired and menial as before, just as wifeless and respectless, same empty house, same disappointment, on a downward curve whose bottom was still unfound. What's to keep him from trying again? asks the brother. He becomes a narrator himself, taking Horace home from the hospital, looking at his first evening in the house by himself, everything the same, the same knives, the rake and the sickle on the cellar landing, the same empty light socket.

What can you do for such a man? says the brother. Give him a new narrator? How can even a psychiatrist do that in three days?

"The doctor seemed to think I should—" said Ruth. Consider my problem, she says. The doctor sees her standing small and black-haired in the immaculate hospital corridor and says, *Wife.* Behind the doctor is the mother, saying, My little failed genius. Who will keep him tactfully away from knives and bottles of pills, open windows and rushing streams with downcurrents, until he feels big and strong again? The doctor and the mother both say, *Wife,* but Ruth said, "It's impossible, out of the question, I can't do—" saying, It is too late for that, too much to expect of me. Telling the doctor and the mother it's not her fault her husband claims he can't live without her. If she allowed that claim she would become a slave. No doubt she is torn between feelings—is that why she backtracks on the telephone and interrupts herself? Not merely the fear of what he might yet do to himself, but some possible regret, still, for the life with him that failed. She speaks of being stringent with her feelings in order to uphold her rights and wonders if there are other cases in the world like this. If not, is she a monster? Yet she knows she must stick to her decision, says Ruth, because it was a considered decision and neither the flight of the lover who briefly assisted her nor the shock of her husband's deed alters the issues by which she made that decision. She knows that if she does go back to take care of him—even if she makes rules and sets a time limit—she will have lost, because that was what he was trying to make her do by killing himself. So it's still dirty fighting, she says, and you mustn't ask me to submit to it.

"Of course I can't go back to him myself. That won't do," she said—with less doubt and guilt, suggests the father, than you were perhaps imagining. "But he shouldn't be alone for a while, I think," she added. "I wonder . . . perhaps Penny . . ." What I really mean is *you,* says Ruth. You and Claudia. Not to embarrass you by putting it into words. But obviously you, the brother, with your children gone to college—as distinguished from Penny, with her children still a houseful. Yes, says the sister, it's your turn. Let Horace go to you.

Quietly somewhere, the wife objects. Speaks of our house, and the private narrative we have been composing together. The mother says Claudia will not object, she's always been good to your relatives and gets along well with Horace. The father says no. Brothers should live in separate houses when they grow up. Horace is ill, but you are a Dean. The deanship is a full-time job, says the father. The serious work of the world. The mother warns in a soft voice: If you don't nurse your brother, whom will you *ever* nurse? Finally Horace speaks. How would I like living in your house? he asks. So you can talk me out of committing suicide? Don't you think I would consider you a patronizing bastard? While Ruth says, You are silent. Again you refuse to help me.

"I think I should definitely call Penny," said Ruth. Since you don't volunteer yourself, and I won't ask you to volunteer, she says.

"Yes, let's see what she suggests," suggested the Dean. Perhaps she doesn't want you to volunteer, says the lover. Forestalling you because maybe she has other ideas for you.

"And how have *you* been all winter?" she now asked. Her voice moved closer, and the narrator recognized times and places in it, making it richer and warmer than before. The brother gave a warning, and the Dean replied without color: "All right. I've been fine."

"And how is it, being Dean?"

"All right."

"Are you being a success?"

"I get my work done," said the Dean. "That's all I can tell for sure."

"You're always a success," she said. Then she said, "I had this friend, this lawyer I told you about, but that didn't last." At the same time she was saying, Remember the softness of my voice which is the same as the softness of my short dark hair and the softness of my small moving body, full of the buzzing summer air lifting a curtain in the open window with the beams and the unfinished walls. "You haven't forgotten, have you?" she said.

Tell her yes, says the sheriff, you have forgotten. No, says the mother, don't lie, though you have stowed it away, filed in albums, not to be looked at until twenty years have passed and all parties are dead. You answer her, says the boss to the manager, who said in a dull contradicting tone: "No, I haven't."

"Can we talk?" she said. He looked at Claudia reading in her chair across the room: she couldn't have heard that, says the watchman. Only an eavesdropper or a wiretapper. While Ruth continues to sound: new things I have to say, new presents for you, in my soft voice full of love.

"No," he said. "Not now." Be blunt, says the sheriff. Don't let her suppose.

"Oh," said Ruth. Notice the disappointment in my voice, says Ruth, the hurt surprise.

Rebukes from the mother, the father, even the wife, made the Dean repent a little. "Sorry," he said. "Some other time."

"Never mind," she said. "That won't be necessary." And then, "I don't have anything to say anyway." Notice the coldness that has now entered my voice, with its fine shading of pride and anger, says Ruth. This is my farewell to you, as hard and beautiful as ice, in my unsoftened, irrevocable voice, says Ruth. My narrator has frozen my memories—has yours?

Explain that Claudia is in the room, says the lover. You can't, says the manager. Surely she knows that. Sure I know, says Ruth. She resents you, says the brother. Bitter, disillusioned after thinking you kind and loving. Now she knows that you are—

Get rid of her, says the boss. It's all right, says the narrator. She'll talk about Horace, but she won't bother you with herself anymore.

Wipe her out, says the boss. What? How can we? asks the manager. The mother is shocked: Are they talking murder in there? The father says surely she doesn't deserve to be erased like that, a nice girl in a tough situation. He defends her to the boss: You always liked her, he says. The boss turns away, denying everything.

24

We found ourselves once more, by arrangement late in the evening, at The Great Wall of China. Ruthie didn't want to eat. She curled up in her booth next to Macurdy to read *Mad* magazine while we ate and talked. This time Claudia knew where I was and who I was with. She said, "It frightens me. Do you have to go?"

I said to Macurdy: "I'd still like to know how you found out."

"You mustn't forget my investigative capability. I have sources in New York who keep track of things. So it came to me that your brother had tried to commit suicide. That's no great secret, is it?"

"No," admitted the boy.

"Naturally I was concerned for your sake. I thought what can we do to help, for it must be a trial and a worry for you."

"Thank you," said the youth.

"The big question that faces us here is this: Is there a danger that he'll try again? That is the natural question that occurs to one in a case like this."

It was frosty fruit-and-liquor drinks in The Great Wall of China at this late hour. Ruthie sipped her drink and read *Mad,* leaning against the end of the booth with her feet up on the seat. After interruptions Macurdy said, "Now, to return to our subject. The question arises because your brother has broken the barrier of normal restraint. If he can break it once, he can break it again. How many attempts has he made—do you know?"

He turned his glass a quarter turn to the left at the end of each sentence and watched the fruit swimming at the top. I had no answer. Three times, four times? "It is now a habit," he said. "And if it is a habit, sooner or later he will succeed." To prove it, he sliced his neck with his forefinger and made a cutting noise in his throat.

"Of course," said Macurdy, "there is also the other side, the side of him that does *not* want to die and saves his life when he gives it a try. That side should be encouraged."

He stirred his fruit with his finger in his glass and thought awhile. "But the risk of accident in a case like this is greatly increased." He took a drink, and lit a cigarette. (Ruthie, behind *Mad* magazine, was also smoking.) He said: "There is an indicated danger here, which since he is your brother we would like to prevent. With all our facilities. That is why we are here."

The narrator wondered, for he was not quite sure why we were here.

"Now," said Macurdy, "the first problem is to understand your brother's state of mind. This is a problem of knowledge, a case for investigation. The task is to investigate that state of mind. Look into it with our professional resources."

"How do you do that?" asked the manager.

Macurdy did not answer. He stared into his drink, frowning and turning the glass. My God, said the father, has this man's investigative science progressed so far that he can use detective processes to weigh the inner balance of a man's mind? With agents and spying and machinery? That's impossible, said the father. Meanwhile Macurdy's face had tightened up in an angry-looking grimace. The grimace passed.

"That's one thing your detective agency can't do," said the Dean.

Macurdy's answer was casual. "You could eavesdrop on his doctors," he said. "Wiretap. Question his nurses. Investigate his correspondence."

"You could go to Horace himself and ask him how he feels," said Michael Morley.

Slowly Macurdy raised his eyes to look at the Dean. The whites showed beneath, and he looked broad, like a frog. "Do you expect him to tell the truth?" he said. And added: "Do you expect him to *know?*"

"Know how he feels? He should know as well as the doctor

knows. He'd know somewhat better than a detective who tries to find out from a doctor or a nurse."

The eyes lowered again as slowly as they had risen, and the frog disappeared. He looked blank, as if he had not heard, and then the angry grimace reappeared, and he said, very quietly, "I hate people who commit suicide. I loathe them more than anything in this world."

That was something real breaking through, all right, said the narrator. The manager showed his surprise. Even Ruthie looked up from her magazine. "Well—" said Macurdy, recognizing the surprise, the grimace gone. "It's because you can't argue with them. They have given up every value." He turned his punch glass around a few times. Then he looked up at the Dean and said, "The reason I hate suicides is that they are trying to kill *me.*"

"Why you?" said the Dean. "You're not God."

"It's very simple," said Macurdy. "When they kill themselves, they destroy the world they live in. I live in that world. They want to wipe me out."

The father considered that logic. Wondered. Did Macurdy depend so much for his existence on being a part of other people's worlds? He said, "But my brother Horace never heard of you."

No answer from Macurdy. Another quarter turn of the glass, then he took a sip. Said, "You're his brother. Don't *you* feel wiped out?"

"Not in the least," said the father. "I feel only sympathy, pity, and concern."

Macurdy's broad grin accused him of lying, and the brother joined in the accusation. The father would not back down, however, so there were the father and the brother, each holding his own view of the case. Meanwhile the angry animal in Macurdy's face had disappeared, smoothed out again in the plumpness. He said, "Of course. And our problem is how to help him, so he won't do it again."

His eyes disappeared, and his voice sounded strained: "Which raises the question of . . . of his wife."

"What about his wife?"

Not looking at us. "I believe she is no longer . . . living with him. Is that correct?"

"You know that, do you?" Narrator said it was odd, the sidelong way in which he looked and did not look at us as we talked about this.

"Her name is Ruth, is it not?"

"I thought you knew that."

"And her maiden name was— You know her maiden name, don't you?"

Quick conference as to whether it was dangerous to reveal it, decided negatively by the narrator. "Morris," he remembered.

"Moffitt, not Morris," said Macurdy, and then back into the veiled voice and unlooking look. "Ruth Moffitt, that was it."

The Dean waited to find out what Macurdy had in mind concerning Ruth.

"And now they are separated," said Macurdy. "So it is unlikely we can get any help for poor Horace from her, isn't it?"

"Unlikely, yes."

He turned around to call the waiter, and with his back turned, said: "This Ruth Moffitt, how well do you know her? Pretty well, would you say?" His voice sounded as if it were coming through a tube with an overcoat thrown over the end, although the words were clear. Ruthie was looking up from her magazine. "Pretty well?"

"A little. Not very well, I suppose."

He turned to Ruthie and remarked, "Same name as yours. Isn't that interesting?"

"Only my name is Ruthie," said Ruthie. "And it isn't really that, either."

"What?"

"Ruthie is my made-up name. What he calls me."

"It's as good as any other name," said Macurdy.

"I'm not complaining. I never complain." She went back to *Mad.*

"This Ruth Moffitt. I suppose I should call her Ruth Morley, even though she is no longer living with him."

"Legally that would still be her name, yes."

"Do you think she'll go back to him?"

"I really have no idea."

"I hope not. . . . You know, when I think of her, I think, What a dish she is. Don't you?"

"What a what?"

"Dish. *D-i-s-h.* That black hair, those boobs" (with a glance at "DARTMOUTH" on Ruthie). "Or doesn't she affect you that way?"

"You've met her, then?"

"You know what she makes me think of whenever I see her? Puts me in mind of?"

"What?"

"Can't you guess?" Macurdy grinning now, after a long transition.

"No."

"Why, screwing, man, screwing. I take a look at her, that hair, that stuff, and I start thinking about screwing, all kinds of screwing, not just me but everybody, the whole damn world." Big sip of his new drink. Grinned at Ruthie, who grinned back. Grinned at me. "It's just the idea she puts into your head. Can't help it. Do you think that could indicate a kind of genius on her part?"

"I wouldn't know," said the Dean.

"No? Doesn't she affect you the same way?"

The question caused confusion, but the manager held on enough to say, "I think of her as Horace's wife."

"Wow," said Macurdy. "And she doesn't make you think of screwing?"

Once more the brother was suspicious, and the manager calculated the safest answer, even if it was (said the boss) rather priggy: "No more than a number of women."

"And you never thought," said Macurdy, "of testing her yourself to see how strict she really is?"

He *knows!* cried the brother, and the manager called in the sheriff: "Certainly not!"

"*Certainly* not!" echoed Macurdy, full of merry astonishment, eyes aglitter with fun. The father charged the manager with perjury. So did the narrator, while the summer curtains rose lazily in the summer air, and the boss warned the manager that if perjury was called for, you'd better damn well make it good. The brother stood by the manager and the manager came back—looking Macurdy as much in the eye as Macurdy's eye allowed: "That's what I said. Certainly not."

And Macurdy backed down, or seemed to. "Well, certainly not," he said, "if that's what you say."

It revived a familiar debate. The brother was sure that Macurdy knew exactly what had happened between Morley and Ruth in the last two summers. The lawyer said there was no evidence for that, even if she might be a likely source for some of his knowledge. The narrator and the detective were almost certain that she was such a source. The narrator was trying to reconstruct his memories of loose narrative talk with her last summer—what in fact had he actually told her so nostalgically about his childhood?—while the detective suggested that she might well have been the one who gave Macurdy his key to the Morley Mythology. The narrator reconstructed this possibility. Consider Ruth, disappointed, hurt, as she was at the end of the summer. Confront her with an ingratiating interviewer (was Macurdy ingratiating?). Conceivable—yet could even the bitterest disappointment and the most ingratiating stranger have induced her to confess her affair with the Mythology's author? Not unless there was a plot—as the brother claimed: perhaps the whole thing *began* with Ruth, or maybe even Horace. Rejecting that (the boss rejected it), the narrator preferred to think it was simply as Macurdy said: when he saw her, she made him think of screwing. Stirred up strong feelings. She had a way of doing that.

Meanwhile Macurdy had returned to Horace, saying: "The only way to make him want to live is to give him something to look forward to. What can we give him to look forward to?"

"I don't know," said the Dean.

"Since his wife can't . . ." said Macurdy. Long pause, then: "Maybe Ruthie could."

She uncurled herself, put the magazine aside, and stretched her arms. Showed no surprise. The youth noticed how large her breasts were, though she was otherwise thin. They bulged in her faded green T-shirt and bent the letters "DAR" and "UTH." She said, "How can I do anything if he lives in New York?"

"He could come for a visit," said Macurdy. Looking at me. "Is it impossible for him to visit you?"

"I don't know." There was disagreement in the chambers.

"Well, if he came for a visit, maybe Ruthie could help."

"Help how?" I said.

She broke into a smile. "You want me to beep beep?"

"Brighten up his life a bit," said Macurdy.

"What's he like? Is he fat?"

"He's an intelligent, well-bred man," said Macurdy.

"Does he look like *you?*" she said to the Dean. "If he looks like you, I could brighten up his life, beep beep. You know." Smiled brightly.

"Intelligent and reasonably cultivated and clean," said Macurdy. "Kind and . . . civil. You don't have to worry."

She looked at me and said, "Would *you* like me to? You know. Beep beep with him?"

It confused the Dean's household, for she was smiling so directly it was as if she had offered to brighten up (said the youth) your own life. While the reader still tried to figure out what *beep beep* meant and how you brighten up somebody's life, the rest of us took it for granted and argued the consequences. On the one hand were those who defined her at last as a simple whore, with Macurdy her pimp, and the meaning of her question was whether *you* want to be a pimp too. On the other hand they were saying these were new times, a different generation, such words as *whore* and *pimp* have no meaning for them: take it as it was meant, a generous offer to cheer up Horace, give some comfort to a man in depression, a generous friendly offer.

The confusion and argument made it impossible to answer the question. But Macurdy had suddenly turned gloomy, the angry grimace again. "He doesn't care," he said to Ruthie roughly. "He doesn't give a shit."

Hostility to us? She gave me a quick glance, eyebrows raised, shoulders shrugged. "I guess it's time to go," she said. In his new mood Macurdy had nothing to say. He seemed, abruptly, to have lost interest in everything. This annoyed Ruthie—the narrator could see it, the first impatience with her boss that she had shown—and she also looked anxious. She got him his coat and took him by the arm as if he were ill. As we left, the gossips stirred. What's wrong with him? asked the mother. What holds her to him? said the sister. Are they really a pimp and his whore? said the brother. Or master and slave? Or patient and nurse? Whatever it is, said the father, she doesn't seem to mind. At the street corner, Macurdy stared at his feet and walked away, saying nothing, but as she went off with him Ruthie turned and waved.

PART THREE

25

Driven by the boy king, the narrator kept rehearsing for Macurdy's tape recorder. It went on all the time, in the midst of other work, under the narrator's other stories. Preparing for a book:

The Morley Mythology. A book of fact and picture. Landscape studies and tours of the Morley mind with emphasis on its origins.

The manager worried about this subversion of the boss, this crazy revival of childhood at the very time when his career was moving to its summit. For more than thirty years the boy king had been asleep or confined, and suddenly this strange Macurdy comes out of the darkness and sets him free. The manager was afraid of a revolution.

The narrator was loyal to the boss and believed in him, yet could not deny the king. Still he kept rehearsing, because he had to, trying to make the reader see with all possible distinctness the detail and vividness of the king's vision.

In the beginning were the two ends of the boy king's world. At one end was the suburban house that looked over the ravine, the dusty streets, the vacant lots of games, the aqueduct in the afternoon. At the other was his grandfather's summer house and the beach, the dunes and the scrubby woods and the harbor with sailboats. Near to the home end was the metropolis—the bridges, the heavy trucks, the subways, the warehouses, the international piers with a smell of sea, oil, and garbage. Short of the far end were green fields and farmhouses and a lighthouse in the early dawn. Between these, every summer, was the night boat. In the afternoon they went into the city by train and taxi, or by car when they had one, down to the lower end of Manhattan, where the streets had railroad tracks in them and smelled of fruit and fish, to the particular wharf they sought. A porter carried their bags through the traffic on the pier. Inside the shed the boy king got his first glimpse of the boat, a section visible through the door, fresh and white with shutters in the windows and a life preserver attached to the net railing, and then the porter led them aboard—across a covered gangplank and down into the rich interior.

Busier than usual, the narrator followed the king everywhere—first to his stateroom and then through all the carpeted corridors, the decorated lounges, the decks. At 5:30 P.M. the ship sailed, pulling out from the pier while its whistle sustained a deep bass chord for at least a a minute. Leaning on the rail, the narrator felt the ship's trembling, its excitement, ever so slightly in his hands and under his feet. Passing ferryboats and tugboats with barges, they rounded the Battery and sailed up the East River under the bridges and past the buildings of Manhattan, on the way to Long Island Sound. The narrator ate dinner with the boy in the dining room and later took him up top to see the Sound spreading out, calm and gray under the fading sky, while the distant lights on the shore receded on both sides. He went to bed in the upper bunk and watched those lights, far off now, watched their reflections in the mirror over the washstand, and listened to the water churning under the paddles. Now and then there was a sound of footsteps on the deck, and near the window a white deck post was lit all night by a caged bulb nearby. Lying in bed, the narrator kept the boy awake as long as he could, so as to miss nothing of what had been so long anticipated and was so long to be remembered. In the very early morning (still dark) the ship stopped at Newport. The narrator woke and watched the unloading on the dock below his window. He saw another steamboat like his own tied up and dark at a nearby pier. This was one of the winter boats and just now was out of service. The journey resumed, and in the early dawn he awoke again as they were passing by meadows on a high shore and a squat lighthouse, just before docking at the city that was the ship's destination.

There was breakfast aboard and then a two-hour train ride to the Cape. There, at his grandfather's house, at the beach, all that day and the next, the narrator found the steamboat everywhere: the house windows were stateroom windows with shutters, the porch was a steamboat deck, the flaring sides of the little rowboat imaged the flaring hull under the steamboat's guards. In his room the boy studied the folders picked up on the ship and read the articles in the company magazine. Though he hated the summer to end, he looked forward to the return trip on the boat.

When he was fifteen the steamboats stopped running. The four big boats were sold for scrap. The king could not believe it. He had traveled on the night boat almost every summer of his life and sometimes in the winter too. It was the adventure of the year. When the boats stopped, he began to study them in earnest. He had not known how famous they were, nor how long they had been admired. Soon there was a book about them. He met an Authority, who had a box full of pictures. As he studied these one afternoon, the steamboats became part of the architecture of the king's mind. His mind was full of their corridors and decks.

The king's Favorite was the steamer *Priscilla,* one of the two big summer boats, second largest in the fleet of four. She was also next to the oldest. His last trip was on the *Priscilla.* For the *Mythology* he wanted to make the reader see that boat not in any old way, but as he saw her. He had pictures of her that he wanted to show, and he wanted to make the reader look at her as he would look at a work of art. For that is what remains of her, said the narrator: you can still call the steamboat a work of art.

The narrator admitted that when he was out of touch with the king the boat in the picture could look pretty antiquated, despite her fresh coat of paint—remote in a lost time with her tall stacks, her open decks, her paddle wheels. Yet if you look closely enough (said the narrator), if you move into the picture and let it spread around you, walk through it with the king, perhaps the steamboat will come back to life.

The narrator presented the reader with a photograph of the

Priscilla, taken late in her career, when she had six lifeboats on each side (in earlier years she had more and her stacks were taller too). Invited the reader to enter the picture, go aboard on the lower deck, where it is shadowed, below the fifth lifeboat. Here will be the entrance lobby, the dining room to the stern, the staircase forward. Let's go up. You will be in the main lounge, two decks high, with a grand staircase and a gallery, all white and gold with red carpeting and curtains and chairs and filigree work and ironwork, with an ornamented white pillar (actually the mast) and an inverted dome of colored light. Let's go out on deck and up the companionway (stairs, says the boy king) to the deck above. See the picture: we are now on the third deck, below the sixth lifeboat. To go forward we must pass through a corridor behind the row of staterooms over the paddle wheel. Select a stateroom: 225, under the fourth lifeboat over the letter *A.* Then along the forward promenade deck all the way to the balcony that overlooks the bow. Good vantage point here, favorite spot to stand as we approach the bridges of the East River or move out into the broadening Sound. From here the boy king can turn and look up over his shoulder to the pilothouse on the deck above—the big nameplate below the front windows, the broad, slightly curved windows themselves, the searchlight on top. As night falls the windows remain dark, the ship's eyes giving off no light themselves. Shall we go up to the top? We must go back to the steps going up just aft of the pilothouse. Now we can walk along the upper deck, past the softly hissing smokestacks and the lifeboats, all the way back, where we can watch the wake, a thick frothy path (so broad and thick because of the paddle wheels) that stretches away across the water as far as we can see toward where we began—watch until the darkness erases it and only a small light burns on the flagpole above us, and the night is complete.

The king says that it is because the boat was a world that moves and thus makes the world around her move. She carried her own geography around, and when she moved, her decks, her walls, her stairways, always stayed in the same relative positions. As if the boat through which you walked were the fixed world while the city and the bridges changing shape, the receding lights, the green farmland in the morning, and all the outspread dangerous sea were the movables, the changeables, the ephemera.

But the steamboat was a living thing too, said the king, and that was another reason. The pilothouse, her head and eyes. The paddle wheels, her feet as she swims. And the undersides of her flaring hull behind the wheels, thighs and bottom not quite concealed. But her sex was a problem. *Priscilla* was a New England maiden and he called her "she," yet to the boy king she seemed more masculine (a sturdy smoke-puffing boat with tall stacks) than the larger yet motherly *Commonwealth* with her full-length upper-deck cabin and her smoother if massive lines. They were not his mother and father, though, as the reader had once suggested. They lived their own lives.

The professor explained the logic by which steamboats could claim to be living things. First: like all living creatures, they existed as an organization of materials rather than the materials themselves. The boat was an organization of separable things, just as a living creature was an organic whole, distinct from the cells that composed it. Second: the boat behaved like a living creature. It moved about, and it moved in an intelligent way, for not only did it heed a schedule; it observed its surroundings and acted accordingly, responding to signals, dodging other boats, participating in rescues. If this was the intelligence of the men who sailed the ship, said the professor, it was exercised by them in their functions as officers and crew, and in those functions they were parts of the ship, just as the brain cells in your head are parts of you. If you object that the crew changed from time to time—so do the molecules of your body. It was in their designated roles that they were part of the ship; apart from these roles they were parasites, like the fleas on a dog. Hence, argued the professor, the only real differences between *Priscilla* and other living creatures were that the boat could not reproduce herself and death could be made final only by the actual destruction of her body. Why, she even carried the magic acid—DNA—in her cells, just as you do, said the professor. It was in the cells of the men who constituted her brain, differing from yours only in being so much smaller a part of the total composition.

Hence it was reasonable to feel grief when the boats died. It was natural rather than violent death—they were scrapped—and they were quite old, yet death was a shock, and even now as the narrator restored them for the reader the boy king's incredulity returned, and the old horror and wonder at the mystery of death remained. Which revived the old question of whether *Priscilla* ever actually did die on the scrap heap, as was popularly supposed. The king knew the other boats had been scrapped. He had seen pictures: the upper decks stripped, the lower ones covered with smashed wood and other fragments, finally only the open shells of the hulls, and then not even that. But his friend the Authority had been to the scrapyard himself and told him that *Priscilla* at that time was still intact, afloat. That was in Baltimore, in September 1938. Though that was almost forty years ago, where was the hard proof, asked the professor, that *Priscilla* had actually died? If there were no pictures to prove it and the Authority had not seen it, was it not possible that she had not been scrapped after all, that the year's delay in execution meant that she had been given a reprieve? The king found one printed claim that she had been scrapped, but it contained an error: a statement in a book published many years later that said that *Priscilla* was scrapped in January 1938. But the same book showed a picture of the *Priscilla's* lounge, stripped of carpets, railings broken, but still intact, with a caption dating the picture in April 1938. And the Authority had seen her as late as September. In the absence of an eyewitness report, said the professor, the only strong evidence we have of *Priscilla's* death is the argument that if she had been preserved, we would have heard: the books would say that she was being maintained as a museum in the harbor at Baltimore or had been bought by a rich man for his collection.

But suppose, said the king, the *Priscilla* was preserved not publicly but *secretly?* Secretly perhaps to escape charges of favoritism from the partisans of the other boats. Granted that preserving secretly a ship the size of *Priscilla* would be difficult, still it could be done if you constructed a hangar to look like a dock, at least 450 feet long, 95 feet broad, and some 80 feet high. And how could you say, argued the professor, that such a hangar did not exist today, if not in Baltimore then in some other coastal city? Sheltering the great white steamboat for that day, perhaps quite soon, when she will be returned to us—decks open for us to go aboard, to inspect her and sit in her chairs, lean against her rails—exhibited as a major work of a hitherto unappreciated kind of art from a unique period in this country's (and the king's) history. Tell this to the reader, said the narrator, to help him understand the Morley legend of the still living *Priscilla* and the dreams that still recur, showing her one dewy morning unexpectedly but not surprisingly paddling her way once more up Mount Hope Bay to Fall River.

Steamer	Length	Breadth	Gr Tonn	Built	Scrapped
Commonwealth	456′	95′	5980	1908	1938
Priscilla	440′6″	95′	5292	1894	1938? (see above)
Providence	397′	88′	4365	1905	1937
Plymouth	366′	87′	3770	1890/1907*	1937

**Plymouth* was rebuilt 1907 after superstructure destroyed by fire.

NOTES. *Priscilla* would be about one and one-half football fields long. She is broader than all but the largest ocean liners. This breadth is made possible by the paddle wheels, with the superstructure extended over the sides to enclose them.

Note the following characteristics of these boats.

The genus (American coastal night passenger boat)

1. White steamboats, steel hull, superstructure partly wood. Three or four decks in superstructure.

2. Hull flares out above the water line along the sides. This overhang is called the ship's guards; it encloses the paddle wheels in ships which have them. The superstructure rises above the guards.

3. Except for sides of main deck enclosing freight section, superstructure walls are everywhere paneled. Railings except on main deck are composed of stiff white crisscross netting. Staterooms have windows rather than portholes, and the windows have shutters that slide inside the windowpanes.

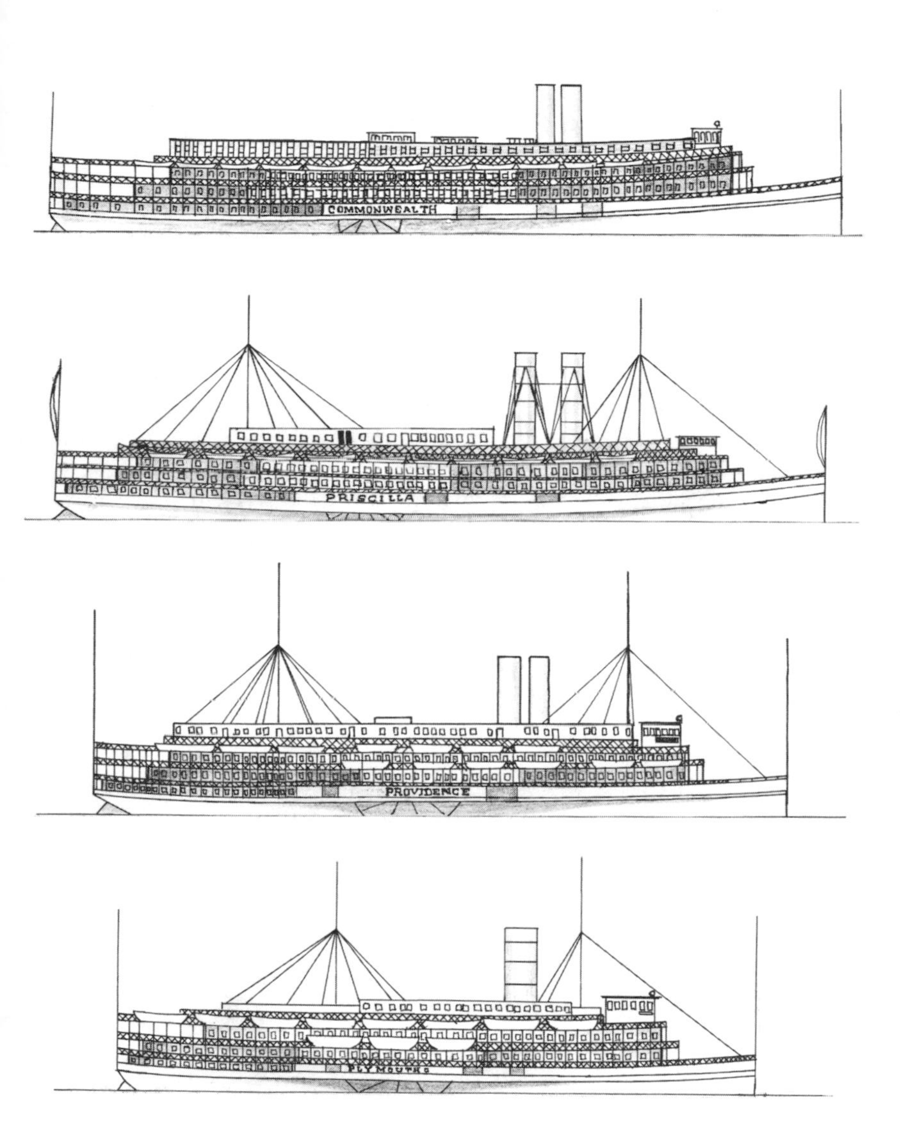
COMMONWEALTH
PRISCILLA
PROVIDENCE
PLYMOUTH

4. The pilothouse stands forward on the upper deck. Flat roof, searchlight on the roof, front curved. No flying bridge by the pilothouse, usually.

5. One or two generally tall smokestacks, plain.

6. Propulsion by paddle wheel amidships or propeller at stern.

7. The main deck, which is the first deck in the superstructure, is usually fully enclosed forward from amidships and is used for freight. Large rectangular freight doors are often visible open on this deck. The after part of this deck is open, and passengers in most ships board here. The line of the railing on this deck is extended all the way forward.

The family (ships of the Fall River Line)

1. Four decks in superstructure. Hull rises high forward, for protection against heavy seas sometimes encountered on route. The second (saloon) and third (gallery) decks have open promenade decks over the guards forward and aft, but not amidships, where there is a row of outside cabins over the paddle wheel. Gallery deck stops short of the bow in a balcony that overlooks the prow. Top deck stops short of the gallery deck and overlooks it. All four decks extend all the way aft.

2. One or two black stacks, fairly far forward, between pilothouse and amidships.

3. Names are painted in black capitals on main deck over paddles. Also on nameplates on sides and front of pilothouse, and on hull at bow and stern.

The individual (the Priscilla herself)

1. Like *Commonwealth,* has a row of outside staterooms on the gallery deck. *Providence* and *Plymouth* have a row of lifeboats here.

2. Alone in having a deckhouse only aft of the stacks on the upper deck. *Plymouth* deckhouse begins forward of the stack. *Providence* and *Commonwealth* have deckhouses that extend from the pilothouse back almost to the stern. (*Commonwealth* has her dining room here, with large windows on upper deckhouse aft.)

3. Resembles *Providence* and *Plymouth* in having three levels on the upper deck, whereas *Commonwealth* has only two. On *Commonwealth* both levels extend forward of the pilothouse.

4. Has two stacks (like *Commonwealth* and *Providence*). *Plymouth* has only one.

26

Somewhere in what was once the future, the narrator, carried by time, will notice with surprise how much has passed already since the evenings with Macurdy and Ruthie in The Great Wall of China. Now as he drives down to the Cape with Nancy and Bobby and his brother Horace, the reader will remind him: that was only March, says the reader. That was before you even knew who Macurdy was. Once again the narrator will be shocked to catch the present in the act of turning into the past.

At such a moment (driving the four-lane divided highway across the flat sand country toward the sea) the narrator will try to rest, listen to the reader for a while, let the reader muffle the shock. For it is the reader who keeps the record. While the narrator is always looking ahead, making stories out of the slippy moving days—new things—it is the reader who follows, listens, keeping what he likes and throwing out the rest. It is the reader who ties the narrator to a certain past, who bridges gaps and labels endings: custodian of an orderly record for the file.

In the car, under the sixty-mile blast of wind against the flap, the reader looks over the Dean's record in the spring season that had not even begun then and is now as completely finished as all other past spring seasons. The Dean's budget. The recommendations for promotions, salary increases, dismissals, new appointments. A new long-range planning report to replace last year's. A new secretary for the office. New colors for the corridors in Old Main University Hall. And the Dean's home life. Easter visits by Nancy and Bobby. Completion of the year's concert and theater subscriptions. Dinners with Claudia, the Redeker party, the Clawson party. Saturday afternoons mowing the lawn and digging with Claudia in flower beds, planting, weeding, watering. Sundays in May going out with Claudia to the Clawmor Beagle Farm, walking in the woods with her, four beagles on a leash. The prime of life, says the reader.

The reader keeps also the letter she received in May—the clean white business envelope with the name of the Musical Institute of Connecticut engraved on it—saying that they must delay their selection of a new director for another year and did she still want to be considered for the job? The laughter when she read that letter, as if it was a relief to have nothing settled. She asked him, *"Do* I still want to be considered?" He replied, "Why not? What have you got to lose?" "Well, quite a lot, as a matter of fact," she said, and once again the Dean encouraged her, as he had the year before: "You're not committed to anything yet, and meanwhile it's an honor, a boost to your career, just to be considered. It can't do you any harm." So she told them she was still interested, and they went out to dinner as if to celebrate. And now she has gone as usual to the Summer Festival, to teach and demonstrate for two weeks, while we go with Horace down to the Cape. . . .

The reader tells of Horace, how he happened to be here with us in this car. Repeats the words that converted Horace's suicide into a nervous breakdown. How he stayed in the hospital three weeks and how his estranged wife dealt with the authorities, the doctors, the Major Medical and Blue Cross, and helped him come home when he was discharged. And then (not to be blackmailed by suicide threats) left. The reader bypasses the two or three shaky yet not suicidal weeks during which Horace lived like an invalid alone in his house, working a little at his editorial job, which he was allowed to keep. Then he decided that a nervous breakdown required a good long recovery, with time to enjoy himself. Two weeks to visit Penny, and then some weeks with us. Finally his trip to Europe, to last as long as his savings held out, looking at paintings, visiting buildings, going to concerts, sitting in cafés. The reader saw him off in April, and he came back at the end of June. He went to spend the rest of the summer in Penny's cottage in Maine. There we found him, says the narrator, when we made our visit. Full of new adventures, claiming that now he knew how to live. That was in his up moods. He had down moods too. He would sit all evening in a chair doing nothing, neither reading nor sharing the games with his nieces and nephews. He would go off on long walks by himself in the woods. That was before he went down to the Cape with us, while Claudia was at the Festival. . . .

Guess who traveled with him all through Europe? says the reader. Ruthie? says the Dean. Be surprised, says the reader: would you have guessed that *Mad*-reading Ruthie Thomas, Macurdy's girl, with the Dartmouth T-shirt, would have become your own tired brother's traveling companion in his great recuperation? The reader wrote his surprise into the record. Tells how Horace stayed, on his visit to us, in the guest room, spending days in the library and after a while going out in the evenings. He found poker partners and went to their houses. One day Macurdy came back to the office with Ruthie (wearing the same clothes, the blue jeans, the Dartmouth T-shirt) and said, "I understand Horace is now here. Ruthie would like to offer her services." The reader made the connection (beep beep to brighten up Horace's life), but the Dean played stupid. "Tell Horace to call this number," said Macurdy, giving him a card and paying no attention to the Dean's stiffness. Cautious and self-righteous, the boss had no intention of doing so. It was the narrator who disobeyed him, acting from curiosity and maybe mischief. He gave the card to Horace when the boss wasn't looking. To appease the boss, he also gave Horace a complete account of Macurdy's strange behavior, skipping only the references to Ruth, and warned his brother not to have anything to do with them. "Okay," said Horace. "Consider me warned." He called her up. "My life could stand some brightening," he said.

Now Horace went out almost every evening, sometimes by taxi, sometimes borrowing our car, staying out very late. Once Macurdy, visiting the boy king in his office, mentioned it: "Aren't you glad that Horace and Ruthie are getting on so well?" I didn't know they were, said the narrator, which made Macurdy smile. At this time Horace was making plans for his European trip, but he didn't mention a companion. Again it came from Macurdy. "So they're taking a trip to Europe," said Macurdy. "Good for them." *They? You mean Horace,* said Michael. "I mean Horace and Ruthie. They're going together. Didn't he tell you?" *No,* said the narrator, *he didn't.* He confronted Horace. "Yes, she's going," said Horace. He had little to say about it. Only gradually did the reader learn. How she told Horace that Macurdy would pay her way. When he wondered why the hell Macurdy would do that, she said because he wanted to. (So maybe, said the reader, it was all Macurdy's idea in the first place.) Well, what of it? said Horace. If Macurdy wants to pay her way, why should he raise questions? That was before we discovered who Macurdy was, but when this came out, probably it helped. The reader saw them off together (Horace and Ruthie at the airport), and followed while they traveled on postcards through London, Paris, Amsterdam, Copenhagen, Zurich, Venice, Rome—cards that always spoke of what *we* saw but never said anything more. Afterward Ruthie came home, and Horace went to the cottage in Maine and never talked about her. "Did Ruthie stay with you the whole time?" asked the narrator at the cottage. "Sure," said Horace. "How did she enjoy the trip?" "Fine," said Horace. Which was the last the narrator heard of her until it was late July, and Claudia went to the Festival, and Horace suggested we go down to the old places on the Cape. . . .

Meanwhile the reader wants you to notice his casual words, twice spoken, about discovering who Macurdy was. Another permanent moment of surprise. Let's go back to that, to the time before you knew. The reader produces a late afternoon when the Dean came home from work, two weeks before Horace's scheduled departure for Europe with Ruthie. And Horace waiting for him when he got home. "I got news for you." Not telling it, though, until the Dean had mixed their martinis before dinner, though he kept repeating: "I got news." Holding off during the cracking of the ice, the measuring, the stirring, grinning like a narrator, although there was anger in it too.

They all sat down—Claudia too. Champion Ethelred of Clawmor climbed up on the sofa and sniffed Horace's drink. "My news.

Do you mean to tell me you don't know who this Macurdy character is?"

"Who he *is?*" said Michael. "Who *is* he?"

"And you really don't know?"

"What is there to know?" the narrator said. "He's a real estate agent and a part-time private eye. What else is there to know?"

"And you don't know, do you? No idea why he picked you for his special investigation?"

Narrator, annoyed by the cat-and-mouse, said, "I've told you what I know. What is this news you have?"

Horace looked into his martini glass, held it glittering between his face and our eyes, and said, "Seems he is a relative of mine."

"Relative?"

"Of mine, not yours—so to speak," said Horace. "More precisely, of my late wife's. More specifically still—" Narrator waited while he took a long slow sip, and then he put the glass down and suddenly, roughly and casually, said, "He just happens to be her bubble, that's all." The word *bubble* was actually *brother,* said the narrator, and he heard it perfectly clearly, and knew what the word was. The difficulty was with its meaning, which was not clear just yet and sounded more like *bubble,* while Michael asked: "Whose bubble?"

"My late wife's bubble," said Horace.

"Which of your late wives' bubble?" asked Michael.

"My last late wife's bubble, my disappearing Ruth's. He's her bubble, that's who he is—this man Macurdy who's become such a good friend of yours."

"You say . . . Macurdy is Ruth's bubble?" exclaimed the narrator's astonishment.

"Half-bubble, to be more accurate."

"Macurdy is . . . Ruth's half-bubble?" As the astonishment began to settle a little (into the past), the narrator grasped more clearly what he had just said: "Macurdy is . . . Ruth's half-*bubble? Ruth's?*"

"You really didn't know that, did you?"

Impossible, said the reader then. Called it impossible for the sake of surprise, but also because we knew all our relatives already. But the narrator reminded us that Ruth's relatives were not our relatives, and already he was hauling out the reader's files to see what would have to be revised in the light of this new information.

"Macurdy?" he said.

"Moffitt," said Horace. "Edward J. Moffitt. Macurdy is an alias."

Moffitt, yes; the narrator remembered someone—Macurdy himself—speaking of Ruth Moffitt as if from secret knowledge. That place would have to be revised. Looked for a reference to such a half-brother in what Ruth had told him of her childhood—and could not remember. Was there something in the fog? Looked again at what Macurdy had told of his own background at The Great Wall of China. There was talk of spying on a girl named Lena, but as for the rest—that too was vague and would have to be revised. The mother said, It should be a relief to know definitely at last who he is. The narrator wondered if it reduced the mystery at all. "How did you discover this?" he asked.

"I met him," said Horace. "Last night. Shook his hand. Fat boy. Remember him well from my wedding."

"You mean you just happened to meet him? Ruthie said I'd like you to meet my friend Macurdy and you said that's not Macurdy that's my old ex-brother-in-law Ed J. Moffitt?"

Horace amused. Explained how Ruthie had told him—"You might as well know"—and after she told him and it was all right, they went and met him. "I knew him slightly," said Horace. "When he comes to New York, which is tolerably frequent, Ruth goes out to lunch with him, but I saw him seldom."

Accompanying the narrator in his search for material to revise, suddenly the reader found words by Macurdy designating his *sister* as a dish, d-i-s-h, who makes you think of screwing. Now, what the hell, asked the sister, is the meaning of that? And other assorted mysteries. No doubt the biggest of these . . . he asked another question. "Will you tell me why, if he isn't really Macurdy, why the hell should Ruth's brother, Edward J. Moffitt, want to track me down and investigate me with anonymous calls and all that? I mean, why me?"

"Maybe because you're my brother and happen to live here," said Horace.

"But still, *why?*" The narrator was burning all the old explanations about his being a candidate for the deanship and the like.

"I guess being Edward J. Moffitt doesn't make him any less crazy than being Edward Macurdy," said Horace.

Already the narrator had begun to compose a series of scenes at lunch in little hidden restaurants in the heart of New York, lunches full of brotherly-sisterly confidences, which might take the place of many a postulated and laborious investigation. (His brother lives in your own city. Shall I look him up? He's very interesting. What's interesting about him? What more can you tell me? Why are you so curious? The more I know, the more I like it.) Meanwhile the boy king was in a panic: What will this do to *The Morley Mythology?* Michael Morley asked: "What does this do to your trip with Ruthie?"

"Why should it do anything to my trip with Ruthie?"

"You're not afraid of being blackmailed or anything like that?"

Horace laughed. "Jesus, what could anybody blackmail *me* for?"

The narrator continued composing private luncheons in secret New York restaurants, offering them to the reader during the weeks that followed this discovery. (Well, what did he tell you about that? Why don't you ask Horace to tell you more, in a very casual manner? Why do you want to know so much about him, of all people? Well, it's interesting to see how things check out. I've always had this curiosity, you know.) He was still composing private luncheons on the way down to the Cape, while the king was asking why we hadn't heard anything from Macurdy in all this time. The king was disappointed that Macurdy had disappeared once his identity became known, and that was why he was glad as they approached the Cape. Meanwhile the narrator . . . (He lives in your own town, you know. I wish you'd look him up and see what he's doing with his life now. Quietly, you know. After what happened last summer, I'd like to know.)

The reader wonders whether to keep or throw out the boy

king's disappointment, which had followed the narrator's own disappointment on learning that Macurdy was more directly connected to Horace than to himself. Were these feelings the boss would authorize? Could they have any place in the final version of the narrative? And yet there was the book about the Morley Mythology, proposed by Macurdy, and the actual interviews, which the Dean had cautiously agreed to, and the reader could not possibly ignore. There had been five meetings, admitted the reader, during which the ex-king talked at length into Macurdy's tape recorder, interrupted occasionally by Macurdy questions. No one yet knew how the book itself would be written. The next step would be to make transcripts of the tapes. Then perhaps Macurdy would write something from that. "Don't worry," he would say. "All you have to do is talk." The king thought there should be many more interviews, for he had told hardly anything to Macurdy yet. He also wondered if Macurdy was paying enough attention to what he was saying into the recorder. Still, he felt good talking about these things, all the old Favorites. It was a feeling of relief and freedom. So that he was definitely disappointed when Macurdy did not come back. Once in June he called to say that he had not forgotten, but he was busy these days with other matters, and maybe later . . . Now, though, you can start thinking about it again. Actually, the king had never stopped thinking about it, never stopped rehearsing for the sessions ahead. He hired the narrator to help and kept him busier than on anything else. He had been sinking deeper and deeper into the Mythology for several months, and all his other narrative tasks, of the deanship and Horace and Ruthie and Claudia, seemed to be skimmed off the surface of the Mythology. Maybe that was why it was a shock to hear the reader recall the past once again, this day while driving with Horace and Nancy and Bobby to the Cape, the sea, and another meeting with Macurdy.

27

Second Rehearsal: The Norwegian Singer

Unlike other Favorites, those of the Third Series were not journeymen competitors, struggling to find a place among inferiors and betters. They were already masters when they became Favorites. For seven years the Norwegian singer was champion of the New York operatic world. She was not the king's Favorite then; he was busier with secondary singers and took her championship for granted. Only when it came into question, when she was challenged by controversy and the passage of time, did she become Favorite. Then she became the prototype of all Favorites who were champions by art.

He was there when her championship began—listening to the broadcast of the New York debut that made her suddenly, at the age of forty, famous. She had sung seldom outside Scandinavia, nor had she ever sung most of the parts that were now to make her name. A few days before, a critic had asked: This "Norwegian soprano, soon to be heard at the Metropolitan, is reported to have sung at Bayreuth. Will some benevolent statistician kindly tell when and what?"

On the radio, the king heard the singing, then the ovation, then the announcer's excitement, calling her a new star. Next day came the reviews:

> The singing we heard yesterday is that of a musician with taste and brains and sensitivity, with poetic and dramatic insight.
>
> . . . She is solacing to the eye—comely and slim, and sweet of countenance . . . a beautiful and illusive re-creation, poignant and sensitive throughout, and crowned in its greater moments with an authentic exaltation. . . .

The crescendo of sympathy and emotion achieved as the first act mounted to its climax were the work of a musician and interpreter rich in all the resources of her art.

. . . superb singing. The voice has the body, the color in the lower register, the brilliancy without stridency in the upper tones to cope with every demand of the role.

Early next week another performance settled the matter. He read about that too:

. . . a transcendentally beautiful and moving impersonation . . . an embodiment so sensitively musical, so fine-grained in its imaginative and intellectual texture, so lofty in its pathos and simplicity, of so memorable a loveliness, that experienced opera-goers sought among their memories of legendary days to find its like. They did not find it.

At that time the most popular composer of opera was Wagner. In the weeks that followed, she took all the leading Wagnerian roles: she was Isolde, Brünnhilde, Elisabeth, Elsa, Kundry, Sieglinde. The audiences came to sold-out houses, and special performances were scheduled for her. They said she saved the Metropolitan Opera from bankruptcy. From the Metropolitan she went out to the rest of the world.

The king looked at her pictures in the paper: dark eyebrows, dark eyes (with a startled look), a straight nose that in profile descended straight from the forehead like that of a Greek statue. Her pictures showed large upper teeth. In costume she was tall and straight, grave and dignified, often gazing (or searching) upward. Out of costume she wore little make-up (at first) and looked embarrassed or shy. He saw what a hard worker she was. During the first seven years of her championship, she sang two or three times each week of the season, and the boy king never saw a bad review.

He heard her frequently in opera broadcasts. He was not a skilled judge of singing, yet he could distinguish her voice from the others by its sound: Isolde's voice had more fullness than Brangaene's. When his mother or father took him to see her in a live performance, they also testified. His sister Penny said, "I can tell

NYT Pictures

she's the best." And his father, not much of an opera-goer, got chills in his spine when the waking Brünnhilde sang her first notes. The king had no doubt about her championship.

During those years he saw her six times: she was Isolde three times and she was each of the three Brünnhildes once. In a later period he saw her once more as Isolde. In those performances she always looked a little different from what the king, knowing her pictures, had expected. She was larger and heavier than the reviewer's phrase ("comely and slim") had led him to expect. Yet as she sang she changed: *large and heavy* seemed to become *tall and stately* and afterward it was easy to remember her as *comely and slim,* which gave him a shock the next time he saw her to find how *large and heavy* she had become again. Her motions on the stage were spare, timed to coincide with the music. Once he sat near the stage when she was Isolde. She wore dark red with flowing sleeves and gold braid and he was alarmed by her anger, with her foot pulsing as she sang about it—as if she were angry not only with Tristan but with the whole orchestra and the conductor himself for his beat. Then the love potion changed her mood. In the moonlit garden, dressed in white with long hair flowing loose, she threw back her veil and smiled for the first time, eager, impatient for her lover to come. Then the final mood, the trance as she sang in the fading light, rising, standing motionless, raising her arms on the final note before sinking down on her lover's corpse. The corpse was the enormous body of the great Danish tenor. After the performance they took bows, the Dane with his arm around her shoulder while the audience stood and shouted, and many came down to the front. She was in a good mood now, anger gone, trance dispelled. She bowed and then curtsied, caught a piece of falling confetti out of the air, and laughed. Not until years later did the ex-king learn of the feud she was then having with the Danish tenor.

The interviewers and raconteurs composed the legend of her personality. What a contrast, they said, to your ordinary vain and temperamental prima donna. This one was modest, shy—a simple, hard-working perfectionist. The king believed in this legend. He knew her well. The narrator kept the record for him. How she fell asleep during a performance of *Parsifal:*

I was so frightened when I discovered that I had dozed off that I kept very wide awake for the rest of the opera, I can tell you.

The memory lapse in one of her early performances:

I was not listening to the orchestra . . . and for some reason I was sure that the phrase began on a C natural. I began to sing it that way. I sang three measures, always transposing upward before I realized what I was doing. I understood later why the dead Tristan's eyes had opened in amazement, why the prompter motioned wildly, why there was something strange in Mr. Bodanzky's gestures.

She said in an interview:

On the stage I am no longer conscious of anything but the music. Wagner put so many, many thousand things into it that you can't simply act, or simply sing. You are Bruennhilde, or Isolde, or Elisabeth. And afterwards, in my dressing room when I am taking off the terrible heavy wig, I say to myself, "Ah, there was so much you could have done."

After the performance she would go to the hotel and play solitaire. She had champagne if she thought she had sung well. "Sometimes I have it even when I have not sung well. It tastes so nice." She said that the most important requirement for a Wagnerian singer was a sturdy pair of shoes and that the main thing on her mind during a performance was to keep her back straight. The legend described her willingness to sing whenever needed, and to work hard at rehearsals. The king had a feeling of great trust. Her success transferred itself to the operatic enterprise itself and justified his participation.

She began to become a Favorite when the rumors of retirement began. The king thought that by being witness to her success he had shared in something historic, and now he was afraid that he would not hear her again. She became Favorite in earnest later on when the controversies began, and he turned partisan in her behalf.

The first controversy was political. The seven years ended in the war, when she went back to Norway to live with her husband. At this time Norway was occupied by the Germans. When she left she said that she hoped to come back, but later sent word that she could not. For four years nothing was heard of her. They said that she was not singing, but was living in retirement, waiting it out. But her career seemed to have ended, and in New York others tried to take her place. The king, remembering what a secure champion she had been, did not believe this possible—others could not take her place.

When the war ended word came that she wanted to return. Now the controversy became fierce. There were charges that her husband, an industrialist, had collaborated with the invaders. There was a campaign against her. The husband died in jail. For several years the controversy continued. Her defense was that she was not political: her place had been by her husband, where she lived in retirement. She had never sympathized with the Nazis. She had never sung for the enemy. The king—who wanted her to come back and reestablish her championship, because it would be like a resurrection from the dead—accepted her arguments and supported her vigorously. She fought to vindicate herself by singing. She came to America and gave a concert tour. At first her concerts were picketed, and one was marred though not halted by a riot and stink bombs. Gradually she overcame the resistance, though it was five more years before she could return to the Metropolitan. The king was in the audience at her concert each year and participated in the standing ovation she always got, though he no longer lived close enough to New York to see her again at the Metropolitan. He persuaded the reader that her victory was complete. After her retirement she reaffirmed her championship in many new recordings. The war taint seemed to have finally disappeared into the past. In her own country she was made manager of the opera company in Oslo. But even after her death the boy king still collected supports when he found them, like this one from a book called *The Singing Voice:*

There was no greater martyr to [the Second World War] than [the great Norwegian], unjustly reviled and demonstrated against in America, the very country that had been first to give full recognition to her peerless vocal and artistic qualities.

The second controversy was artistic. In contrast to the other it was quiet, scarcely noticeable unless you looked closely. It turned on the charge that she was not the greatest singer of them all, that there were some limits to even her art, some important things that other singers could do better. At first the king thought such suggestions ridiculous, for they seemed to deny her well-attested championship and ignored the great historical sensation he had lived through. Yet those who cast doubt all seemed to be making the same point. They said that the Norwegian's singing, though beautiful and technically perfect, was "austere" or "cold." "Glacial," said one critic. "Emotionless," said another. "Sexless," said a third. Other great singers were warmer, more interesting, more exciting.

Such criticisms alarmed the king, and he tried to suppress them. As if they threatened the integrity of the Mythology. Even in his long dormancy, the boy king would hear the personal threat when such a criticism was sounded, and wake up enough to ask the critic —*our* critic, the boss's critic—to defend the old champion. Yet now in this resurgence of the king, the critic is more independent than he used to be. He likes to remind the ex-king that if other distinguished critics find her singing cold, there must be some basis to the charge. The king replies that most of the negative criticisms he has heard were based on the singer's recordings: he does not recall such objections to any actual performance. Bring back the live performances, he tells the narrator, the recitals as well as the operas—recall the excitement of the audience, the excitement he felt, the singer's own held-in and subtly released excitement. With such a stir, how could it possibly be cold? He says that the singer's recordings do not reveal either the bigness of her voice (requiring a large space to expand in) or the way her intensity would increase in the course of a performance. The father calls that a hard argument to sustain when you no longer have anything left but records to back you up. Meanwhile the critic has grown strong enough to express the heretical opinion that there are times when he would actually rather hear some other singer. Times when, on the same long-familiar recordings, suddenly her singing, despite its technical perfection, sounds detached, her voice, despite its beauty and richness, tired. Such judgments are subjective, admits the critic. The truth is that the same record that sounds exciting one time will sound tired another. The same detail will be entirely different. It depends on ourselves, suggests the father, which one of us happens to be listening.

And while that argument developed, along came a third controversy. This one was inner, between the narrator and the boy king. The narrator had doubts about the great singer's modesty and simplicity, which the boy king had always admired. He looked at the beginning of her dictated autobiography:

> I have never really wanted to write a book. I don't think my life concerns anybody but myself. I don't care one bit what my reputation will be when I stop singing . . . . Immortality as an artist means nothing to me. Fame, glory—they are empty, meaningless words. . . . I am extremely simple, the complete opposite of complicated. I am not a bit difficult. I am just the average person who walks the earth.

No doubt this is what she supposed, but the narrator didn't believe her. She was not the average person who walks the earth, and he doubted that she was indifferent to fame. He did not believe in her legendary simplicity, in spite of her reported fondness for movie magazines and games of solitaire. (The king was bothered by the movie magazines too. They didn't fit with the legend of the singer's good sense or her intelligence—the quick brain that learned Kundry in three weeks and the three big Brünnhildes in a few months. What that means, said the narrator, is that you are a snob about movie magazines.) The narrator had heard stories enough to wipe out the old legend forever: people turned away from her dressing room, slights given thoughtlessly or wantonly, shyness so extreme as to become rude, grudges held, unpredictable changes and shifts of feelings. The narrator advised the king to accept a new legend: complexity instead of simplicity, tractability mixed with stubbornness, modesty mixed with pride and vanity and even grandeur. Is that a fact? asked the king. What are facts? said the narrator. What do we know but legends, and how can we choose except one that holds the pieces together? Asks the king: How real are *you,* for that matter? How much of a fact are you in the final Morley reckoning?

The critic, who argued that all great singers were individual and could not be ranked, wondered why the boy king didn't bring others, some of the great more recent singers, into the Mythology. The king resisted. Said that it was not only a matter of *singing.* The Favorites of the Third Series were recognized champions, publicly acknowledged, and the point of the Mythology was to defend such established eminence against the erosion of forgetful time. The Favorite was a token of the boy's kingship, the narrator said. Each Favorite was an intimate part of his history and enlarged his kingdom. By watching her as she won acclaim, he became participant, and the event belonged to his history as well as hers. She was the voice of the king's own unrealized work, the possibility of achievement, of perfect accomplishment.

Why a woman? asked the reader. Because no sound was as beautiful, said the critic, as a woman's singing voice when well produced and controlled. The singer was the full-throated ease of emotion that professional skill makes possible, said the narrator. She expressed the feeling, the sensuousness, of being professional.

Uninterested in analysis, the king wanted to follow through her championship to the end. Tell about her recitals during those five or six years after the war—the shock renewed each year when she first came onstage because she was so much heavier than he remembered, her face round, her neck fat, and how he rediscovered her through her intensifying eyes, her familiar smile, and then her voice, shaping her through her singing to what she had always been.

Tell also how she began, late in her career, to sing classical parts, such as Dido in Purcell's opera. She sang this in London for friends, in a small theater with a contract in which she was paid "two pints of oatmeal stout *per diem.*" To show how deep goes the championship quality of her art (said the king), tell about her recordings after retirement, in her late fifties and sixties, and how well her voice stood up, how little it was affected by her age. Tell how in her sixties she learned the mezzo roles in the *Ring* for a new recording in which her own famous soprano roles were to be taken by the great Swedish soprano who had replaced her on the Wagner stages. Tell about the surprise of her young colleagues on this recording when they heard this old lady, known by name only, sing her first notes. Tell also how she went out in the streets of Vienna at five in the morning to vocalize (vocalize: *mi mi mi mi mi*) so as to be ready for the recording session at nine-thirty without disturbing her neighbors in the hotel.

She died of cancer at the age of sixty-seven. Her death prevented her from continuing with the mezzo roles in the *Ring.* The Danish tenor sent a wreath. Though more than a dozen years have passed, the boy king still finds it hard to believe she has died. But actually, of course, she has not, said the boy king, as you can demonstrate with the phonograph whenever you like. As he listens to her, singing again Dido's lament, the boy king is secure and confident that she exists, and he is full of her sadness:

> When I am laid (am lai-ai-ai-aiaid) in earth,
> may my wrongs create
> No trouble, no trouble in thy breast!
> Remember me! Remember me!—But ah-ah-ah!
> forget my fate!
> Remember me! But ah-ah-ahaah!
> forget my fate!

CRITIC'S REPORT. Drawn up by the critic at the king's request for the reader to keep an enumeration of the primary qualities of the great Norwegian's art.

1. *Power* of voice, the ability to project clearly, loud and soft, in the largest of houses, to cut through the full Wagnerian orchestra. Nothing

sounds strained. There is always the suggestion of more in reserve.

2. *Accuracy:* close attention to detail, the pitch of notes (her pitch was infallible), their rhythmic values. You could see this by following the score. You could rely on her to give you an accurate version of the music as written.

3. *Beauty* of voice, considered simply as a musical sound. It was both rich and clear all the way up and down its range. Some tones astonished the critic, they were so full of color and other qualities, and he could find no words to describe them that satisfied him: purple? gold? sweetness?

4. *Control.* A critic said she handled her voice like a fine race horse. No breaks between upper and lower registers. The vibrato was restrained, sometimes suppressed altogether. In slow music she emphasized control by allowing tone and vibrato to develop deliberately after she had attacked the note. She shaded her tones with a variety of colors. No fear that she would falter or break.

5. *Authority,* the impression she gave on stage as in concert. Of being in charge. Of enjoying herself. The intensity of her characters emerged through simple acting, spare graceful gestures, and her respect for the music.

28

Said the reader:

Now in late July, during our visit to Penny in Maine, while Claudia was at the Music Festival, Horace and I took Nancy and Bobby down to the old places on the Cape. There was no house to visit now, no grandparents, and we stayed at a motel.

The trip was Macurdy's idea. At first I would not go. I said: (1) If we are going to visit the Cape for old nostalgia, why not wait until Claudia can come? (2) Why make a special trip all that way to see Macurdy, who is still untrustworthy even if I do know his real name now? (3) Why should old nostalgia be complicated by his presence, when I still don't know what he wants? (4) If it's

Ruthie you want to see, why don't you go see her by yourself?

The arguments against me were these: (1) We can't postpone the trip because this is the only time Macurdy will come. (2) He wants more interviews for your Mythological book. He wants to see the places that were important in your Mythology. (3) You have given him interviews and you were disappointed when they stopped. (4) Ruthie won't come to the Cape without Macurdy. So if I am to see Ruthie, you have to come and see Macurdy. (5) This won't interfere with your vacation. Anytime you and Nancy and Bobby want to go to Martha's Vineyard or Provincetown without me, feel free. (6) Nancy and Bobby want to go. (7) Claudia thinks it would be a nice trip for you while she is gone.

We drove the heavy-trafficked loop around Boston and then the long straight divided highway across the flatlands with miles of scrubby trees growing out of sand. Across the high arched canal bridge and along the top of the scrubby woods, with glimpses now and then of the bay to the west silvered by the afternoon sun beyond sand bars and silhouetted houses. It was five o'clock when we got to the motel. I could feel the brightness of the water without seeing it, and knew where the beach was, out beyond the houses and the harbor, as if I had just been there. At the motel desk Horace asked, "Is there any message for Horace Morley?"

"No, but there's a message for Michael Morley."

It was a firm white envelope. The first item was a passage Xeroxed from a book, with a note above and below. The note above read as follows:

Did you know about this business between the members of your Mythology?

Then the passage:

In the cast for that performance Flagstad made another specific request which the Metropolitan graciously granted. She was devoted as a friend and colleague to Madame Dorothee Manski and she wanted Manski on the stage with her that night of celebration.

(Ha, said the king, they were friends. This would please him when he had time to think, he said, this devotion between the greater singer and the lesser, both reflecting himself. . . .)

It was one of Flagstad's real sorrows later on that Manski proved to be such a bitterly disloyal friend to one who had shown her such affection.

(. . . and then enemies. The king caught the words "bitterly disloyal." The shock of personal betrayal. Whose fault was it?) Meanwhile time rushes on to the fine handwriting of the note below:

Gives you a shock, doesn't it? I found it in a biography. Isn't it interesting to find true things like this about the people whose lives you have been imagining for so long? I hope you don't find it disillusioning.

(Not in the least, said the king, already guarding himself against the reader, who would want to settle the question of blame. No, said the boy king, it makes no difference. Two people in the Mythology diverge. Is there any reason why everybody in the Mythology should be sweet and loving to everyone else?)

The second item in the envelope was a letter:

Hello. Thought I should look over your Favorite place with my own eyes. I'm staying at a cottage which I found by the beach. Would like to discuss Horace with you before he sees Ruthie—and also have an interview about the Cape—so how about coming over this evening by yourself? Send him and the kids to the movies. They are showing a movie called *Don't Look Now* in Falmouth. Give me a call at 262–0717, and I'll come and get you.

Tell Horace that Ruthie doesn't arrive until tomorrow noon. She'll call him when she gets here.

Macurdy

29

The reader's report:

First we went to the beach for a swim. The bay was to the west, beyond the long sand bar that blocked the horizon and protected the harbor. A road from the village went out to the sand bar. It crossed a little bridge at one end of the harbor, and then bent to the north, running along the sand bar just over the beach. At the north end of the sand bar was a bulge of land, with trees and gardens and a dozen big houses. The houses all had gray shingles and white trim. Most of them had been there in the time of my childhood. From the road on the sand bar you could see my grandfather's house half a mile away, facing the village over the harbor. (Give to Nancy and Bobby, said the narrator, as well as Macurdy: the high hedges like walls on both sides of the road hiding the houses, the lawns, the gardens, until suddenly they came to the opening to Grandfather's house. Then the wicker furniture, the kerosene lamps, the bookcases, the sweet woody smell of the house. After being served tea and sugar cookies on the screened part of the porch, the boy and his sister and baby brother went exploring. The grass on their bare feet was prickly, like pins. A lawn sprinkler zigzagged in the front. Led by the boy, the children, lifting their feet delicately because of the prickles, went down the grass to the back of the house, past the laundry yard and the pear tree into the garden, surrounded by heavy underbrush, and shaded by trees, with benches, a wooden swing, a sundial. After the garden a narrow path took them through the thick wild bushes to a wooden dock with the rowboat tied up, with sailboats moored in the harbor, and houses in the village across the way. This was the ultimate center of the Favorite Place, the center of all location, the place to which the journey on the night boat had brought you. You stood on the dock and looked across, watching the smoke from another train as it moved through the village, waiting for a glimpse of the engine between the houses, with its tiny gold numerals too far away to read, while up on the porch your parents sat with your grandparents, who were still alive.)

So we went out to the beach, to swim in the late afternoon. The beach was long and white and stretched away for miles to the south. It was almost empty now, though the sun was still high. The breeze coming off the water was chilly, and modest breakers, the size of a man, were rolling against the shore. We saw the remnants of a hot day on the sand: a large gull walked around a waste barrel, searching in the plastic bags for picnic remains. A diving float bobbed in the waves off the shore, facing a row of bathhouses. Three men tried surfboards in the breakers. I looked down the beach beyond the bathhouses to the cottages and wondered which one Macurdy had taken.

As I sat on the beach, I kept hearing questions about the long-ago incident in Macurdy's letter. Why, after all, did Manski turn on her friend? Was there some provocation? Was it a misunderstanding? And why was it mentioned in the book—this book written after the Norwegian's death by one of her best friends? Was this retaliation for something? Such questions were painful. I said I did not really want to know. I said it was important not to get personally involved with the real people behind the Mythology.

Back at the motel, I called Macurdy. We made arrangements, and after dinner, after the others had gone off in the car to see *Don't Look Now,* Macurdy came for me with his car and drove me to his cottage. It was down the beach about a mile from where we had been swimming. We drove on a narrow dirt road with grass in the middle. "I just happened to find it," he said. "A week's rent —cost me a bundle."

In the car he showed me another Xeroxed passage. Here the great Norwegian was rejecting a bid for reconciliation from her former colleague the great Danish tenor. "I will never forgive him!" she said. "Never! Never!" Macurdy laughed. "Well, she finally did," he said. "It says they corresponded with each other in the end." That was good, but still I wondered. What had the Danish tenor done to deserve such bitterness? And why was I so concerned? Like quarrels in my own family, threatening me? Meanwhile Macurdy was saying: "They are all dead now. All we need is a little historical perspective."

As we drove out through the dunes the narrow road crossed the railroad tracks and ran beside them. This was the line where my trains used to run. It ran between fields of tall grass, and now the grass grew between the rails themselves. The rails were rusty and uneven and nothing traveled on them now. I remembered how the boy used to watch them and wait. How he knew the direction to the tracks from wherever he was, from the house or the beach or the village, and how alert he was for the sound of the train, knowing always where to look or go so as to see it riding across the dunes or crossing the road on the way to the station. Paying most attention to the engine.

1001 (1907–?) Steam passenger locomotive of the New Haven Railroad. Class I-1, 4–6–2 ("Pacific") wheel arrangement. Driving wheels 73". Tractive effort 31,550 lbs. Tender capacity 14 tons, 6,000 gals. Locomotives of this class (numbers 1000–1031 of which 1009–1029 were built by Baldwin, the rest by Alco, all in 1907 except 1030 and 1031, built in 1910) served originally in main line express service on the New Haven and later on local and light express service out of Boston. In Morley's time they shared with the larger I-2's (1300–1349) and the smaller G-4's (numbered in the 800's) most passenger service on Cape Cod and southeastern Massachusetts, including the trains that met the Fall River boat. In Morley's judgment the I-1's were good-looking engines. The stack was taller than in the later, heavier engines, which is an advantage, and the surface was less crowded with pipes and gadgets. The two domes were well spaced, the engine well proportioned. When Morley knew them, the I-1's had been changed in several ways from their original appearance: the cylinders were modernized, the headlight centered on the smoke box, pipes and tubes were added, the number and the name "NEW HAVEN" were painted in gold block letters. Michael Morley believes he chose 1001 for Favorite after watching it back up to a train in Woods Hole, but that is a very old memory and he is not sure. Later he kept a record, according to which he saw (from 1935 through 1940) all but nine of the 32 engines in the I-1 class. The nine he did *not* see were 1001, 1005, 1010, 1012, 1013, 1023, 1025, 1029, and 1031. As a result, Morley is not sure that he *ever* did see 1001, even in the years before, though he kept hoping to. Sometimes he wondered if 1001 really existed. Had it been wrecked? scrapped? abandoned? Was it a mere fiction, an imaginary number? A friend reported seeing 1001 in Boston in 1935, but if the friend knew that 1001 was the Favorite, could the report be trusted? According to a book he had, three of the I-1's were still alive in 1950. Which three? Though he knew that soon after that, all steam engines on the New Haven were withdrawn, he would have liked to know the specific fate of each one.In the absence of a direct sighting of 1001, he decided to give all I-1's collectively the status of Favorite in the Mythology.

30

It was almost dark when we got to Macurdy's cottage, with a weak memory of the day still in the sky over the water. The cottage was small, with lights on. When we came in, there was Ruthie in blue jeans, coming to greet us. She turned off something loud on the radio. "Well, brother!" she said, holding out her hand.

"I thought you weren't coming until tomorrow," I said.

They looked at each other. "We wanted to see you before seeing your brother," said Macurdy.

I asked why.

He looked about and made a face, grave. "We're worried. You know. His suicidal tendency."

I thought Macurdy looked different from the last time. Not just the informality of his clothes (his loose checkered shirt), but his eyes, the bags under them looking bruised, and then I realized he had lost weight. He seemed more nervous too.

I said that I hadn't noticed anything different in Horace, although he had been rather quiet, perhaps.

"Ruthie spent three weeks traveling around Europe with him," said Macurdy. "He's in a bad state of mind. Right, Ruthie?"

She shrugged her shoulders.

"We think it's serious, no telling what he might do. We think you should know, in case you want to take measures."

"What measures can I take?"

"That's a problem to think about, certainly." He was frowning, thinking hard, and then Ruthie began to frown too. It worried me a lot, but suddenly the frowning annoyed me, and it occurred to me to ask: "How come you never told me who you were?"

The frown broke into a grin. I waited, but he did not answer. "How do you like our place?" he said. Waved his hand around. Pine furniture, a table, a couch, a few chairs. A small radio on the floor. Indian blankets hanging as curtains to the closets, and a stairway going up. There was a door opening out to the beach, opposite the door we had come in.

"I went to the real estate lady and asked, Have you got anything on the beach available for a week, beginning now? These beaches are great. You know what the beach always makes me think of?"

"What?"

"Why, screwing, man! Screwing in the sand, all out in the sun and wind, not knowing whether anyone can see you or not."

I didn't say anything. I remembered something else that made him think of screwing.

"Well, what does it make *you* think of?" he said. "Drowning?"

I said, "What do you want to interview me about tonight?"

He gave me a look as if I was being difficult. "That can wait," he said. "Let's take a look at my beach!"

We went out, down the steps to the concrete wall and down from that onto the beach. We looked at the lights farther down the shore and walked a little toward the inlet and back. He pointed out the stars to Ruthie and identified the constellations. After a while I said, "Hadn't we better get started?"

He kicked the sand a couple of times. "I don't know as I feel like it," he said. "I think I'm coming down with a headache."

My easy annoyance with the outrages of Macurdy began to warm up. "I left my brother and kids to come out here tonight," I said.

"We'll make it worth your while," he said. He looked again at the bay. "What a beautiful night," he said. "Let's go swimming." Turned to me: "Want to?" I didn't know what to say. Then to Ruthie: "Ruthie?"

"Sure," she said.

"Maybe a swim will fix me," he said.

Now the narrator rehearses this particularly for Claudia.

As I watched, not knowing what to say—because I did not want to go swimming in the night, even though the wind had died—suddenly I saw him undo his belt buckle and drop his trousers, and in another moment his shirt was off. Then, standing in his shorts, off with his shoes, while I heard thinking: Wait, wait, are we going naked? Is he? Will *she*? Then yes, down with his shorts, and there he was with his potbelly and bare white behind. Now what would Ruthie do? There she was, undoing the big pirate buckle at the front of her jeans. Does she mean it? Is this what is happening? She was pulling her T-shirt over her head (no bra! someone noticed), then dropped her jeans and (give me time) her underpants. So there she was too, beside Macurdy, thin and white with breasts and a dark patch, taking off her glasses, putting them with her clothes on the concrete wall by the house. They both looked at me.

"Aren't you coming?" said Macurdy.

"I have no bathing suit."

"Neither do we," said Macurdy.

She laughed.

I felt community pressure to conform. Someone warned me not to trust them even now—though the naked girl with the long hair had traveled three weeks around Europe with my brother, and the naked man with the potbelly was my brother's ex-brother-in-law. Someone else said that I looked stupid—Bureaucrat, Administrator, Dean, Prig—standing there in my clothes without joining in.

The girl beckoned. "Come on!" she insisted.

I thought, What would I do if Claudia were here? But Claudia was not here, so I thought instead, What would Claudia expect me to do? Then the community pressure tightened, and I began to get undressed. "Hooray," said Ruthie. I realized that I had not gone skinny dipping since the men's pool in college, and I had never gone skinny dipping with women in my life. I was worried about revealing the Dean in a state of erection.

They went ahead of me into the water while I undressed, taking care not to drop coins or keys in the sand. The air was colder than I liked. As I went down to the water she turned and looked at me. I still regarded myself as lean and athletic, but when she looked I thought that my potbelly must be even larger than Macurdy's. I noticed that she was looking at my penis, which felt very sensitive in the cold air. I walked in quickly, up to my shoulders. The water was warmer than the air.

Nobody could swim very well. I don't know if Macurdy could swim at all. He bounced on his toes, bobbing up and down. He wore his glasses still, thick, dark-rimmed. Ruthie would swim two or three strokes at a time, and then pull up to catch her breath. My only stroke was the side stroke. After a few minutes Macurdy said something to Ruthie and turned back to the beach. I started to follow him, but Ruthie called, "Don't go yet." He turned and said to me, "Please stay. I don't want her to go swimming alone."

So it was a matter of doing the responsible thing. From the water, I watched him carry his clothes up to the house. I kept covered in the water while Ruthie played, splashing, ducking, trying strokes, gasping and laughing and bubbling.

She said, "How come you like this place so much if you can't swim?"

I was shivering and soon I noticed that her jaw also was trembling. "Isn't that enough?" I said. We went out together and up the beach. I tried not to avoid looking at her and also not to look at her except in a natural way. At the wall she found two large bath towels that Macurdy must have brought out. We dried ourselves. She stood up straight (facing me, frontal) and rubbed the towel through her hair, long and wet and stringy. "Where did he go?" I said.

"Migraine," she said. "He gets migraines. Can't stand it, so he has to lie down in the dark."

I was aware that I was alone on the beach with a naked girl

named Ruthie Thomas, and that I was naked too. I thought of all the hundreds of people who would misunderstand this if they knew. I said, "I guess I should go home, then."

"Stay awhile," she said. "I'll give you some sherry before you go. We can talk about Horace."

She sat down on the wall and draped the towel over her shoulders. I picked up my shorts. "Don't do that," she said. What? Oh, she meant my shorts. I let them go.

"Sit down," she said. "Relax and enjoy it. The beautiful evening."

She smiled as if I were being lovably ridiculous and she were full of sympathy. Still feeling community pressure, I sat on the wall beside her—not too close. She gave me a big smile. "A little uptight, aren't you? Take a deep breath."

I mumbled something. It occurred to me with a shivering shock that if I touched her, I could probably have her, just as she was—right now. It occurred to me with another shock that this was probably just what she expected, what she was waiting for—right now. The news of this shot through my body and made me swell up. I took a deep breath—

"That's better."

—and draped my towel across my lap.

Now it occurred to me that if this was what she was expecting and hoping I would do, and if I didn't start doing it soon, she would be disappointed, and her friendly, considerate behavior would change: she would turn cold and formal, maybe even ironic and mean. And then here I would be, sitting on the beach in the night without any clothes on. The shock of this situation made me shiver again—how had I got into this anyway? I said (to myself) it had happened too suddenly, I needed time to think it over, to look up my policy for a case like this. I knew I had a policy; I just couldn't remember it. But then I did remember it, as it had been fixed finally by last summer's developments with Ruth. Policy: To recognize that it was Claudia who was at stake in times like this. Did I wish to gamble with her or put her painful warning to the test? *Never again*, said the policy—which had been settled then with no reason to be changed now. Therefore. . . I considered Ruthie's disappointment and wondered how disappointed I might be too. Would I be proud of my control or would I be wondering for the rest of my life what it would have been like? Would I too turn cold and formal, ironic and mean, against myself, for turning down such opportunities? I began to wonder if maybe my policy should be more flexible.

Meanwhile she was looking at the towel in my lap. She said, "Are you cold?"

"A little," I said. (Actually, it was my back and shoulders that were cold, although I hadn't noticed it until she asked.)

"What I mean is, I hope you're not covering yourself on my account."

What she meant was, community pressure again. I thought, here is this Dean of the College trying to conceal a partially erect penis from a young kid not very different from a student, which in some communities would be an extremely foolish position for a Dean to be in. On the other hand, I felt the approval of my penis from everyone that mattered—from Ruthie herself, who disapproved of my hiding it, and from Macurdy and from Horace and from the night itself, with only some uncertainty about Claudia, my deep ignorance of what she would expect me to do. Or my pretended ignorance.

"I hope you're not ashamed of it," said Ruthie. "There's no reason to be ashamed of it as far as I'm concerned." It was too reasonable to argue against. Seeing how clear she was in the night, her breasts with their nipples and the dark hair in her lap, I felt ridiculous and put the towel around my shoulders as she had done.

"You mustn't be ashamed of your body," she said. Well, now, that broke the spell a little. A child was lecturing me on complicated lessons learned and qualified before she was born, as if I had never heard of them. Yet I don't think the lesson was the important thing here. For suddenly she reached out and touched the back of it quickly with two fingers—just once. "You mustn't be ashamed of *that.*"

Now it occurred to me with a real shock not merely that she

would be disappointed if I didn't rise to the occasion—she was actively trying to seduce me. And therefore this was a trap. It meant Macurdy was in on it too. I began wondering how dangerous a trap it actually was, and whether there might not be some way to submit cagily, to have the benefit without getting caught. Meanwhile I had to answer her. Truculent: "I'm not the least bit ashamed of it. Never was." I recognized a game that had rules. I put my hand on her thigh—felt once more the unfamiliar softness of another woman—and said, "Aren't you ashamed?" at the same time as I tried to think what to do about this trap that was being set.

Suddenly she shivered. "I'm cold," she said. "Let's go in to the house." And jumped up, away from me, scooping up her clothes. I felt as if I had been kicked, but then I followed, thinking, What a relief! Up there Macurdy was waiting, and what a fool I had been to suppose seduction when all it was, obviously, was a bit of new-generation didacticism.

She went naked into the lighted living room, and I followed. Macurdy wasn't there. "He's gone to bed," she said. "It's all right." Threw her clothes on the couch. Perhaps I was mistaken still. I said, "How do you know he's gone to bed?"

"He always does when he has a migraine. And anyway—"

"What?"

"Don't worry," said Ruthie Thomas.

The empty living room, the lights on, the doors and windows open. Bare feet upon the prickly fiber rug. She shut the outside doors. The hair on her head was still clumped into long wet strings. She had her glasses on and nothing else, and her skin looked healthy and fresh and pinkpeach in the light. I realized that my feeling of relief had been a false alarm, that the license we got from natural skinny dipping had just about expired. We should have put on our clothes before coming in, someone said. She went to get some sherry, but still no move to get dressed. I glanced nervously at the open windows. "Who's around for miles and miles?" she said. I thought that if I was being seduced, it was already too late to escape. Therefore. I realized also that my feeling of relief a few minutes before had actually been a feeling of disappointment and my feeling of fear now was actually a feeling of relief. I went back months and remembered looking across at her in the booth of The Great Wall of China and how her breasts distorted the letters "DAR" and "UTH," and how cheerfully she spoke of brightening up my brother's life.

She went upstairs to check on Macurdy. While she was gone I put on my shorts—it was easier when she wasn't there. When she came down she said, "He's asleep. It's a bad one, and he's going to sleep until morning." Then she said, "Take those off."

"What?"

"I'll give you a rubdown," she said.

Wouldn't it be simpler, someone suggested, to leave it up to her—let her decide what the dangers are? So (having decided that) I let my shorts drop. We sat down beside each other and sipped sherry. Then I stretched out on the couch and she knelt by me and rubbed me down with alcohol. I sat up and drank some more sherry. I felt the warmth of the sherry, and it was as if everything had been transformed, as if my usual views of myself were wrong, my policies stiff and foolish, my fears unreasonable, my suspicions blind and narrow. The heavily funded protection of my home and career and self-esteem and the orderly discipline of my emotions were merely feudal. All was changed as she went and came back with the sherry carafe, refilled my glass, filled her own, and set them both down on the coffee table. I made room for her on the couch. She said, "Is there anything else you'd like me to do?" I said, "What would you suggest?" For a moment she looked at me as if I were the one who was teasing, making jokes, and then suddenly, taking off her glasses, she said, "Oh, well"—cheerfully—and lay back on the couch. I was expected to bend over her while she put her arms around me and brought my face down to hers. I felt this combination of strange and familiar, this almost-child that I scarcely knew, with her strange connections, her odd indifference, her funny willingness, who tagged along for unknown reasons after the almost-monster Macurdy to make him seem at times almost human, who listened to long conversations bored yet not complaining, who read *Mad* and listened to rock, and traveled all over Europe with my brother—doing *this,* no doubt. I moved forward upon her with the same astonishment I used to feel in the old exploratory days when I found some new girl (which didn't happen so very often, after all), with arms around me and legs and bodies all pressed together.

"Aren't you glad you came?" she said, and had a fit of giggles. After she caught her breath she said, "I figured I ought to do something to make up for you not having your interview."

"Is that the reason?" I said. She did not reply.

"You can get dressed now, if it makes you more comfortable."

31

The reader also rehearsed this for Claudia and possible others.

After I got dressed we sat on the couch and drank sherry and talked. Still naked, she refilled our glasses and settled down beside me with her feet up on the ottoman. "Tell me," she said, "what do you really think of Macurdy?"

"I don't understand him," I said.

"What's to understand?"

"What he's after, what he wants."

"What do you mean? Why should he be after anything?"

"This pursuing me. This peculiar interest in the inside of my mind, and all these things from my childhood. What's going on?"

"He told you. I remember. Wasn't that clear enough?"

"No," I said. "It doesn't explain it."

She was looking at me, smiling. "It doesn't?" she said, in a tone of surprise. Of mock surprise, I realized. As if I had stumbled upon some obvious thing that everybody knows—and she found it funny.

"Why," she said, "don't you remember? He got interested in

you because—because—what was it? I forget." She laughed.

"He likes being private detective," I said.

"That's true enough. God, yes, he likes being private detective."

"And you help him, right?"

She took hold of her long hair and covered her face with it. Her eyes in her glasses peeked out at me through the strands.

"Sometimes," she said.

"And what kind of work do you do for him?"

She shrugged her shoulders. "Research," she said. "Sometimes I ask questions. Or—I look things up. Or—other things." Giggle.

"Sometimes agent provocateur?"

"What?"

"Nothing. Why do you do it?"

She leaned back farther, her head over the back of the couch, hair hanging down, breasts shallowed, with nipples and pubic tuft bright in the light. Finally, in a voice like a child, she said, "He likes me."

"And do you like him?"

Another long naked pause. I thought perhaps she wouldn't answer, but she said, "We get along."

I said, "You don't feel exploited?"

She sat up abruptly. "Exploited, shit!" she said. For a moment I thought she was angry and was going to break off, but she leaned back again, crossing her arms over her breasts. "I mean, I'm a little sick of all this *exploited* jazz," she said. "I'm a grownup; I can take care of myself."

"Sorry."

"Tsokay."

She stared at me for a while with curiosity or some message. I was embarrassed, not knowing how to meet her eyes or avoid them without being noticeable. Gradually she began to grin again.

I pulled myselves together and brought back the main question. "Will you tell me what—what is it Macurdy wants from me?"

"You don't think he's a private detective?"

"Sure he's a private detective, but what of it? Why is he dogging me?"

"You don't like this Mythology he's making for you?"

"Making for me?" I hesitated and decided to ignore that. I said, "That's beside the point. The point—"

Silence. She had mannerisms. She liked to move her long pointing finger around her body as if following a trail. It went around the edges of her glasses, then along the side of her neck. Now it was tracing circles around her two breasts.

Ask a hard fact. "Why did he make all those nuisance calls?"

"Why don't you ask him?"

"I did ask him."

"Well, what did he say?"

"You were there. You heard him."

"Maybe—" she said, and stopped. Her pointing finger had moved down her body and was now tracing large triangles around the original one.

"What?"

She got up and went to the stairs, looking up. Came back and sat down. "Just checking he can't hear."

"Ah," I said. Conspiracy and relief.

"Do you think he was sore at you?"

"Sore?"

"Pissed off," she said. "You know."

"Really? What for?"

She considered. "You *do* know who he is, don't you?"

I thought it over. "You mean that he is Horace's—I mean Horace's wife's—that is, Horace's wife's *brother?*"

"Good for you, sonny boy. Right. The one named Ruth. My namesake. You know that."

"He's her brother. I know that."

"Right. Half-brother or stepbrother," said Ruthie. "Which is which? I always get them mixed up. Half-brother is when you have the same dad and a different mom or the same mom and a different dad. Right? And stepbrother is when you have both different moms and dads. No, that can't be because then you wouldn't be anything at all—"

"No—"

"No, right! Stepbrother is when your mom marries another time to some other dad and he has his own children—or vice versa—so that you have different moms and dads both. So with Macurdy and that Ruth it must have been half-brother, because it wouldn't have been incest otherwise."

"What did you say?"

"I mean if it's a stepbrother and stepsister it wouldn't be incest, would it? It would be just ordinary illicit relations, right? It wouldn't be incest unless you were actually related, like I mean had the same mom or the same dad."

"What incest are you talking about?"

"So if it was incest they must have been half-brothers instead of stepbrothers. Although in *Hamlet*—when we studied that in school—when the uncle marries his brother's wife, don't they call *that* incest? Yes, I remember: incestuous sheets. And they weren't even related. So that maybe they could have been stepbrother and sister instead of half-brother and sister. Although I guess customs change, and I guess you wouldn't call a man with his brother's wife incest nowadays, would you?"

"What incest?" I said again.

"Macurdy and his sister?" She put it as a question.

"Macurdy and Ruth? *Incest?"* Although I had seen a lot of incest in literature, I had never heard of a real-life case.

She nodded and grinned. Strands of the long hair pulled around her nose.

After a moment I said, "Real incest or imaginary incest?"

"That's what I'm asking you," she said. "Although I don't know why he'd waste his time on imaginary incest."

"You're asking *me* this?"

"Well, you remember that Lena he told you about? That he used to spy on. Well, actually that was Ruth." She watched to see my reaction. "Slightly altered," she added. "I mean, she was about fourteen and he was seventeen. Living in the same house. He didn't live with her as a child, but then he went back when she was like thirteen or fourteen, and he got to watching her. You know, used to follow her and watch, driving him crazy. You know." You know. "So finally one night when she came back, he asked her to do it with him too. So she did. I guess she didn't mind the incest and all because it wasn't as if they had grown up together. Or he told her it didn't matter. You know. She didn't care. I guess she thought if I can do it with other guys I can do it with him too. Why not?"

Triangles. Circles too. And points. She stuck her finger in her navel.

After some reflection: "Or maybe you're right; maybe she didn't. Maybe he only imagined it. Maybe it's only what he wishes he had done—you know."

"Did he tell you this?"

"Or maybe he threatened to tell on her unless she did. Like because of what he had found out spying on her. He went up to her and said, You better do that with me too or I'll tell."

"Would he do a thing like that?"

"He's capable of it."

"He is, is he?"

She looked at me a moment, and said, "Uh huh." Then, "It must have been so sad. She went off to college and had men and he came out to Ohio and went into business. She married this guy in New York and divorced him and met your brother and started living with him and finally got married to him. Right?"

I said, "Does Horace know about this incest?"

"I guess that depends on whether anybody ever told him."

"And Macurdy told you?"

"Many times. I thought you'd know if it's the truth or not."

"You thought I'd know? How should I know?"

"I just thought you might have heard something. Horace never heard of it, either."

I thought back and asked, "What's all this got to do with Macurdy being sore at me?"

"Sore at you? Who said he's sore at you?"

"You did. Pissed off, you said."

"Oh, did I? Well, maybe he's a jealous type. You know."

"Jealous?"

"Oh, he's not jealous of *everything.* He doesn't mind who screws me, for instance, as long as I keep him informed—it's what he expects of me, it's part of our relationship. But where Ruth is concerned . . . Maybe because of the incest. Even though it was only a childhood romance—you know—if that's what it was. He can still get pretty mad when it comes to Ruth. And when he gets jealous—"

I had that heartbeat again. Uncomfortable surmises. I took my time and put the question carefully. "Just exactly what—whom—is he jealous of in connection with Ruth?"

"Well—*if* he's jealous," she said casually, "I suppose he's jealous of you."

"Me? Macurdy is jealous of *me?*" My voice was pale. "Why me?"

She looked at me, full of knowledge. "You know why," she said.

I thought, My worst fears are confirmed. In a moment I'll feel them and they'll destroy me. No question what she knew now, so I said, "How did he find out?"

"About you and Ruth?"

I took it and said, "Yes."

She shrugged. "I guess she told him."

"She told him?"

"Who else could have told him?"

"No one, I hope."

"Well, so it was her. What made you think she wouldn't? He sees her whenever he goes to New York. Every couple of months. Days —what?—at the zoo? Who knows? He had lunch with her."

So I knew I was cornered, and it didn't seem fair. I said, "Why not Horace? It's Horace she married; why isn't he jealous of Horace?"

"Don't ask me," she said, as if it were hopeless to figure out. "Maybe because he's used to Horace. There's nothing secret about Horace's relation to Ruth."

"You mean after all those other men in her life, he still gets jealous?"

"I don't know if he's jealous," she said. "I haven't any idea."

"I thought you said he was."

"I said he *might* be. How should I know what he really thinks?"

I considered. "So she told him about me, and he moved to Ohio so he could go after me?" Jesus!

"No, no, relax!" she said. "We've been in Ohio for years. His agency, you know. It was the coincidence that interested him. Here she had this affair with Horace's brother who lived in the same city as we did. How could he resist that? If you hadn't lived there, he would have forgotten. It was the opportunity. And after he had called you up once, the whole idea got more interesting. I mean, the idea of being detective and finding out everything."

"Playing with me."

"In a nice way," she said. "He never meant you any harm."

"I've never been able to believe that."

"Why not? He's very fond of you. (Most of the time.)" I noticed the parenthesis in her speech. "You're forgiven, if that's what you're worried about. No—if he really wants to hurt somebody, that's different."

"What do you mean?"

"Well, you know! He has a mean streak, like anybody else. But you don't have to worry. He likes you fine."

"And did Ruth tell him about my childhood Mythology?"

"I guess so," said Ruthie. "How else would he know about it?"

"I didn't know *she* knew about it," I said. "I don't remember mentioning it."

"So maybe she got it from Horace."

"Maybe she did."

"You were close to Horace once," she said.

"Is that how he puts it?" I asked. "I was close to him *once?*"

"You consider yourself close *now?*" She was surprised.

I felt a little ashamed. "Well, listen," I said. "Does Horace know about—about Ruth and—" I tried to avoid saying *you know.*

"Ruth and you? I don't know. I don't believe he ever mentioned you," she said. She began to giggle. "You know, that was a workout, that trip."

"How?"

"Keeping him from committing suicide. Cathedrals and museums and back to bed. Making love so he wouldn't kill himself. My God, I was *busy.* I thought I would die!"

"Oh." I thought of something else. "Will Macurdy be jealous of me again now?"

"Because of me?"

"Yes."

"Nah. He won't care." She gave me a soft look.

"You sure?"

"He doesn't care about me. You don't have to worry."

I said, "Is Macurdy really interested in my Mythology?"

"Why, sure," she said. "Don't you think so?"

"I had an impression he was getting bored by it."

"Is he? Well, Macurdy has his moods, like everybody else."

"Does he really?"

"I went all over Europe with your suicidal brother, and I live all the time with Macurdy. I get along well with these suicidal types."

"Is Macurdy suicidal too?"

"Nah. He has his days, like I said." I was disappointed by her retraction. She was saying, "It's time to drive you home now."

As I watched her putting on her clothes, I remembered the drastic unprepared thing that I had done with her, whose memory was still attached to my body. All that peaceful assurance. It drowsed my mind as I struggled to see through, trying to keep awake by asking questions. Asking how much of a fool I would prove to be and what kind of a trap I had fallen into. Unreal questions. Meanwhile the brother asked the narrator if he believed anything at all that either of them had said.

And in the night the boy king, oblivious, continued to look forward to his postponed interview.

32

Third Rehearsal: The Opera

The boy king wanted to put the opera itself into the Mythology, but the boss objected. It embarrasses the boss, said the narrator, that the boy king's favorite composer was this particular German, and he would like to dissociate himself.

At first there was no Favorite among the composer's operas. The boy king preferred those that had gods and dragons and parts for secondary singers like Manski. Gradually, though, performances by the Norwegian soprano and the Danish tenor brought *this* opera into the Mythology as Favorite. This meant that if he had to save only one he would save this one. He knew it best and thought it was the most characteristic, most concentrated of this composer's work.

The boy king took the narrator and the reader once again to the high balcony in darkness as the prelude begins—begins in the low strings amid the shaded lamps of the orchestra pit while the footlights glow upon the curtain. The narrator described it: Often the first note in the cellos is so soft you can't hear it. Then it rises into the famous first dissonance, dissolving upward and dying out. Pauses, repetitions, upward transpositions. The orchestra grows, the slow rhythm has a repressed passionate quality, new themes develop out of those already established. The mood is one of waiting—rising toward a climax that never arrives, sinking down again to an audible stillness in the bass as the curtain rises. On stage everything is still: the princess is transfixed with her head in pillows on the couch, the offstage voice of a sailor sings a melancholy air without accompaniment. Then a burst of violence from the orchestra as the princess springs up, and the first act is under way.

The opera hurries slowly through three long acts, a performance that with intermissions will last almost five hours. The music is always moving, riding ahead on the passions of the princess and the knight. In the first act she is full of anger—hurt, insulted, outraged, scornful—which the music depicts in detail. She loves and wants revenge on the knight. So she gives him the death drink which turns out to be the love potion, and the orchestra overflows into the next mood. Now (Act Two) she waits in the garden in the pale blue light of the moon. There is a long tryst with garden and moon and night music of love—until the crash, the exposure, and the shame. In the third act the knight waits on the battlement under the hot sun, wounded, thirsty, and delirious, longing for death, which is the only way to solve his love. He remembers, and the music remembers with him, what has gone before—the music of the ship, the music of the garden, which is all changed now. The climax is his death when the princess arrives, and then it is down to the final darkness as the soprano sings the famous concert piece that subdues the tumult in rich orchestration. It is the death they have been longing for, death in love, which can only be satisfied in death.

Originally, the boy king remembered, when he first tried to listen to the music, it frightened him. It seemed full of pain and suffocation. When he got to know it better, the pain became splendid and delicious. The characters' emotions, which came out of the music rather than the words or the situation, felt like his own. They tore him apart, or so he thought. The movement of the music in a performance was a journey from one place to another—transportation. The opera was a place in time, a geography, or an architecture. You go in one door and you find your way through familiar rooms, all in their order, with mysterious lights and scents and expected surprises, until you come out at the other end.

Can you take the reader on this trip? the king asked the narrator. Make him see those colors, feel those emotions? The narrator was doubtful. You could play the music, but that's no guarantee, he said. All the performances you have ever heard are part of the emotion you hear when you go through it again, performances when you were a child or a young man, with singers now dead, all in a time now gone. The emotion you think is the music's is really your own—said the narrator to the king.

Now the advocate intervened. This was a critic hostile to this composer, one who had grown up on phrases, sentences, articles, from critics, musical scholars, friends—he was a body of critical lore not sought out but acquired by accident or in reaction to some aggression by the king, and brought together into his person, like a file. In the old days the king kept him locked up, for he was afraid of his influence, but in the dormancy the boss released him. Now with the boy king's revival, the boss said that the advocate should also have a voice in the book, for they would have to live together henceforth. The advocate read off an abstract of the accusations that had accumulated:

> It is documented that the man who composed your opera was personally a scoundrel. He never paid his debts; he betrayed his friends. He was anti-Semitic. He was loved by Hitler, who took him for his inspiration. . . .

(When you told Macurdy that he was totally innocent of the use the Nazis made of him, it was—said the advocate—not all that certain.)

> Considered artistically, the literary quality of his librettos is poor (characters express their emotions by naming them: "yearning," "bliss," "pain"), his plots are unsympathetic, his work glorifies passion over reason and intellect, his characters glamorize suicide. His operas are too long. He had a bombastic conception of art, a faulty philosophy of the union of the arts.

In the old days the king thought he had to answer these accusations. He made fine distinctions (man and artist, inner and outer man). Then as he sank into dormancy, he took the scores with him, rolled them up, and slept with them while the anti-Wagnerian years went on. Occasionally he woke to hear a little of the old music, filtering through a leaky radio or an open spot in a symphony concert or framing the sound of some singer he wanted to hear again. The narrator noticed how aged it sounded now, with the retired king so close to sleep. Almost dead, as he said, faded sounds remembered like the old photograph of an old steamboat, the *Priscilla.*

But now that the boy king has revived, said the narrator, so has the opera. The old king has listened to the records and polished up the music, and finds it is more alive than ever, because he knows more and hears more than before. The king says the advocate's objections no longer matter. They have nothing to do with what is going on here, as the king makes his way once more through the carved time of the opera. The king says his conscience is clear, as if it were a moral matter.

The reader asks why—why does the absurdity or faultiness of the plot no longer matter? The narrator tries to understand: What actually happens to the boy king in the opera? He says: As you ride through the events of this opera (which are emotions), you think that they belong to the characters—the knight's despair in the third act, for instance. Yet it is not the simple misery described by the libretto. The emotion comes from what the musical journey has added to that. The real story is not the relationship of the knight to the princess, but the relation of both of them to the music on which they are traveling—this music which makes such a point of the fact that they are being taken for a ride.

All along the way, adds the narrator, this journey has landmarks, moments of light and darkness. You know they are ahead, you wait for them, you watch as they go by, and remember after they have passed. Moments—a few notes in the orchestra, a short passage sung—in which are concentrated the process of future turning into past. Each performance discovers new landmarks, waiting on the landscape like bridges and streams, taking their place among the others previously discovered. I found a new one last time, said the king, never noticed before: when the princess describes the relief that the poison drink can offer—

für tiefstes Weh', für höchstes Leid

—how the voice from deep and low leaps up like a cry on the word *höchstes,* yet falls short of the octave it is aiming for. And another:

the effect of perfumed suffocation as the princess identifies the death drink she wants the maid to prepare:

The landscape is most complicated in the third act, when the boy king lies wounded on his couch. His wound is his obsession—madness—in which the memories of past music are darkened by present loss, by a general overwhelming sense of total loss, loss of all music, as the boy king associates the shepherd's pipe not only with his present misery but with the deaths of his ancestors. Still there is the present music, which burns like the sun: he is obsessed with the painfulness of sense itself, with music itself as pain. So he curses the love drink, curses himself for drinking it, caught as he is in the burning music without a cure.

The critic asks, Do you mean that the hero's real obsession is *not* with love but with the music in which he is embedded? The medium in which he exists? In which his princess also exists? Which becomes your medium (boy king) while you listen. The grief in the third act is grief for the remembered music of acts one and two, memory all distorted and melancholy. The hero's longing is his longing to stop this movement of time, so that the moments past, the landmarks, will not disappear. The death he seeks is the end of the opera, whereupon the parts will recompose themselves into a final memory, and decomposition will cease. The love potion is consciousness itself. . . . It would follow, said the critic, that this is what the music does to a story which would otherwise have been merely a morbid tale of suicidal self-pity. It shows how emotions and relations look when subject to the consciousness of time. The consciousness of time is music, whose beauty is its own self-mourning grief, which blackmails you into sharing. He remembered the king's melancholy as the last act hurried toward its close: how the opera was getting away from him and soon would all be gone. How sad that always was, said the king. The narrator remembered the philosopher (Nietzsche, that is, said the reader) who spoke of the composer's "genius for finding the tones peculiar to the realm of suffering, oppressed, tortured souls." There was more:

> No one equals him in the colors of late autumn, in the indescribably moving happiness of a last, ultimate, all-too-short pleasure. . . . As the Orpheus of all secret misery, he is greater than anyone.
>
> . . . our greatest melancholist in music, full of flashes, tenderness, and words of solace in which none has anticipated him, the tonal master of a sad and indolent happiness.

Still, could this explain the boy king's enthusiasm, what made this painful experience a Favorite in the Mythology? The narrator asked, What happened to the scoundrel when you listened to this music? You heard a composer, but who was he? Did you ever find in that music of his maturity any voice or tone of the man you had read about? The boy king said no, it was all absorbed, washed clean. Then the narrator recalled how sometimes in performance the king took his eyes from the stage to look up at the proscenium of the house and hear the music reverberating there, and then he would become aware of the audience sharing what had now become *his* music, all his, the magic of his Mythology sounding in this house for everyone to hear. The scoundrel in the composer did not matter because the boy king himself had become the composer. It came out of the depths of his mind. That was what it meant to be a Favorite in the Mythology.

This embarrassed the boss even more. Let it be clearly understood, he said, I do not authorize and take no part in the boy king's claim. I did not compose the opera, nor did the boy king nor any of our constituents. It was composed by a man in another language, another century, another country, another world, a human being but no relation, a stranger. . . .

The king had stopped listening. He wanted to get down to the hard factual business of the Mythology. List the singers he has heard in this opera:

As the princess—*Live:* Flagstad (4), Traubel (2), Lawrence (1). *Broadcast:* Nilsson, Dernesch, Barlow.
As the knight—*Live:* Melchior (6), Svanholm (1) . . .

The king deplored the cold indifference of the boss, which had prevented him from attending a live performance in almost thirty years. Now that he was awake he wanted to go again to hear the new singers, see the new productions. Hearing the music alive again in his head, as fresh as it had ever been . . . while suddenly the narrator was asking, What was the difference (can you hear it?) between *then,* as the boy swam through the third act to the death he both longed for and dreaded, swam through heated gold to that oncoming death that was really life, liberating him from that moment, making him forget in the outdoors, on the aqueduct, with his friends—and *now,* as the man swam once more through that same gold to that same death, which was really a memory of being young, of all things gone, while the actual death, unknown, blank, and silent, waits not at the end of the well-known score but somewhere beyond it, around some corner, near or far, who knows?

33

And the reader must add this, telling how we went down to the beach the next morning, Horace and Nancy and Bobby and I. Horace did not want to go, afraid of missing the message from Ruthie, until I said that she would not arrive until afternoon. I felt the lie in this—I did not like it, but it was what Macurdy and Ruthie had told me to say and I couldn't get out of it. It satisfied

Horace, I thought, and we all went down together.

I sat on the beach in the sun, facing the sea, which was really the bay stretching out west and southwest to a blank horizon, and lay in the sand planning how to tell my children (who also lay in the sun, not noticing) about my lying here in this same place years ago—how, never a good swimmer, I mastered the beach by sitting here and looking and letting my consciousness swell. How this was the place that filled my mind in old times when I considered such matters as the difference between my existence and that of the rest of the world, the place best remembered to illustrate distance while at rest and to display how small I was in comparison with how far I could see. Remembered as the place in which I would look at the farthest land visible with only clear air between and recognize how invisible I must be to whoever at that distance was invisible to me. With the sun blazing down on me and the cool breeze from over the water threatening to shut my eyes and dry up the outer surfaces of my mind, I would observe some sand-crusted remnant of former fish washed on shore, and make the comparison, as if I knew how it was to be the beginning of life itself, a chemical molecule rising out of water and stone and step by evolutionary step becoming aware of itself.

And point out to them how little the beach itself was changed—despite the constant action of waves breaking on the shore and the unrememberable shifting of the dunes. Today it is calm, the little breakers only a few inches high as they roll up the shore at an angle. Tell how in geology no ground is more perishable than sand bars and beach, all shifting and washing away in a brief flash of geological time, though even after almost fifty years it is still the same: the same white beach stretching in a long curve miles to the south, bending into a long point of land that disappears gradually into the horizon. Far down that shore on a bluff still stands the old gabled hotel that was always there, and farther to the right a stone water tower near Woods Hole, eight miles away. Directly in front of us, the nearby green water turns bright blue farther out, and far away one can faintly see, off to the right, the opposite shore, coming into view, pale and blue but expanding and becoming more solid farther to the right. A high white lighthouse stands on a pile in the water between that shore and us, miles out. In the clear blue sky white streaks merge into white haze toward the horizon, reminding us of commerce.

I looked at these things with my grown children, ignoring what I saw with Horace—the number of cottages breaking up the woods above the shore to the south, all white trim and gray shingles and gables. And unsharing even with Horace, I tried not to look at the nearer cottages among the dunes beyond the bathhouses on our own beach, nor the one cottage, gray and small and distinct among others, whose existence I had discovered last night.

My brother was morose and preoccupied, as usual since he came back. And I was nervous with a feeling of danger that I told myself was not real, only the effect of my active imagination. I found Claudia in my mind, close but silent, head turned away, waiting. I remembered how zestfully my penis had pocketed itself in the other girl last night, and the thought shocked me with old-fashioned guilt. What have you done? As if I had taken something belonging to Claudia and given it to a stranger. Of course I hadn't given it away: I still had it this morning, and of course I could say that it was not Claudia's property anyway. Perhaps she would agree. But still there was this fear, and it had to do mostly with her presence, there in my mind. What would she do if she found out? Or was it not her behavior that I feared, but what she would *feel?* Or what she would think? I didn't want her to find out, I knew that . . . But then I wondered if the danger I feared was not something quite different. Not what Claudia might do or think, but what might happen to her because of me. Fear not of her but for her. What could that danger be? I did not know, yet I thought I must have done something thoughtless, even brutal, by exposing her to it. It made me feel sad for myself too, as if that brutality had changed my character and I could not go back to what I was. I was surprised to find myself worrying about the brutalization of my character at the age of fifty. I tried to laugh myself out of it, and yet it would not go away, this uncomfortable feeling that the damage threatening me was not only outer, but inner.

After sunning myself for a while, I went in to swim, joining Nancy and Bobby, while Horace remained behind. The water at first seemed cold, but I soon warmed up. The bottom was smooth with little ridges of sand. It sloped gently, and you could walk a long way before coming to the depth of your chin. I stayed in a long time, because I thought it would be good for me, and because we had driven all this way to enjoy the beach. And because Bobby and Nancy were staying in long, and because I was hoping that Horace would come in soon. I thought I wanted to be in the water while Horace was swimming. I was also remembering swimming in the dark, last night, down the beach, with a pebblier bottom and other things.

We were swimming near the north end of the beach, near the rocks, away from the crowds. This was private beach belonging to the occupants of the houses at the end where my grandfather's house used to be, and we swam here now at Horace's insistence by right of tradition, he said, since this was where we used to go as children. Below the high tide line was public, he said. It made me uncomfortable to ignore the signs, but Horace said they couldn't keep us out, so I let the responsibility rest with him.

After I had been in the water several minutes, I looked back at Horace on the shore (bulging white over his black trunks, with hair and beard dark all around his face), and I saw two people walking up the beach from the south. They were a short stocky man dressed in a dark business suit and a slim childlike girl almost naked with white skin (untanned) in a minimal bikini (yellow). Both wore dark glasses. In their grotesquerie I thought that I had seen them before. Then I thought they looked like Macurdy and Ruthie, and I wondered what they would be doing here. It proved how obsessed with them I had become, and then as I saw Horace getting up to meet them and Horace shaking the man's hand, I realized that they were in fact Macurdy and Ruthie and they had walked up the beach from their cottage—at least a mile. The sight of them filled me with vague stupid fright—if I did not join them immediately something bad would happen—and I struggled and pushed my way through the water and up the beach to where they sat.

"So here you are," I said.

"I just got in this morning," said Ruthie in a loud reminding voice.

I sat down. My brother did not look at me. Macurdy sat with crossed legs. He looked odd on the beach in his business suit, his dark glasses, his coat and tie and black leather shoes. Between Horace and Macurdy sat Ruthie. Her yellow bikini concealed almost nothing (making vivid the recent memory), though her dark glasses concealed her eyes. I was surprised how little pleasure Horace showed. He sat upright, jiggling pebbles in his hand, staring at the sand, no less morose than he had been before she came. So my blind fear in the water, which had not subsided, began to shape into blobs of questions. Is he angry? it began. Is he hurt, depressed? If he kills himself, will he blame me? Will I blame myself? What did I do? Did I do anything? Could I have done differently? When did my blame begin? Did it begin last night, in the cottage on the beach—or on the sand before the cottage? Or did it begin when I answered Macurdy's note at the motel, or, more precisely, when I let Macurdy take me to the cottage and allowed myself to enter when I saw Ruthie there—instead of saying to Macurdy, you are making me lie, take me back to the motel? Or was it before that? Did it begin when I began making tapes about the Morley Mythology with Macurdy, or before that when I let myself have dinner with him at The Great Wall of China? Or let him into my office? Or answered when he first broke his silence on the telephone? Should it be pushed back even before that, back to last summer, or the summer before, at Penny's cottage, back to the upstairs room, theirs, hers, back to the nod of my head, or to my sympathy, to my simple willingness to listen, even to that? All this subsequent blame that arose from that, was it? Or should I go all the way back, with stations of blame all along the way, back to the earliest when little brother first became little brother and someone said to me, Take care?

That kind of question. Also a resentful counter question: Why blame me? Was I my brother's et cetera? Then all these big questions spinning suddenly pulled away to open up (again) a core of inner questions about right now, right here. Was Horace satisfied with Ruthie's explanation that she had just arrived this morning? What had they told him to explain where she had arrived, how she had traveled, how she had been met? Was that in fact why Horace was so glum—because he could not believe them? Or had they, rather, told him more truth than I knew? Betraying me, perhaps, by admitting that Ruthie had in fact been here last night? In which case I was exposed already as a conspirator for not having told Horace myself. Of course in that case Ruthie would not have made such a point of having just arrived, in such an ostentatiously loud voice. No. But next I wondered how Horace could possibly believe that she had arrived only this morning—hurrying from the airport, I suppose, to the cottage to change in haste, so as to be able to stroll up here so casually and sit in the sand in her minimal bikini: how could Horace believe that? And wouldn't he recognize (having traveled all over Europe with her) the lying tone in her voice, which was so obvious even to me? And therefore know also my own lie, with whatever conclusions follow from that.

This made me wonder again why I had gone along with the conspiracy at all—why in fact didn't I tell Horace that Ruthie was already here last night, why didn't I tell him myself? Well, the answer to that was clear enough. The next question was whether Horace could figure this out, if he hadn't figured it out already. He would know I had lied about Ruthie because he could tell she had lied. Now, *why* would I lie about Ruthie? Must be because I had shared something with her that must be concealed from him. Now, what could anyone share with Ruthie that had to be concealed from Horace? So he would figure it out. Considering how morose he had been all morning, he must have figured it out already, before she even came up the beach. How could he? Detected it last night, just from looking at me when I came in, quite late, after they had got back from the movies? In the sand where we sat, I noticed her thin thigh muscle stretched toward her crotch as she sat cross-legged, and I noticed my own white and hairy knee, fat, with droplets of the bay still undried, and I noticed Horace sitting between us, and the memory of last night passed around him on both sides between her thigh and my knee, and I dared not look to see what he was looking at.

I wondered how to find out what he knew, how to make sure. I wanted to ask someone, but who? And with the four of us sitting here, not to mention my two kids not far away, it was not possible to talk about anything at all. Macurdy in his black glasses, his suit, Horace bare white, fat, with black beard, Ruthie also bare with black glasses—I was facing the idea that perhaps the lie was not Ruthie's and Macurdy's and mine to Horace, but Ruthie's, Macurdy's, and Horace's to me. What lie would this be? I didn't know, I couldn't imagine, but as I tried to figure it out, it occurred to me —with shock as if for the first time—that Horace must know what had happened in the cottage the last two summers when the others were away. Must *know*—not suspect or guess or wonder, but know. And not possibly, but probably, most likely, almost certainly. And not suddenly now this morning for the first time, but for weeks, all summer. For they had traveled all over Europe together. And it all began with his jealousy, not of him but of me. And he knew it and told her and she told me. And they traveled all over Europe together so she would have told him too. Therefore if he had not learned it earlier directly from her he would have learned it later when she told him, and therefore he certainly knew it and knew it all summer, knew it against me. So whose conspiracy was it now? Would he not see me as lying to him once again with her whom I (yes, I) had offered to him, taking her back in simple spite? Wouldn't he see us all linked together against him, obscurely and for unknown purposes, his estranged wife, her brother, his brother, the girl, all joined up in a plot to destroy him? Or was it rather a conspiracy against me? If Horace knew so much, was it perhaps all a scheme devised by him, in collaboration with his friends, to hurt my self-esteem and destroy my marriage—in retaliation for what I had become?

We sat there not talking. The sand and the sea were so bright

I could hardly keep my eyes open. I was stuck in my questions, blind: how could anyone ever know what anyone knew? And what did Horace mean by his ever-deepening gloom?

Finally he got up. "I'm going swimming," he said.

We watched him go down to the water. He waddled. I saw Ruthie and Macurdy exchange a look, as if she was questioning him, or they were questioning each other. After a few moments she too went down to the water. I noticed as she turned how even thinner she was than I had realized last night. Again the small piece of yellow cloth reminded me, and suddenly I realized that I shared this familiarity with both men here, with my brother Horace in the water and this man Macurdy who remained fully clothed on the beach. All three of us. But they knew her unwrapped better than I did, much better. This was disagreeable, I thought, as if I had been forced to settle in a foreign country with a hostile government. A moment of revulsion against my memory of last night, as I saw the girl fading away into the two grim men who seemed to sponsor her. The revulsion subsided as she reached the water's edge and looked back at us to wave.

They were spaced apart in the water. Farthest out was Horace, who had walked in until the water covered all but his head and then continued, swimming, only his head visible, going out into the bay. Halfway to him were Bobby and Nancy, ducking and splashing, and partway to them was Ruthie, still wading gingerly. Now the whole bay, the beach, the sky, seemed to have become very quiet. I noticed to the right, where the opposite shore was visible as a pale-blue strip, a series of sharp pointed white triangles posted against the shore—a row of sailboats far out, having a race. The lighthouse was to the right of them, standing in the bay: it was white, shaped like a pyramid, placed upon a large red-brick base that stood high above the level of the sea, and it looked enlarged by distance. Still farther to the right I saw a large freighter coming into view. It had come from the canal, out of sight to the right, and was now moving down the bay, somewhere in the middle, toward the sea. It was miles away, pale and blue and half transparent in the light haze, yet it stood up surprisingly large and high as if viewed through a magnifying glass, and I could discern its rusty sides as well as the plume of water tossed up by its bow, though it seemed to stand motionless.

"I apologize for my headache last night," said Macurdy.

I mumbled something, no clear words in my own mind.

"I hope your evening wasn't totally wasted," he said.

Quick sharpening of question: Did he really know what happened? Or not? Then suddenly I thought, Here we are alone and for the first time I know who he is and what his motives are. Or at least what she had told me last night his motives were. Ask him about that—and checked myself with the thought that he was mad and it would be dangerous to talk about anything real.

"It wasn't a wasted evening, was it?" He seemed to want an answer to the question.

The freighter was approaching the lighthouse. Now you could see the motion that was previously undiscernible, you could measure it against the lighthouse. I wondered whether the freighter would pass inside or outside the lighthouse and guessed it would pass outside. In a moment it came even, and I was right, it passed on the far side and looked actually as if it were a great distance beyond the lighthouse. It looked indeed as if the freighter were almost standing on the horizon and were not its actual size but magnified like a mirage over the distant shore and the distant sailboats.

I looked for Horace and saw him still heading outward, his head now just a small dot in the water as he swam without splashing, keeping his arms under water. On the other hand, my suspicion of Macurdy was probably itself slightly mad, paranoid, and I ought to overcome it.

"It wasn't wasted, was it?"

"No, it was a pleasant swim," I said. I realized I was getting nervous about how far out in the water Horace was swimming. I said, "He's going awfully far out."

"Did you have a nice talk with Ruthie?" he asked.

"Yes."

"What did you talk about?"

I didn't like the question and tried to avoid it. "Nothing special," I said. The freighter standing high, I noticed again its spouting plume at the bow and also a part of the propeller above the water level kicking up spurts. It was approaching the row of white triangles and again I wondered on which side it would pass. Probably it would pass on this side of them. Probably the freighter was not a mirage though it looked like one, and probably it looked so large because it was actually closer than it seemed to be. And Horace's head, going out toward a distant point that the freighter now was approaching, Horace's head was only a small dot, and I was nervous about his being out so far. "He should have turned back before now," I said. "If he goes out too far he won't be able to get back."

"Horace?" said Macurdy, looking out. "He won't drown himself now; he's got Ruthie."

The freighter was catching up with the row of sailboats and now it caught them, the first one and then the rest, swiftly, one after another, mowing them down. After another moment they appeared again, behind, one after another, the same as before.

"I got something I'd like to give you," said Macurdy.

Now even before I saw the envelope he took out of his pocket, and then still more as he handed it to me without looking at me, I felt that something nasty was about to happen, again the tangible swelling of the surface over the fear which had been lying underneath, breaching now like the back of a whale—reminding me of its existence with the thought that here it comes.

"Wait a moment," said Macurdy. "Before you look, I want you to understand this as a gesture of my good faith to you. I'm giving them to you; you can do what you like with them."

I opened the envelope and found a group of dark snapshots. Dark with dim white figures: pornography. The first shock was unpleasant (the first glimpse of pornography always is, said the narrator), followed by a momentary relax of relief, which was swept away in a new suspicion that made me look at them rapidly —five or six pictures which I turned over, one after another. They were all taken from the same angle in a dim yet clearly lit room, with a couch in the middle, a table and chinaware and glass cabinet in back, the familiar style of Cape Cod cottages. The pornographic couple were on the couch, a slim girl with long hair and a portly gray-haired man with an enlarged belly, naked in all the pictures. In the first picture the man was lying on the couch and the girl was kneeling on the floor, bent over him with her hands on his thighs. In the second they were both on the couch and he was leaning over her with his hand in her crotch while she held his member. In the third they were sitting up and she was leaning over his member and holding it, with her long hair concealing her face. In the fourth he was lying upon her and her legs were raised over his hips. In the fifth they were leaning back on the couch side by side, naked, exposed, their feet on an ottoman and his hands clasped behind his head with a complacent smile upon his face. His face in all the pictures was either earnestly or grinningly complacent, and I disliked him on sight. His elderly nakedness was offensive for reasons not yet clear. Then I realized that he reminded me too much of myself, as if he had concentrated the qualities I had worked all my life to get rid of—stupidity and selfishness and blindness. And then I realized (even before I got to the last picture, where the faces came into plain view) that it was of course myself. It took me a moment but only a moment to figure out the situation, who my partner was, when and where it had taken place, quickly eliminating Claudia from the picture and also Horace's Ruth, before recognizing what I already knew without having to recognize, that the pale white girl with the long hair was Ruthie and the reason the room looked familiar was that I had posed for these pictures last night.

So it was in fact a blackmail plot, and I had fallen into the trap.

"You took these?" I said.

"Somebody took them."

"Where were you?" I said. I could not figure out where the camera could have been.

"That doesn't matter," he said. I thought it did matter. Only later, while other things were more in front of my mind, did I realize from the angle of the pictures that they had been taken from the window. I remembered that she had shut the doors but she had not drawn the shades, and he was outside with his camera.

"You recognize these pictures?"

"I . . . never saw them before, if that's what you mean."

"Naturally not. I just developed them. Nobody has seen them but you and me. You recognize what they are?"

"I . . . suppose so." Fact was, my mind was too noisy at this moment for me to be certain of anything.

"You recognize the man? And . . . the other person?"

Was there a chance I was mistaken? No. "Is that—" I waited, hoping for him to complete the sentence. He did not do so.

Was he laughing? I couldn't tell because the glare was too bright. "I recognize them," I said at last. "What am I supposed to do with them?"

I heard him mumble, "For the Mythology." That is what I heard, and in the instant I saw the whole project of the past months come falling down. A crash followed by fire. I saw a burning of the books, pages and pages in flames, all the pages of my Mythology which I had entrusted to him, and it was as if wiping out finally all memory of my childhood. The flames became rage, and I thought for a moment that there would be a murder on the beach. I felt it coming, though I did not yet know who or by whom or why.

34

That was one moment, but even before I had time to recognize it, fear slammed down like a fire bulkhead, concealing the rage of the burning Mythology. It would go on smoldering out of sight, I knew, but first I had to cope with this. I repeated my question: "What am I supposed to do with these?"

So he changed his answer. This time his voice was clear and bland. "Whatever you like. They're yours. I give them up to you."

I saw Ruthie in the water, a small figure (and checked once more for my brother's head, a tiny dot out in the brilliance of the bay). "Does Ruthie know about these?"

"Ruthie has no interest in them," he said. "I give them to you as a gesture of good faith."

Good faith, good will—I was relieved. If he said it was a gesture of good faith, it must be so. But I wondered, I couldn't figure it out. I said, "I don't understand."

"I'm giving them up to you. Giving them up. That's what I mean by a gesture of good faith."

"Oh," I said. "I see."

"I want to make sure you understand that."

"What?"

"I know you have been suspicious of me," said Macurdy. "No doubt at first you had good reason. But it has been difficult for me to prove my good faith."

"I see," I said.

"I understand your suspicions. Perfectly. I think it was wise and sensible of you not to let your guard down too swiftly."

"Oh," I said. I thought. I looked around him, the dazzling beach beyond. Finally I said, "Of what have I been suspicious?"

"Why, it's the most natural fear in the world, I suppose. The fear of someone knowing too much about you. I suppose the blunt and vulgar word for that is blackmail. The power someone has over you if he knows too much. I understand it very well."

I stared at the sun shining on his face, though not at his eyes, concealed behind dark glasses.

"So now you hope to blackmail me?" I said. My words were carefully chosen. I had first thought of saying, "What do you want?" but that sounded as if I considered myself vulnerable, which would make me so. Then I considered, "So now you are blackmailing me," but that too seemed to concede too much, so I changed to "hope to blackmail," in my own hope to protect my bargaining position, until I could figure out just what my position actually was.

"You misunderstand me," he said. Gesture of the hands; how

difficult it is to be understood. "I am giving up to you the evidence that I could blackmail you with. That's what I mean by a gesture of good faith."

I said, "You think I could be blackmailed by those pictures?"

"I am telling you I have no intention of blackmailing you."

"That's not what I'm saying," I said. "I'm asking if you think I could be blackmailed by such pictures—if you did have such an intention?"

He looked away, "I think that's a matter between you and your image," he said. "I'm giving you the pictures so that you can feel perfectly safe and trust me with any secret, even the most damaging ones. I want to allay your suspicions once and for all."

"Oh," I said. I recognized my tendency to believe what anyone tells me. But also my suspicious tendency, my sensitivity to mendacity and deceit, as also to irony and sarcasm, which made me now both believe and disbelieve him. My powers of analysis were lagging behind both belief and disbelief. I said, "So you're giving these pictures to me to do what I like with, and that ends the case, eh?"

"I hope that you will trust me better from now on," said Macurdy.

I said nothing. Sat there, silent, and Macurdy also silent, and I looked out over the bay to the place where my brother's head had been. The freighter in the distance had passed on to the left, smaller now as it moved down the horizon. I remembered the steamboats that used to go between New Bedford and Woods Hole, crossing the horizon to the left, barely distinguishable silhouettes on the horizon, with a trail of smoke beginning as a narrow line and spreading out into a wash across the sky—steamboats that had not run for many years. I remembered the banked fires of the insulted Mythology and asked: "What did you mean about the Mythology?"

"What about the Mythology?"

"About putting the pictures in the Mythology."

"What? You want to put those pictures in the Mythology?"

"Certainly not. That's what you said."

Why, he laughed. "I never said any such thing."

"I heard you. You gave me the pictures and said, 'For the Mythology.' You said it, and I heard it, and I feel—" How? I groped for my shifting anger and self-defense.

"That's your imagination," he said. "Why, that would have been outright insulting, and I wouldn't blame you for taking offense."

Well, my mind following along slowly in the heat of the sunshine found another question to ask. "Well, then, why, if you want only to prove your good faith, did you take those pictures in the first place?"

"I told you," he said.

"I don't recall."

"I took them so as to prove to you once and for all that you can trust me. To prove my good faith."

I repeated the explanation to myself: He took the pictures so as to give them to me and thereby prove that he had no intention of blackmailing me. He was outside the window with his camera, equipped with fast film, in order to do this. He took the pictures not in order to blackmail but in order not to blackmail me. I listened to my explanation and it seemed to me as if my explanation was the opposite of what I was explaining to myself. I said to myself, If he is blackmailing me, what damage can he do? I asked myself, Are we prepared for a catastrophe, or do we need more time to get ready? Then I noticed the silence that had come down between Macurdy and me. I thought, He thinks I am not polite for not having thanked him for not blackmailing me, therefore I had better. I said, "Thank you very much."

He shrugged his shoulders. It's nothing, that's all right. I wondered if he wanted me to apologize for my adventure with Ruthie—for wouldn't that be painful to him? Wasn't he showing forbearance in not accusing me, even going to such lengths to demonstrate his good faith? I remembered how generously he had offered Ruthie as a companion to my brother. I looked out at the bay, the blue water beyond the green, where my brother's swimming head had been. Would he find my apology outrageous for falling so far short of my injury to him? Was that why he took the pictures:

to prove how nobly he could control his indignation for the offense I have given him—to show me that he knew the offense, and in spite of that was willing to forgive, to forgo? In a trembling of injury, he must have come downstairs from his migraine when he realized what was happening, taken his camera, gone outdoors—yet he could not have come downstairs, not while we were in the room. He must have been outside already, before we came up to the house. With his camera. Therefore. Suddenly I was explaining to myself the real reason why he had taken those pictures—for that was the question that ought to be asked: not merely why he was giving the pictures up, but why he had taken them—and suddenly it seemed very clear to me why he had taken them. Why, it was so that he could—

Suddenly I looked again at where my brother's head had been —*had been* rather than *was.* Because I couldn't see it. Realized I had been looking there for several minutes, all the while thinking about something else—all that while trying to pick up the reappearance of Horace's head out there where it had so quietly disappeared. I realized that the flat surface of the bay out there was not as flat as it looked, for besides the glittering of the blue, there were small waves invisible from here behind which specks on the surface could hide. But they could not be big enough to conceal so long the speck I was looking for—they could not conceal it at all. *He ought to be visible out there,* there was nothing in the way, *and yet I could not see him.* I began to lose my sense of where he had been. Particular points in the water dissolved, everything melted into everything else. I looked at the wide band of shallow green water closer to shore where the others were, looked quietly for him there, but he wasn't there nor should he be because he had been swimming farther out, which I knew because I had been watching him until he disappeared.

A cruel idea of what had happened had already formed in my mind. It had formed actually the moment I first noticed his disappearance, or possibly it was the forming idea that first called his disappearance to my attention. But I was not yet ready to let that idea speak. It was still only the kind of idea that occurs to you when something unplanned appears, of the drastic extreme that is always a possibility to change everything forever. Usually I don't grant respectability to such ideas because they are so common and cause so much dissension. The important thing was to look for Horace and find some less drastic explanation for why I could not see him. And say to Macurdy, quickly but without alarm: "Where's Horace?"

He looked up. Looked at the bay through dark glasses. "Isn't he out there?"

"I don't see him," I said. I could see he was looking at the green water where the others were, and I looked too, and counted: Bobby, Nancy, near each other, Ruthie apart.

"He was swimming far out, and now I've lost him," I said.

"Far out?"

"He was swimming straight out. He kept going out further and further and now I've lost him." There was a little of the cruel idea getting into my voice now, cutting away some of its foundation, making it shake a little. I got to my feet, thinking that would increase my range and bring him into view. It didn't.

I saw Macurdy scanning the bay. Saw him looking down the beach toward the left where the other people were, down toward the bathhouses.

"He didn't go that way," I said, though I also looked there. "He was swimming straight out. He kept going further and further."

Macurdy also got to his feet. "He must have come back."

"He couldn't have. I would have seen him."

"Well, he isn't out there now," said Macurdy.

Again I looked at the people in the water far down the beach —but it was impossible he could have gone down there—and across all the visible surface of the sea to the rocks on the right, and then I looked up and down the beach itself—though I would certainly have seen him if he had come back, nor could he have come so quickly. I looked up to the road where the car was parked —if he had gone up to the car, though he could certainly not have got back from the water and up to the car without my seeing. And if he had not come with us to the beach this morning or if he had not come with us to the Cape . . . but now I could think of no reason for not seeing him except my cruel idea, which was pressing me now with pain, and I asked myself, Is this an emergency?

I wanted to ask Macurdy if this was an emergency, and I said: "He was swimming straight out. He kept going out further and further and then disappeared."

"Are you sure?"

"Yes, I'm sure."

"He must be out there, then."

"He can't be. I don't see him."

"You said he was out there."

Now the idea finally hit the surface and became an emergency, statable in words, "He must have gone under," I said. "He's been under too long."

"You think he's drowning out there?" It was Macurdy who said it, not I, not I, but once said it became my own idea too. The sea looked too placid to contain a struggling man, and my mind worked with the word *drowning,* which was not the same as the word *dying,* I said to myself. I knew that the real impact of the catastrophe would strike me later, for already it was a catastrophe and probably already finished. Meanwhile I wondered what to do about it.

"What should we do?" I said.

"Are you *sure* he's out there?" said Macurdy.

"I *saw* him and now he's gone!" I said. Thinking fast now: since he could not possibly be anywhere else he must be out there, and since I couldn't see him he must be under water, and since he must have been under water for many minutes he must be drowning, and if he was drowning this was an emergency and it was probably already too late for help, but since that conclusion was unacceptable as yet because too sudden, too unwarned, too final, too overwhelmingly terrible, it was necessary to do something worthy of the emergency so that it wouldn't be on your conscience for the rest of your life. But what could you do? Call for help? Call the authorities, those who rescue people—but who were they, where were they? Who was there to give help but those of us who were here, and what could we do?

Go out and get him, I said to myself. You should be in the water now, rescuing your brother, bringing him to shore.

Now that I knew it was an emergency, I felt free to rescue him.

"Call help," I said. "I've got to find him." Still hesitating a moment, since Macurdy in dark glasses simply looked at me, I realized that I was now committed to rescue, and began to run.

I ran splashing into the water and ran or struggled to walk through the shallow water that held my legs back, pushed heavily through the deepening water, turning my body from side to side so as to move faster. Shouted to Bobby and Nancy and Ruthie as I went: "Go help Horace! Go help Horace!"

They did not hear me, and then one by one they did, looking at me across the water with puzzled faces. I raised my arm and pointed and shouted, "He's drowning out there! Help me find him!" I saw Nancy understand first and begin to follow, and then Bobby. Farther away, Ruthie made no response. My children were behind me, at a distance, as I pushed outward.

I came to the depth of my chin and realized that now I would have to swim. And I did not know in what direction to swim. At this depth I could see the surface of the water for only a few yards around. It was milky and lightly disturbed by ripply folds. I would have to cast off and swim and I had only the side stroke and not much endurance, and I did not know in which direction to go. I knew that whatever direction I chose, if I was not aimed just right, the divergence between my course and his would increase with every stroke, and suddenly I knew it was impossible for me to find him, hopeless. I stood there at the limit of my depth and bounced on my toes trying to see farther, though I had seen much farther when I was standing on the shore and had seen nothing. And that was why I was out here now in the water seeing less.

I waited while Bobby and Nancy came up, and while I waited I recognized that my cruel idea had become an historical fact. My brother Horace was dead. That was the fact. *Already* dead, I said, making a point of it against the possibility that he might still be only dying, in the last throes of struggle out there somewhere. But he could not be still dying, I said to myself now, making a point of the fact that he was already dead.

The fact was terrible, but it was too soon to feel it—only the knowledge that it was so, that the present had defaulted on a debt to the future. The fact was a boundary line, I knew that. It marked a line between the age in which Horace lived and a new age in which he did not, and already we were in the new age. I did not like being in this new age, so suddenly, with so little warning, with so little consideration, and no opportunity to choose or turn back —not yet. The new age had no character at all, it was fresh and empty, while Horace's death stood behind me like a wall cutting off all the time that I had known and lived in. I couldn't think about it yet, though, because I was out here standing in water up to my chin, my children coming out to me, with the problem of what to do next (which was the eternal problem of my life). I had to keep bouncing on my toes so as not to get a snootful of salt water.

"Where is he?" said Bobby.

"Out there." I waved loosely. "Out there somewhere."

He leaped up to look around and then plunged outward swimming the crawl, strong and fast. "No, no," I called after him, and Nancy called too. After a few moments he stopped and once again leaped up for a look and continued swimming. A new and worse cruel thought began to form. "It's impossible," I said to Nancy. "We can't find him, we don't know where he is."

The next time Bobby paused to look around I called him. "Come back," I said. "It's no use." After a few moments Bobby was back, and we stood there together looking out and at each other.

"It's hopeless," I said.

"Hopeless?" said Nancy. "Jesus!" I saw that she was crying. I was surprised, for no sad feeling had yet broken through the stone wall of shock that contained this moment in my own mind.

"He's been out of sight too long, and we don't know where to look." I asked myself, Would that explanation, which seemed so reasonable here, stand up under my own intensive questioning in years to come?

We began walking through the shallowing water to the beach.

"We'd better call the police," I said. "Send someone out in a boat."

"Why, is there still a chance?" said Nancy, cutting herself off as she realized what the boat would be looking for. "Oh!" she said.

"Why did he go so far?" asked Bobby. I don't know, I said. "Did he call for help?" asked Nancy. No, he just disappeared. I was watching him (what was I doing, actually? I tried to remember. Talking to Macurdy), and then suddenly he disappeared. "So there's no possibility," said Nancy, "except that he's drowned out there."

"Do you think he did it deliberately?" said Nancy. There was another dark idea—he had finally succeeded—not respectable until Nancy had spoken it. I took it.

"How can anyone know?" I said, although actually I had already accepted it. He had simply headed out and not being much of a swimmer, swum as far as he could without turning back until exhaustion pulled him under.

Now what to do next became the question of what to do about this catastrophe which had defined itself as a definite event and could therefore be stated: Horace had drowned at the beach at the Cape. Probably a suicide. The first task was notification. Whom should we notify? First the police, to send a boat to find the body. (There was a spark of shock given off by applying the word *body* to my brother Horace.) Then send word to Penny. Then Claudia —call her. Would she be expected to leave the Festival for whatever it was that we would be doing? What in fact would we be doing? Send word to Ruth? Was this necessary, was it expected, should anything be expected of her? Who else to notify besides Penny and Claudia and possibly Ruth? I wanted to notify Mother and Father, but since they were already dead themselves, I could not. As we approached the beach, I saw the three of them standing there watching us—Macurdy in his business suit and the other two in their bathing suits—and wondered if they would help us take care of whatever had to be done. I began to think of *arrangements.* Who would take charge of them? Was this my responsibility? Funeral matters? Coffin? Where should the funeral take place? What money? If I had to take charge, would Penny help me? And yes, whose money would I use? I was glad to have my children here as well as the three I saw on the shore—Macurdy and the girl and the fat man with the beard—to help me with what had to be done.

Under all this rapid movement of thought, I heard another current trying to decide what to do about Horace. Repeating, my brother has died. Can I believe it, can I stand it? I heard one faction trying to wake up another faction out of its sleep with the news, which the other seemed unable to hear. I heard another faction trying to reach back into the time when Horace was alive, trying to keep it from sinking into the past.

I noticed the real things around me, the water still dragging against my legs, the white sand up ahead of us, the car parked on the road above the beach, the air, the sky, all things which existed in a world in which I existed, and I had to tell myself that Horace, my brother Horace, did not exist in this world. All these things I could see, this water, the sand, the car, the sky, the day itself, all this which he had known was still there, but his knowledge of it had died. I felt the shrinking of the world by his going out of it. I wondered how much love I had left for him in a lifetime of drawing apart after so close a childhood and I wondered how much live grief this event would arouse in me. Then I realized he had been one of the real things around me like this water itself or a rock on the sand, my brother Horace, cranky, personal, irritable, abrasive, with whom I had struggled just as I struggled with the tangible world which pulled against my legs or scratched my feet like the pebbles I walked upon as we neared the shore. I realized that it was terrible for him to be dead, and would always be so even after I had forgotten about it, and soon it would reach me, the feeling and the reason for it. Suddenly I remembered at breakfast just this morning, Horace telling Bobby and Nancy about a walk we took, the older brother and the younger, when we were still boys, up to the pair of water towers in the woods—and the momentary feeling I had then (only this morning) of being closer to my brother than I had been for a while, and now the memory was a sudden whiff of first grief rising like underground water in my throat with warnings of more to come. But this was checked abruptly by a sudden question as I noticed Ruthie standing on the shore (between Macurdy and Horace, watching as we approached), since suddenly I remembered again what had happened to me last night: the question whether Horace had indeed committed suicide because of that. The question was shocking: did he swim out there to die because his brother had deceived him? I wondered, will I be able to stand that possibility once it comes home to me? We were stepping out of the water onto the sand, and I looked up the beach to where they were waiting, with a feeling of dread that spread to them now—what if it should also occur to *them* that Horace had committed suicide because of me, what if it had already occurred to them, and was this why they were standing there now looking so disapprovingly at us, and then Nancy said, "But there's Uncle Horace now."

I had been looking at him for at least a minute without realizing it.

35

"Wow! what a relief!" cried Nancy, and Bobby too, and they leaped like animals up to where Horace stood with the others. I too felt the relief for a moment, all the air lightening and a great physical pressure in my body seeming to disappear. Oh, yes, it was a great relief, I said to myself, to let all those thoughts, those adjustments I had already begun to make, all that shock and that dread of emotions yet to come—to let all that wash away in one swift recognition, the sight of my brother alive again with no boundary lines after all between the world as it now is and as it was an hour ago. A great relief, though not as great as I thought it should be, while the residue of shock and the vague sense of something unpleasant about the whole experience remained.

"What the hell is going on?" said Horace.

"We thought you had drowned," said Nancy.

"Drowned? Why the hell should I drown?"

I was out of breath. "I saw you swimming—you went straight on out and then you disappeared. We couldn't see you anywhere."

"Where were you?" asked Nancy.

"Nowhere," said Horace. "I swam over to the rocks and walked back."

"I didn't see you. I saw you swimming straight out and then you disappeared. We looked and looked."

"What a stupid thing. I was over by the rocks."

I looked at Macurdy for confirmation. I realized that I didn't want to talk to Macurdy, though I didn't know why. I overcame this and asked: "Isn't that right? Didn't we look and not see him anymore?"

He said, "I tried to call you back when I saw him on the rocks. You didn't hear me."

"What a stupid thing," said Horace.

"Well, Jesus, Uncle Horace," said Nancy. "We were scared to death!"

"Sorry!" said Horace. Then he softened a little, as he realized what a shock we had been through for his sake. Or so he did with Nancy and Bobby, though I could not tell whether he meant to relax with me. They sat down and someone said something funny and they laughed, but I could not pay attention because the relief I had expected to feel from Horace's recovery did not come. Something bad had happened in spite of Horace's rescue, though I could not remember what it was. I knew I had better find it or it would get worse, and then at last I did remember. I looked at Macurdy, who sat in the sand tossing pebbles. He tossed one pebble and tried to hit it with the next. He stared at the sand in his dark glasses.

After a while Horace spoke to Ruthie and they walked off down the beach. Nancy and Bobby stretched out on their backs to expose themselves to the sun. They seemed to be asleep. Macurdy reached into his pocket and again handed me the envelope.

"Don't you want this?" he said.

I took it. "What is it you want from me?" I asked.

"Nothing. I'm giving you these pictures to show my good faith."

I knew better. It was clear to me now. His good faith was his proof that he had the goods on me and would only take his time before exercising his power. His denial of blackmail was his polite way of informing me that I was his prisoner and could expect to hear later rather than just now what his terms were. It was clear to me because I knew that he had planned to take the pictures in advance, because he had himself arranged for everything that happened last night, and I knew also that his giving me the pictures in good faith was his way of telling me that he had other copies, as well as negatives. It was clear to me also that once blackmail started it would never stop, for the hold on me was tangible. I was his slave. I saw myself facing a ruin that he would bring about—in his own time, unaffected by anything I could do. I realized that in the economy of blackmail, slavery and ruin were alternatives—I could avert ruin by being a slave or avert slavery by accepting ruin—but on the beach then it was clear he meant me to take both ruin and slavery.

Still, I got over the worst of my gloom before long. I began to think how to fight back. I did not know how I could, but I thought it should be possible. I thought a Dean should be able to thwart a blackmail attempt based upon such foolishness as those pictures exposed. It would depend on what I was willing to sacrifice in order to fight back. I did not know, for how could I, until I knew what demands would be made?

In the afternoon, I found a moment to be alone in the motel, and then I burned the pictures. I knew it made no difference, because Macurdy had copies, but at least it got them out of my hands. I enjoyed pretending that I was burning the episode out of my mind. There was a big task ahead of me, for my narrator, but that could wait.

In the meanwhile, I turned my curiosity, idly, to the question of what had tricked me into believing that Horace had drowned. But I couldn't concentrate and I got nowhere with it.

PART FOUR

36

Thus went the story which by constant review the narrator made firm and gave to the reader—to pass on to Claudia if needed or keep for its value as a secret. The reader rehearsed it constantly during the weeks that followed. When autumn came he studied it less frequently. In November, days went by when no one looked at it at all. It would reappear (reflections of it) sometimes on a quiet evening while we sat reading another book.

What was the trouble with me? Simply that my voice was absolutely buried. I would wake up and find that I could barely speak. . . . I would dig for that buried voice of mine, actually dig. I estimated that I brought it up one tone every half-hour. To loosen it faster, I would go into the bathroom and yell out as long and as loud as I could. I could sing quite freely in my hotel suite, but I believe my neighbors could hear me when I let go, with what feelings I dared not speculate.

Some slippery spot in the road, something the narrator had forgotten about, we thought.

I hated so much to have anybody listening when my voice was in such bad shape. I didn't want to have them say they had heard Kirsten Flagstad screaming in her bathroom. I must have sounded like a sea lion. So what do you suppose I did? I turned on all the faucets of the sink and bathtub and made as much noise as I could to cover up all that yelling.

It was taking our breath away, this forgotten thing, and for a time we did not know what it was. She sat in the other chair reading, and the boss was content, except for this short-breathed fear like ice forming over something cold that the narrator had buried. Then suddenly the narrator remembered the rusty railroad track between sandhills with grass growing up between the rails, and the ghostly engine, and he dropped through to the beach, at night with heads bobbing in the water and one head moving in toward shore leaving the other two behind, and dropping through again right into the reader's library, where the story fell off the shelf, pages open, complete, shocking, just as he had put it together last summer, already four months ago.

Four months without a word, said the narrator. The more time passes, the safer we shall be. You really forgot it good this time, in the consternation over the loss of the great singer's voice. (Sounded like a sea lion, did she?) Would there be no blackmail after all? Full of hope, the mother asked the question, and put the narrator to work again.

Said the narrator: How terrible the fright was, even more than we knew, after the false death of Horace and the man Macurdy's denial of evil motive. I went back to the motel, burned the pictures, and waited. How swiftly then Macurdy and Ruthie disappeared from the Cape, leaving only a brief message, and how uncomfortably we—Horace, Nancy, Bobby, and I—remained and stayed our week. Then we returned to Maine, to Penny and Claudia, who had come back from the Music Festival, and Horace went back to New York and we all came home in the car. Waiting quietly all the time. Macurdy to make his move. Since it did not reach us in Maine, it would be waiting for us at home. Since it was not there when we got home, we would still have to wait.

The narrator remembered how hopefully the manager asked him to repeat Macurdy's words about good faith. The manager believed those words, because words are powerful, and if people don't believe what other people say, then the world will go to chaos. And also because the air was still clear at the beach and the sky continued bright and the sea remained calm and people still kept going to the beach to lie in the sun and we ourselves were still lying in the sun. So at first it was between the simple acceptance of good faith affirmed in the sun and the assumption of an invisible catastrophe that you could do nothing about, and the simple acceptance seemed more natural.

Only there was always the narrator to remind you of the trap that had been set, the pictures taken, the impossibility of composing a rational narrative that could be squared with good faith. Soon the narrator had destroyed Macurdy's good faith completely, and the only problem was not whether it was a catastrophe but what kind it was. This was the question the reader kept asking. What is the actual disaster, what ruination has it actually caused? Who has been hurt by it? What cost? It's coming, said the narrator. *What* is coming? insisted the reader. The worst, said the narrator.

Let's go through it, said the narrator. Because of the pictures you are subject to blackmail. To prevent his using the pictures, you must meet whatever demands he makes. He will say, *Do this,* or I will destroy you with these pictures, and you will *do this* so as not to be destroyed. After a while he will think of something else: *Now do this,* and it won't matter what you have already done for him, *now* you will *do this* too. And each time you *do this* you will be more vulnerable, more corrupt, than before. He will say you *did that* because you were blackmailed into it, and now I have you for that too. He will blackmail you just as God blackmails living creatures for their lives and health.

But what does he stand to gain? asked the manager. What can he get from us? Does even a Dean, asked the brother, have money enough to make it worthwhile to a professional blackmailer? Simple power, suggested the narrator. To make you aware of him, your weakness against his strength. Perhaps he can give orders to the deanship. Make you do something as Dean you wouldn't otherwise do. Take some stand you wouldn't otherwise take. Countenance dishonesty in some planted case, suspend charity and generosity in another. Because he still nurses the old grudge, he wants to humiliate as many of us as he can, said the narrator to the rest of us.

This must not be permitted, said the father, in a firm voice. To preserve the integrity of the organization, the blackmail must be refused from the start, and if it hurts us externally, so be it. These words revived the boss, who had been near to fainting. Right, he said, the threat must be resisted. He gave orders to the manager: ask the narrator what is the best way to resist.

So in November the narrator went through it all again, this inspection of possibilities, as he had been doing constantly since the summer. *Do nothing and wait,* he said. Sooner or later you will hear. When he calls, you will refuse, you will decline to be moved. And what will Macurdy do then?

What can he do? said the narrator. The worst he could do. He takes his pictures to the newspaper, the board of directors, the President of the University, the alumni director. To make a fuss on behalf of parents. Moral turpitude. Corrupting our children. The Dean exposed in all the bareness of his ass. Could you be fired? asked the reader. Public embarrassment forcing you to resign? So the blackmailer would hope, but the narrator had doubts. Probably the newspaper would refuse to print the pictures. The member of the board (or the President), being wise and civilized, would recognize the malice. Who is that naked man in the pictures? he would ask. Is it our Dean? Well, it might be, but can you really be sure? If you can't prove it, it seems to me you would be wiser just to turn around and . . . etcetera, said the narrator.

So where's your catastrophe? asked the reader. A little ridicule, a little shock for a while if it gets that far. Sexual slipups seldom make catastrophes nowadays, said the reader. They embarrass, but they don't destroy. The narrator tried again. All right, he said. What the blackmailer will do is give the pictures to Claudia. That's the scare he's got up his sleeve. He can't destroy your deanship, but look what he can do to your home.

What happens now? asked the reader. Let's try and see, said the narrator. First the blackmailer shows Claudia the pictures. Says,

Have you seen these doings at the beach last summer while you were at the Music Festival? How I admire the cool disregard with which you give your husband his freedom! You *did* know, didn't you? Hope I am not giving away secrets. Of course she recognizes the viciousness of the blackmailer. That's not her husband, the pictures are a forgery. So she hopes, perhaps for several days, in a desperate effort which she can't keep up against the truth, which forces itself upon her finally—her undeniable recognition of what the pictures show. Still she tries to protect him, for she knows that this is a frame-up—how could her husband (not a total idiot) have got caught in such pictures unless he was lured, tricked, trapped? And thus perhaps she disappoints the blackmailer—but the damage has been done anyway, said the narrator, as she continues to reflect on what the pictures, trap or not, reveal. My husband smacking his lips at a girl with long hair. The concreteness of the pictures, dim and blurred though they be, narrows the track on which her imagination can ride. My intimate Michael with his privates showing, pointing them at an unknown girl with bare breasts, navel, and privates of her own. How ugly it looks! It reminds her (said the narrator) of her own bare breasts, navel, and privates, of Michael the same after a quiet evening, of his look and his touch full of their twenty-five years. Now she realizes that whatever trickery was worked on him, he is in the picture enjoying himself and he could not have been trapped unless he had led himself into the trap. Drawn by this other girl's breasts, navel, and privates—giving obvious proof that her own gift of these parts, freely given for so many years, was not enough for him. Perhaps she tries to snuff out the quick anger that this thought provokes, but that's hard because already she will have recalled—she will remember this instantly—the shock of last summer which has hardly had time to subside, with all its explanation and counter-explanation, its groping confusion of threat, promise, and forgiveness. It occurs to her that perhaps we are not dealing with some lapse on Michael's part, not some momentary forgetfulness nor even some foolish overpromising that he is unable to keep, but with a whole unsuspected secret way of life, a deep concealed habit. Perhaps she lives, has lived all along, only on the outer edge of his private life, perhaps his life is full of private cells with women in them, unknown to her.

Such a thought will make her dizzy, said the narrator. Who is this man to whom she has given everything? The narrator saw her stagger, frightened, running up to the room she shared with him, falling upon the bed, struggling with her desire to scream. Talking to her beagles about it, confiding in Ethelred and Clawmor's King Arthur what she could no longer confide in him. The narrator projected into this easily, assisted by memories from another time, of a young husband with doubts about his young and new wife in times before there were children, when she was so little known, so scarcely understood. After a while she will try to recover the calm appropriate to a master musician and candidate for a directorship of a musical institute. Hours each day of intensified practice at the piano, not even reading the newspaper, nor books, shaping her hands and fingers into Czerny and Chopin and Beethoven while her thoughts try to find new slots to settle in. She makes an effort to subdue irrational fears. Whatever else he is, she will say, Michael is still Michael—predictable in his open parts. She will try a light attitude toward the whole question, the liberal modern view that a man with a lot of women might wish his wife to take. Well . . . if he is the kind of man who needs a continual replenishment (new samples) of breasts, navels, and privates, so, she will try to say, that's the kind of man he happens to be. Trouble with that, she can't get rid of the idea it's a humiliation to her. She will have a bad time erasing the image of all those young girls offering their sympathy to the poor husband for his old wife (*not* laughing at her, though, she won't let herself imagine that), girls flattering themselves that they are relieving the poor man of some deep need (younger, or simply *different,* breasts, navel, et cetera) that the old wife can't provide. She uses Chopin's Polonaise to destroy their complacency—it is good for the purpose—making the piano tremble with military rage, with chords crashing on their heads.

She will grieve (and the narrator grieved with her) for the illusion that what she shared with Michael was the knowledge that they were both crazy—she with her beagles, her companion and utility dogs, he with his "mythology," both with their egos, their ambitions, their deanships and directorships—and that all this was healed in the secret life of their bed at night. But since that is no longer private (projected the narrator), it is as if the craziness is no longer shared, and they are all floating off into their separate isolations.

Now she will remember (the narrator got it back from the reader) what they said the other time. She broke off from the Polonaise (that time too) and said, "You must give me some warning if it happens again." He said, "It won't happen again." She played the opening chords again. "If it does I couldn't stand it." *Bang*--didiBang! "I'd have to divorce you." Di-biddybiddy-*Bang*-didiBang. "Then after I divorced you, you and I could have an affair in peace."

Now—said the narrator—she finds herself challenged on the seriousness of her threat. Forced to ask herself: Do you mean to carry it through? Are you required to? Then she will begin to see (the narrator began to see) her husband's real answer (this, not the feeble promise of his words) to the threat she had made in her anger. It was his demand that she choose: divorce if you must or yield me my right to entertain girls with long hair and new (different) breasts (et cetera) when I wish. And when she gets that message, so indirect, devious, won't it then become possible, even likely (as she continues to reflect) that it was no stranger blackmailer who sent her the pictures, but her own strange little-known husband himself, a blackmailer of a different kind? Could she, so confronted, protect herself from even such a dark suspicion as that? Terrified, repulsed, will she divorce him finally not simply from disappointment, nor even from disgust, but from fright?

This must be stopped at once, said the boss. So the narrator tried again. This time, to forestall the blackmailer, you show her the pictures yourself. No, you burned your copies in the motel. Instead you tell her about them, taking her into your confidence. One evening, quiet, face to face in our living room. How Macurdy, and then Horace, and how when we got to the Cape. There was a note, and I called, and Macurdy said, and we thought it was only. So we went down to his cottage on the beach—tell her that—and Macurdy suggested, and how foolish it seemed, and we, and then again we, and then Macurdy had a migraine and disappeared, and then she, and you simply could not help. How foolish you knew, even then. And afterward more so. And then when you saw the pictures. You never meant. So you tell how she was just an easygoing, free with herself, with Horace also, but dishonest, obviously. And how it means nothing, absolutely, as to you and me. How we could make a solid front against. How nobody means anything to me as you. How you ask her, how humbly, please. The narrator described her sympathy. Disappointed of course that you at your age of life after so much. Annoyed perhaps at your stupidity in allowing yourself, in not being able to see, to foresee. Nevertheless, sympathy, solid front. And then, said the narrator, the blackmailer will withdraw defeated, for if Claudia is on your side, what harm could he possibly?

So you recommend, said the manager, that we tell her all, to disarm the blackmailer in advance? Tell Claudia everything at the earliest opportunity. The earliest opportunity did not come, however. At the cottage, first he had to wait until Horace had left. Then he couldn't do it, because it was vacation and they were Penny's guests, and the rooms were too small and the walls too thin. Wait until we get home. On the way home, the narrator warned that the blackmail message might be waiting for him, might even be in the mailbox when he arrived. The manager decided to make the revelation that night in the motel, yet when the time came the opportunity vanished because they were tired and Claudia wanted to read in bed, and he had a hard day's drive ahead of him tomorrow. The next day in the car the narrator said he had missed his last chance, for you can't discuss it in front of Nancy and Bobby. Yet when they got home, he was still spared by the blackmailer, and the narrator said he was lucky and the manager resolved again to find an early opportunity.

After that maybe it was the narrator himself who prevented the manager from carrying out his resolution. The manager was most resolute on the first day. In the morning the manager announced that he would tell her in the evening, after a day's work and dinner —in the quiet of evening in the living room when she had got back from visiting the kennels. Yet when the quiet evening actually came, first she played for half an hour with King Arthur on the floor (rolling around on the floor allowing him to bite her) and then she began to read a new book (*Communicating with Your Beagle,* bought on the trip), which the narrator said she would not want to interrupt. Not even for important business? said the manager. The narrator replied how calm, how peaceful (despite the snuffling and scratching and snorting of beagles on the floor around us) —in this time which will soon be left behind, leaving only a trace. How sad, said the narrator. He looked across the rug at her. A moment before she had been smiling at you, with an anecdote about Clawmor's Venerable Bede, known as Ralph. The narrator looked at her forehead, her eyes drifting down from the book to look at Queen Anne (Susie), who looked back up at her with love —her eyes, familiar and friendly, her total ease with curled-up legs in the chair, and then he predicted the change in her look as we began to speak: *This summer at the beach a certain girl . . .* The narrator predicted how she would turn to him, how her eyes would change as the meaning of his words entered her mind— how, changed, they would recede and freeze, her face would stiffen, the lines no longer familiar nor friendly, the ease gone or taken away, her whole person taken away from him as without a word she turned herself into a stranger. This will happen, said the narrator, so the manager decided to wait until the evening was over and they went to bed. But when that time came, the narrator predicted a painful discussion that would go on for half the night. I can't afford that, said the manager, I need my sleep and so does she, and he postponed it until tomorrow evening. When tomorrow evening came the narrator said that the situation was identical with the previous evening. He predicted that there would be more time in the weekend for them to go through every aspect of the question. The manager decided to take her out to dinner on Friday night, a festival occasion to relax their spirits and make it easy to raise the question—quickly, in a way that would get rid of it quickly. When Friday night came and they were seated in the restaurant, the narrator said that to broach the subject now would ruin our digestions and our festival. Tomorrow night instead, the manager promised. That evening, however, the husband was aroused and wanted to make love to his wife, especially as he had not done so in three or four nights, and once again the manager put the question aside.

One evening when he and Claudia were again sitting in the living room, the narrator said, It looks like you're caught in a procrastination deal. Manager protested: I haven't had a chance. Narrator said, You've been letting your opportunities slip. Said, This is an opportunity now. Manager said, I need time to prepare. I can't plunge in without planning. On the following evening, the narrator asked, Are you prepared now? Narrator predicted that if he didn't do it now he'd never do it, and then Macurdy would make his move and you'd be ruined. All right, said the manager. Tonight I'll do it. In five minutes I'll do it. As soon as she comes into the room. When she came into the room she went to the piano to practice. I forgot about her practice, said the manager. Can't interfere with her practice.

For several nights the manager seemed to forget, until one evening the narrator reminded him. Not very loudly, though, just a whisper: You could do it tonight, said the narrator. Why did you remind me? said the manager. Couldn't you say that I forgot again tonight? I didn't hear what you just said—what was it you said? Okay, said the narrator, let's put it down: Tonight we forgot.

One night the narrator said to the manager, A whole month has gone by and you haven't spoken to Claudia. I bet you never do. The manager said, But we haven't heard from the blackmailer, either. What do you think? Do you think he won't do it after all? The narrator admitted, Perhaps our chances are better than we supposed. Added, Perhaps your resolution was more panicky than it needed to be. If the man is a blackmailer he won't start by throwing away his ace. Maybe you don't have to tell Claudia anything until the blackmailer makes his demand. And if he never shows up, then nothing will be lost.

This lasted for several days. But the narrator was always seeing things in new ways. One night he attacked the manager without warning. What terrible stall is this? Letting it go and letting it go, as if the blackmailer were a reasonable man who would act quickly or not at all. See him ripening his plan, see him grinning as he watches your delusion that you have escaped, while all the while he refines and refines, devising a better squeeze. And every day only makes it harder to explain to Claudia, aggravating the question she will certainly ask: Why did you conceal this? And why do you tell me now? And the increasing impossibility as time passes of answering either one.

At times it seemed to him as if she must have guessed—by observing his edginess, by hearing his thoughts. As if she were more distant, more reserved, looking at him in a funny way. He felt it—the narrator asked about it, some new formality in her, or some caution, and he stirred the manager's fear: You must delay no longer. There was a day of storm, which died, and the manager forgot his resolution again. After that, still sometimes the narrator would stir up his fears, but each time it was easier to ignore, and when he mentioned it, the manager usually replied, Perhaps we're lucky.

Sitting in his chair, the narrator once again went through it—what happened four months ago and perhaps would not have any consequences after all.

I shall have three places to enjoy my privacy when I go back to Norway to stay. The house in Kristiansand will be my regular home. About two and a half hours' drive out of Kristiansand, away off the main road, I have my little cottage, surrounded by forests and lakes. I shall go there, as I have in the past, when I need absolute peace and solitude. . . . And in Oslo there will be an apartment waiting for me. I shall be there whenever there is a concert, an opera, a play, that I want to catch. . . .

. . . I am eager to come back [to America] now as an ordinary visitor. I shall learn to know Broadway and its fascinating theaters; I shall go to the City Center for the beautiful ballets and operas and plays I have heard and read so much about. . . . I have only one misgiving about that. If only I could be completely unknown to the audience, just one of them. I may be abnormal that way, but it bothers me to be recognized and accosted in public.

37

On a gray cold afternoon, with December in the streets, Claudia called from her office in the School of Music to us in the Office of the Dean. "Michael?" There was a distinct pause before she said it: "I just got a letter from the Musical Institute of Connecticut."

Telephone isolates the deliberate lowering of her voice, and exaggerates the pause, the tense understatement of feeling. We wait.

"They want to know if I'm still interested."

"Well, you are, aren't you?" What was she understating, and why was the narrator so nervous and on guard?

"This is different," she said. "They want to know if I am *seriously* interested."

Still we wait, quiet under the boss's orders. She mumbled as if she were ashamed of it: "They have narrowed it down to three candidates. I'm one of them."

"You're one of three?" said the husband, cautiously. "Good for you."

"Yes," she said. Her voice was a warning. "But they want me to commit myself."

The Dean said, "You can't commit yourself until they make you an offer."

"They've told me the offer—if they make it." She summed it up. New programs, good future, responsibility, prestige. We knew all that before. Directorship: A charge to hire and organize, start and develop. Salary, $42,000 a year, travel expenses, fringe benefits.

"That's more than I'm making, " said the Dean.

Yes. Three-year contract to begin with—more to follow, maybe. To begin next September. If.

The Dean said: "They should either make you an offer or leave you alone." The lawyer was on guard. The sheriff was also ready, though confused, uncertain what services were needed.

She explained. "They were very very nice about it," she said apologetically, as if the equivocation were her fault, not the Institute's. "They've reduced us to three outstanding candidates—that's what they said, 'outstanding.' They have to present our names to the board, for *them* to make the choice. So that's why they have to know whether I'd accept or not. That's what they want to know: if they make the offer, would I accept it?"

While the lawyer scrambled looking for precedents, the father was saying, If that's how they run it, that's what you have to go through. The father was elated, already predicting her victory. If you're already one of three, you're almost there, he said. And whether you are in or out, it's good news. The wife was worried; she thought the ground was shaking under her feet, but the father said it was only her nerves, such good news could not be bad, any upward movement of career . . . The narrator was surprised, and the manager spoke to the narrator sharply, demanding, Where were you? The narrator said it was a loose thread, but it's not loose now. It sure ain't, said the manager, full of rue, but don't worry, repeated the father: any upward movement of career as big as this . . .

Then suddenly she said, "What should I tell them?"

The Dean did not expect to be asked that question. "Well, you're—you're still interested, aren't you?"

"Yes, but—but . . ." What? "We're down to the end. Am I *that* interested?"

The wife said the ground was shaking, grabbed the husband.

"That interested?"

"Am I ready to accept an offer if given?"

"Are you asking *me* that?"

"I'm going to have to decide. I want to know what to decide."

Suddenly the wife screamed, and the husband felt panic, felt them falling together. I thought you had it solved, said the wife to the manager, I thought you said there was nothing to worry about. The manager confronted the narrator with the same question. The narrator groped after Claudia on the telephone: Doesn't she have a solution? What did she *expect* to do if she got an offer? Again she said, "What shall I do?"

I said, "That's your decision to make."

"Is it really? I mean, yes, I suppose it is. All right. I'll have to think—talk—I mean, think about it. Talk." Concluded: "Let's talk it over tonight."

All afternoon the news was flashed around, back and forth, in the rooms, while the commentators went to work predicting how Claudia would decide and what the consequences would be. That evening after we came home, we went out to eat at The Great Wall of China. This was Claudia's suggestion, as if she did not know of our dinner once long ago with Macurdy and his Ruthie. She looked younger than usual, her brown eyes large and full with her success. How pretty she is, said the husband, how taken for granted. But there was also something else, some eye-dodging shyness—as if she were ashamed.

I reached across the table and took her hands. "Whatever you decide," said the husband. "I think you have every right to be pleased with yourself, what a great honor this is. I want you to know how proud I am, I couldn't possibly be prouder."

The shame that made her look down, shake her head, and then in a small voice she said, "I have to tell you something."

Watchman: "What?"

Now she looks at us. "I have already written my letter of acceptance."

"You what?"

And looks away. "I wrote and told them I would accept. *If* they make the offer, I mean."

While the wife and husband fell through the open ground.

Crash. "I thought you intended to talk it over first."

"Yes, but then I decided it was my decision to make and I realized what my decision would be." Looking away, turning over forks and spoons, upside down. "So I wrote the letter."

"We were going to talk it over."

"You said it was my decision."

"Yes . . ."

"Do you want me to change my mind? Retract?"

How gloomy was the Dean now. "You can't do that if you have already accepted. It's too late."

"I haven't mailed it yet."

"Oh!"

"So we can still talk it over, if you think we should."

"But you've already decided what you want to do."

She stared at her martini before answering. "Not necessarily," she said.

Through martinis and won ton soup and beef chow mein and sweet and sour pork and egg foo yung and egg rolls with soy sauce, with bean sprouts and noodles and rice, we debated innerly on what to do while the external conversation with Claudia bounced off the subject to other things, to dogs and music, and back again, touching it from time to time, gingerly.

"The problem," said the Dean, "is."

In the silence that followed she said, "I know."

He heard the wife crying. The narrator heard it and realized that she had been sobbing for perhaps months, unnoticed. She said, Are you going to let her get away with it? Aren't you going to stop her? The husband put his arm around her. The lawyer said it is a question of understanding what kind of a marriage she thinks we have. The father said there must be a way, there always is.

Prompted by the father, the Dean said, "We must consider whether it would be possible to commute." She smiled and shook her head. He ignored the shaking and pursued: "Commute for weekends, I mean."

"It's out of the question," she said. "I've already looked into it. It's utterly impossible."

Well, then—

"The only way to avoid . . . long separations" (narrator noticed her difficulty in speaking of that) "would be if you could also find a job in Connecticut."

The Dean felt a blast of wind. What was that? A cry from the Dean: What, You'd fire *me?* "Perhaps a professorship in geology at some college might be available," she said. *Geology,* cried the Dean, roared the Dean from prison, moaned the Dean from the ex-Dean's grave, all the Deans asking, How can a man retreat, back off into his own past, as if the past were not always something it is necessary to escape from? "But I don't think you'd like that," she said, "because of the position you've established here."

Damn right! "Yes, yes, that would be hard . . ." while the wife murmured, Thank God she understands that, so maybe now she will also—

"There's no way out," said Claudia. "If I take the job, then we have to separate for the greater part of the year." As if to console him she added, "I should also have to give up the kennels." Then she looked at him so openly, with such a question in her large brown eyes, that the father jumped to her support. You should give her assurance, back her up, stand by her. Now she will be nationally known, added the father.

The Dean felt a speech coming on. "I don't want to interfere in what is best for you and your career," he said. She smiled. "I wouldn't want old-fashioned prejudices to get in the way of your opportunities." Solemnly declare. "I want you to know that I expect your career to be fully as important to you as mine is to me, and I recognize that importance." Stamp his speech with the Seal of the Dean. She smiled again.

"And yet—"

"I know," said Claudia. Her voice was soft. "It wouldn't be forever," she said. "We'll have summers" (narrator noticed the quick look she gave him on the word *summers*) "and vacations. And . . . later."

The wife said marriage was living together. How could you separate like this with so little of a quarrel—how could you be so cold? The child asked, Can people be apart for long periods of time and still be together? The lawyer tried to think of other couples who do it, but couldn't find any. The mother said it was like saying goodbye to children when they leave home to seek their fortunes. How she hated that, how dreadful to let the people you love take their lives away to other parts of the world, while the years eat them up—but that is what we do with children, said the father, we drop them down the chute into time. So it is possible, said the father. It can be done. Sailors do it. Public figures, musicians, actors, politicians. Salesmen do it. Soldiers. Explorers. Baseball players. Kirsten Flagstad did it, and was criticized when she tried to stop. Surely, said the father, you can live alone for a while in your prime of life, knowing that it is for the good of you both. You, at the top of your career, can grant her this portion of her own, which I remind you is neither an angry separation nor a lasting one. There is no quarrel, repeated the father. She will also give up her dogs. You will share vacations and summers and the permanent reunion later, when you descend from your careers. This is work time, said the father, summer, with the shining sun and the hot day and the ripe fields. Winter will be time enough to sit around the rug talking of old days.

Again the Dean spoke: "In brief, as far as my own feelings are concerned, I would rather you turned it down. Purely selfish reasons. But I don't want to interfere with your opportunities and certainly this is an opportunity. So I think you have to decide for yourself in terms of what will be best for you." He heard his words echoing back to him, coming together like cars on a Dodgem floor: your real opportunities for purely selfish reasons in other words if you really want to know and therefore we ought to consider but because of other considerations I would rather not your decision but otherwise and else.

The next night when she came home she sat in the living room with her drink and said, "I mailed the letter."

"That you would accept the offer?"

"That I would accept it if given."

In our house no one spoke for several moments. We waited for the wind. The boss bowed his head and knelt. The manager looked around the inner room, which seemed much larger and emptier than usual, and saw the others lying on the floor. He heard the father speak, his voice still calm, though hidden behind one of the pillars, advising him to say something to Claudia, to recognize the gravity of her decision and indicate support, but the manager couldn't think of words that would do this.

She said, "I probably won't get the job, but if I do I'll get an apartment in Connecticut and you can maintain the house. You can use Angie to keep things clean and cook for you. I'll withdraw from the kennels, and you can send the dogs back if you wish. We'll have holidays together. I'll come home for Christmas, and there'll be a week or so in the spring. Perhaps I can even come home for Thanksgiving. And of course we'll have the summer vacation. Perhaps after a couple of years we can plan something special with our extra money, like a trip to Europe. It's not forever. And if it doesn't work . . . Tell me, do you think I am being wise and fair?"

The Dean said, "Now you can't change your mind."

"Yes," said Claudia.

At dinner that evening, there was little to say. Frightened on his own behalf, the boss asked the narrator to spell out what it would be like alone in the house on mornings and evenings after Claudia had gone. The narrator looked ahead. A cloudy morning, you rise from bed in the empty house, shave, wash, dress with the doors open before going down to the large and empty kitchen. Cook your breakfast, leave the dishes. When you come home, they will still be there. Milk crust on the glass and bowl. Unless Angie has been by. Perhaps she will cook you a meal, and you can sit down to the same table where your late wife and former children used to sit. In the evening you will sit in the living room by yourself, and when it is time for bed, you will turn off the lights and go upstairs and spread yourself across the double bed. The mother will say, The house is a mess. The father will say, It won't be, not with Angie to take care of it. The chief problem says the wife, is who to talk to. You have this busy narrator and all the rest of us, but no one to talk to. The pile-up of a day's work, hundreds of words filed in the Dean's cabinet, take-home words, but no one to receive them, nothing to do but let them bounce around, looking for a listener.

On the other hand, whispered the boy king . . . What a chance for me! You could work on the portfolio without having to explain it. You could spread it all over the living room floor. You could turn the stereo up loud. There was also the bachelor—the old youth sneaking back, whispering. You could call up Ruthie, he said, invite her over. *Ruthie?* cried the lawyer. Good God, have you totally forgotten? It doesn't have to be Ruthie, said the bachelor. It could be somebody else. While Claudia in her Connecticut apartment (said the brother) does likewise. And who might she invite? asked the brother. Some young music student, some delicate pianist with mustache and long hair, proficient in Chopin or the Russians, or perhaps a harpsichordist, specialist in Vivaldi and Scarlatti, with a little pointed beard? Would he perhaps, unknown to you, move into her apartment and keep it for her (practicing the harpsichord in the evening) while she makes her Christmas and Thanksgiving visits? What will you do then? asked the brother. Will you call back the jealous young husband for a new edition of those questions from the first days of marriage? Asking (because he remembered how complacently she had let him into her room at the Euphoria Motel) what complacencies might still be going on in the practice rooms of the School of Music. Or would you worry only that the delicate harpsichord lover, adopted to fill up the empty part of the year, might grow big enough to take over the rest of the year too and file his claim for the years to come as well? Hearing this, the wife challenged the manager bitterly for his negligence. How could you have let this happen, let her get away after twenty-five years? Why, she's as much a part of the group as any of us, said the wife. She has even become a part of the narrator. The wife heard Claudia's voice in this vocal resounding house of the Dean, the constant sound of her, talking, singing, sometimes laughing, sometimes soothing, always asking questions, offering suggestions, making judgments. Who are *you* anyway? said the wife. Just who is this character we call Dean or this even older, though younger, character we call Michael Morley? Who is this *person,* this entity that claims to see and feel and think and speak for us all, this organization, this institution, this college and hospital and government that calls itself a self—who is this that thinks it can let a charter member like Claudia go off and set up a separate residence in Connecticut? Couldn't you have stopped her? said the wife. Wasn't there a word strong enough to save her?

The Dean said, "Is there nothing I can say?"

She looked at him (with pain on her face, said the wife) and looked away. Said quietly, not looking at him, "Maybe they won't give me the job. It's only one chance out of three."

After dinner, in the living room, she crouched in front of King Arthur and Ethelred. She held their chins one in each hand and looked into their eyes. She made kissing motions with her lips. She said, "I would have to give up my beagles." Added after a moment: "Also." The dogs whined, wagged the tips of their tails nervously. After a moment he saw that Claudia was looking at him. Maybe her eyes were shiny, wet—he hoped that's what it was.

She got up and came over to where he sat, knelt by his chair, leaned on his shoulder. "I'm sorry," she said. "I—thought . . ."

"Thought what?"

"Thought you might prefer it."

"Prefer for you to leave? Jesus Christ, why?"

"Prefer for me to take the job. I don't know. Never mind. I'm just sorry." She bowed her head—hiding something? Observe the top of her head, the part of her hair.

(What made her think a damn fool thing like that? demanded the boss. Somebody's going to pay for this!)

Then she said, "No I didn't. I did it because it's my career that's at stake." Suddenly she lifted up her head and said, "Damn!" She went to the piano.

She began to play the Chopin Polonaise as loud as she could. *Bang*-diddyBang! Then Ethelred and King Arthur stuck up their noses vertically and started to howl. Moving up from the alto into the soprano range. "Ow-oo-oo-oo!"

"What the hell?" said Claudia. All around the house the six

beagles started to howl. She laughed.

"It's a fire engine down the street, started them off," explained the narrator.

"They're grieving," said Claudia, laughing. "Everybody's grieving."

Meanwhile the father was advising the wife: If anyone asks, you can talk about the analogies. The sailors and the officers of ships at sea. The captains of whaling vessels a century ago who sailed on three-year voyages from New Bedford and Nantucket, while the widows walked their widow's walks. Soldiers at war and on foreign missions, wives waiting faithfully. Explorers to the Arctic, the Antarctic, and the Amazon. Remember the Flagstad case.

Remember, this is the prime of your lives, said the father.

38

Churning through the water like a ship, a great white paddle-wheeler like the *Commonwealth,* Claudia's decision left a broad wake, full of foam and whirlpools and mushrooms of blue water. Popping up in one of the pools of this wake soon came Macurdy's old remembered pictures from a summer at the beach now suddenly as old and far behind as all previous summers—events that had become part of the past. They popped up, held by the narrator, who liked to go fishing in the wakes of great ships. Look at these things we were forgetting, he said. All that blackmail. Yet suddenly in the wake of Claudia's decision, the threat of blackmail seemed to scatter and dissolve, until the narrator with surprise announced that it was over, no longer to be feared. Why not? asked the reader, wanting to be relieved but afraid to. Maybe foolish escapades on the beach no longer make a difference, said the wife, if you are going to live apart for the greater part of the year.

The manager said that wasn't settled yet, she was still only one of three candidates. That doesn't matter, said the narrator. What matters is the strength she showed in making that decision. That is the strength that will disarm the blackmailer. Along with the change of weather, the change of season, the time that has passed —the blackmailer's failure of nerve, his flight. There was a muffled celebration (not too loud) at this good news, in the midst of which the boy king reappeared, nervously going from voice to voice asking questions. Where's Macurdy? asked the old king. (Where have *you* been? asked the narrator.) Where's the Mythology, asked the king, where's the portfolio? Macurdy's gone, said the narrator, and good riddance. Be glad we're free, said the manager. But the king, who never believed in blackmail, was disappointed. Macurdy was going to help us with the Mythology, he said. Have we driven him away with our mistrust?

One day the Dean decided to find out. He looked up "MACURDY, Real Estate," in the telephone book, but the number turned out to have been discontinued. So he wrote a short letter to his brother Horace in New York. He had not written to Horace since the summer. It was a polite letter, ending thus:

P.S. Do you know how to get in touch with Macurdy, whom I have not heard from since the summer? His phone here is disconnected. Or if not Macurdy, Ruthie?

The reply came quickly, not from Horace but from Ruthie herself —with spiderlike handwriting on scented notepaper:

Hi. Glad to hear from you. Horace okay, happy at last, new job in bookstore. Overqualified, but what the hell. You'd be surprised his good spirits. I have a secretarial job in a doctor's office. Not bad. Guess you didn't know I'm living with him in his new apartment. Since September. Best thing for both of us, might even get married, that is, he wants to and I'm leaning toward it. Marriage is not so binding as it used to be, divorce is easier, so why not? You know. Don't know, actually. Maybe. I'm writing instead of Horace because he's embarrassed or whatever it is. In any case, don't worry. I said your letter ought to be answered, families ought to stay in touch with each other, brothers. As for last summer—enough said. Okay?

As for Macurdy. Frankly I haven't heard from him since we broke up last September. Last I heard he was at home. His real estate went out of business, which may be why you couldn't reach him by his office home. His home phone was 738-3773. If you get him, give him my love, tell him Ruthie sends her love. To you, too—brother.

Love, Ruthie Morley

Not until after Christmas, after New Year's, well into January, after visiting children had gone back to college, while we waited (week added to week) for some response to Claudia's commitment —after the chatter of voices talking of blackmail and desertion both had quieted and settled into routine, and Ruthie's letter itself had hardened into an artifact from the past (unincreased by further word from Horace)—only then on a January evening snowing outside while Claudia was attending a rehearsal at the School of Music and the boy king was impatient again for the unfinished business of the Morley Mythology, to put the steamboat and the singer and the locomotive in a book and make their juxtaposition tangible to the world—not until then did the Dean finally decide to call that number and find Macurdy again. The decision to call was made several days or a month ago. The decision was not made until just now, this January evening. It was made secretly, without debate, and presented to the manager as a *fait accompli:* this has been decided for you—as if he had nothing at all to do with it.

So he went to the phone and dialed 738-3773. While dialing, he heard a voice asking: Are you deliberately—have you been always —trying to get yourself destroyed? The voice was suppressed, replaced by some fast-growing fright which grew still faster as the phone rang in his ear. He wondered what he was afraid of. It made him want to hang up, but that would look like panic and might make the recipient think he was being harassed. Which suggested another question: had Macurdy felt the same fright as he listened to the ringing, back in his anonymous days? And did his own fright, his own beating heart, give him a thrill of pleasure perhaps?

Click, the phone lifted, and in the pause the beating heart pounded at his breath, trying to knock out his breath by its thumps, until the voice sounded, dark and nasal: "Hello?"

Now be silent, said the sheriff. But the manager was too firmly in charge for that, and he spoke: "Is this Macurdy?"

"Speaking." Colorless, no expression.

"This is Dean Morley."

"Who?"

"Michael Morley." Pause, wait for recognition, no response. "Haven't heard from you for a while, thought I'd call you up."

The silence that forced this speech out of him got worse with each word he spoke. Then he waited. Macurdy said, "What do you want?"

"I . . . just wanted to see how you were."

"I'm all right."

"And . . ." Pause. Check instead: "This is the right Macurdy, isn't it? Ed Macurdy? You know me, don't you?"

Heard the Macurdy voice, still colorless. "What else do you want?"

"Well, I just wondered why I hadn't heard from you for so long."

Pause. "Nothing to say," said Macurdy.

"Well, I was wondering if—"

"I thought you didn't like to be pestered by me," said Macurdy.

"Well . . ." The manager said this was rather difficult. The narrator recalled references (Ruthie's) to Macurdy's bad moods, which we had never seen. Was this one? The Dean tried anyway: "I was wondering if you had forgotten about *The Morley Mythology?*"

"The Morley what?"

"You remember. That book you suggested, of things that interested me when I was a child." How foolish it sounded now in the hostile cold of the telephone!

"Oh, that," said Macurdy.

"Maybe you have lost interest in it," said the Dean.

"Yes."

"What?"

"Yes. I've lost interest in it."

Astonished, the manager asked the narrator to explain, and the narrator, equally bewildered, could only grope. Something bad must be happening, he said.

The Dean asked: "Why is that?"

"I never was interested in it," said Macurdy. "I thought it was boring."

"Why? You never told me that. You always said." The manager couldn't make the Dean say what it was Macurdy had always said.

"I guess I lost interest in *you*," said Macurdy.

"Really?"

"You ought to be glad. I haven't pestered you for a long time. You always called it pestering. Aren't you glad I stopped?" Nothing to say, silence in argument. Then Macurdy spoke again. "You got my unlisted number from somebody. Turn around and pester me? Why should you do that?"

"Sorry," said the Dean. "I didn't think it would be pestering." The sheriff loaded the words with the tone of irony, as if the very idea were ludicrous, despite the sister saying that the irony proved nothing and would fail. Better hang up, said the father.

"Fact is, I don't like you very much," said Macurdy. "In fact, I don't like you at all."

These words hit the boss in the stomach like a bullet, opening up a cold numb place before pain. They also struck the narrator a heavy blow. Threatened to knock down the structure of his whole Macurdy narrative which he had worked so hard revising and rebuilding for so long.

"I'm sorry," said the Dean. "I didn't realize you felt that way." These words were also supposed to have irony in them, said the manager, which got lost on the way out.

"In fact," said Macurdy, "I never did like you."

Not like me? said the boy. How could anybody not like me?

"You never . . . told me," said Michael Morley.

"It's not the kind of thing polite people tell," said Macurdy.

Ask him why, said the boy, why he doesn't like us. The Dean objected, said the question was abject, said we ought to get out of this at once. The manager took the boy's question, bounced it off the Dean's objection, picked it up again, painted it with another coat of irony, which immediately faded and vanished, even as he spoke: "I'm sorry. I didn't know I had offended you."

"You think you've offended me? Your word *offend* offends me!"

"What have I done to make you angry?"

"I didn't say I was angry. I said I don't like you. Never did. Can't stand you. Hate your guts."

"But *why?*"

"Why what?"

"Why don't you like me?" Don't ask that! said the Dean, but it was too late. The Dean wanted to hang up, this was pointless degradation, but there were too many other interests to allow this.

"Why don't I like you?" said Macurdy. "Why should I? You think I *should* like you? What the hell have you ever done to make me like you? You tell me, name one thing you've ever done to make me like you."

"I never did anything—I never asked you to—I never expected to—I'm not asking you to—I'm merely expressing surprise—"

"Surprise that I don't like you? That figures. It would surprise you, wouldn't it?"

"I'm merely expressing surprise because you always sounded friendly to me. I took—" Dean at work saving pride and dignity, mustering some force. Said, "I took your word for it."

"Did you really? I don't think so. I think you were always looking around for the ulterior motive. Do you want to know why I don't like you?"

Tell him no, said the Dean. It's not your business to stand around and be insulted. The others objected: Yes yes yes, they all said. Tell us why he doesn't like us. It's what we ought to know. Unable to settle on a style, the manager did not speak.

"Well, there are lots of reasons," said Macurdy. "The more I think of it, the more reasons I find. I keep thinking of new reasons. I really do find you repulsive. It makes me squirm and sets my teeth on edge to think of you. You know, like a fingernail on a blackboard. Repulsive is a good word for it. Disgusting? I'm not so sure about that one. Maybe so, maybe not. I'll tell you, the main reason I don't like you is I hate your guts."

"You expect me to sit here and listen while you insult me?"

"Hang up anytime," said Macurdy. "Feel free. You always used to hang up on me, you did it all the time. I don't care, that's the way you are. But if you want to know why I don't like you, I'll be happy to tell you. If you don't like it, then you can hang up, and leave it to your imagination."

Against the Dean, still advocating hanging up to avoid the insult, was the narrator leading the rest of us, saying there must be a motive and we'd better hang on to find out. Remembering not only old blackmail dangers but habitual cautionary tactics of a lifetime. Fury like this has a reason: you'd better find it out.

"I've never done a thing to harm you, to my knowledge," said Morley. "If you think I have, I wish you'd tell me, because to my knowledge I have never done nor intended you the slightest harm."

"That's typical. Always trying to be in the right. Always perfect. How the hell do you know whether you've done me any harm? I'm the only judge of that."

"Well, how have I harmed you, then?"

"You know one thing I can't stand about you is your assumption that you are better than me. You take it for granted, it goes without saying. Your very conspicuous assumption. From the very beginning, when you used to hang up on me with such outrage."

"Jesus Christ, you were harassing us."

"Come on, knock it off."

"What?"

"That's your excuse. Later when you discovered I was really a human being you went on the same way, always looking for the suspicious motive, always talking to me in a certain tone, to warn me I'd better not try any funny business because you were on to me, yes you were. Always wondering what terrible thing I might do that you wouldn't do. Always making sure that I knew you were on guard, for fear I might kidnap you or blackmail you or set a trap for you or steal from you or kill you—always the wicked thing I would do to satisfy your fixed idea that you were better than me. I'd damn well *better* do something you wouldn't dream of doing yourself. Do you think I liked to see you thinking of me like that? There was also the problem you had, whenever we met—with very few exceptions—as to whether you should consent to talk to me or not. Don't deny it. Your face gives you away. That cautious hesitation, that flickering fright—it shows. I hear the tightness in your voice when you start to speak. I know what it means: should you contaminate yourself by speaking to me, or not?"

How does he know? asked the student. The Dean, embarrassed at being caught, shut his door. The father, however, said there was a reasonable answer to at least some of the man's complaint, and it ought to be made.

"You seem to forget," he said, "the peculiar way in which you first made my acquaintance. Don't you realize—"

"Certain telephone calls . . ."

"Damn right."

"What you call harassment. You think that makes me an inferior being who might do something you wouldn't do."

"It's bound to arouse suspicion. Certainly you can understand that."

"If someone is capable of doing a thing like *that,* God forbid, who knows what else he might do? Wow! Pardon me, sir, that's bullshit. The only thing it proves is that you're not capable of it. You're not capable of it, and you can't imagine anybody doing anything you're not capable of. Only that's bullshit too. Who says you're not capable of it? You're just as capable of it as I am, only you choose not to, so as to feel superior to me, for instance. So you can enjoy thinking about all the other things you aren't capable of that I might be capable of—all the other ways in which I am to be mistrusted, scorned, avoided, looked down upon, used."

Asked in a low voice, half humble: "What would *you* have done if someone harassed you on the telephone like that?" Pause. "I'd like to know . . . if there was a better way to do it."

"That worries you? Now in your perfection you wonder if there might have been a still more perfect way, and you'd like to know what. Maybe you hope I can't answer you, which proves you behaved in the best possible way, as you have been insisting. There's just one thing wrong with that—namely, that I am a human being and do not share your low view of me."

"Why did you take those pictures in your cottage?"

"To blackmail you, of course. That's another case in point. Immediately you jump to the conclusion I mean to blackmail you, and nothing can shake you of that idea, because you begin with the notion that I am a blackmailing type, in contrast to yourself, who are not."

"But why did you take them? If you didn't mean to blackmail me, why did you take them?"

"Impulse. I like pictures of people screwing."

"Is that a reason? You expect me to believe it? When I find a trap has been set for me, do you expect me to decide it wasn't blackmail because you say it was only an impulse?"

"Have I blackmailed you?"

"No, you haven't."

"Yet you assumed I would. That's what I mean."

"Because at the time, in the circumstances, no other explanation made sense. The trap set, the bait, everything fixed up to suck me in. What kind of an impulse was that?"

"Trap, you call it?"

"What else could it be? You were supposed to be upstairs with your migraine, whereas actually you were waiting outside the window with your camera, where you knew you'd get a good angle, where it would be all set up for you."

"I like pictures of screwing. Why should I waste my time on blackmail? You think I want you to taste my power, hey? Why should I bother? There's your arrogance again—you think you're so important that I would go to the lengths of blackmailing you for pleasure."

"I know you haven't blackmailed me," said Michael Morley with care, "and I also remember your calling it a sign of good faith. But I don't understand. I just don't understand, and if I have offended you, you'll have to explain it to me because I don't understand it. I don't understand why you set it up like that, I don't understand your impulse, I don't understand what you meant by good faith."

"You screwed my girl, but you're too good to take responsibility? That was simply a trap you fell into, was it? Another thing you wouldn't do but I would, right?"

"Is that the trouble? Jealous because of Ruthie? I see, I see. Then you'd better ask her what she did that night, how she behaved. And what about—what about—what about my brother Horace, for instance, if you're so jealous on Ruthie's account?"

Macurdy's voice quiet. "Who said I was jealous?"

"You suggested it just now."

"People don't fall into traps like that. They step into them. You knew what you were doing."

Morley held his fire.

"You pretend it was a trap," said Macurdy. "That's what I don't like about you."

"You were only innocently taking pictures, accidentally, as it were? And only accidentally, coincidentally happened to let things fall out so that I would be there to have my picture taken?"

"Well," said Macurdy. "Maybe I wanted to prove that you would react as I knew you would. Maybe I wanted to prove you would react the way you actually did."

"What kind of reaction were you trying to prove?"

"Thinking you were being trapped and about to be blackmailed, perhaps."

"Wait a minute. You set a trap to prove that I would think you'd set a trap?"

"You wait a minute," said Macurdy, talking slowly now. "That was no trap. You stepped into it. If you stepped in, not knowing what you were stepping into, then you are stupider than I have given you credit for. It was you who decided to call it a trap, which was exactly what I might have been trying to prove, if I had wanted to prove anything."

"Why such animus?"

"It's no animus. I just don't like you very much, is all. You like yourself and expect everyone else to like you the same way. Well, I don't, and I resent your expecting me to, is all. I tell you this because you called me up. I didn't ask you to call me up. If you hadna called me up, I wouldna said a word. You'd have gone on protected from everything, and you'd never known, but when you come around asking me why the hell I'm not licking your ass anymore, why, I'll tell you. You know, I don't like much of anything about you at all. I don't like how you look—you middle-aged types with glasses and trained wrinkles, twisting your face up to suggest that you're *thinking* all the time, and puffing on your pipe to suggest that you are calm all the time. How can you be calm, Jesus Christ! Calm because you control the world, unlike the rest of us, who don't. I don't like how you talk—your voice has a nosy edge that irritates me, and you have a pompous way of stuttering. I don't like how you walk, and I don't like your gestures, your hands always squaring things off, imaginary blocks in the air, as if your mind was full of architecture—as if you wanted people to think how architectural your mind is, how neatly divided into segments, one two three four, everything in its own place. You see, I just don't like you very much—I don't like your shirts and I hate your suits, and if I see someone else wearing a suit like that, one of your colleagues, it reminds me of you and makes me want to puke—but that's not the main thing. That's not important, really, that's only personal, compared to what I really can't stand about you."

Again the Dean asked, Do we have to listen to this? Yes, said the father. The father said this was a madman talking, but we'd better listen, because who knows what a madman might know? But why should he hate me? said the boy. How can anybody not like me? The boy was splattered with tears, crying loudly, but there was also another voice, penetrating the sound, grim and harsh: You'd better listen, because nobody has ever told you such a truth as this. He's saying what he thinks, by God, and you'd better know it. If he doesn't like you, he's got his reasons, said the voice. Maybe I don't either—addressing first the boy, then all of us: Maybe I don't like any of you, either.

The manager recognized the voice of the martyr, who used to be prominent but had not been heard around here lately, and when Morley spoke now, it was at the martyr's direction: "What can't you really stand?" he asked.

"Can't stand you sitting in that office being Dean."

"It's my job."

"Sitting with your ass on a ladder with a few people above you and more people below you, enjoying yourself and thinking everything is just great. Doing your bit to keep the educational institution functioning, to keep the social institution alive, to preserve the privileges of your position of superiority."

"Education—to preserve the heritage of civilization—"

"Smug," said Macurdy. "That's it. You occupy a position of privilege and power. Since you profit from the system as it is, you share responsibility for the wrongs it creates. I wouldn't care if you took some honest position. If you said it can't be helped or you don't give a damn. Even if you just said it was a problem you're working on. But hell—that's not you. What you do is, you turn your back on it while pretending that you are not. Pretending that you are good and generous and doing all that you can for the world."

"Turn my back on *what?*"

"The world's misery that you profit from."

"I didn't know you were a revolutionary," said Morley.

"I'm not."

"I didn't know you were a political activist."

"I'm not. It's your smugness I don't like. What a nice guy you are. Says you. And then that precious childhood of yours, that Mythology, as you call it. That goddamn Mythology! The conceit of it! Frankly, it makes me sick."

"Makes you sick?" cried Michael. "For Christ sake, you started it! I never would have thought of it if it weren't for you."

The reader questioned the narrator while the crowd stood around, listening, waiting, puzzled. That's true, isn't it? said the reader. You remember, don't you? Remember how he offered to put himself at our service? How he brought to you, without being asked, pictures of the ballplayer, the opera singer, the boat? How it was Macurdy (not the Dean) who said the Morley Mythology would be fit subject for a book, a book of detail crammed full of facts, rich in impressions and memories that made childhood such a crowded and fascinating world. If you're interested enough you can arouse anybody's interest, remember that? Remember, you are a fan, the world is full of fans, and *The Morley Mythology* is to be a book for all fans?

Yes, said the narrator, and the crowd grew angry. Remind him, tell him, said the leader of the crowd. "It was *your* idea," he said. "It was you who thought it would be such a great book." Press home, said the leader. "A book for all fans," he said. "Remember that?"

"What a lousy idea that was!" said Macurdy. Sputter. "A book for all fans. What an imbecile."

"It was your idea, not mine."

"You know what's wrong with it? All those things you are a fan for are dead and gone. Your steamboats were junked thirty-seven years ago. Your ballplayer pitched his last game almost forty years ago. All your singers are dead. Your opera is neither revolutionary nor fashionable, but a museum piece for special occasions. Your steam engines—Jesus, every damn one of those things in your book is something dead."

"You said—"

"Listen, buddy, it's your Mythology, not mine. Don't try to foist it off on me."

"Are you trying to *deny* that you suggested, you encouraged—"

"Let me tell you something. Nobody could have encouraged you to do such crazy things unless you wanted to be encouraged. So I found out something about you. Or say I confirmed something I already knew. Boy, did I confirm it!" He waited to be asked what it was he had confirmed, probably. Since the manager kept silent, he said it himself: "I found out what a baby egotist you really are."

You mean he deliberately lured us on to expose ourselves? asked the narrator. A lousy con game? What for? Can't believe it. He didn't lure me, he lured the boy king, said the boss, uncomfortably, while the sheriff said, Ask him, and the manager said, Silence. Macurdy: "A grown man, nursing your past like that. Not the great past. Not the heritage from the past, whatever that is, or whatever history we are supposed to know so as not to relive it—none of that. Only your own special narrow coddled baby past full of its steamboats and its cows and its Nazi idols—"

Nazi? Is he reviving the old arguments yet once more? Sheriff broke through the manager's guard: "Hold on there. I resent that!"

"Resent away."

"You know damn well how unfair and ignorant such suggestions are."

"So maybe they are. I'm talking of feelings—associations people have."

"Well, I don't have such associations."

"Okay. And some people do. And you don't care."

"If I tried to adapt my life to avoid crossing the feelings and prejudices of everybody in the world—"

"Seems to me that's what you keep trying to do. And so you retreat into the nursery. Retreat, then get me to write a book about it, cram your goddamn nursery down everybody's throat."

"I don't see what harm my Mythology does to you. Or to anybody."

Speaking slowly and nasally, Macurdy said, "Well, let's see. On the question of harm, perhaps it will take another generation of consciousness to determine the damage done to the world by such behavior as yours. I don't care about that. I didn't say you were doing harm—you may be, you may not be. What I am saying is that it is goddamned repulsive. To me personally it is repulsive. If you were an old man, I could excuse you, saying you were senile. But you, Christ, you're supposed to be at the peak of your career, you have power over people, you claim to be an intellectual, a leader in the society, and what do you do? You play with your toys and glorify your toy basket by calling it a mythology. Then you take me and try to use me as a public relations man and take the responsibility off your shoulders."

The manager favored silence again.

"Here's something else," said Macurdy. "On that old steamboat of yours, you had a black man who carried your bags and led you to your stateroom, and another black man who served you in the dining room. The ship was powered by steam produced by stokers shoveling coal into the furnace all night long, all the while you lay in your comfortable upper bunk listening to the waters. In the morning you landed in the depression town with the closed textile factories, the tenements and the unemployed, and you looked the other way as you left the elegant steamboat on your way to your private summer place. Then your operas. Music of passion to take you out of the real world as far as you could go. Selfish music. The music of solipsism. You know what solipsism is? You bet you do, a Dean like you, solipsizing away while people fight and starve and die and the whole world goes crash. You know something? You really *do* believe you are Richard Wagner, don't you? You composed those operas and you deserve to be praised for them, don't you, just as you should be praised for designing those steamboats, captain, O my captain. I also hear your sinuses in the voice of that singer you admire. That's you incarnate in her voice, even though she was a woman and is now dead. You want the credit for her discipline and artistry, don't you?"

"Why are you doing this?"

"Why are you letting me? You asked, so I'm telling. Consider your marriage. You take such goddamn pride. As if it were a great achievement and your wife a great work of art like an opera or another steamboat. I know what it means—your big private house, your lawn, your cars, your dinner parties, your vacations, your beagles with the cute names. That's your big boast, your marriage as if it were a great accomplishment instead of the weak dependency relationship it actually is—"

"What do you know about my marriage? What can you possibly—"

"Right. What can I possibly? How private. Secret. Sacred. Sugar. I know your old-fashioned marriage—as old as if you lived a hundred years ago; you haven't changed a bit in all that time. Your wife is yours. You treat her with noblesse oblige. You share your privacy with her. You built privacy together to exclude the outside world—you *use* her to create a privacy, so that you can have privacy without being alone. I also know that even in privacy you aren't as intimate as you pretend."

"What makes you think you know that?"

"I happen to know. Well, for instance. Take your fear of blackmail, for instance. Your fear of blackmail, which is the fear that you might have to violate the rules of the game, or maybe change them because things aren't quite what you say they are. I happen to know something about the rules of your game, you know, something about what you and your wife are willing and not willing to have between you. I have concrete evidence."

"What concrete evidence?"

"Never mind that. My secret. It won't hurt you. Just like I happen to know you are afraid of being blackmailed even though you never actually said so."

"Okay—how do you know that, then?"

"Same way. Happen to know—using my intelligence. Which is considerable, by the way. You have never properly assessed the true level of my intelligence. You know what I really like least about you? It's the complacency of your guilty conscience."

"My what?"

"The complacency with which you enjoy your feelings of guilt. Most people can't afford a guilty conscience, or if they do it drives them mad. But you, you take pride in yours."

"Where do you get these crazy ideas?"

"Oh, shoot, man, it's obvious. Why, this blackmail thing, now: your indulgence in that. What a luxury. Your indulgence in me, for Christ sake. But that's not the worst thing, the really detestable thing."

He stopped. Michael Morley waited.

"Aren't you going to ask me what the really detestable thing is?"

"I thought I might as well wait for you to tell without being asked."

"Now, there you perk up a little. It doesn't help your case, though. I'll tell you the worst thing first, and then I'll tell you the detestable thing."

"There's both a worst thing and a most detestable?"

"Right. The worst thing is this notion of privacy you have, this idea that you have a right to keep yourself to yourself and still keep a place in the outside world. This idea that if someone calls you up, he's in the wrong."

"You don't believe that?"

"It's a complacent prejudice," said Macurdy. "The notion that you have some integrity as a person that sets you apart from other people, that you are different from them, that you can live in the world, this crowded modern urban world, like some old Victorian mansion behind a stone wall covered with vines and rosebushes, like Sleeping Beauty. Privacy is dead, man, no one believes in privacy anymore. Privacy belongs to the stone age, or the robber barons, the notion that you have a privilege or right to cut other people out of your mind. Which you can't do, because we're all going to be together from now on, man, everybody in it together or dead, that's how it's going to be."

"Is that so?"

"Psychological capitalism, that's what privacy is. As inefficient and corrupt and cruel and dated as economic capitalism. The fallacy of free enterprise and the fallacy of individualism, fallacies both. So that's the worst thing about you. The most detestable thing is something else."

"Of course."

"The worst thing—privacy—is worst because it impedes progress and holds back change and compounds injustice. The most detestable thing, now, that is what makes people squirm when they see you, what makes them turn clammy and want to puke and try not to think about you, what makes people really want to loathe you."

"People? Others besides you?"

"Anyone, man, anybody. Just ask anybody if it isn't so. What I mean, the most detestable thing is this notion that you are the victim of an injustice somewhere. You sit in your Dean's office, with your ass sticking out, high up on your ladder, congratulating yourself on what a success and what a fine marriage and what a nice childhood and how nice of you to share it with others, and all this time at the same time you keep thinking how unfortunate you are, what a victim of injustice, how unfair that someone would want to call you up or take pictures of you, even though you are screwing his girl. And you moan and groan how unfair it is that you should grow old and die, and not only that, but how beastly mean that somebody you know should happen to dislike you and even go to the length of telling you, quite honestly—though it was you who called *him* up, not vice versa. So—you know—that's the really detestable thing about you."

"That's it, eh?"

"That's it. All I have to say to you."

"You can't think of anything more vile to say about me?"

"Oh, I can think of a few words if you'd like me to. I can call you a sonofabitch, a bastard, a goddamn prick, a motherfucker. Expressive words, but I doubt they add much to your knowledge."

Is the barrage ended? asked the manager. May we ask? Step in, said the boss. Now. "May I say something, then?" asked Morley.

"Feel free."

"I don't understand. There must be something you haven't told me—"

"Surely you don't want *more?*"

"I say there must be something else, because I don't understand what I have done to provoke such a reaction."

"Good God, and I've been spending the last half hour trying to tell you."

"There has to be an explanation. Such a bitter, angry, *violent* feeling—"

"Who's angry?" said Macurdy. "This is not a violent feeling. This is a calm, cold, steady feeling of permanent dislike. I don't like you, never did."

"Why me? Why me?"

"Ha ha. Because you're the one I don't like—okay?"

"You came after me as a complete stranger."

For a moment the telephone was silent.

"No, sir; not quite, sir."

He tried to remember what Ruthie had told him.

"I didn't intend to dislike you in the beginning. That was only after I got to know you and found out how dislikable you were."

"I'd like to know what I did to set you off like this."

"Set me off? I've *told* you. Why should you care anyway? I'm just a stranger who started invading your privacy, right? Isn't that what you always thought?"

No word from Michael Morley.

"It's what you always thought. So why should you care?"

Still no word from Michael Morley.

"Only remember in the future. Privacy is dead. Individualism is dead. The species takes precedence over the specimen from now on. Don't forget it."

Silence from Michael Morley. Just hold the phone and let the other cope with it.

"If you had hung up on me the way you used to, you wouldn't have had to listen to this. Not yet for a while anyway. Your own fault."

No speak.

"For a while anyway."

Why did he repeat that? Broke Morley's silence: "What do you mean by that?"

"Who knows what the future may bring?"

"What are you trying to say?"

"Who knows what the future may bring. I'm not trying to say, I'm saying."

"Is that a threat?"

Macurdy silence. Then a low whistle. Then the shadow of a laugh. Then: "That's you again. In the beginning I only wanted to play a little game with you because I was curious. But you started coming over me with theories of invasion of privacy and depravity and blackmail . . . even *incest,* for Christ sake."

Incest? The detective jumped, reached for it, but it got away. Macurdy continued: "What do you think I could do to you?"

Sudden fear of what he might have foolishly provoked in the man's mind. Said: "I'm just trying to figure out what you're saying."

"Vanity. Vanity. Why should I waste time making threats to you?"

Be still again.

"All talk," said Macurdy. "That's all you are, isn't it? All talk and think, talk and think, think think think. Think about yourself all the time. Threats are talk. If I want to do something, I do it."

A growing urge of anger, moving fast down into Michael Morley's fingers. Sudden full-grown birth of desire to murder. Still held in check for a second by cautionary forces, which were then scattered by a loud voice asking what worse could be prevented by continuing to let him live? The murder gathered in the Morley fingertip, which moved and poised itself over the receiver button.

"It's a dumb stupid life anyhow," said Macurdy. "That's the trouble with you. You don't realize—"

Finger touched the button, with the slightest force killed the voice that was speaking. Act of murder, followed by silence. There was an instant of alarm while they asked what important thing he was saying that you did not allow us to hear, until we recalled the buzzing dial tone that would now be sounding in his ear, interrupting his idyll, jeering at him mechanically.

After a moment Michael Morley released the button to see if the connection had truly been broken. He heard the dial tone himself, rigor mortis in the voice he had finally managed to kill.

39

In the night the manager said, You're not asleep. Turned again to ease the tightness in the calf of his leg. The room was still, the window open a few inches, frost reflecting moonlight on the other window, a fresh trickle of cold air passing over his hip, and Claudia's breathing deep and steady. The room was quiet, but there was a commotion in the house and a shambles of wreckage. In one corner it sounded as if someone was shouting (without sound), wild, swinging a chair around. Macurdy, said the manager. The manager said that Macurdy had joined the group, his voice would be heard regularly from now on.

The father spoke above the confusion. You knew from the beginning that the man is a madman, he said. A madman's hate—let it go. Projecting his innards onto you, something in himself that he hates, transferred and imposed onto you. It's his own problem; let him keep it. But why—asked the mother—why should he choose *you* for that projection?

The reader remembered what Ruthie had said, that night at the beach, of who Macurdy really was, with the real name of, and the brother of, and the jealousy that fixed later, so they said, not on the husband but on the. So he called you up for the gratification (said the father) and them himself got sucked into it. Jealousy jeopardized, the integrity of his madness threatened?

Still it was a savage attack, and the manager felt his wounds and they were deep. Am I to blame? he said. He looked around at us all. Which one of us (he asked) is the guilty one, which one is it that the man is attacking? The boy, the father, the mother, the narrator, the brother? Or the boss himself? I'm only trying to keep order, said the manager. Is that so terrible?

I always said you were too conservative, said the sister. The madman has a point. See yourself from the point of view of a poor native of India. Fat, well-clothed, surrounded by space and goods and birds in your well-protected estate: the rich man! You *are* the rich man in the eyes of the world, said the sister, little though you think so yourself.

The manager complained. How difficult it is to be political, when all sides have so many flaws. Too late. Fifty years old, habituated. Rational. Fixed in geology and the ship of Dean. Civilized. Don't defend yourself, said the father. Assert. Man of intellect with a responsibility to maintain the continuity of civilization. Macurdy is an ape man, said the father.

But *you* were always too private, said the sister. Hiding in your room with your needle and ring—I saw you! She sang:

I know something you don't know!
Michael is a solipsist!
He is nothing but a mist!
Ya ya!

It was his mother defending his privacy on the grounds of things inside himself too fragile for the world. Arguing with the sister. *Sister:* You must admit those boats and trains and things look childish. Cows too. *Mother:* But he became Dean. Grew up normally and then took a backward look. *Sister:* Ran hiding inside himself. Would the father still defend him, seeing how much the Mythology had grown and wrapped its foliage around the modern world of the Dean? Was it still the continuity of civilization, of life, of the Dean himself, now that Macurdy had sliced it with his hate?

How can you live when someone hates you as much as all that? said the mother. Should we consider giving up? said the manager. Giving up what? said the father. Everything, said the manager. Michael Morley—giving up *him.*

Whoever he may be.

In bed the tightening of the leg muscles made him turn over again. Stirred Claudia, breaking for a moment the rhythm of her sleep. You're blushing, said the mother. The heat of shame, even in the dark. And trembling, cold—the fright of waking up suddenly in an unknown place. Of finding people changed, unrecognizing you, or seeing not the familiar parts of you but different parts, parts you never thought they could see—making enemies of them. Still there was the father trying to speak calmly, saying, You are reacting to his attack rather than trying to understand what made him behave that way. He's piling it on you: why does he accuse you of making up the incest story, when you got it from Ruthie who got it from himself? The question is not whether he told any truth about you but whether he (the madman) is still dangerous. What more can he do?

What has he done, for that matter? asked the narrator. He has expressed dislike, in a direct manner. The father said, Strong people can always stand the hatred of others. It is natural to be hated. You have to trust the boss, put your faith in him. Again the twitch, the spasm kicking his leg out straight in the end of the bed. He opened his eyes upon a firmer awakeness. Saw the frosted window again, the glisten of the night light, moon. Close by was Claudia's arm, bare, pale, upon the sheet as she lay with her back to him. And still the chattering voices. You still have a wife, said the wife. Ask her. Ask her what? said the manager. Ask her, Is it only a weak dependency relationship? Ask her if *she* likes you.

In the distance Macurdy (swinging chairs) laughed. Connecticut, he sang. Connecticut forever. And suppose he goes directly to her now, said the sister. Not now with cheap blackmail pictures taken on a beach, but with the harm you did her career by marrying her? Suppose he persuades *her* it is a cheap dependency relationship? I'll fight that, said the sheriff, drawing his guns. Insults for the enemy—bang bang bang, go the guns, working up a good rage. But there was no order in it. Let's get rid of the boy king, said the sister. Let's get rid of the Dean, said the boy king. The Dean accused the brother. The brother blamed the old-fashioned mildness of the father and mother, who in their various ways had failed to grasp the meanness of human nature.

All the voices that speak for me were in a riot that night in the quiet bedroom beside the sleeping Claudia, everyone accusing everyone else. Injuries. Heart's blood. Deep wounds. After a while they all began to surge toward the manager, making him their scapegoat. Led by the brother, intending to lynch by carbon monoxide, hanging, an overdose—whatever would do the trick. You don't want me, you want the boss, said the manager. I only carry out orders. But they couldn't find the boss. They broke down the door to the boss's office, and there was nobody there. Empty, gone. This was a great shock to all of us, as if we had learned that there had never really been any such thing as a boss, only a myth with a voice in the loudspeaker faked by the manager or whoever else could grab the microphone to pretend a little authority.

The narrator ran away, left the shocked and bleeding crowd

behind. Outside he found the boy and took him on the train to the wharf, where the steamer was getting ready to sail on her last trip. The train came into the covered shed on the wharf and as they stepped down to the platform, they could see the lower decks of the steamboat—the white sides and cabin walls, the brown shutters in the staterooms, the net railings, the companionways going up from one deck to the next. The life preservers on the railings and the lifeboats three decks up, between the davits. It was late afternoon, and on an upper deck they heard the great free voice of the singer announcing the departure of the ship. The boy was full of expectation, but as they drew near the gangplank, the way was blocked by a man, swinging a chair. No admittance, said the man. They backed away, off the dock, into the depression-struck textile city, and the boy's disappointment, the disappointment of both of them, was keen. In the distance they heard the whistle blow. It swelled up into a chord in the strings and woodwinds and faded away, waiting for the next phrase, and in a few minutes the voice of the singer joined in, but they could no longer hear her, and they knew that the boat had left without them.

"Michael?" Real voice, Claudia, leaning on her elbow in the dark. "Are you all right?"

Woke up sharply. "Can't sleep, is all," he said.

"You've been tossing."

"I'm sorry. I woke you."

"Can I do anything for you?"

"Guess not."

"Would you like a back rub?"

"Yes, that would be nice."

According to the narrator, this was unusual. Once, years ago, she gave him a back rub when he was ill. Macurdy said, You are letting her comfort you.

"Is something troubling you?" said Claudia.

He heard someone speak for him: "My God." The need to answer the question shocked him. In an instant his whole organization jumped back into place, with the narrator scolding the manager, saying, Now you've done it! What are you going to tell her now?

Tell her everything, said the manager.

40

The narrator told her, beginning while he lay on his belly in the night as she rubbed his back. First Macurdy—he said, "You remember Macurdy?" She remembered: the anonymous caller who turned out to be Ruth's brother, companion to the girl Horace traveled through Europe with. She knew also that Macurdy was looking things up from the Morley childhood, though why he wanted to do this she could not understand.

The narrator narrated. "He called me up tonight. It was a very simple message: he hates my guts." The reader interrupted: *He* called *you?* Narrator hesitated, saw his mistake, wondered whether to correct it, postponed the question. "Explicitly, in so many words. He told me in a variety of ways what a loathsome character I am. He called me *repulsive,* like a fingernail on the blackboard. Accused me of being always in the right. Pompous, selfish, egotistical. Said I make a fetish of privacy and live in a fantasy world. Blamed me for being reactionary and racist and sexist and living off the exploitation of the poor."

The back rub stopped. After a moment, she said, "Why did he do that?" Quiet. Tense, observed the narrator. Alarmed.

Repeat her question back, in exasperation: "Why did he do that? I don't know why he did that. He accused me of complacency, of feeling superior to everybody. He accused me of exploiting *you,* of impeding your career, of using you to create privacy for myself, so I can have privacy without being *alone*—that's what he said. He accused me of enjoying feelings of guilt, of being complacent about them. He ended up calling me names."

No back rub. She was sitting up, perfectly still. The Dean waited for expressions of sympathy. She said, "He called you up to tell you this?"

The Dean had an obligation to the truth. "Well, no. Actually it was I who called him."

"You!" Her surprise. "Why did you do that?"

"Why?" Narrator also surprised. "Why, because I hadn't heard from him for a while. I had no idea he felt that way about me."

"You didn't?" Narrator: Why does she question that? Why does she sit back like that, so suddenly cold and skeptical?

"Not the slightest. It was a complete shock to me."

"You don't regard Mr. Macurdy as an enemy?" In the narrator's surprised silence she continued, "You never thought he was dangerous?"

"Dangerous?" said the Dean. Yes, exactly. The narrator's astonishment was not with the idea but that she had it. So he admitted, slowly, uncertainly, "Probably he is dangerous."

"You never thought so?" she said. "*I* think he's dangerous." Then she changed that: "I *know* he is dangerous!"

"You know that?"

"I'm astonished that you didn't know it," she said. "I'm astonished that you called him up."

Unable to see her face in the dark, a dark oval, featureless, black silhouette against the window. "*How* do you know he is dangerous?" he asked.

"I know more than you realize," she said.

The Dean turned and sat up. Light a cigarette in the dark to adjust this uncomfortable time, to steady it. Give her one too, light it for her, get a glimpse of her face in the glare of the match. It told him nothing. Get used to the dark, to making out expressions on her face even in the dark.

"What is it you know?" he asked. He waited for her to answer. She took two or three long puffs on the cigarette and dipped it in the ashtray that she had placed on the bed between them. Getting ready to speak and then not speaking. Finally she said, "What is there for me to know?"

"How do you know he's dangerous?"

"I don't know," she said. "What harm could he do?" Retreating? Trying to force him . . . ? Tell her everything, said the manager, but first find out what she claims to know, said the narrator. So he waited awhile without saying anything, in hopes she would add something to explain what she meant.

Meanwhile her confirmation that Macurdy was dangerous—however she knew it—multiplied the narrator's sense of that danger. It seemed to the narrator that the crisis was at hand, for she would receive the blackmailed pictures in the mail tomorrow. Of course she would! That was the inevitable result of digging up so foolishly the privacy of Macurdy, who had gone into his own kind of hiding. Such a hate he had unlocked, what even Macurdy himself had perhaps not suspected. "Oh, my God," said the Dean.

Yet if Claudia knew that Macurdy was dangerous (in whatever way), perhaps just that would give her the sympathy to understand his fears, suggested the narrator. Just saying the word: *dangerous.* It sets up a bond between us, which might protect us a little against the actual danger.

The manager suddenly: "I've been afraid he would try to do me harm," said the Dean.

"What kind of harm?"

"Harm. Talk . . . Gossip."

"Gossip?"

The Dean groping to say and not to say—then suddenly slipping it in, as if hoping she wouldn't hear: "Blackmail."

She heard. "Blackmail?" she said. Her voice colorless now, her carefulness, in the dark, as if it were a contest between them. With a touch of irony? "What could you be blackmailed for?" Yes, definitely there was irony there, as if the estrangement he feared had already begun to open up. The narrator drew back, seeing how afraid they all were. Fear that caught the manager, interfering with his work, the boy's fear of her anger and estrangement, and the husband's fear, he said, of the hurt she would suffer, the injury she would feel when he told her. And the narrator's own fear of the unspoken things on her mind even now, before he had told her anything, which had made her seem now so suddenly cold and wary and concealed.

She waited for an answer. Finally he said, "I got into a messy situation last summer."

"Then it *is* true," she said.

"What's true?" He looked at her.

"Nothing," she said. "What was this . . . messy situation?"

He could see her now in the dark, and she looked at him gravely—so gravely, the wife told him, she must already know what you are going to say, must know it from what shows in your voice. Or worse, continued the wife. Your solemn preparation is making it worse, and her gravity is really fright as she wonders what you are getting ready for her.

Out with it, said the manager, but the narrator wanted to build up the background. "When we got to the Cape, there was this message from Macurdy. He wanted me to come down to the beach that evening without Horace—by myself." That sounds mysterious, conspiratorial. Can you account for it? "I thought it had to do with our project—you know." God, said the manager to the narrator, are you too reduced to *you know* because it doesn't make good sense? "I went."

"You went?"

"I went down to his cottage to see him. It was on the beach; he had rented it." Her eyes in the dark looked at him . . . waiting for more. Well, now— "Well, now—" The narrator prompted: Ruthie was there. You had not expected her because Macurdy had said she was not coming until tomorrow. Said: "It turned out Ruthie was already there. I wasn't expecting her." Why not? Claudia's eyes staring at him, her body as rigid as if he had already shot her. "Because Macurdy had said she was not coming until tomorrow." Narrator: Part of the trap, clearing the way to set the trap. Said: "That's one thing to make me think it was a trap."

"So it was a trap, was it?" she said.

Narrator: Actually you knew Ruthie was either Macurdy's girl or Horace's or probably both, but you on the other hand were Claudia's, so there was no reason to suspect a trap. Said: "It didn't occur to me it was a trap." Narrator: Then you went swimming. Said: "Then Macurdy suggested we go swimming." Narrator: Skinny dip. Said—Hold on, here. Narrator: Macurdy's suggestion. Said: "He suggested—" Narrator: Community pressure. Emphasize the simple logic as it looked in the night. Said: "I had no bathing suit. He suggested we go without." Narrator: So you went. Said—is there any need to say it? Said— Mute. Claudia spoke: "So you went without."

"Right."

"You and Ruthie."

"And Macurdy. Only—" Then Macurdy got a migraine and left us alone. Said: "Then Macurdy got a migraine and went inside."

"A *migraine?*"

"That's what he said." Narrator: And left us alone. "And left us swimming by ourselves. I should have stopped then. But—" Narrator: He insisted. She insisted. Said: "They insisted." Narrator: After a few minutes, you went up to the house with Ruthie, who seduced you in the living room. "After a few minutes we quit, came out to dry off. Went up to the house." Narrator: Up to the house with Ruthie, where she seduced you. "Up to the house." Narrator: Too wet to get dressed. Up naked to the house. Her fingers, quick touch, arousing. Mutual nakedness in the dark, then the light. He tried to speak, but voice halted.

"Where you screwed her," said Claudia. "Right?"

Her voice was tense and quiet. Narrator said: We are now on the dangerous threshold—now she knows—steady, now. "Yes," he murmured.

He began the apology or the words of assurance: "I want you to know, I never wanted, I did not intend, I have never done, ever, with anyone, except—"

"Never mind that!" she said sharply. A quiet, tough harshness in her voice. Adding, quieter: "Never mind the bullshit." Then she said: "What do Macurdy's pictures actually show?" Take a good look at her, look well. The staring Dean. She said: "That's the question you want to consider."

She knows. He looked a good long time before speaking. She was staring at him with a severe, cold look on her face. He decided not to speak at all. She saw his bewilderment and said: "He offered me a set."

The narrator guessed immediately what a burden of work this revelation placed upon him. He thought first that the feared catastrophe had finally struck. The man had done exactly what he had most feared and had thereby destroyed everything: her cold tension covered the fury and grief of their end. His second thought, directly following, was that although the worst possible had been done, it had done no harm, and the Macurdy terror was over at last. The man had sent his pictures to Claudia, who had kept it to herself. The coldness was what was left of the fury and grief that she had kept to herself. The second idea followed the first and the first came back and drove out the second, and for a while the two ideas alternated. Meanwhile the narrator became aware of great unknown narrative territory stretching out, requiring quick reconnaissance. Everything depended most of all on how long she had known it, and he asked (voice in a gasp): *"When?"*

"September," she said. "After we got back. I got a letter."

September? Four months or more ago! Then already we're safe, said the narrator, seeing it through all the dazzle and confusion. If she's hung on to that news for four months or more, keeping it to herself, it doesn't much matter how angry she gets now that it comes out—she's already accepted it. Trying to catch and make secure that one clear point of relief amid all the shock and fright of confrontation. How noisy it was in the stillness of the bedroom in the dark, with Claudia sitting there like a stranger (not his loved wife of so many years), so alien now with her knowledge, and her reproach, and her judgment.

The lawyer and the sheriff were quick. "September!" he exclaimed. "You've known about this since September."

"Yes, my dear," she said.

"And you never told me?"

"No, I never told you."

And now the sheriff, outraged: "For God's sake, *why* didn't you tell me?"

"Why didn't *you* tell *me*?" she came back instantly. (Now you could find the edge of that cold suppressed anger coming out.)

"Tell you *what*?" That was the sheriff, in the general bewilderment outraged by the suggestion that he had ever withheld anything from her.

"Tell me *what,* did you say? What? what? Don't you know what? Tell me of your little mess last summer—if it was only last summer. That's what I mean. Why didn't you tell me about little Ruthie and her skinny dipping and the traps you fall into and Macurdy and his opportune pictures? Why should I tell you? Why shouldn't you tell *me*?"

"Claudia!" The voice was weak, but the name was flung out across the estrangement, like a rope flung from a ship. To pull her back, to keep her from drowning (or himself?). Hearing the rising of Claudia's anger, the narrator could not trust his own assurances of the moment before. Nothing terrified him like anger in Claudia, not because that anger was so terrible in itself, but because of the estrangement that all anger opened, and the lost feeling of being estranged. When Claudia is no longer Claudia but a stranger, and you are alone on a boat drifting out of sight of land. He threw her name at her like a rope to pull her back. Then the question: "I didn't tell you because" (abject) "I was afraid—"

She cut him off, gruffly. "It doesn't matter now," she said. "Just one thing I want to know. Are you still carrying on with that little—"

"Still carrying on?" Sheriff to emphasize the utter absurdity of that suggestion. "It was just that one single evening on the Cape, just that one solitary occasion—which was a trap, I tell you. Why, don't you know she's been with Horace all fall?"

She said nothing for a while. Dark silence, puffing new cigarettes—as if face to face with what could never be said between them.

"Were you aware he was taking pictures?" she asked after a while.

"Certainly not! I'm not that stupid." Sheriff again, saying questions like this are signs of the estrangement—her sudden ignorance of what might or might not be possible to him. Explained: "I thought he was upstairs with his headache. I thought—"

"You didn't know you were being photographed?"

"Of course I didn't know."

"But he did show them to you later?"

"Right, yes, he did. How did you know that?"

"I gathered it from his letter. And how did he try to blackmail you? What did he ask when he showed you the pictures? What threats did he make?"

She asked these questions like a dispassionate lawyer. The narrator said it was part of her effort to be realistic and rational under stress, to face facts and ignore the feelings that were tearing her up.

"Nothing," he said. "He just showed me the pictures and said he meant no harm. I've been waiting ever since."

"Waiting for what?"

"For the ax to fall. Or whatever he intends." The narrator looked at Claudia and told the manager. Said to her: "Looks like it fell without my knowing. Looks like he never waited to get something in return. He just went ahead and did his nasty business without waiting to ask."

She said, "Do you want to see his letter to me?" The narrator leapt up, eager, and the others all followed, with some apprehension and trembling. Claudia got up. "Let's go down to the kitchen," she said. He got up and followed her downstairs in the dark. Her motions as she moved (said the narrator) were jerky, somewhat like a machine. On the way down she stopped at her desk. He went on to the kitchen and turned on the light. She followed him in. Her face looked solemn and harried in the harsh kitchen light. She thrust a crumpled piece of paper at him. All her motions were abrupt, jerky, lacking her usual grace. She went to the refrigerator, yanked the door open, while he opened and began to read the paper she had given him.

Confidential. Dear Claudia: As you probably know, I find myself in possession of certain photographs of your husband and my assistant Ruthie engaged in therapeutic games of an intimate personal nature, taken on Cape Cod this summer, the night of July 31. Since your husband does not seem interested in these pictures, and I have no use for them, I thought maybe you would like to have them, to dispose of as you see fit. I offer them up to you free as a gesture of good faith. The pictures are of moderately good quality, showing a variety of steps, if only the most standard positions in the therapeutic process, along with some good body shots (frontal) and recognizable faces. If interested, simply return this note to my office. Yours, E.M. P.S. If you would like me to take pictures of your husband and yourself in similar positions, I'd be glad to oblige.

"You knew who E.M. was?"

"I knew that must be Macurdy."

"Therapeutic games?"

"It didn't take long to figure that out."

She had the milk out of the refrigerator and slammed two glasses on the table. She picked up one glass and tossed it to him. He caught it in the air. She filled the other until it spilled over and then handed him the milk carton. The narrator said, She received this letter in September. She has had it for more than four months. The knowledge—of the therapeutic games, of the pictures taken, of the attempt to blackmail the husband with the pictures, rejected—has been in her head all during those more than four months. During that time she has made love with her husband many times, they have been out to dinner together often, they have been to movies and concerts. They have discussed the elections and the early frost, they have been out to the kennels and brought back a new beagle named Lipton, they have visited Nancy in Milwaukee and met her new boyfriend, and they have discussed her commitment to the Connecticut job. All this together, while the concealed knowledge of the girl Ruthie and the mess on the beach remained unmentioned, as if it made no difference. No difference until now.

It was the narrator trying to understand what was this knowledge that she had kept to herself for so long, and then the brother, the sheriff, the lawyer, all together taking offense, surging forward aggressively: "I can't understand why you didn't tell me when you got this."

She rapped the table hard with her hand. "I was waiting for you to tell me."

They were saying (brother, sheriff, lawyer) that if she had reason to be angry, she had given him reason too by keeping it to herself for so long. He said, "If you thought I was being blackmailed, why didn't you come to me? Why didn't you at least ask me?"

"Are you blaming me for not troubling you about it? Blaming me for trying to consider your feelings? For protecting you?"

(The narrator said, Suddenly they are shouting at each other. The Dean and his wife, Michael and his Claudia, shouting at each other for the first time in years.) *Claudia:* I thought if you're in trouble you'll tell me about it. Why the hell didn't you tell me you're in trouble? *Michael:* I've been living in terror that he'd take it to you. *Claudia:* Terror? Terror of *what,* for heaven's sake? *Michael:* That you'd misunderstand. *Claudia:* Baloney. I mean, bullshit. What's there to understand? You were playing around again, that's all. *Michael:* That's what I mean. It was a malicious trap. *Claudia:* Ha ha. *Michael:* Well, it was, damn it. *Claudia:* So you say. *Michael:* Didn't that letter strike you as the least little bit *strange?* Didn't it strike you as dangerous? *Claudia:* Insane. Yes. Of course. Yes, yes, yes. I didn't know what to believe. *Michael:* Then why didn't you ask me, for heaven's sake? *Claudia:* Couldn't *you* tell that he was a madman, too? Wasn't it just as obvious to you? Why couldn't *you* tell me? I was waiting for you to tell me. *I was waiting for you!*

Then sat down hard in the hard kitchen chair. Nervous gestures of her hands, brushing hair. Taking breaths. Silence, going back. Was this the scene they should have had several months ago, or had the intervening time changed the scene? Who is she? said the narrator. Who is this stupid Dean? said Macurdy. Where did Claudia go? asked the wife. All these voices were faint and timid. Michael Morley seemed empty, echoing. No one knew where anyone was.

She began to talk again, a different tone now, as if trying to think, trying to understand, trying to mend. She said, slowly: "No. I don't know why I didn't tell you. I think I thought the best way to deal with a madman like that would be to ignore him. I thought, he's trying to make trouble between you and me. So the best way is to pay no attention."

Meanwhile the narrator and the lawyer were quietly arguing whether it mattered that she had not told them. Arguing whether that was only a false issue to conceal the guilt he felt. That the only real feeling to protect now was the great relief that she had not confronted him with it when it was new and fresh. Lawyer saying that her keeping it quiet so long was all to his advantage.

Meanwhile she said, "But then I thought there must be some truth to it. I mean, he wouldn't talk of showing pictures to *you* if there wasn't some truth to it. I thought then, if that's what you want, if you want to go on having your Ruthies without telling me, then that's the way it has to be. *Who am I* to interfere with your way of life? I thought. You want to keep it secret; okay, we'll keep it secret. I won't breathe a word. No doubt it was a great mistake for me to berate you over Ruth the way I did. As long as you don't tell me, I won't tell you. I'll keep the letter to myself."

He said, "In fairness to me, shouldn't you have tried to find out whether it was true or not?"

"What then?" she said. "It *was* true, wasn't it? You didn't say you didn't screw Ruthie, did you? So what's the advantage of asking you?"

"Claudia, you're angry."

"Am I really? I *was* angry, that's sure. When I thought of you and Ruthie and Macurdy and all the fun you were having together, screwing and taking pictures and getting all blackmailed together, I felt pretty damned left out of things. I thought if you could be made to squirm a little for your stupidity, it would serve you right. I didn't tell you about Macurdy's letter because I thought it would serve you right. To squirm a little."

"That's vindictive," said the Dean. "I never knew you to be vindictive, Claudia."

"Of course I'm vindictive," said Claudia. "I'm full of vengeance and fury. That's the way I am."

Then after a silence she said, "Listen, Michael, I did mean to tell you about that letter, sooner or later. When I first got it, I meant to tell you right away—it never occurred to me that I wouldn't. I don't know why I didn't tell you. I kept putting it off."

Concede. "I meant to tell you too."

"About Ruthie?"

"About the mess—yes. I meant to tell you and kept putting that off too."

"Well . . ." She shook her head. Then suddenly she was the dispassionate lawyer again. "The only question now is what the pictures actually show. How recognizable are you?"

"Recognizable enough."

"We have to anticipate what he's likely to do. I still don't see why you wanted to call him up. Deliberately inviting trouble."

The Dean said, "I don't think there's anything much he can do now."

"Well, frankly," said Claudia, "neither do I. He could try to embarrass you at the University, but I doubt if he could get away with it."

"He's done his worst," said Morley.

They turned out the kitchen light and started upstairs again. On the way Claudia still talked. "There were times when I was angry and I thought it would serve you right to make you stew and worry. Or maybe that wasn't it. Maybe I was afraid of the hassle I would get into with you if I told you. All the issues we would have to face. Which we still haven't faced. You realize we haven't really resolved any of our problems here? Even now we haven't. But I did mean to tell you. I really did. I just kept postponing it and forgetting it—that's all."

They climbed back into bed in the dark. The boss was shaky, trembling. He felt as if we were all estranged. Everyone from everyone else. Spoke of canyons between everyone, with slippery edges—how dangerous, easy to fall into. He reached over and touched her shoulder, and his arm was like a flimsy bridge. But you are not estranged from Claudia, said the father. That's the whole point, right now, that she is here and you are talking, and you are not estranged.

She said, "Do you mind telling me now how long your affair with Ruthie lasted?"

"Never," said Morley. "That one night—that was all. As I told you."

"Uh huh," said Claudia.

"Don't you believe me?"

"Sure, I believe you," said Claudia. But of course she does not believe you, said the narrator. Not with conviction, not with certainty, nor will she ever believe you in that way. And always she will be wondering things without speaking, and afraid of what is unspoken, just as you are, and therefore even Claudia and Michael are more estranged than you like to say, in spite of the bridge your arm makes to her shoulder.

In the night, the narrator went back to Macurdy with his new knowledge. He saw: Macurdy would know from the nature of our call that Claudia had never mentioned the pictures to us in all these months. What would this discovery have meant to Macurdy? Could that frustration have been enough to ignite—or merely fan—what was on fire tonight? And going back before that: What did it mean to Macurdy in his long autumn silence, wondering what rift he had opened between this man and his wife? With the discovery that all his wonderings had been in vain? In the following days the narrator kept returning to these questions. They added their secret dimension to the public knowledge of Macurdy's death: to what extent was the knowledge that Claudia had never told us about the pictures in Macurdy's mind when he died? From this, the narrator went on to Horace, asking, for instance, if the pictures had been offered to Claudia, wouldn't they also have gone to Horace? The answer came right back, with stunning shame for the narrator: of course they did. Went to him probably that very first day at the beach when they had also been given to us, just before or just after our hallucination of his drowning. Was that why Horace had been so surly and distant since then, and why he had left it to Ruthie to answer his inquiry about Macurdy? If all this was so, finally, what did it mean that after Macurdy had offered the pictures to all three of us, to Horace and Claudia and ourselves, we kept them secret, by some solidarity of privacy and respect, all three of us—what did it mean to Macurdy's deathward-moving autumn, including, if it did include, his girl Ruthie's desertion of him in disgust and her flight to Horace (who bore falsely perhaps the reputation of being the suicidal one)? The narrator went through such questions often, from that first time in the kitchen at night when they leaned against the sink still talking and into the days following, in the aurora of time around Macurdy's death and later too in the time after the Connecticut question was settled. They kept him busy for a long time.

41

The narrator keeps forgetting that it was not immediately, not the very next day, but two or even three indistinguishable days later, and once again narrative movement was propelled by a voice on the telephone. This time it was Ruth.

"Ruth?"

Ruth Morley, yes. Not Ruth—or Ruthie—Thomas, not Macurdy's Ruthie, nor Horace's Ruthie, but Horace's *former* Ruth, remembered (said the narrator) for bare summer afternoons (longer ago now than when last remembered) in the upstairs room at the cottage when the others were away and it was warm and breezeless and sunny. Also for a confusion of mind later which gradually dissipated through a low buzzing fear, as well as another phone call, also in confusion, about some suicide attempt that his brother had made. Who called now to ask if he was going to the visitation.

What visitation?

"You didn't know? I'm sorry. It's at the Durwood Funeral Home tonight from seven to nine-thirty, and the funeral tomorrow morning at the same place. Yes, I called to say hello, of course—old friends—but also to invite you to the visitation if you would care to, feel free to come, and the funeral also if you can. I hope I get to see you."

Whose funeral?

"Whose?"

Did somebody die? (Everyone tightened up. Someone whispered, *Horace!* He's done it at last! Shut up! said the others.)

"You haven't heard?" She seemed to wait, although actually she was speaking. "My brother. You didn't know?" Still meaning seemed to wait, though still she spoke, and no one could remember who her brother was. Horace? Horace, yes—but Horace was our brother, not hers. Her ex-brother? But no, Horace was her ex-husband, not her ex-brother. "He died Sunday. In his sleep. I thought you knew. I'm sorry."

Whose brother?

"Mine," she said. Pause. "You don't remember him? You knew him—he knew you. Ed Moffitt. He knew you well."

Ed Moffitt was a stranger's name and blasted out of sight whatever faint recollections of a Ruth's brother might have been gathering. Damned if I knew anyone named Ed Moffitt, said the narrator. Don't admit it, though, said the manager, for she will be upset that you can't remember. Asked instead: "New York? I should come to New York for the funeral?" The funeral at most, said the manager. How could she expect him to fly to New York in time for a visitation tonight—not to speak of going all that way to the funeral of someone you can't even remember knowing? She said: "New York? It's not New York; it's here. I'm in town, the Marble Plaza Hotel. I got in a half hour ago."

I had to tell her. "I'm sorry, I'm blocking on your brother. Did I know you had a brother?" Narrator said yes, someone had told him once about a brother for Ruth Morley. Something disreputable about the telling itself, whoever it was, as well as about the brother—as if illegitimate, or retarded, or put in jail.

"My half-brother," she said. "Oh! I guess you probably knew him by his play name."

"His what?"

"The name Macurdy that he used—is that how you knew him?"

"Macurdy?" Yes, I told you—said the detective.

"A name—one of his play names, to give him greater freedom." Sure, said the detective, recognized at last, who from the moment she said the word *brother* had been trying to remind the narrator of Ruthie on the beach and the well-known connection between Macurdy and this other Ruth, but was blotted out by the static of someone else's mysterious death followed by someone else's incomprehensible name. Now the narrator realized that he had not only a predicate—someone had died—but a subject as well. They did not go together, however. He said:

"Macurdy? Died?"

"You knew him as Macurdy, then?"

"I knew Macurdy. He *died?*"

That's impossible, said the Dean, you are speaking nonsense words. I knew it all along, said the brother, I knew all along he was dying. And now he is dead, said the narrator.

"Very suddenly—Sunday night."

The narrator felt guilty, blind, stupid, not to have foreseen it. Even stupider for not being able, even yet, to figure out what clues could have helped him to foresee it.

"In his sleep, you said?" I asked.

"In his bed."

"What was the cause?"

"I think they are trying to find out. I shall ask the doctor later this afternoon."

I picked up Ruth Morley at the Marble Plaza Hotel. Claudia stayed behind, because she had never met Macurdy and thought it better not to go. On the way, the narrator quizzed Ruth for whatever could help him revise his story to the facts. Sudden death in his sleep, what could be the cause, what do they suspect, what do you suspect? Well, she said, they did an autopsy, but she didn't know the results. The narrator, avoiding one possibility, tried other kinds of suddenness that might come in sleep: Stroke? Heart? Wasn't he too young for that? Oh, nothing like that, she said. Narrator wondered why she was so sure. (Hepatitis? Extreme alcholism? Alcohol poisoning—ask, was he alcoholic? said the narrator.) Meanwhile she said they were looking to see if it was sleeping pills or some other drug. Was he on drugs? asked the narrator. (Overdose.) Who knows? she said. Could be. Quite possible. Or sleeping pills—the narrator picked it up gingerly, the possibility he had been avoiding. Asking first, An accidental overdose of sleeping pills? Unlikely that—don't mention it. Sleeping pills, said the narrator, coming to the possibility at last: They suspect he took his life?

"Oh, they know *that,*" said Ruth. "That's certain."

Certain? cried the narrator. How could it be certain when you don't know the autopsy results? Oh, but Ruth meant only they don't know what means he used. They know it was suicide because there was a suicide note. A note, she said, to the girl who's now with Horace. That's how they found him. The note said, By the time you get this I'll be dead, so she called long distance to the police, who broke into his apartment and found him. Dead in bed. Two days already by the time they got to him. What a terrible, what a shock, how little they suspected, they had their differences, lately somewhat estranged, never quite understood, but her brother nevertheless, often close. It made her cry.

The reader asked, What are *your* feelings? The manager was puzzled, since he couldn't find any feelings yet—the news just now was all questions of business and what to do. There was the question of escorting Ruth, whom he had not seen since that summer, to the visitation, the question of behavior and tact at the funeral home, the question of taking her back to the hotel afterward. Also whether he should attend the funeral tomorrow, and who else he would meet, and how to fit this into his deanly schedule. Also the immediate question with Ruth of how to talk to her, how to look at her (she wore a rose-to-purple short dress and was strong in flowery scent, with her eyes enlarged and richly decorated and violet)—though the problem was disappearing since she talked so much herself, so preoccupied, with no remembered embarrassment between them. So said the manager, but the narrator said the manager couldn't see the obvious signs of feeling, how tight he was as he drove up the parkway from downtown, not to speak of the leaping incredulity repeating, which was really a good strong feeling of excitement and pleasure.

She told how she heard the news and how she arranged to get off work, and she talked about her job and the settlement of her relations with Horace and her lawyer friend, but the manager could hardly hear because the narrator was so busy trying to answer the reader. How do you feel? Relieved? asked the reader. Yes, said the narrator, great relief. Inexpressible relief, he admitted, taking a great breath. Relief because he can't blackmail you anymore? specified the reader. And can't hate us, added the narrator, or perplex us wondering what he will do next. Be glad of his death, said the narrator, an unexpected liberation.

I'd feel ashamed of those feelings if I were you, said Macurdy.

The manager heard that and began to worry, wondering about shame. Did he feel it, should he feel it, and if so, why? Meanwhile the narrator spoke of the excitements of change, how it quickens the spirits and stimulates the voices. The narrator thrived on change, he especially enjoyed this astonishing suicide of the old enemy.

I'd feel ashamed of that if I were you, repeated Macurdy. He died suffering, said Macurdy, and your life is shorter than it was. You can't talk to me any longer, said Macurdy. That's a loss.

Macurdy's death was the punishment he deserved, said the brother. Now we are vindicated—against his hate, against the evil traps he set, the evil pictures he took, the evil use he made of them, against his evil accusations. A just death, said the brother.

I'd feel ashamed of such feelings if I were you, said Macurdy. You overlook that he chose to die. Was there a punishment for *you* in that?

Maybe he's watching you right now, said the boy. Watching how you keep your secret, said Macurdy, from the woman my sister who sits beside you, thinking that you and he were the best of friends. Now he watches you, said Macurdy, slipping into your car and catching your thoughts, smiling to see how carefully you hide from her any clue as to your fear or his contempt.

Now he knows the mysteries that you know nothing of, said the boy. Sees the universe and the shape of time past and to come, looping out and circling back, and he looks over your shoulder, into the mortal back of your mortal brain.

No, said the father, we don't believe in ghosts. There is no Macurdy, said the father. There is no father, said Macurdy.

The main thing, said the narrator, is the unbelievability of his death. Three days ago he was berating you on the telephone and now he does not exist. Three days ago—or make it last summer, or last spring at The Great Wall of China—this man Macurdy inhabited your time. The narrator remembered what he had said when Horace was thought to have died, only this time it was Macurdy—telling how Macurdy had made use of your time, shared it, measured himself by it just as you did. This same connected fabric, said the narrator, still linked by blood vessels with that in which he lived, yet not his time, nor will he ever hear of it. Stimulated by death, the narrator lectured, speaking of history, where all events are frozen into the rigor mortis of the past like statues, and told of his own part in freezing them by his constant drip drip dripping of narrative cement in the liquid bowl of memory. This he contrasted to the present, which is not of course an infinitesimal moment for a geometer but a swimming wave-filled sea of voices and people jostling each other. The narrator said it was his business to petrify this shifting field as it recedes into the distance, so that it will look solid and historical. Not too fast, though—the narrator hates to make history too soon, to let life go too rapidly. Let Macurdy swim a little, yet, in the waves. It takes a while to believe that he will actually not come back again with more tricks, or that the telephone will not ring with his silence, his insinuations, or his hate.

As we parked by the Durwood Funeral Home, the boy hung back. The funeral home was a large white Victorian house with ornate eaves and a bright illuminated sign in front. The boy's fear had been growing all the way, but the manager would not listen. The boy was afraid of dead bodies. He always had been, ever since he was a boy. For a long time he had never seen one, and he was afraid that if he ever did, his father would die. Eventually his father died, and he saw him lying dead in a hospital bed. After that no one paid any attention to the boy's fears, but they still remained, and the manager had to drag the boy by the hand as we went up the walk to the house. As we went, Macurdy began asking nasty questions, blaming the Dean for his death. You hated Macurdy, didn't you? he said to the Dean. You wished him dead, and he died. Therefore you killed him.

As we went into the room the boy said, Maybe it wasn't Macurdy, maybe it was someone else who died. The boy hoped not, he hoped it was Macurdy who had died. We looked until we saw him, yes, in the opposite corner. Lying with the light on him, upon satin, with cream-colored satin above on the inside of the open lid. The rest of the people in the room were strangers, but Macurdy was familiar, a silent host to the visitors. We went and looked. Recognized him because the narrator had said in advance it would be Macurdy, that the one lying in the coffin would be Macurdy. Recognized him because he looks like Macurdy, said the manager: I remember him and this is an excellent likeness. Not because he looks like but *is,* said the Dean, not a likeness but an identity. Yes, said the boss, convinced: That is actually Macurdy, the man himself, and his death is complete, at last. They all looked at him, his round face, his closed eyes. Smaller than remembered, in his neat gray business suit with clean white collar and dark tie. His face was sober, with something not quite right, not quite as remembered, about his hair. The boy said, He doesn't look dead to me. See him breathing. See his lips, and the slight scowl on his face, looking as if he were about to speak, to say something sharp and pointed, contrary to what you thought he would say. But the wife denied that he looked alive. That's Macurdy with a change, she said, and the reason you know he is dead is not the coffin, nor the narrator's word, but that he looks dead. Inanimate, stuffed, powdered, prepared, designed—a work of art resembling life. The boy agreed: It's perfectly possible to look at that and know that Macurdy isn't here.

Looking at the body, the narrator called it a body and compared it to a photograph. It was a residue that gave a concrete picture of a particular moment, that time when Macurdy put himself permanently to sleep with despair pills. This was the real proof that Macurdy had committed suicide. The horror, the depression, the unbearable feelings—whatever they were—had been in that fixed face. They had swarmed beneath that powdered brow and closed eyes, until he had taken his pills and developed them. It is the moment of silencing that is photographed here, said the narrator. Inside, said the doctor, the process of disintegration is far advanced. The cellular network in the brain (all the fine distinctions) has begun to collapse. Yes, said Macurdy, it's dark in here. The floods of light that used to pour through the windows, the electric signs that lit up the corridors, the voices arguing, laughing, contending for power—it's all quiet now, said Macurdy. All dark, musty, cobwebby, swampy, rotten, collapsed, stinky, and dead. You'll have to quarrel by yourself from now on, said Macurdy.

Most of the people in the room, said Ruth, were business colleagues, associated in Macurdy's ventures. There was an old woman standing by the coffin. She was short and her face was plump and surprisingly smooth, and she had soft white hair curled in ringlets all over the top. "That's Mother," said Ruth. Suddenly she turned and looked at me with a bright smile. "That's my boy," she said. "Did you know him? Boy! Don't you think he was intelligent? Boy, was he intelligent! Was he smart! Boy, he was the smartest boy I ever saw! It makes a mother proud, how smart he was. You can still see it on his face—look!—how smart he was, if you look closely."

42

I kept going back to look at him. Later when I was standing by him Ruthie appeared beside me. "So," she said. "I wondered if I would see you." She wrinkled up her face. "Oogh!" she said. "Did you see what he did to himself! Yuck!"

She was wearing a dress for the first time and looked small and inconspicuous. Now they are both here, announced the manager, both Ruths, each of whom in her own way squeezed into the cracks of your married life and invited you to squeeze into her—the one decorated, ornate, sullen, the other casual, simple, careless, young, each giving the narrator a memory of nakedness and sex with some heavy tugging, and all gone now for both of them. Look at them now in the same room with the corpse of Macurdy, said the manager, avoiding each other. The narrator had his conversation with Ruthie on chairs in the adjacent room, where it was quieter.

More news for the narrator to play with. She said that Horace had not come because he didn't want to run into Ruth. She said no, Horace did not want to be estranged from his brother, but yes, she did notice the coolness you speak of. You are probably right about the reasons, she said: last summer at the beach when all those things happened. But he is better now and would like to be on good terms. And what a surprise *this* is! she said with excitement, pointing to the coffin. Can't get over it, how wrong we all were to worry about Horace committing suicide when obviously the real suicide person was you-know-who. It all goes to show, she said. Doesn't it? Said Horace was fine actually, the thing about Horace was his all-out way, his no-compromise, his anti-hypocrisy. His zest for life, and that was why he sometimes seemed suicidal. No fake feelings, let every feeling have its voice, including honest despair. That's why he tried to commit suicide, it was to live life as fully as possible, true to the feeling of the moment. Now that we are happy together, she said, you don't have to worry about Horace—as long as it lasts.

As for Macurdy. "He was a little bit odd," she said. Living with him had its exciting and wonderful moments that she would never forget. You know how tender and loving, how very gentle Macurdy could be (well, as a matter of fact, the narrator did *not* know this). But also moody, as I told you last summer, fighting depression. I guess he lost that fight, said Ruthie. She was honored that he had sent his suicide note to her, out of all the people that he might have sent it to. She had it in her purse and showed it to the narrator:

Dear Ruthie, By the time you get this I'll have done what I should have done four years ago or better still my mother should have done to me when I first saw light. Sorry I've been so slow getting to it. Don't worry, there's nothing you can do to stop me, it's already done by the time you get this and the processes of decay are well under way. The only thing for you to do is call the police by long distance phone. Tell them to come to my apartment, walk in, the door will not be locked. I'll be in bed waiting for them. You'd better do it quick because if you don't, I'll begin to stink, and you don't want that on your conscience.

I know the conventional thing for people in my circumstances is to apologize to their loved ones for this terrible thing they are doing. But what's the point of doing a terrible thing if you have to apologize for it? And what makes you think I have any loved ones? I'm sending this to you because I figure your feelings would be hurt if I sent it to anyone else, even though why should I worry about hurting your feelings after all you have done to me? Hell with that, anyway.

My only regret is that I shall never know whether you learned any of the lessons I tried to teach you. Think about me sometimes, will you? Give me just a little thought, now and then? Okay? Think about me as you travel around the world trying to prevent people from doing themselves in.

If you think the world stinks enough without me, don't forget to call the police. All my love for the rest of my life.—Boots.

The manager was embarrassed. "Bitter letter," he said.

"Bitter?" she said. "That's what Horace said. That's not bitter. That's just Macurdy, the way he always talks."

"Does he?" The narrator did not know that. He had never heard Macurdy talk that way until the last night, the last telephone call. The reason the call was such a shock was this: he had never heard Macurdy talk like that. So he told Ruthie about it—what a surprise it was with its load of unsuspected hate. "I never dreamed he felt that way about me."

She considered awhile. "He was blinded by suffering," said Ruthie. She looked uncomfortable and embarrassed. "He liked you fine," she said. "You know." Her voice was muffled. "He always wanted to please you."

The narrator wondered whether this was a whole lie or part lie, whether there was any possibility of its being true. It was a difficult job being narrator in a case like this.

Meanwhile Ruthie had picked up a different kind of narrative question. "Did you say Saturday night? He called you Saturday night?"

"No, I called him."

"Do you know—it means you may have been the last person he ever spoke to, just about." She broke into her smile. "Maybe that's why he did it," she said. Beaming. "Your fault! You drove him to it!"

Smiling, sassy eyes. Joke, said the father. She smiled and patted him on the arm. Still the boss ducked, and the mother tisked about Ruthie's bad taste.

"No," said the Dean, answering as if she had meant it seriously. "He was halfway there when I called him. He was on his way, already sinking, already deep on his way down. Only of course I didn't realize that."

She smiled and again patted him on the arm. The boss warned the narrator: I refuse responsibility for that. Whatever else you load on me, I will not be blamed for that.

The detective wanted to question Ruth. Did you and Macurdy ever talk about me? he asked. But the manager censored the question. She will call you nervous, paranoid, he said. The detective tried another question: Did you ever tell him about the Mythology or about the needle and ring? But again the manager censored him.

It could have been Horace, said the narrator. It could have been a family evening, Horace and Ruth and Macurdy, and Horace telling interesting psychological things about his brother. It could have been.

"I appreciate your kindness," said Ruth. The detective wanted to ask if she had told him about the breezeless summer afternoons at the cottage. The manager prevented that. You know the answer, he said, and it wouldn't make any difference. The lover wanted to ask Ruth about the life she was leading now, but the manager stopped that too. She prefers to keep you wondering, said the narrator. Let her be.

They all went back for a last look at Macurdy. So there he is, said the narrator. See how he has changed. In the beginning he was a presence without a substance. Now he is a substance without a presence. And he will never bother us again.

The Dean left both Ruths and drove home. The reader asked the narrator; Do you know why he killed himself? The narrator said, No. *Reader:* Do you have a theory, can you make a guess? *Narrator:* He got depressed. He hated himself. He was angry. He was frustrated and ashamed. Who can say? *Reader:* Do you know why he invaded our life so aggressively? *Narrator:* No. *Reader:* Can you make a guess? *Narrator:* Ask Ruthie. Ask Ruth. Ask Horace. Ask the father, the mother, the sheriff. They have theories. *Reader:* I heard a rumor that he was jealous of our privacy. He didn't like the way you and I and the rest of us keep to ourselves, excluding him from our discussions. *Narrator:* Maybe. Or maybe we just happened to stumble over his psychosis at the right moment. *Reader:* Is he really dead now? We'll never hear from him again?

"You saw him?" said Claudia, when we got home.

"Yes."
"And Ruth?"
"Yes."
"Did you see anyone else?"
"I saw Ruthie."
"But Horace stayed home?"
"Yes."
"Are you going to see Ruth or Ruthie again?"
"No."
"Good," she said. Then she added slowly: "I guess I don't really enjoy these adventures you get into." Well, said the wife, promise her it won't happen again. Promise in good faith, firm conviction. Certainly, said the manager, but the father intervened. Can you make that promise in good faith, he asked, if she goes away for the greater part of the year, for three years or even more?

In bed the Dean's wife held the Dean in her arms as if she knew he had had a shock. Then she turned over and went to sleep. Again he looked at the frost on the window, the stillness of the curtains, the pale outside light, the silhouette of the bare tree partly obscured by the mist and frost on the window. The wife said, You have had a shock, and the narrator wondered what kind of a shock it was. (It's cold, said Macurdy. It's a blank and cold and empty world from now on, he said. Aren't you afraid?)

The patterns of frost rose up in little jagged peaks from below. Some of the peaks were clear and sharp, others turned misty and vague. Below, the frost all merged together and became opaque and blurry and you could hardly tell it was frost. The Dean where he lay could not see the bottom of the window where the frost began. The reader asked, Was this a narrative that had been completed this evening? Beginning with an anonymous silent call, ending with a man's death. Macurdy in, Macurdy out. The reader asked what he should include between that beginning and that end? A strange vague threat, flattering, tempting with bait, to hook you into a self-destructive act, and then the threat destroying itself? The prime of life reaffirmed? Or should you look rather at all those broken selves pulling themselves almost but not quite apart? Or was it those nervous fears, the paranoid anxieties, rising like a geyser and falling back upon themselves? What should you do about the boy king? asked the reader. Was he in it too?

Never looking back, the narrator ignored these questions. He turned and told the others what the boss was feeling now. The boss is resting comfortably in a feeling of great relief, he said. He expects you all to get back to business soon, after your necessary rest. He thanks you for your cooperation and is grateful for the new wisdom that you have stored up for his future use. (Bullshit, said Macurdy. He'll never be rid of me.)

The mother said it was cold. The narrator admitted it. It made him uncomfortable to recognize the end of one of his narratives, even though he was always trying to make things end. The trouble with an end was the blank that followed, the sudden unemployment into which it threw him.

The narrator admitted it was cold. Now that we have reached our prime of life and cleared away whatever was threatening it (what was that? said Macurdy), the narrator looked to the time ahead. The fulfillment of his deanship and whatever might follow from that. The narrator saw himself cashing in on the prime of life, converting it into the culmination of career. Coming attractions for the Dean: power—power in the institution, power in the town, the society, power over people. This would be his best time yet. So it would be also for Claudia, if she goes to Connecticut—admitting that it would be cold, a hard and austere time of concentration, these next few years.

She lay beside him in bed, asleep, her shoulder raised in silhouette, blocking his view of the lower edge of the windowpane where the frost began. The brother remembered an urgent question he had been wanting to ask her. It was in September, he would say, when you received the note from Macurdy advertising his free pictures and your husband's alleged summer infidelity. It was later than that, December, when you committed yourself to Connecticut. You knew of your husband's adventure at the time you made that commitment. My question (said the brother) is this: Did such knowledge influence your decision? Did you choose to go because of what you knew? Because you thought he wouldn't care? To serve him right, a little? You must ask her, said the brother to the narrator. You must wake her and ask her; it's too important to ignore. Tomorrow, said the narrator. He was getting sleepy and forgetting what he was trying to say. Now at last we are ready . . . ? The boss resting comfortably in a state of great relief. Macurdy resting comfortably in his coffin?

The narrator heard the brother complaining. Speaking out of a sharp pain or so it sounded. Why haven't *we* ever been allowed to commit suicide? asked the brother. Or discuss it as a workable alternative, as Horace did, as Macurdy did? Why has it always been such a taboo? Can't *we* have a breakdown too, go batty or mad? Why can't we collapse as Horace did, as Macurdy did?

It would be no fun, said the father. It would hamper my work, said the Dean. But the Dean isn't the only one who has to live in this house, said the brother. Neither is the father. We want a policy that gives *all* of us more voice. The manager was sympathetic, but he explained the problem to the brother. It was that the boss was too strong. Neither the brother nor the boy king nor any of the others could stand up against the solidified power of the boss and his supporting favorites: the Dean, the father, and the narrator. Sometimes the manager himself was tempted to try something wild, but in the end it was always the same: he was the faithful servant of the boss. Democratic though we seem to be in our sleep, the regime was still at heart a dictatorship.

The Dean reached out and put his hand on the Dean's wife's shoulder. She was asleep and turned away from the pressure. The brother said, Wake her, force her, but the father with great calm said, Let her sleep, and the boss and the manager sided with him.

EPILOGUE

The ending to that narrative is still mostly firm—it still ends, despite the new things that happen—and the reader has it well in mind. Sometimes the narrator, who keeps shedding himself like a snakeskin, would like to go back and interfere with himself then, to tease him with the things he never knew. What difference would it have made to your narrative (he would like to ask) if you had known that Claudia's offer from Connecticut would never come or that by now (this quiet evening in September) the Dean would be an ex-Dean? If you could have seen us now, as the Professor sits in the living room with Ethelred and Queen Anne, looking forward to bringing Claudia home from the hospital tomorrow and meanwhile reading geology to get himself back into shape?

Our own body has been called a museum of relics. The ear muscles, for instance

The narrator and the manager and the Name were all making plans, for tomorrow and next summer and the years ahead. Your interrupted career as a geologist, said the Name, who was out of breath from running hard, while the narrator preferred to speak of travel plans. He wanted to work on a trip to Europe, something next summer for the ex-Dean and his wife. It was planned as an epilogue (a celebration) to the happy ending of Claudia's illness, also to compensate for frustrations and disappointments that last year's narrator never guessed. Meanwhile the Name, pursuing his own ends, was trying to make up for lost geological time:

Until the nineteenth century it was the custom of natural scientists to believe that all the events they were beginning to read in the record of the rocks had to be crowded into a few thousand years. No wonder

The narrator was pleased that he was still able to come up so frequently with happy endings, and he wanted to collect them as long as they would come. He showed Claudia's illness to last year's narrator: described the shock when the routine examination required the not-so-routine tests, followed by the warning of the doctor. A stranger was present, said the doctor, occupying her with malignant intent. Fortunately they knew this stranger and how to deal with him. In the hospital Dr. Feeney was jubilant and shook his hand. "We caught it in time, thank God," he said. "You can look forward to a long life together." That was the happy ending, said the narrator, but it came out of the terrible scare, the several weeks in which he did not know what the ending would be and lived in fear that this time it would be different. This time it was not Horace that was threatened nor a stranger named Macurdy dying, it was not a parental past dropping back into the distance—this time it was Claudia herself. . . . Nor was it a decision she had to make, not a question of will or feeling; it was the cold far future forever reaching into the present and stealing from him. On the night before she went into the hospital, said the narrator, Claudia and Michael held each other in their arms like Hansel and Gretel in the woods. I was holding her so tightly to keep her from the witch, while she clung to me to keep from being stolen. Out of a long silence I heard her whimper, like a child, a word I could not understand—was it "Help . . . Michael"? She moved and woke, still warm, still living, and we held each other and comforted each other as we had done for twenty-five years. The boss and his perilous, fragile golden prime of life about to be smashed.

After the happy ending, Macurdy warned, Don't think you got away for long. The endings will not be happy forever. That's why the narrator wanted to get on with the European trip, while the Name worked so busily studying geology. He would propose it tomorrow when she came home. A narrative itinerary: three full summer months (with the whole winter to get ready for it). Fly to New York in June, then London. Two weeks there, then north through Cambridge, Lincoln, York, Durham (the narrator will take Claudia through the checkpoint at Kennedy, down the long ramp, through the tunnel that stubs up like a worm against the plane, into the cabin, spacious like the inside of a ship, down the aisle looking for their stateroom. When they are stowed, the narrator will take her out on deck and they will wait for the overture to begin) to join our narratives together, hers and ours. Meanwhile the Name objected: You don't have time for such sport. Not after all the dispersion of your energy in the past.

No wonder many of the geologists of the late eighteenth and nineteenth centuries belonged to what is now called the catastrophist school. They believed that the earth's history was a series of extraordinary catastrophic events.

There was a petulant tone in the voice of the Name that the narrator thought was ungrateful. He said, we have her back, we ought to make the most of her. He was still not free of the Macurdy suggestion that her illness was really his punishment for supposing a happy ending on the day she got her letter. They were standing in the kitchen while she opened it. She handed it to him without saying anything. He tried to embrace her, but she pushed him (not roughly) away. She went back to the beagles without saying anything. That evening he took her to dinner, the restaurant with the Diomedes décor. "Frankly," he said, "I'm relieved." "And I'm disappointed," she said. "The sons of bitches. I didn't want their goddamn job anyway." He said with all the sympathy the mother, father, and wife could produce: "It's the blow to one's pride that hurts." "Oh, hell," she said. "My pride is intact. I wonder about theirs." He asked her: "But would you have taken the job if they had made the offer?" She replied: "I was committed." In the weeks following, she never gave a different answer. He made love to her that night, though, and the narrator insisted that she was not long unhappy.

Light glares on the slick pages of the book, the figures, the diagrams, photographs. Eyes squint, pages move, and somewhere Macurdy growls to the reader: Ask why he censored the sinking of the ship of Dean. Was that a happy ending too? The narrator denied censorship. It was only the boss, he said, sensitive on the question, wanting to put an end to loose talk. As for the happy ending, yes, said the reader, of course it was a happy ending—this return after so long a distraction to his chosen career, his geology, his teaching. In the glare of the light on the page, Macurdy snorts and growls: Return to his chosen career, hell. Tell the reader the Dean was fired. Tell the boss he's an incompetent geologist too.

The narrator was weary of the argument. That's over, he said, past. Now it's time for new things; let me give you new things. Night after night he has been working out itineraries in bright vivid images of place: out to the lakes in Switzerland and up to the mountain village opposite the black and crystal glacier mountain where we shall lean against the railing on the deck waiting for the overture to start. Meanwhile the Name's

perspective of geological time had been deepened, sure of the validity of the concept of uniformitarianism, first set forth by James Hutton at a time when there was no evidence to support his hypothesis of the great vista of the history of the earth.

He looked back over the narrator's itinerary and saw

The history of any group of fossils (brachiopod, fish, cycad, trilobite) . . . shows progress from primitive forms to more and more complex, or, one might say, more advanced forms, and usually ends in a steamer with four decks above the guards and in most cases a pair of black smokestacks, fairly tall, situated forward.

The Name suddenly asked the narrator, What are you doing? Asked because

The history of any group of steamboats shows progress from primitive singers to more and more complex, or, as one might say, more advanced forms, and usually ends

The Professor tried to continue, to pick up the sense

usually ends in

and went back again because the narrator was distracting his attention trying to bring the conductor to the podium so that the boat could leave the wharf and the journey begin before the Professor could find the word

usually ends in extinction.

The Name asked: Are you out of your mind?

The question rang through the lonely evening and tolled the narrator back to his self, which he occupied alone. The Name's question gave him a shock. You have been running amok again, said the boss, and the narrator knew. The king has come back, he said. He has brought back his Mythology to take the place of the deanship that sank. He wants me to sail again on the old white steamboat, to go again (with Claudia, with you) to the opera with the great Norwegian and Danish singers, to ride the train behind the I-1 locomotive with its two sooty domes, and watch the pitcher convert body motions into statistics. He has overcome the Macurdy-shock and more than ever keeps pestering me, invading my narratives, tearing up my itineraries, replacing them with his own.

Perhaps he wants you to do it in the old way, like when he was in control, said Macurdy. This was one evening among many, and the former Dean was reading

extraordinary catastrophic events such as volcanic eruptions, earthquakes that tore open the canyons of river valleys, floods which overwhelmed the land, and mass extinctions and recreations of life. Not until the geologists' perspective of geological time had been deepened could they be sure they had lost

have we lost?
are we losing?

A more realistic attitude toward the processes of erosion and sedimentation and of astrophysics convinced many geologists and astronomers that

My God, are you losing your mind? asked the reader, when he heard what was being proposed. The former Dean put down his book

convinced many geologists that such a limited time span was inadequate, and by the middle of the nineteenth century the earth's age was estimated in terms of

and listened to the boss's order: Test him and see. My God, said the reader (while the man put down his book, went to his study desk, and began rummaging), if it has to be tested, the test is already flunked. The man is already crazy.

Then one lonely evening while his wife Claudia remained still in the hospital the late Dean of the College of Arts and Sciences rummaged in his desk until he found a piece of string, a penknife, and a pencil. With the knife he cut the string into a short length; he closed the knife and put it away, and tied the string into a loop with a heavy knot at one end. Inserting the pencil into the loop, he jiggled it in a reciprocating (back and forth) motion, which with the aid of a slight twist was transferred into a circular motion for the loop of string. Spin, said the boss to the narrator. Let's see if we have lost our minds.

What do you see? said the boss to the narrator. Only an old man, said the narrator, trying to see if he can still work a child-time kick. Can he? asked the boss. No, said the narrator, who could not see the king or even a boy playing needle and ring, but only a pencil and a loop of string. Come on, said the Name, you've got work to do.

Good, said the boss, we are still sane. Now we can get rid of the boy king. The narrator was sorry. He felt depressed. He wondered if he would miss the old king, if the landscape would be dull without him. The Name went on reading:

These rocks, he supposed, represented the original crust of the earth, and therefore he called them Urgebirge. . . . Directly above these was . . . the Flötzgebirge. . . . Above these . . . the Angeschwemmtgebirge.

Proud distinctions, said the reader, and at least you can praise him for the fine Dean he was and the fine geologist he yet has time to be. Competence and accomplishment, said the Name. *If* he was a fine Dean, said Macurdy. Adding, slyly: Is it possible he was fired because of certain pictures sent illegally through the mails? There was a racing of blood, a hot blush through all the rooms, and everyone was shocked. My, I never thought of that, said the mother. In the commotion the father spoke firmly. Impossible, he said. If that had been the reason, you would have heard. The narrator introduced the President: "new needs, new policies, a new team . . . to permit you to go back to your natural preserves which all your training . . . your true abilities . . . a younger, more energetic operation . . . time to refresh your spirit . . . things falling behind, not paying attention to your . . ." Your honest, authenticated incompetence, explained Macurdy.

Get to work, said the Name. Only fourteen years left. With the manager he agreed to map out a program of study, of retraining and future research. To refresh us all, said the narrator. Read books, go places, learn new things, replenish the reader's files. Get back into the world after your long Deanly exile. Yet not tonight, not this week. For though he had been defeated, though he had been banished, the king had not left, and now he was demanding his own time to share and borrow from the Name. He had been everywhere during the past week. He appeared at faculty meetings: a professor speaking leaned on the rail in front of the podium, and the king placed a lifeboat and davits beside him. In the hot gassy air of late-afternoon traffic he built a panting locomotive waiting on the platform. He took the Mythology into the ex-Dean's conversations, flipping its pages, looking for opportunities. In competition with the Name, he harassed the narrator with demands.

It looks like you're going to have to live with it, said the manager. The narrator agreed. Likely we'll have both of them with us from now on, the Name and the king, both making demands. But what woke up the boy king? asked the reader. Why did he ever come back? The narrator had been wondering about this for a long time. Do we see in the boy king now a pattern of the senility to come? As he led the way up into youth, so will he also direct our descent into age? Will that same bright light of the child reappear as a glaucoma fog to blot out (gently, gradually) the world, while the boy king, the mad old king, recaptures his throne?

Will you someday go to Baltimore looking for the preserved and unscrapped steamboat waiting for you in a secret shed?

The narrator recommended compromise with the king, to keep the peace. For the sake of the peace you can make collections, with pictures and memorabilia. You can buy specialist books. You can write little essays for the journals of historical societies, for assuredly you are not the only one with a boy king in your house. You can find steamboat buffs and opera buffs and fans for almost any singer. You can find railroad fans who will locate and charter an old steam locomotive for you. You can place even your boy king in the modern world if you don't ask too much for him. Keep it modest—a small madness to protect us all from worse.

And tonight, while the Name still reads (always reading, over and over, trying to catch up), the narrator sketched another itinerary for Claudia when she comes home.

The medial Tippecanoe sea . . . was shallow . . . and its floor was continually within range of wave and current motion. In such an inland sea minor warpings of the crust or small changes in sea level could shift the shoreline hundreds of miles, and either lay bare hundreds of square miles of sea floor or inundate the land.

New York
Rome
Florence
Ravenna
Venice

Milan
Lausanne
Geneva
Paris

Then while the narrator took Claudia on the train from Paris an hour out of the city to visit the cathedral at Chartres, which we had never seen,

Kings, princes, barons, citizens, peasants and labourers took part in the building, giving their money or their strength. This effort enabled the cathedral to be finished in 25 years . . . thus ensuring for the main building a degree of unity almost without example in the ogival style.

the old king knocked on the stateroom door and told us it was time to get up, it was already light out and the opera would soon be over. From the upper bunk we looked at the stateroom window and the mirror over the sink, which reflected a further view from the window, and now the shore was close with factory buildings and warehouses moving by rapidly in the pale clear light, and we jumped down from the bunk to dress quickly because it was our last trip and we did not want to miss anything. When we got out on deck the last act had already begun. The deep chords that sound like a steamboat whistle, full of the melancholy thirst of the hero's dying, had given way to the melancholy piping of the shepherd, mournful unaccompanied, while the hero lay in the parched sunlight under a blasted tree, unconscious, and his loyal servant (Macurdy, baritone) waits. And we all wait. Standing on the forward balcony, overlooking the prow of the ship below us, overlooked in turn by the pilothouse behind and above us, we watch the city as it gathers around us on both sides of the East River, cool and gray. The deck is still moist, the rail damp and solid and still registering the slight transmitted vibrations from the engines. The hero wakes. Moment by moment the music passes through the anticipated landmarks on its way to the end, and after each moment has passed, it is gone. We clutch at each moment (damp and solid and cool) and try to give an even more concentrated attention to it, as if this will slow it down or keep it once it is gone.

The ship turns the bend and now the open harbor off lower Manhattan comes into view, and everyone knows there are only a few moments left. The joyful piping of the shepherd signifies the heroine's approach, and we know that this brings with it imminently the end, the hero's last words, soon to be followed by the death-song of the heroine as she stands and raises her arms over the orchestra. The pier where the ship will dock comes into view. The ship will pull up to the end of the pier at her starboard side and then back slowly into the slip—slowly, while the workmen handle the hawsers. Soon now, very soon, she will come to a complete halt, and that is the last we shall ever see . . . while the narrator tries to remember, Where were we? Planning for Claudia: Paris.

Then how about

Mont Saint Michel
Dinard
Jersey
Salisbury
Wells
Chester

While the Name carries on as usual:

The figures are given more realism by means of an analogy. If we condense time by a factor of a million so that one year represents a million years, we can compare the four billion years of geological time to the four thousand years since 2000 B.C. The oldest rocks of the earth's crust would be forming at a time equivalent on our condensed scale to the period of the Middle Kingdom of Egyptian civilization. The Pre-Cambrian eras would then, following this analogy, include the Egyptian, Greek, and Roman empires, and the Dark and Middle Ages, up to the beginning of the Renaissance or about 1370. The time of the Hundred Years' War and the heroic deeds of Joan of Arc would correspond roughly to the beginning of the Ordovician Period. The end of the Paleozoic would correspond to the mid-1700's. The end of the Mesozoic would correspond to 1904, when Teddy Roosevelt was starting his second term as President. The Cenozoic Era would correspond to the 65 years since then. On our scaled-down calendar, man would have arrived on the scene just last year.

The manager plans: Tomorrow, if you tell the guard that you are going to pick up a patient, he will let you park. They will give you a receipt to take to the cashier, while she is getting dressed. You will come down with her in the elevator, and in the evening you can talk over your plans. You will have all the evenings to come, all the rest of your time for talk, for as long as your good luck holds.

PS3573 R49 M6
+The Morley mytho+Wright, Austin M
0 00 02 0211227 2
MIDDLEBURY COLLEGE